Chasing After KNIGHT

HEATHER BUCHTA

Penguin Workshop

For Leo and Alex

—HB

PENGUIN WORKSHOP
An imprint of Penguin Random House LLC, New York

First published in the United States of America by Penguin Workshop,
an imprint of Penguin Random House LLC, New York, 2022

Visit us online at penguinrandomhouse.com.

Library of Congress Control Number: 2021048261

Printed in the United States of America

ISBN 9780593384954 (pbk) 10 9 8 7 6 5 4 3 2 1 LSCC
ISBN 9780593384961 (hc) 10 9 8 7 6 5 4 3 2 1 LSCC

Chapter One

I met him at junior-high summer camp.

Despite his current reputation as an A-list actor who only dates models, and despite summer camp's reputation for romance, we never dated back then. To be honest, since that seems to be my new hobby, you might as well know we *never* actually dated. But once in your life, if you're lucky, someone comes along when you least expect it and knocks the wind clear out of you. By the time you catch your breath, your entire life is messed up. Maybe that's just me. Or maybe that's just love. Either way, four years later, I'm still learning how to breathe again.

★★★★★

"Memories are what you hold on to when you have nothing else." I'm sitting in my twelfth-grade Creative Writing class listening to Ms. Meckel, who enjoyed one-too-many outdoor concerts in her life—the kind with tie-dyed shirts and "helium-filled" balloons.

"Alexa," my best friend, Lindsey, whispers from a nearby desk, "you look like you smoked out with Ms. Meckel last night." She leans forward, hoping for a good story, always hoping for a good (and preferably wild) story, but I smile and shake my head. I'm not about to tell her that this dumb assignment kept me up until dawn.

Ms. Meckel looks over at us. She knows we've been talking, but she just turns and stares out the window, probably imagining a kaleidoscope or something "far out." She moves her head like she's listening to some groovy tune, and it makes her stringy hair swish back and forth when she talks. "Memories shape you." *Swish. Swish. Swish.* "Please get out the homework from last night to share with the class. Alexa? Lindsey? We'll begin with you."

Our assignment was to bring a memory to class, an artifact that shaped our character, and to write a short story about it. I actually spent the whole previous day working on my AP Spanish project, not Creative Writing. Creative Writing was my last priority, but for top colleges to accept me, I needed a creative elective, like art or theater. Beginning art was only for freshmen, and theater—not an option. Ever since junior-high summer camp and the *incident,* I won't go near a stage. I won't even watch television—Netflix, Hulu, even YouTube—because I don't want to chance seeing *him.* My high school offered Creative Writing as a senior elective, which was fine by me. I used to like writing. I used to *love it,* actually. But that was before ninth grade, before I realized writing often involved remembering. And that wasn't something I was ready for.

Finally, at ten last night, after finishing my other homework, I rummaged through an old box in my closet, searching for my first Girl Scout uniform. A perfect artifact. Something that had shaped my character. But then, underneath some baseball caps and my mom's Nancy Drew books, I saw the familiar blue-and-black plastic lanyard bracelet with the metal clasp. I stared at it for a minute before the memories erupted, and I almost got sick to my stomach. I threw it away before we moved to Vegas the summer before ninth grade. I know I did. "Mom?" I hollered through closed doors. Moments later, I walked across the hall to my parents' bedroom. The two of them lay side by side with their own reading lights. Mom looked up from her book.

"What's this?" I asked her.

"Isn't that one of those lanyard arts-and-crafts majiggers?" Dad answered for her.

"I know what it is, *Dad.*"

"Honey," Mom said. "Don't use that tone with your father."

"Mom."

She waited a moment. "It's been in a box for three years." Another moment. "No harm done."

"I threw it away!"

Dad set down his *Sports Illustrated* magazine. I pressed my lips together and waited. If Dad interrupted his sports, it was serious. "Then throw it away *again*. Understand?"

I nodded. Discussion over. No more arguing with Mom; Dad was sure of that. Mom knew it, too, so she added, "You two were so close, Alexa. We were in the middle of moving when I found it in your trash. I thought you might change your mind eventually."

"Well, I haven't." I emphasized each word like they were three separate sentences.

"Carson *gave* that to you. It was a gift."

"I don't know any Carson," I murmured, then gently closed their door so Dad wouldn't ground me for *attitude.*

I could hear Dad through the door. "Carson . . . Isn't he that actor kid?"

It was after 10:30 p.m. The September heat tidal-waved over me as I left my air-conditioned house and entered the garage. All the boxes looked the same, untouched and unmarked since the move. I was away at math summer enrichment on those last days before we left. Dad had packed up my bedroom and done his best to label things, but what did I expect? You could barely see the floor of my bedroom back then. I scoured every box, but that darn uniform was nowhere. When I came across a box of old letters, I didn't dare sift through it to see if my one postcard from Carson was still tucked away, too.

The dry heat was too much. I walked out of the oven and back into the cool of our house. It was close to midnight. Enough already. I'd sit down and write the memory, then be done with the assignment and any thought of him. How hard could it be?

I flipped open my laptop and wrote, *I met Carson at junior-high summer camp.* The corners of my mouth lifted into a smile, but I shook it off. I meant to jot it quickly—how much would I really remember, anyway? But as I started writing, it was like a dormant volcano woke up. It was alive all along, and nothing, not one shred of his face or his eyes or his voice had left me. Five hours later, when I finally paused and looked up from my laptop, the desert sun was peeking through my blinds, reminding me I had school in an hour and a life that needed Carson as far away as possible.

★★★★★

Alexa Brooks

Period 4

September 15, 2021

I met Carson at junior-high summer camp. It wasn't just any summer camp, either, but an island summer camp, twenty-six miles from the mainland, complete with two dances and no parents. I had been to Girl Scout Camp for the past five years, but this summer, the summer before ninth grade, I forgot to sign up on time (big surprise), so I searched the internet for a camp and found one on Catalina Island. *With boys.*

Sometimes it paid to be irresponsible.

On the day I was supposed to leave for camp, I woke up to an alarm beeping somewhere beyond my closed bedroom door. "Alexa!" Dad hollered. "You're past the alarm!" Shoot. I kicked a shoe and a couple of balled-up socks as I rolled out of bed. On the floor, I dug through the piles of clothes until I found a pair of jeans. I wiggled into them, then slapped a piece of duct tape on the side of my sleeping bag. With a thick Sharpie, I wrote "Alexa Brooks" on the tape.

I could hear Dad's alarm beeping again, and his sock feet stomping to go shut it off.

"It's eight already?" I yelled, smelling the armpit of a T-shirt before slipping it on. I looked at my phone. Dead. Forgot to charge it overnight.

"Yep!" he answered. "Eight-oh-one! You're gonna miss the boat! Let's hustle! You packed?"

"Completely!"

I pulled an empty duffel bag from underneath my bed and began taking handfuls of clothes from the floor and stuffing them into the bag. I opened a drawer and tossed in a few T-shirts, pairs of underwear, and a bathing suit.

I dragged my duffel to the bathroom, snatched a toothbrush and towel and shoved them into my bag, stepping on my clothes to scrunch everything inside. Next to the sink, my goldfish swam in a four-inch circle in his glass bowl.

"I hope you survive, Fish," I whispered, and I stuck a Post-it, reminding my parents how much to feed him, on the side of his bowl. With my unzipped duffel slung over one shoulder—clothes spilling over the top—and my sleeping bag under my arm, I grabbed the fish bowl and carefully walked downstairs. I placed the bowl on top of the TV, on top of ESPN, Dad's lifeline to the athletes he yelled at every day (athletes he just knew he could beat). Fish would be safe and well fed next to the remote control. I grabbed Dad's car keys and noticed my Apple Watch on the counter. Should I bring it? This was beach camp. I didn't want to chance losing it—but Dad shouted from the top of the banister, "Go, go, go!" like the starter pistol just fired for a race. He soared down the stairs, and I snagged my watch and followed him out the door.

As soon as Dad turned the ignition, the car's digital clock stared back at me. I checked it with my watch.

"Hey," I said, "it's only eight-oh-one."

"Exactly." He punched me in the shoulder before reaching for his seatbelt. Dad knew me well.

It was a short drive down the 110 Freeway to the San Pedro

boat terminal, just enough time for me to text Beth that I was on my way. All my good friends were away on family trips, which left Bethany Gordon to come with me, and she cried a lot at school, but maybe she wouldn't cry on an island. I stuck to two people at school: Kara Walker, the easygoing type who'd giggle at anything, and Paige Connelly, who was kinda Hollywood-ish because her dad was a top casting director, but she was still fun. This week, though, I had Beth Gordon, neither easygoing nor Hollywood, but I didn't mind: I had a friend.

When we finally docked at camp two hours later, a man wearing a pirate costume greeted us. "I'm your captain," he called from the pier with a funny accent. He forced a fake burp, and all two hundred of us groaned. We dumped our luggage onto a large field before following the captain on the camp tour.

Mostly this was a beach camp: snorkeling, waterskiing, kayaking. The camp looked like a bunch of barely-watered football fields attached by dirt roads and a smattering of sagebrush. We followed the camp counselors and the captain along the dirt roads, where he introduced us to the "ARRRGH-chery station" and the "ARRRGH-ts and crafts building," and a short hiking trail—Hiker's Peak—going up a hill to an ocean lookout: "Stay on the trail. No walking the planks, aye?" After the tour, we walked back to the field for our stuff, so we could settle in our cabins and change into our swimsuits.

I passed the swim test, which wasn't saying much because basically you passed by not drowning. You swam around ocean buoys—six laps of a pool—and if a lifeguard had to rescue you, you had to swim the rest of the week with a life jacket.

That entire day felt like everything was in fast-forward, and on days like that, you never think that the guy of your dreams is going to waltz in and push the pause button. Beth and I were watching people get out of the ocean, giggling at their "Ows" and "Oofs" as they stepped onto the painful rock beach. Suddenly, my laughter hitched as my eyes met a tan-skinned guy slicking back his wet brown hair. His teeth were so white, whiter than any I'd ever seen—*I can see them from here*, I remember thinking. And what fourteen-year-olds are that tall?

At that point, another boy asked to use my towel because he'd left his in the cabin, and I said okay. Well, really, I didn't say okay. I just handed it to him. I was a deer in headlights, stuck on the tall, dark, and handsome almost-ninth-grader walking out of the water. The boy with my towel said, "What's your name?"

"Good," I said, because I'd thought he was going to ask me how I was.

"Your parents named you 'Good'?"

I turned to the voice. Standing before me was this adorable, skinny kid with blond hair that flopped in his face, the soft hair that looks brand-new, like it does on two-year-olds. Before I could correct myself, he laughed.

"My last name's Knight," he said. "What if we got married?"

"Okay," I said, but then I got it. My first name, "Good," his last name, "Knight." His eyebrow lifted as if to say, Get it? He laughed again, and I instantly loved the sound. He reminded me of someone I knew, but maybe he just had that friendly face.

"Mr. and Mrs. Good Knight?" I held out my hand. "We have to get married!"

"Right?" he said. "Great. Well, then." He shook my hand. "Hello, Goodnight."

"Hello."

Then I looked back at the ocean, searching for the guy with the smile whiter than pearls.

★★★★★

When I finish reading my essay, Ms. Meckel's eyes are all misty. "That's deep. I feel your vibe. Say the last line again."

"Then I looked back at the ocean, searching for the guy with the smile whiter than pearls."

"Mmm," she sighs, sipping her herbal tea. "Sounds like the guy of your dreams. But you were looking in the wrong direction, weren't you?" Lindsey stifles a snicker by pretending she's sneezing.

"What?"

Ms. Meckel constantly searches for deeper meanings, but usually she speaks unicorn—all halos and auras and dream catchers, stuff that feels like she ate one too many mushrooms as a teenager. This doesn't sound like nonsense. This sounds like she means my eyes should've been looking at the skinny, floppy-haired kid next to me. She thinks like Mom does, like it was Carson, not Dylan, I should have dated. I thought that, too, once. But no one ever found out, and thank God. Who'd believe me after what I did to him?

The bell rings, and a hand slips around my waist as we file out. "You were looking in the wrong direction because the guy of your dreams wasn't at camp, was he?"

"Hey, John," I say without looking. My boyfriend touches a strand of my hair before returning to fix his own. Our brown hair matches, our eyes match. *We* match. Luckily for him, he has three inches on me, still short for a first-string tight end, but not hobbit short. He stops, and I realize he's waiting for an answer. We've been with each other for over a year, so I didn't think he'd be worried. I lean in and kiss him. Our noses touch when I say, "John, it was *junior high*. How do you even know what the guy of your dreams is like at that age?"

We head to the lunchroom, thirty rectangular tables inside a multipurpose room. The gymnasium doors are to the left. The boys' ninth-grade PE dismisses at the same time our lunch begins, mixing the cafeteria with smells of casserole and basketball sweat. Yum.

My other friends join us—Lindsey, Kim, and Heidi's boyfriend, Ryan. Heidi's not here yet because she stops every day to pick up her cello from the band room. Before I sit, Kim's already searching everyone's eyes and doing her usual emotional roll call, asking how everybody's doing. Lindsey and John say, "Fine," and Ryan just shrugs, which is more than you usually get from him. I punch him in the shoulder, and he grins, rubbing his thick bicep like I hurt him.

"And you?" Kim asks me, tilting her head. Her straight black hair falls across one eye, and she leaves it there. I think she's going for mysterious, but it comes off slightly sultry, which is just weird. Everyone's staring, so I must've spaced. "Are you good?" Kim coos, pouting her glossy lips.

"No, I'm fine," I say, and everyone giggles. After three years, they still haven't realized that I never call myself good. Not anymore.

Chapter Two

It's funny how memories fade, but your brain still holds on to certain things. And not even the interesting ones! I remember my green toenail polish and the circular tables in the dining hall. I remember eating dinner the first night with Carson, the blond kid who borrowed my towel. I don't remember if Bethany was there or not.

"The food's good," Carson said between mouthfuls.

"Good like me," I said, and he spat out part of his food because he was laughing through his nose. After Carson first called me "Good," I started to call him "Night," but then I began changing it up. Like, instead of saying, "Hi, Good," he'd nod at me and say, "Good." I'd nod and say, "Riddance." He liked that one. Over the course of the week, we greeted each other with "Good Fellas," "Good God," "Good grief," and when I was amped on a sugar high, I shouted, "Ness-gracious-great-balls-of-fire!"

On the second day of camp, a Tuesday, I remember sitting on the waterfront wall looking at the ocean as the sun rose behind a bunch of clouds. Sunlight shot through three places where the clouds parted—three fingers of yellow laser beams touching the glassy water. I heard a splash and turned toward the boys' villas on the right. Carson, in a T-shirt and flannel pajama pants, was skipping stones into the ocean. To a fourteen-year-old girl, the rising sun had nothing on who was standing behind Carson, leaning against the short stone wall surrounding the villas.

The guy from the swim test.

Carson saw me and waved me over. I walked barefoot across the stone beach, barely noticing the pain from all the rocks. "Good!" he shouted.

"Morning!" I shouted back. He ran over and threw his arm around me.

"Nice one. Hey, this is my best friend, Dylan."

Dylan hobbled gorgeously over the rocks toward us. "Hey," he said. "I heard about you."

This guy of my dreams had *heard* about me. I couldn't stop smiling. Suddenly Carson popped me playfully on the shoulder. "Good, you better get. That lifeguard's waiting to start his safety talk." Behind us, my cabin of girls, a villa of boys, and a lifeguard in red shorts stood watching. I hurried back but didn't hear a word of "ski-boat safety." *Something* was playing pinball in my ribcage. My heart only slowed when Beth leaned over and whispered, "Who's the tan one?"

★★★★★

"Hullooooo!" Lindsey shouts in my ear, bringing me back to the warm cafeteria and my twelfth-grade friends. All staring at me. "I asked you about the bracelet," Lindsey says. "Was it his ex-girlfriend's, and did she catch you wearing it?" I shake my head. "You told Ms. Meckel that some sort of bracelet was your artifact. What's that got to do with anything?"

I reach into my pocket and feel the familiar plastic braiding and the metal clasp. Somehow I forgot to turn it in with my assignment, which throws me because I don't forget things like that. Not when it comes to grades. Heidi appears, dumping her cello next to our table with a *thwump*. "Nice job, William Faulkner," she says, a compliment with the tone of an insult. She's one of those girls who helped me understand the word *paradox*. She gets higher test scores than any of us, but I never see her study. She also loves to grows plants—there are at least twenty in her bedroom—but then she litters all the time. And if you point that out, she says, "I like plants, not the environment."

Heidi sits next to her boyfriend, Ryan, and she kisses him on the cheek. "Way to make us all look bad," she says to me with a grin. "We were only supposed to write two pages. That was like a two-hundred-page novel. And yeah, what's with the bracelet?"

I never got to the bracelet part. I never got to a lot of parts. My story was about the first day of summer camp—listening to a cheesy pirate, handing some kid a towel after I swam in the ocean—hardly about an event that changed my life. But that was the thing about Ms. Meckel. If you could take her on an emotional journey, she'd forget that you didn't follow directions.

"I made that part up," I say, tucking the bracelet deeper in my pocket. "It was late last night. I didn't have my assignment done."

"OMG. Alexa!" Lindsey squeals, her ponytail flip-flopping as she bounces in delight. "Ohhh. Emmmm. Geeee. You made that up! You acted all NBD. The story, the guy . . ." But then she stops, like she doubts herself. "Wait, really?"

"Brilliant," Heidi says, shaking her head. "I shoulda thought of that."

I see John's shoulders relax. "I'm at football till four today," he says, thankfully changing the subject. "Need a ride home after cross-country practice?"

"Nah, I'll just go with Linds."

"Sure," Lindsey says, still eyeing me. "You positive there was no bracelet junior-high fling thing?"

I hold my hands up in surrender. "Do you see anything on these wrists? No bracelets. No spicy eighth-grade dirt on me. Just extra writing practice before I send in my Boston College personal statement."

"Ha," Heidi snorts. "Overachiever."

I excuse myself to the restroom, splash water onto my face, and look in the mirror, wishing I'd made up the whole thing. I shake my head at those memories creeping up out of nowhere. I open my planner to check my week's homework schedule, when a student enters and tapes a flyer to the mirror. "Hey, Alexa!" She waves even though we're two feet apart, and I smile. I recognize Jillian from one of my classes last year.

"Hey there," I say and look at the flyer. Instantly my smile is gone.

"You feel okay? Do you want me to get someone?" I shake my head and back into a stall, locking the door and collapsing onto the toilet seat, but there's a duplicate flyer taped to the inside stall door: auditions for the upcoming theater production.

★★★★★

Every night at campfire, a few cabins and villas performed skits with their counselors, but I only recall the second night. Carson and Dylan surprised us by walking onto the camp stage, and Beth and I screamed like we were at a rock concert. They performed a simple skit about two guys camping, one in a tent and one outside the tent. A motorcycle gang appears and robs the guy outside the tent, but the guy inside sleeps through it. He thinks the guy outside is making it up because he's scared, so he switches places and lets the scared guy have his tent. They fall back asleep, but this time, the motorcycle gang appears and decides that they've robbed the guy outside the tent enough, so they decide to attack the one inside the tent . . . the guy they've been robbing all along! Carson played the guy sleeping in the tent who thought his friend was making it all up. I remember how much everyone laughed whenever Carson did or said anything. I remember how proud I was, even though our friendship was only two days old. I also remember that whenever Dylan appeared onstage, Beth and I tried to out-scream each other.

★★★★★

The bell rings for fifth period, jarring me back to my

bathroom stall. When I exit the bathroom, the hallway's empty. That was the late bell, officially announcing the first tardy of my high-school career. My physics teacher doesn't care, but I still can't believe it. She lets me come back after school to make up the negative tardy points, but by the time I get outside, all my friends are gone, my cross-country team has already run off campus without me, and John is probably in his football gear, sailing headfirst into blocking sleds and tackling dummies.

Instead of doing my own workout, I take the late bus home. There are only three, instead of the six early ones, so you're covering twice as many stops, which means at least an hour longer ride. I could wait for my team to return and get a ride with Lindsey, but I'm not ready for her questions about why I missed cross-country practice for the first time ever, which will lead to how I got my first tardy ever. She'll know something's up. She won't even have to see what's in my pocket.

Today the bus goes to North Las Vegas first, then heads south on the I-15, passing by the big casinos that tower above the east side of the freeway. I crack open a textbook, but I'm transfixed by the tall buildings, remembering high places and views, and someone who can take over my entire day, even when I haven't thought about him for years.

★★★★★

After breakfast on the third day, Carson, Dylan, Beth, and I walked to the arts and crafts tent. We picked colors for plastic lanyard bracelets and sat on the benches overlooking the ocean. The wind was blowing wisps of Beth's hair, and I noticed for the first time that Bethany Gordon was pretty. Maybe I never noticed because she was always crying about something—losing a homework assignment, getting a detention, being picked last in PE. Sometimes she'd even get teary if you forgot to wait for her after class. But when she laughed or stood where the wind hit her wispy hair, she was pretty. I think Dylan noticed it, too.

I showed Dylan my bracelet and made a funny face. "Mine looks like knots."

"You should take lessons from Beth," he said. I smiled but felt crummy when he said that.

"I love knots," Carson said. "Boy Scouts give badges for knots. There's not a *bracelet* badge, now, is there?"

I giggled. "Nope."

"See? Here, give me your knots. You can have my bracelet." He fastened the blue-and-black plastic braid around my wrist next to my Apple Watch, and in that moment, it was better than a hug.

That afternoon, all the color teams competed in something called Oatmeal Wars. Five kiddie pools on the football field were filled with oatmeal. On "Go!" everybody ran to the different pools and fished through the oatmeal for Legos that matched their color team. Then they had to run the Legos to the slab of concrete in front, where the counselors had to construct a Lego cube. The biggest and most accurate cube-shape won. I wanted to play, but Bethany was standing on the outside of the pandemonium, and she asked me to stay with her. Together, we watched oatmeal fling in every direction. It quickly became less about making a Lego cube and more about shoving oatmeal down people's shorts and in their faces.

"Not into sports?" Dylan called to me, oatmeal dripping from his fingertips. A dried clump of oats was stuck to his forehead. Oatmeal never looked so good.

"Hey, Good!"

I turned to my left but too late. Carson had filled a Frisbee with oatmeal and pied me in the face with it. I could hear Bethany and Dylan giggling.

"You're done, Knight!" I yelled, wiping away the slimy paste just enough to see him bolting across the field. I caught up and dragged all ninety pounds of him across the grass. He was laughing too hard to put up a fight, but he broke free next to the purple team's kiddie pool. I charged into him the way my dad taught me to push someone into a swimming pool. *Stay low,* he'd say. *You get under them, they got nothing on you.*

I launched Carson into the kiddie pool of oatmeal, but he held on to my tank top, and the two of us toppled in. I felt little plastic Lego pieces jabbing my butt as I swiveled, glancing to see if Dylan was still around. Kids were shouting at us to get out so they could find the Legos. Carson switched to a strange accent. "I love these spa treatments; absolutely fabulous on my complexion." I laughed so hard I snorted, which made us laugh harder. "Gross!" Carson held out his hand full of slimy goop. "Look what you did! Get a Kleenex, for God's sake."

As I crawled out of the pool and onto the grass, Carson

turned serious. “He’s over there,” he said, gesturing behind him.

“What?”

“Dylan,” he answered. “You were looking for him the whole time we were in the pool.”

That wasn’t true. It was only once, and I couldn’t believe Carson had noticed. I hoped Dylan didn’t. “Yeah, right,” I said. “You’re smoking something.”

“Oatmeal,” we both said at the same time and laughed like there was nobody funnier in the world than us. I waited until Carson wiped his face with a T-shirt, and then I looked where he had pointed. There was Dylan, talking to Bethany near the blue team’s tub. When I turned back to Carson, he was walking away.

★★★★★

“This your stop?” the bus driver hollers. I look through the cloud of dust kicked up by the late bus and see the parked semis. I’m at the 76 Station truck stop, one mile past my house. Somewhere between lanyards and oatmeal, I’ve missed my street. “Last stop before the bus yard,” the driver barks. “If this ain’t it, I can’t help you.”

I sling my backpack over one shoulder and climb down the steps onto the hard-packed dirt, three hundred miles away from junior high and three years from one lousy mistake. The revving diesel engines hum around me, a circus of semis trying to drown out the sound of my voice back then.

“It’s not what it looks like.”

I had actually said that, like they do in the movies, only it wasn't the movies. And it was another lie, because it *was* what it looked like.

Whatever. I drop my backpack to the ground and fumble through it for my iPhone. Where is the darned thing? Finally, underneath my stash of ten perfectly sharpened number two pencils, I excavate it and text John and Lindsey: Meet @ my house 2nite study ACT. Then I open the audio version of *The Great Gatsby*, one of our AP novels, and start my walk along the dusty roads back home.

★★★★★

"Hi, Lexie," Mom calls when I walk through the door. I follow the warm scent of onions and peppers into the kitchen, where Mom stands over the stove, stirring the turkey chili and leaning over the pot, eyes closed, her face wrapped in the turkey-chili steam. "Good for the pores," she says, as if she can see me staring at her, which sometimes I'm convinced she can. "I made enough for John, if he's dropping you off after practice." She calls toward the entryway, "John?"

"Not here," I say. "But he's coming later. Just texted."

"Speaking of texting, Lindsey texted me." Mom says it casually, like it's normal for friends to text their friends' mothers. "She said you weren't at cross-country practice today, that you weren't answering your phone."

I make a mental note to kill Lindsey later. "I took the late bus. Had to study instead of practice today. The ACT's in two weeks."

She glances at the oven clock, then pulls out her phone from her pocket to make sure the oven's right. "Huh," she says, which is her way of saying, *The late bus shouldn't take this long. Where were you, really?*

"I missed my stop. Got off at the truck stop and walked home."

She steps away from her chili and scrutinizes me.

"You missed your stop. *You.*" I nod. "Hmm." She looks back at the chili and stirs it again, slowly this time. "You and John have a fight today?"

"No. He's on his way over."

"You get a B on a paper or something?"

"Mom! Seriously. No. I just missed my stop. I was studying. I got distracted."

Her arms drop, and she frowns like I've told her something serious. "Ohhh," she says, but I haven't said anything, so I know she's doing that climb-in-my-head thing. I walk fast to my bedroom, trying to outrun what I know is coming, but her voice catches up at the end of the hall. "I'm really sorry about the bracelet, sweetie!"

Chapter Three

Every time Lindsey walks into my bedroom, she says it reminds her of a library or hospital, or a hospital's library, or a librarian's hospital, depending on her mood. But to me, my room carries its own mountain air to clear my head. I have two floor-to-ceiling bookshelves, symmetrically placed on either side of my bed and framing the window above my headboard. In the corner of my room is a rectangular desk, the same dark wood as my bookshelves and headboard, with my laptop on the right and five red pens, five blue pens, and five mechanical pencils in a porcelain cup on the left. Organized. Together.

This is fake, I hear a voice tell me. I shake my head and rearrange my books not by author or title, but by color of the binding, and the colors go from the top of my shelf to the bottom like traveling clockwise on a color wheel. I exhale and smile at the world I know, so perfectly ordered. "See? I'm fine," I say to my books.

The only things that change daily are my closet doors. I have the sliding kind, made out of giant mirrors, and every night before bed, I write my to-do list in dry-erase marker on them, along with a vocab word to use at least seven times that day. Today's word: *disparate*. Different. I haven't used it once so far. *That's disparate*, I think. There's one. But other disparities start creeping in: the disparity between Dylan's and Carson's personalities, the disparity between Carson and me at the beginning of the summer versus Carson and me at the end, the *disparity* between—*What am I doing? Stop!* I sit on my bed and pull out my flash cards, and for the next half hour, I lose myself in ACT math problems. Numbers make sense. There's a definite right or wrong, no room for interpretation or misunderstanding. I tap my fingers on my scientific calculator, and it acts as a soothing tonic to my muddled thoughts. Soon I lose myself in equations rather than feelings.

★★★★★

"Hey," Carson whispered. "Good, wake up."

I woke up and had a brief freak-out—forgetting that I wasn't at home, that I was actually at camp in a sleeping bag—and I flew up to a sitting position, wide-eyed. Unfortunately, I was on the lower bunk and whacked my head on the wooden plank above me. "Ohhhhh," I groaned, falling back down into my bed.

"Shit," Carson whispered. "You okay?"

I looked up at him, rubbing my head. "I've never heard you cuss."

He snickered. "Never. I know. In all the years we've known each other."

"You're dumb," I said, but we were both grinning.

He looked down at the mountain of clothes covering me and my sleeping bag. "If you're cold, they have extra blankets," he joked. Then he lifted his foot. Hanging from the toe of his sneaker was my bathing-suit bottoms. We giggled, and he gently covered my mouth with his hand.

Two beds over, the sound of snoring stopped, and someone shifted in their sleeping bag. Carson motioned to follow him. I had no idea how he sneaked across camp to the girls' area in the middle of the night, but I grabbed my shoes and followed.

"Where we going?" I whispered when we reached one of the dirt paths.

"Up," he whispered back.

He took my hand. Nothing felt weird about it, but I remember thinking it was weird that it didn't feel weird. We had a flashlight but didn't dare use it. Going out after hours was a serious offense, and Captain Jack Sparrow made no "arrrgh" jokes when he discussed that at orientation. We came to the trailhead of Hiker's Peak.

Carson whispered, "Can you do this without a light?" I stared at him like he was an idiot. "Alrighty, then," he laughed, and turned up the hill. I focused on the small reflectors on the backs of his tennis shoes, my heart beating a mile a minute. I'd never felt this kind of adrenaline rush, this mix of doing something dangerous *while* breaking the rules. We didn't say a word the entire way up, but our shoes found a common rhythm, making the same *chhaw* sound in the dirt every time we stepped. Fifteen minutes later, we reached the peak.

"This," I said breathlessly, turning in a full circle to take in the view. You could see the entire island. On one end, about ten miles away, the lights from the main town, Avalon, danced across the water. Behind us, just beyond a sign that read "No Hikers Beyond This Point," a steep cliff dropped down to an empty cove, normally pitch-black. But tonight, every time the little waves would crash, plankton lit up the shore with a bright, fluorescent green glow. We sat down on the dirt and let the wet air fill our lungs, the cold breeze gently wafting through our pajamas.

"I wish I didn't have to go home," he said.

"Why?" The thought hadn't occurred to me. I loved camp, but it was camp. I mean, I didn't want to live in a sleeping bag.

"What's there?" He tossed a rock off the cliff. I heard it hit a rock below and then another, but I never heard it splash, like it just disappeared, or found a home somewhere else on its way down.

He made me a little nervous because he always joked, and now he wasn't, and I didn't know what I was supposed to say. I bit the side of my cheek and played with the bracelet he'd made me, twirling it around my wrist.

"You know I didn't pay for camp."

"Me neither," I said. "Duh, your parents pay for it."

"Parent," he corrected. "I live with my mom."

"Oh." I waited for him to say more, but he didn't. "Is she nice?"

He shrugged one shoulder. "Sure." He tossed another rock toward the hillside. It ricocheted off a bench built to overlook the view. "She didn't pay for camp, either."

"Oh." I unfastened the clasp of my bracelet and started playing with it.

"We got a *scholarship*." He spat out the word *scholarship* like it was some disease.

I understood what that meant. Carson was poor. My parents weren't rich, but I knew they weren't poor. Not the kind of poor that required a donation to send their kid to camp. I took the plastic bracelet and stretched it long like a pencil, then dragged it through the dirt, making squiggles.

"I want it to be different when I go home. Only I know it won't be."

I could feel how bad he felt, but everything I wanted to say sounded stupid in my head. I wanted to tell him that maybe his mom would get a better job, or maybe they'd win the lottery. I wanted to mention something about his dad, but I didn't know if he even knew him. So I just sat there, tying the plastic bracelet into a knot, then untying it again, staring out at the view as if I could find the answer there.

"You could act," I blurted.

"What?"

"I don't know. I mean, I do know. I mean, you were good—your voices in the oatmeal pool? And your skit at campfire was the best one there. And you're funny."

"You just think I'm funny."

"No, you're funnier than anyone I know, even adults. I bet you could do stuff like commercials. There's money in that. My friend Paige—her dad is one of those casting guys who pick the people to do commercials." My heart thrummed with excitement.

"I have a cousin who acts," he trailed off. "He hasn't done anything, but he has this agent, and they send him on auditions."

"Yes! Auditions! Carson, we've got it!" My bracelet

accidentally sailed out of my hand and into a sagebrush plant. I stood and walked off the trail to grab it, but my foot slipped. Suddenly I was sliding, not toward the cliff—thankfully—but down ten feet into another sagebrush. Carson laughed.

"Mmm, sagebrush, you're gonna smell good."

I threw a pebble at his foot. "Shut up, dummy."

"You know, the Native Americans used sagebrush as deodorant."

"Hand, please?"

He reached down and grabbed my hand. On my way up, I lunged for the bracelet with my free hand, but my foot slipped again, and I planted my hand in a cactus. I howled. Carson had my other wrist and must have used every muscle in his ninety pounds to pull me up. I wrapped my good hand around my other wrist and squeezed, trying to cut off the circulation from the hand with the cactus spikes. The tears sprang forth before I had a chance to think about it. "Hold up," he said. He walked me over to the bench that looked out at the harbor. He laid me down across the bench and sat next to me. Placed my head on his lap. "Just look out there, okay?"

He turned his mini flashlight on, sticking the end of it in his mouth. With his free hands, he tenderly picked the cactus spikes out, one by one. After he finished, he didn't say, "I'm finished," or sit me up right away. We gazed at the rippling dark ocean. I thought he was thinking about his home and his money problems, or maybe wondering where his dad was. But when he finally spoke, I was way off.

"Why do you think people like views so much?" His voice was soft.

"I dunno," I said. "'Cause they're pretty?"

"Maybe." Then he went quiet.

I sat up and faced him. "Why do *you* think?"

He shrugged. "Who knows." Then he said, "Like, who knows why you wear a watch?" He lifted my wrist and showed me the black face of my Apple Watch. "It's been dead for more than a day."

I smiled that he noticed. "It was a gift from my parents. Trying to help me be more on top of things."

He laughed. "Hold on, stay there." I thought he might be going to the bathroom, so I didn't look behind me, but when he came back, he took my hand again, refastening the bracelet next to my dead watch. "When I'm famous, you can tell everybody I gave it to you."

We walked down and sneaked back into our beds, barely before daylight. Nobody ever knew. Something shifted in us that night, and it seemed small. For the rest of the week, I refused to charge my watch. He started thinking about acting. But now I know it was bigger than that. Sometimes I wonder if his entire life would've been different if he hadn't had the guts to sneak over to my cabin, if I hadn't had the guts to break the rules.

Chapter Four

“This isn’t the inkblot test.” I look up. Lindsey’s in my room standing over me.

“What?”

“You’ve been staring at that card like you can see something in it. The answer’s not going to change into a butterfly. It’s too average to change anyway.”

“Yeah . . .” I trail off.

“That was a joke, Lex. Get it? The problem was asking for the mean of the test scores. Mean. Average. It’s not going to change because . . . Oh, never mind.” She smacks me over the head. “Ugh, what did you do to your books? Your room is so sterile. Seriously, at least get a hot doctor for this hospital.”

I half smile. “He’ll be here after football practice.”

“Speaking of hot doctors.” She kicks her shoes off and flops onto my bed. “Did you hear about Marvin Hillcrest, the doctor from the soap *St. Louis Hospital*?” She doesn’t wait for a response. “Of course not, because you’re weird and the only teenager in America who doesn’t know who he is. He just got *arrested* for hiring a call girl—that’s a sex worker, in case it’s not on your vocab list—and he’s been happily married for twelve years. Like *happily* happily, too, because he was doing talks and interviews on how to make a marriage work, and now we *know* how he made that marriage work! Ha! Can you believe him? That's not even it." She ignores that I've grabbed my flash cards again. "That call girl was found dead yesterday. They say it was an accidental overdose, but you know what I think?"

Here we go. She knows something's up with me. She always tells me a crazy celebrity story when she's trying to snap me out of a funk. If she only knew the irony. "It's not an overdose," I guess.

"No, silly, it *is* an overdose, but it's not accidental! I bet she was pregnant, and Marvin's wife found out. So the wife takes money from their joint savings and hires a *hit man.* When Marvin notices there's money missing, his wife blames him and says he used the money to hire a call girl, but the truth is, she was a call girl, but he never *hired* her. The call girl was his mistress! And they were actually in love, and when he discovered she was pregnant, he was going to leave his wife and rescue this call girl from her life of prostitution. So the hit man that his wife hired breaks into the girl's house and switches her prenatal pills with poison pills, like arsenic or Rohypnol or both."

"Definitely both," I say. "How is it that I'm lying down and still dizzy from your story?"

"Come on, Lex," she says, resting her head on my stomach. "You know it could happen."

"Definitely," I say. "It definitely *could* happen." I groan and get up. "Come on, let's go eat my mom's chili."

"Jeez, why are you so uptight today? Everybody can see it.

You're like in *Mars of the Living Dead*, which makes no sense to you because my best friend is allergic to movies."

"I'm not allergic. I just. I like to live life rather than watch it."

"Hm," she says, "I have a theory about that."

"No!" She finally gets a laugh out of me. "No more theories! Let's go!" I drag her to the kitchen.

Dad comes home, and the four of us sit down to eat. Lindsey dishes about all the upcoming events and school gossip, but only the PG stuff, thank God. I like my parents, but if I ever watched movies with them, I wouldn't watch the ones with make-out scenes.

"—And the Christmas dance is coming up!" she adds.

"Linds, it's September," I say midbite.

"But I'm in charge of planning it! Dances are where couples ignite, memories are made, lives are changed!"

★★★★★

Thursday night at camp, we had a dance under the stars. The dance floor was the basketball court, and the deejay mounted his speakers on the sports-equipment storage boxes. Girls and boys walked back and forth like they were searching for a friend, when, really, they were just trying *not* to look unpopular. After a while, the counselors got everyone onto the floor by playing the songs that uncoordinated people could participate in, like "Y.M.C.A." and "The Chicken Dance." After Carson and I jumped around with some redhead girl who joined our dance crew, the deejay switched to a slow song. Carson rolled his eyes and looked at me. "Well?"

I shrugged and began slow dancing with him. I was just above his eye level, just high enough to look—

"He likes Beth, ya know," Carson snapped.

I felt my face warm, and for the first time, I was mad at Carson. "I don't like Dylan," I lied.

"Who said anything about Dylan? I was talking about God. God likes Beth, ya know." He grinned, and suddenly I wasn't mad at all.

I laughed. "You're so dumb."

"And why don't you like Dylan? I like Dylan. I like Dylan a lot. I mean, he's my best friend."

"Again, you're dumb."

"So you shouldn't talk bad about my best friend. I can't have my two best friends hating each other."

I stopped dancing. "Best friend?"

"Okay, sure, I guess you can call me your best friend."

We stood like statues, eyes locked, while everyone swayed around us. A smile cracked the corners of my mouth. He wrapped his skinny arms around me and we hugged each other tightly like it was a moment, like we'd just gotten married or something. Then I pulled away and slapped him softly against the side of his head with my open hand. I didn't think back then that four days was too short to call someone your best friend. I only knew the name fit. I'd met my best friend.

★★★★★

Lindsey kicks me under the table. "Of course she's going,"

she says, helping me jump back into the conversation. "She has a boyfriend. It's a formal dance. She's a senior."

I nod. Focus on my chili.

"About time you did something fun," Dad chimes in.

What? I look up at him. "I do fun things." All I hear is the clanking of silverware. "Lindsey. Back me up."

Lindsey nods. "Sure. Of course you do. Of course she does." More clanking silverware.

No one's looking at me. "I go to football games."

"Isn't that required in your, uh, society?" Dad asks.

"Student council. Yes, but still. My boyfriend plays. I'd still go."

Lindsey mumbles something, but I only hear "cards."

"What?"

Lindsey looks up. "You bring your index cards," she says. "You study."

"I . . . that's not . . ." In my mind, I see Carson looking at me. His eyes, sad, confused, right before they turned cold. "Look, *fun* doesn't get me into a school like Boston." I feel a tension settle over the table, the kind that comes whenever I mention East Coast colleges.

"There are some good schools closer to home, like maybe in California?" Mom suggests. "Stanford, Berkeley—"

"I'm not going to California," I say.

She concedes, but not before looking at Dad and saying, "California's bigger than Hollywood."

"Hollywood?" Lindsey pipes in. "What about Hollywood?"

Mom picks up on my death glare, but Dad's too busy enjoying his food. He doesn't bother to finish his bite before he starts giving me the before-game pep talk. “I say you *make* yourself go to college in California. You fall off that horse, you get back on. You throw—”

“Dad,” I say through gritted teeth, but he’s twirling his spoon in his chili.

“You throw an interception, you stay in the game. Good coaches don’t pull you out. Lesson being”—because, of course, every football story has one—“no boy is worth avoiding an entire state for, especially some Hollywood pansy—”

“Dad!” I shout. He stops chewing.

“Honey . . .” Mom touches his arm to tell him he’s said enough.

“What?” he says. Takes another bite. “What.” He looks at Mom, then me, then back at Mom. He has no clue that he’s broken a three-year code of not mentioning Carson.

“I want. To go. To Boston College,” I say.

“Then go to Boston College.” He takes another bite. “Crappy football team, though. I mean, nothing like back in nineteen ninety-three when they beat number one Notre Dame in a last-minute field goal. You see them lately? Really, Alexa?” And just like that, we’re back to normal. Well, except for Lindsey, who glances at my dad and then mouths to me, “Hollywood pansy?” I roll my eyes to convey that *all parents are crazy*, but instead of smiling, she looks down and moves her spoon around in the stew.

Chapter Five

John arrives after dinner. He opens the refrigerator and scoops up a plate of leftovers, because he knows my parents are okay with that. I guess at this age, I should have more drama with my parents, but why bother when they're not all that dramatic? I have a curfew, but it's more like a *suggestion*.

Dad believes curfews are for kids who need supervision. He knows I don't drink or smoke, which is more than he can say for himself at my age. Plus, since we moved to Vegas, and I got on what he calls a "straight-A streak," it's like I'm his favorite team, and he doesn't want to kill my mojo. Once, when my mom suggested a curfew, he said, "If you're watching a basketball game on one foot, and your team starts winning, then you stand like a flamingo until the buzzer, dammit. You switch feet or sit on the couch, and your team loses? You got no one to blame but yourself." His lesson: If I started high school with straight As and no curfew, why start a curfew now? I'd end up with bad grades for sure, and he'd blame himself.

They don't mind that I have a boyfriend, although Dad did pull John aside once while they were on the couch watching college football. I was in my room getting ready for our once-a-week dinner date, when the deafening volume of crowd cheering suddenly stopped. I found out later that Dad muted the TV during a timeout.

"Listen up," he said, using his coach's voice. "Don't get my daughter pregnant. Understand?"

"Yessir," John said.

"There's only one way to make sure of that," he said, pointing the remote at John like an accusing finger. "This isn't some football game."

"Yessir."

And then, to prove that it had nothing to do with football, he used a football example. "You don't run that play. You take a knee. You get me?"

John hardly touched me that night and probably would've avoided high-fiving me had I not called him on it. That's when I heard the embarrassing exchange that took place while I was applying mascara in my mirror with the vocab word *celerity* scrawled across it. *Celerity*. Speed. John wouldn't be running the make-out bases with any *celerity* in the near future. He barely made it to *first*, and that was probably because I took him by the hand and walked him there.

★★★★★

After clearing the food, my parents take off for their evening walk, while John, Lindsey, and I sit at the kitchen table and bury ourselves in polynomials. The dining-room light reflects off the sliding-glass door to the backyard, our images blurry and hunched over our work. John stands, punching and ducking at his reflection, having a boxing match with his counterpart. Lindsey punches at his reflection, and he acts like it hits him in the face. "John," I say. "Come on, help me with this problem."

He sits back down to help, rubbing his jaw, which makes Lindsey laugh. He figures the problem out easily, then looks at the glass again and flexes his bicep, as if his brute strength had somehow helped him with math.

"So Boston College?" Lindsey asks, but she's known it's been Boston College for years. What she's really asking is, *What was all that about at dinner?*

In response, I nod once, and I'm thankful she knows not to press the issue.

She puts her head in the book and mumbles, "If we keep studying this much, you're going to have to hire me as your publicist to fix the damage you're doing to your social life."

I throw a wadded-up piece of paper at her head but bury myself back in my notes. John squeezes my arm and winks at me through the reflection. He loves this side of me. Predictable. Responsible. And I do, too.

★★★★★

Two hours later, we've finished, and I'm busying myself with setting reminders on my phone. John's massaging my shoulders, and Lindsey's leaning on an elbow, watching me curiously, which, of course, I'm ignoring. Thankfully, John's phone rings.

"Mom," we all say.

John's mom is a stickler about his 9:30 p.m. curfew on weekdays. It's 9:32, and we've lost track of time as usual. He ignores her call and then texts: Driving. Be home soon. I walk him out while Lindsey heads to my room to get her shoes. "This Saturday?" he asks. "The Glass Café?"

"Of course." I lean back against his car door. Every Friday is football, so Saturday is our night out. We rotate between three restaurants. I tip my head back to kiss his lips, but his vibrating pocket interrupts us.

"Mom again," he says and kisses my cheek before getting into his car. Still no sign of Lindsey, even after John drives away. I walk back inside and find her in my room sitting on the edge of my bed. Her shoes sit by her feet next to the crumpled-up jeans I wore to school.

"Don't be mad," she starts. "It's just weird, seeing your jeans on the floor. You're a neat freak."

She's right. I don't even remember changing my clothes after school. I was stuck in a memory somewhere. She lifts her hand, dangling Carson's blue-and-black lanyard bracelet.

"You went through my pockets?"

She ignores the question. "There's a story, isn't there, Lex?" She holds the bracelet up to my eyes, trying hard to contain her bubbling excitement. Her body wins, and she reaches up and tackles me so that we're lying on the bed like two grade-school kids at a slumber party. The bracelet flings onto my pillow. "Come *onnnn*, Lex, don't lie to me, please? Your dad said something about avoiding California because of some guy?" I gnaw on my lip. The memories are starting to ache with no one to tell. "Were you in love?"

I nod, and her eyes light up like Fourth of July sparklers. "I *knew* it! I absolutely *knew it*! So the bracelet *did* belong to the hot guy with the green eyes. The one walking out of the ocean. Or wait! It belonged to his girlfriend, but he gave it to *you*!"

She's starting to stress me out. I don't know if I can handle disclosing the truth, much less trying to unwind it from Lindsey's web of conspiracy theories.

"Okay!" I say, and cover her mouth. She grabs hold of my wrist with both of her hands and squeezes. "Okay, I'll tell you. But you can't talk." She nods very fast and covers her mouth with her own hands. From there, I tell her the beginning, the whole camp story, and then I take her into the summer after camp, closer to what I want to forget.

★★★★★

After camp ended, Carson and I started talking every night before bed. The first night we watched *Saturday Night Live* together, and he added his own dialogue. Maybe I was just a good audience, but I laughed until my sides cramped, and then we talked until I fell asleep.

My battery went dead, so the next night, I plugged in my phone. We talked again until we fell asleep, but this time, he was still on the phone when I woke up. "Morning, Good," he said, his voice groggy with sleep. That was another tradition we started. Since he called me "Good," we started saying "morning good" and "night good" instead of "good morning" and "good night." Only we understood why, and that's all that mattered.

Unlike our friendship, Bethany and Dylan's relationship lasted only two weeks and five Kleenex boxes. Dylan and Carson lived in downtown LA, and we lived in Orange County, and at fourteen, anything beyond a bike ride might as well have been a different galaxy. Bethany could no longer waltz over to Dylan's villa in her bathing suit or meet him behind the archery range for a kiss. The new girl with the olive skin and wispy hair was now just someone who texted Dylan nonstop. Everybody knew that texting someone that much was stalker-ish. Unless you were best friends. Like me and Carson. Then, it was almost required.

"Hey, I gotta go," I told Carson. For the past three weeks since camp, we'd been calling each other daily, even when we had nothing to say. We'd talk about funny-looking people we saw at the mall. Or dumb videos we saw on YouTube. Who gets the armrest at a movie theater. Best hashtags. "Beth's calling."

"Yeah, Dylan told me about that."

I wanted to ask more, but instead I put Carson on hold and answered her call.

"He keeps ignoring me," Beth said through hiccups and sniffles.

"Aw, Beth. Maybe you should leave him alone a bit. Maybe he'll call you when he misses you."

I heard her swallow. "Kay."

"Carson's calling," I lied. "Can I answer? I want to see how his audition went."

I already knew, but I didn't know what else to say. Carson texted me the second he'd gotten the callback: Might be in a

Mazda commercial. My pretend parents and I dance around the car. Zoom zoom. Lol

Beth sniffled a goodbye as I clicked back over.

"She's crying again," I said.

"Yeah, big surprise."

My body jolted. Dylan's voice. "Hey, Dylan. Sorry, I thought it was Carson."

"No problem." The way he said it, I knew he was smiling. "Carson's in the bathroom. He told me to hold for you."

And that was our first phone conversation. I imagined him lying on Carson's bed, elbow bent, one hand behind his neck.

"What's up?" I asked.

"What's up?" he repeated, which made me laugh. "What's funny?"

"Nothing," I said. But I couldn't help thinking that Carson would've understood why I was laughing. I waited for him to tell me what he and Carson were doing today, or to ask me something about my day, or even to state something useless, like the color of his backpack. Finally a loud *thump* broke our silence, then shuffling. "What was that?"

"Dropped the phone."

"Oh."

I watched the clock above our piano. Thankfully, I heard another sound. Music. "What are you doing?"

"Playing guitar." His words were smooth, like his voice was strumming the strings. I melted: He was hot *and* a musician. "So I was thinking." He stopped like it was the end of a sentence.

"Yeah?"

He strummed a chord before continuing. Whatever he was about to say was good, the guitar made sure of that. "Maybe we should talk more."

Says the guy who hadn't said a word. Once again, I wished for Carson to be my audience so that he'd get it. I knew what Dylan meant, that we should hang out more—that he was interested—but I couldn't stop giggling. Again, he asked what was so funny.

"Nothing. Sure," I said. "Let's talk more. Get my number from Carson's phone."

"Yeah?" he said.

"Yeah."

"Cool."

"Cool."

I filled my cheeks with air. He strummed the guitar. What should I ask him about? Hobbies? Family? School? "How's life been since camp?"

"Good."

"Hmm?" I responded, but "Good" was *Carson's* nickname for me, not Dylan's.

"Huh?"

"Nothing. Sorry." I looked back at the clock. I could hear it ticking. On the other end, Dylan started finger-picking high notes.

What was taking Carson so long? Finally, I faked like my mom was calling me and told him I had to go.

Weird. I never thought about what to say with Carson. Why was it so hard with Dylan? That night, I opened my journal, and instead of recapping the day, I jotted down things to talk about. While I was writing, a notification lit up my phone. Carson had sent me a message. I opened Snapchat.

KNIGHT33
| Good

LEXYGURRL
| Sundheit!

KNIGHT33
| Thank you. What r u doing

LEXYGURRL
| Nothing

And that was the first lie. I wish I knew why I lied right then. Carson was my friend. I could tell him anything. I never had to make a list.

Maybe deep down, I knew Carson wanted to be the guy I'd make a list for. Now that I'm seventeen, that's easy to see. But in that moment, Dylan was taller, darker, and more mysterious. And I was fourteen. So I made a list.

Chapter Six

Two weeks after that first phone conversation with Dylan, Carson and I were on the phone as usual, falling asleep ear to ear.

I said, "Doesn't it feel like we grew up together?"

"What do you mean?"

"I mean, I thought I knew you when I met you. Like you reminded me of someone. And now it's like we've always known each other. But it's only been a month."

"Yeah," he said. "For me, too. Night, Good."

"Night, Knight."

"Wait," he said. "Wanna go somewhere?"

"Right now?"

"Yeah. Come on!"

"Carson, it's after midnight!" But I was up, slipping my shoes on. "Where?"

"Up, of course."

He said he was climbing to the roof of his apartment complex. My room was on the second floor. With some squeaking, I removed the screen and straddled the windowsill. Above me, the roof sloped fifteen feet higher.

"This is dumb," I said, putting my phone on speaker. But

I started crawling up. "So dangerous."

"Local teen dies on cell phone," he joked. "New law passed. No cell phones on roofs." Then he added, "Be careful." With shaky legs, I reached the peak and sat with my back against the chimney. Below me, streetlights winked, congratulating me on my climb. I felt that crazy-alive feeling again, like when I'd held Carson's hand and we ventured toward Hiker's Peak. I didn't want to share Carson with anyone in that moment, so I took him off speaker.

Ear to ear, we looked out at different views, but I felt closer to him than ever, too close to talk. When he finally spoke, he was quiet, like he didn't want to wake the world. "You can see the Hollywood sign from here."

"Really?" I exclaimed, totally forgetting the quiet rule.

"Shh."

"Amazing," I whispered. "You can't see any signs from here. But you can see mountains behind our street. Just the outlines. The canyons."

As the canyon breeze ballooned through my oversize T-shirt, a car drove by on the street below. Carson heard it. "Where do you think he's going?"

"Home?"

"From the bar." Carson always tried to guess what people were like by the cars they drove or the items they bought at the grocery store.

"What if he doesn't drink?"

"Oh, he does."

"But he's driving slow," I pointed out.

"Guilty. He's coming home from a strip bar."

I laughed. "I wish talking to Dylan was this easy."

Carson suddenly went quiet. Had my phone hit a dead spot?

"Carson?"

"You talk to Dylan?" He tried to sound casual, but something sounded wrong.

"No," I lied. "I meant back at camp. He always wanted to talk to Beth, remember?"

"Yeah, well, not anymore." I stayed quiet, so he added, "He got your number from my phone."

"Yeah?" I tried to sound like this was news to me. "Maybe he'll call then."

"Do you want him to?"

"I dunno. Do you care?"

This time, *he* stayed quiet. Carson shouldn't have cared if I was talking to Dylan. I shouldn't have cared if Carson knew. But we both did. More than "friends" should.

So I didn't tell Carson how Dylan would call me. Didn't tell him, either, that most of those "talks" were spent in silence, me writing stories or catching up on summer reading while Dylan plucked away on his guitar or smoked a cigarette. He liked to smoke, which was gross, but maybe that's what musicians did. Sometimes we'd talk, but our words didn't *click*. Maybe Dylan and I just needed to hang out in person. Still, the hot guy from the swim test back at camp—*that* guy—was paying attention to me, and it was new and exciting, and I didn't want to jinx it. Besides, there was nothing to tell. We weren't dating or anything.

"I should go. If my parents find me up here, I'm toast," I said.

"Be careful. And Lex—" I felt it then, the serious way he said my name, that he wanted to say more. Maybe he knew I was lying. Maybe Dylan had already told him. But instead he said, "Watch out for sagebrush."

★★★★★

Luckily, Beth left for Michigan to visit her aunt for a month, so I didn't have to hear her cry about Dylan while he called me on the other line. I felt so rotten, but Dylan was calling me, and no way was I going to tell him to stop. We finally did hang out in person, and I searched for that magical *click*. It never came.

Dylan, Carson, and I would meet up with a group of friends at Magic Mountain, a public park, or the beach. Carson had gotten his first commercial, and I insisted on treating him like a famous Hollywood star. At Magic Mountain, we'd yell in line, "Oh my gosh, it's Carson Knight!" and we'd all scream Carson's name. Crowds of people would crane their necks, looking for this famous "Carson." He always slugged me playfully when I'd yell or ask for his autograph, but I know he loved it because he never told me to stop.

Carson never wanted me to come inside his apartment, so we'd take his puppy, Cooper, to the park, and roll around with him and play tug-of-war, or climb trees while Cooper barked and whined at us from below.

We kept to our traditions: calling me "Good" instead of Alexa, climbing to high places, going to sleep on the phone, but he always surprised me with something new. Once we met up at Hollywood Hal's, this 1950s diner where the waitresses are mean to you, and it's supposed to be funny. My parents sat at a separate table with my grandma. I introduced Carson to my "oma," which means *grandma* in German. Carson smoothed his hair back and stood taller, straightening his shoulders. He shook her hand. "Wie gehts," he said, and they exchanged three or four sentences in German.

"I didn't know you spoke German," I said when we sat down.

"I didn't know you had a grandma," Carson said.

I laughed. "You're so dumb."

★★★★★

"Wait, wait, wait," Lindsey stops me. "Just Carson met up with you?"

"No. It was his friends and my friends."

"So what was the hot guy doing during all this? Where was Dylan?"

I blink. "I don't remember. Probably next to me. Can't remember if he sat by me at Hollywood Hal's. Maybe across from me?"

"What was he wearing?"

"Dylan?" I ask. "Gosh, Linds, I have no idea. Why does it matter?"

"Because it *does*! Because he's hot, and you'd remember that. I mean, you remembered Carson's *posture*, for God's sake." She sucks in a mouthful of air like she's been underwater too long. "Oh my word." She slaps her forehead. "Your artifact." She lifts the bracelet off the pillow, pinching it between her fingers. "You started liking Carson."

My body stiffens. I take back the bracelet. "Not right away. Or maybe right away. But I didn't realize it until we kissed."

"You kissed?" She leaps to her feet on my bed and then sits down cross-legged. "What about Dylan?"

I give a half laugh and tuck the bracelet under my pillow, out of eyesight. "Dylan was there."

Lindsey's eyes grow so wide, her eyelids disappear.

"It was just a *dare*, Linds. Not a real kiss. We were all—" Lindsey's hand shoots up like she's in class, dying to be called on. I roll my eyes. "Yes, Lindsey?"

She drops her hand. "So let me get this straight. After you started flirting with Carson's best friend, you started liking Carson. But only after you kissed him . . . in front of his best friend."

I wince. "Gah, when you say it out loud, I sound awful."

"You mean *awfully* awesome! Lexie, you're better than Hollywood! Tell me you confessed your love, and then you and Carson made out under the stars in the rain."

I feel a deep pang in my gut when I think of Paige's party. "You can't see the stars when it's raining."

"Don't change the sub—" She gasps, and her mouth drops wide open. "You never told him."

I think of how I tried. The memory pulls down my eyelids, and I swallow, then snap my eyes back open, resolute. "I was moving away. No point."

"Oh. My. Gosh." She rolls over onto me and looks up at the ceiling. Then she bounces up to her knees. "Lex, you have to find him."

"What?"

"Do you know where he is?"

I laugh and it comes out like a cough. "Yeah, I have an idea."

"Los Angeles, right? That's why your dad made that comment. Come on, road trip!" She dances on the bed like she's at a nightclub.

I shake my head. Carson used to live in Hollywood. Not the glamorous part, either. He lived at 402 Franklin, Unit 201, in the stack of apartments that looked like they were stapled together. I'm sure he doesn't live there anymore.

My phone chimes a jazz tune, and Lindsey stops dancing and glares at it. "Which one is that? Study time?"

All my friends know I have a separate alarm for everything in my life. Tonight, I'd already ignored the "Review Ch. 4 Calc" alarm and the "Plan outfit for tmrw" alarm.

"No, bedtime."

"But—"

"Forget it, Linds. I have debate this Thursday, cross-country on Saturday, ACTs in two weeks, college apps due in a month, and you want me to hunt down some kid from junior high who hates me, for all I know."

"It didn't sound like it," she counters.

"I never got to that part!"

"So let's get there! I'm waiting for it to get good." And by *good* she means *bad*, but I flinch at the word and head to the closet to plan tomorrow's outfit.

"He doesn't matter anymore," I say, tugging a blouse off a hanger.

"Obviously."

I stop and look at her. "I have a boyfriend now, remember? You're friends with him." I pick up her shoes with one hand and her backpack with the other, and walk to the front door. Her sock feet pad down the hallway behind me. "I've spent three years planning my road to Boston College, and I admit, the past few days have been shaky, but I'm not letting some stupid junior-high romance screw that up. Not now." Focus. I start to see tomorrow's checklists popping up in my head. "I don't care about him anymore."

She hugs me super tight, tipping me side to side as she says, "Fine," as if there are five i's in the word. "But I know things about Marvin Hillcrest that even TMZ hasn't discovered yet." She lets go, slips her shoes on, and pokes me in the chest once with her index finger. "I know love stories. And I know that if you really didn't care, you wouldn't have made Ms. Meckel get all cry-faced, and you wouldn't have lied about the bracelet." She slaps me softly on the side of the face. "And you *would've* told me the rest of the story."

"That's not true, my alarm—"

"Forget it, Lex." She opens the front door and walks out. The heat rushes in with her last words. "Bedtime, right?" She shuts the door behind her, so true to her personality, always looking for the last dramatic word, that Hollywood ending that leaves everyone begging for more.

Her words won't leave me alone. Even after I change into my pajamas and plug my phone into my charger. I drown them out with my electric toothbrush, but as soon as it shuts off, I hear her again: *"You* would've *told me the rest of the story."*

Lindsey with her crazy theories, what does she know,

really? I don't care about him anymore. "That's right," I agree with my thoughts.

"What's right?"

Mom pokes her head in my bedroom door. "Oh, nothing." I shuffle some papers on my desk as if I'm finishing up. "Just this calculus problem. I did it right. Correctly, I mean." I stack the papers and slip them into my backpack. "I was checking my answer with the book."

"Okay," she says. "Good night, then." She hesitates. "Lexie?"

"Hmm?"

"The calculus book you just checked your answers with? It's on the dining-room table. I wouldn't want you to forget it tomorrow morning."

"Right. Okay. Thanks." I walk to my mirror and start erasing my vocab word as if she hasn't just called me a liar in her sweet Mom way. *Disparate*. Tomorrow will be *disparate*, and to prove it, I wipe the word off my mirror with one sweep of my hand. I turn to the next word from the Kaplan study guide. *Obdurate*: stubborn. What a dumb word. It doesn't even *sound* stubborn. I skip to the next, swearing to myself that I'm not being obdurate. *Bilk*: to cheat or defraud. What kinds of words are these, anyway? Finally, I find one that I write on my mirror: *Tenacity*. Resoluteness; the state of holding firm to a purpose. That's right. I scribble my schedule for tomorrow, then snap the cap back on. I change my mind and pull the cap back off. I write down my long-term goals:

Straight-A streak. No losses.
ACT: 34? At least 32.

Valedictorian speech? Not cheesy.
X-country: Qualify for State

There's still more mirror space, so I scribble my goals for the week. I don't abbreviate on purpose, so I can fill up more of the mirror:

ACT book: 10 pages/day; all 4 subjects
X-country Saturday meet: 1st or 2nd
Personal statement— revise
Saturday date with John

I stop. Why do I categorize my date with John as a weekly goal? Something about that feels wrong. My thoughts feel muddy in my head, so I hop to the other sliding mirror and write my daily and weekly assignments, a different color for each class. After drawing one hundred seventeen beautiful squares, I discover that I still know the entire periodic table of elements by heart. I stand on a chair to reach the last twelve inches of space in the upper left-hand corner and write daily to-do's like *shower, eat dinner with family, go to school.* I even throw in *sleep* as if I wouldn't do it otherwise. When I'm done, there's barely room to peek my eyes through the loops in my cursive l's, but I step back and admire the view: My life is ordered, organized, and so full I can't see my reflection. I feel calm again and ready to attack tomorrow with *tenacity*.

Chapter Seven

In the following days, I erase each goal after I accomplish it: Revise my personal statement. Check. First place at Saturday's meet, turn in every school assignment, work on my ACT book—especially the science section. Check, check, and check. Sure enough, as I fall back into my usual routine, my mirror clears up, and there I am again in full view. This morning, as I sit in my first-period AP Lit class, my trip down memory lane with Lindsey two weeks ago already feels distant.

In class, we're studying Stephen Crane's "The Open Boat," the story of four men trying to find their way to shore in a little boat. Simple enough, until our teacher Mr. Kucan speaks. It's always simple until he speaks. My friends and I call him Captain S because we joke that he's secretly a sadistic supervillain. He loves giving extra assignments, especially if it involves punishing the whole class for one student's blunder. He's also notorious for knocking students out of valedictorian status, but so far, I've gotten nothing less than an A- from him. "Obviously, this was taken from a real incident," Mr. Kucan says, as if we all knew that. He paces the room, pausing at certain desks just to make students nervous. "Stephen Crane once was shipwrecked for thirty hours. He was with three other men." He stops and looks down at John, then taps his finger on John's desk. "One drowned while trying to swim ashore." John swallows, and his Adam's apple bobs up and down.

Mr. Kucan crosses the room and stops with his back to us. "This was written in the late nineteenth century, on the back end of the Industrial Revolution. We had made so many breakthroughs in technology that we believed we could dominate and conquer any force of nature." He turns on one heel. Faces us. "Enter four men in a boat, who learn too quickly that no amount of technology can save them from the forces of nature: a wave, a current, the wind, a shark—even starvation or exposure."

"Or love," Lindsey whispers, nudging me in the side. I'd hoped that she would've let it go by now.

"Interesting observation, Lindsey." Somehow, across an entire classroom, Kucan's supervillain ears have heard her misstep. The class groans. He strolls to the board and writes one word: *love*. "Is love a force of nature?" he asks. "Is it controllable by choice, or are you at its mercy? Can you avoid it?"

"Why would you want to avoid it?" asks Chad, the captain of our Varsity Club. He winks at the first girl who looks his way. I know he has no clue about the noun *love,* but Lindsey says he's well acquainted with the verb, at least according to the freshman cheerleading squad.

"A worthy inquiry," Mr. Kucan responds. "But perhaps Alexa, who found your question base enough to sardonically smirk at, could answer you."

My words tiptoe out of my mouth. "I didn't realize," I say,

which I hadn't, "but I can think of many reasons to avoid love." John looks at me, but I pretend not to notice.

"Name them," Mr. Kucan challenges.

"Pain," I say.

He waits, but I press my lips together. He says, "I thought you said many. Does the class need to write an informative essay on singular versus plural?"

"Regret," I add. "Loss. The feeling that you can never quite make something what you want it to be, and yet you can never go back to what it was."

"Well, well." He claps his hands slowly in mock applause. "Spoken like a typical teen movie."

"Maybe," I acknowledge, but his eyes bore into mine like I've sassed him. "I mean." I try to correct myself, but it barely comes out. "I don't watch movies."

"Then that will be the class assignment. Watch the new adaptation of *The Open Boat,* which was released in theaters Friday." For once, the class doesn't groan. Only I do. Who else would complain about watching a movie for class credit? A couple girls giggle and clap quietly.

Lindsey raises her hand.

"Miss Kenzington?"

"The movie is actually called *Open Boat,* not '*The* Open Boat' like the classic title."

"And I'm sure that won't be the only thing lacking," he responds. "As you know, this movie will be an atrocity to the classic, and Mr. Crane will be writhing in his grave during every reel. This is a teen adaptation, correct?"

The class collectively nods.

"Lovely," Mr. Kucan says drily. "Is there even a shipwreck?"

Lindsey's hand shoots to the sky.

"Yes, Miss Kenzington?"

"The story is about a high-school prom that takes place on a large yacht off Long Beach Harbor." She sounds like she could be reciting straight from IMDb. "Unexpected winds pull the boat off course, complications ensue, and the yacht sinks."

"Tragic," Mr. Kucan says.

"And four guys must make their way to shore on a lifeboat."

"And let me guess: They're from completely different social coteries in school and of course would never fraternize normally."

"Yes! But they need each other to survive."

"Of course they do." Mr. Kucan takes a moment, closing his eyes and swallowing like he just ingested one-hundred-proof whiskey. He opens his eyes and turns in my direction. "And lest you think I give credit for going to the cinema"—at this he glares at me—"you will write a critical essay delving into each of their motivations for reaching shore and answer the question of whether love is a force of nature as strong as the natural elements they face."

"Great, Mr. Kucan," Eric, a guy on my right, says. "We get to take our girls to watch two hours of Cayden McKnight." His words slap me in the face. I grip the sides of my desk tightly, trying not to react.

Mr. Kucan smiles at no one in particular. "Ah, yes. Mr. McKnight. The picture of upstanding citizenship." I don't know what he means by this, but I recognize the dripping sarcasm, and I feel defensive.

"Hey!" I shout, and then immediately snap my mouth shut. Mr. Kucan's feet stay planted, but he turns his neck slowly to face his challenger. "He's nice," I add softly. "I mean, I hear. I've heard." He cocks his head at me, amused. I'm tripping over my thoughts, and he knows it. Loves it. "He speaks German." I can't believe I just said that out loud, but my head is swimming in nausea.

"Ah, Germany," Mr. Kucan retorts. "A country with an impeccable moral reputation. Grand example, Alexa Brooks."

"Sir, I can't—" But I'm interrupted by an office aide who enters with a note for a student. Mr. Kucan is momentarily distracted, and I turn to Lindsey. My weak words spill out in a rushed whisper. "I can't watch a movie with Carson Knight."

"Carson?" she whispers back. "No, Lex, it's Cayden Mc—"

She stops, puzzling over the evident terror on my face. Then she looks down at her desk and pieces the names together under her breath. "Cayden McKnight, Carson Knight. Knight, McKnight. Knight, McKn—" Her eyes grow wide as golf balls, and her mouth freezes in a giant *O*. She turns to me with a look that says, "You kissed the hottest actor in America, and you never told me." Luckily, I don't have time to agree, because I can feel my breakfast coming back up, and I bolt out of the classroom.

The janitor later verifies to Mr. Kucan that my breakfast did, in fact, make it into one of his trash cans, so I'm not penalized for rushing out without a pass. When I drag myself from the nurse's office to second period, no one mentions anything except the usual, "Nice job at the meet on Saturday." In fourth-period Creative Writing, Lindsey sits across the room, and amazingly, she leaves me alone. She doesn't even offer a sideways glance when John approaches my desk to see how I'm feeling.

"Do you need anything?" He sounds insecure, like he's talking to a girl for the first time in his life. I realize I've never really needed anything from him.

I shake my head, and he visibly relaxes.

"Great. I mean, okay, let me know." But it sounds like he hopes I won't.

When I get to lunch, Lindsey swings next to me on the lunch bench. "Look whose color is back in her face!" she chirps.

"I say crazy things when I get sick, too, don't worry," Kim says, and then leans in like she's about to reveal a sexy secret. "One time when I had a fever, I told my dad to tell Leonardo DiCaprio to get out of our freezer." Everybody laughs, and Ryan gives me a sympathy pat on the hand, a lot coming from the king of apathy.

They all know what happened in Kucan's class.

In a panic, I scroll through our group chat, but thankfully, Lindsey didn't mention any Hollywood stars of my past. Just a text that I was so sick, I talked back to Captain Sadistic. I smile weakly at everyone. John keeps a short distance between us in case I'm contagious.

"Big game this weekend," he says to make sure I understand, and I do. It's logical, and that's us. But is that enough? I catch myself thinking this, and I cough. It startles John, and he looks at me like, *Are you getting sick again?* I shake my head, and he sighs gratefully. Should I be annoyed with this? That his game takes precedence? I feel, well, I don't feel. I mean, I don't feel bad. At all. I excuse myself from the table, but it doesn't help, because the person I want to get away from right now is me.

All this talk of boats and shores and Carson brings back a distinct memory, one of sand and lifeguard towers and first kisses. It feels like the memory stands over me the rest of the day, hovering, waiting for me to look up at it. Not a chance. After school, our cross-country team heads off on a ten-mile loop through Spring Valley. Lindsey, my usual running partner, doesn't show up to practice. I'm the same pace as our fifth guy runner, but strangely, he's absent as well. Instead, I'm left alone with no distractions, just neighborhoods with rows and rows of semi-custom homes. A memory catches up, matches my pace, and I can't outrun it.

★★★★★

I met Carson Knight on June 10. They say that at camp, you often have a "mountaintop experience" where you feel changed, transformed, and on top of the world. It lasts for a short bit until regular life swallows it up, and you end up more depressed than ever. My "mountaintop experience" lasted the rest of June and all of July. I had a perfect best friend, a secret almost-boyfriend, and a new tube of waterproof mascara.

Then Mom and Dad came home one night and told me the unthinkable. It was August 1, and my aunt had been watching me for a few days while my parents visited their friends in Las Vegas.

"We're moving," Mom said.

Chapter Eight

"What do you mean?"

"I mean we're moving," she said, as if repeating it would somehow explain it. "The market's low over there, and we got a great deal. We've been looking for a while. We started when you were at camp."

I felt dizzy. My parents couldn't just *move* me right before high school. "You're kidding, right?"

Dad shook his head.

"I'm starting high school in a month!"

Dad nodded.

I was annoyed that he wasn't talking at a time like this, just shaking and nodding his head like the baseball-player bobblehead on his dashboard.

"Which is why," Mom responded, "we're moving now. We don't want to move you midsemester."

"Why would you move me midsemester?! Why ever?! Why can't you wait until I go to college?"

"Financially, it's the right time."

"No, it's not! Not if you did your finances better!"

"Lex," Dad finally spoke—a warning. I stormed off. A minute later, I came back into the family room with the licorice tub I'd filled with all my babysitting money and spare change from the past three years. I dumped it onto the couch, and quarters bounced onto the carpet. Dimes slid between the cushions. I grabbed a fistful of dollar bills.

"I can get an apartment."

Dad started to speak, but Mom touched his arm, and he stopped. The money didn't get me a new apartment or a way out of Vegas. But it did get Mom's sympathy. She said, "Why don't I drive you and your girlfriends to the beach tomorrow before work? You can meet up with your friends from camp." I nodded miserably, then called Carson immediately to break the news.

★★★★★

The next morning, we arrived at the beach when the sand was still cold. The wet, salty air brought me back to camp, and camp reminded me of Carson, and suddenly I couldn't wait for him to get there. Then, because he always seemed to know, he tackled me from behind. My face pressed against the cold sand, making an imprint, and I laughed, rolling over and hugging the guy I felt like I'd known since birth. I was shaking the sand from my hair when I stood up to hug Dylan. He was still beautiful, but I wasn't so shocked by it. Maybe because we'd been to Magic Mountain and Hollywood Hal's. Maybe because at all those places and even on the phone, his one-word answers never changed. I knew he looked at me differently now, like he was paying attention, and he did it that morning at the beach. I was embarrassed that others might see, so I looked away.

We ate breakfast by the pier. When the check arrived, I slipped Carson a ten-dollar bill, and he didn't get mad. Under the table, he linked pinkies with me, and I knew it was his way of saying thanks. Then Dylan, sitting on my other side, slid his foot around mine and locked legs with me. Neither knew what the other was doing under the table. I didn't let go of either—fingers locked with Carson, legs locked with Dylan. It felt wrong, but in that moment, I didn't know who I should pull away from, so I stayed locked with both.

After breakfast, we played Frisbee and jumped around in the water. Dylan dunked me repeatedly, and Carson rolled his eyes. There were six of us: Dylan and Carson brought their friend Phil, and I brought Kara and Paige. We all basked in the morning sun, soaking in the heat and one another. I felt like we were seniors in high school on one last vacation with old friends before we left for college.

Dylan stood up. "Anyone wanna go back in?" He motioned toward the waves. Phil jumped up, and Paige reached for Kara.

"Come on," she said, pulling Kara up. Kara dusted the sand off her legs and grabbed the Nerf football. Phil ran toward the shore for a pass, and the four of them took off. Dylan looked back.

"You guys coming?"

"Soon!" I said. The sun was a warm blanket. Carson felt the same as I did; I could tell even without looking at his closed eyes. I tapped his shoulder and pointed out an empty lifeguard tower. "Wanna go up?"

"What a dumb question," he said, standing and walking toward it.

"*You're* a dumb question!" I shot back and hip-checked him once I caught up. At the top, we climbed onto the railing and hung our legs over the edge. We watched the waves reach for us like fingers stretching for the tips of our toes, collapsing and falling back to try again.

"I'll miss you."

It was the first time he mentioned the move. Somehow he knew I hadn't told anyone else. I rested my head on his bony shoulder, thinking back to his question: *Why do people like views so much?* We sat there for minutes, but this silence was different than the silence on the phone with Dylan. This quiet felt like home.

"Do you like Dylan?" His question caught me off guard.

"No." *Lie.*

"Does he call you?" he pressed.

"No." *Lie again.*

"Has he told you he likes you?"

"Nuh-uh. Why, *does* he?"

"If you don't like him, why should it matter?" I could feel his shoulder tighten under my ear. "You know that nobody ever talks about me that way? You and Beth are always asking about him. Dylan this, Dylan that. Tall, dark, and handsome Dylan—that's what Beth called him, right? What did she call me?"

I cringed. "I don't know."

"Yes, you do! You were there. *Cute* Carson. Cute. Really, Alexa?"

I was so shocked at hearing him call me by my actual name that I didn't notice he'd started climbing back down. "Come on," he said. "Let's go find *Dylan*."

Everyone was back at their towels when we returned, so thankfully we could slide back into the group conversation and drop the discussion. Paige finished her bottle of soda and spun it on the sand. "I know what we can play!" she said. She flattened a square of sand and spun the bottle like a pinwheel. No one wanted to admit we were nervous, so we all acted like spin the bottle was as common as brushing our teeth.

It landed on Phil. Paige spun it again. It landed on Dylan. Everybody laughed between chattering teeth, which was good, because it released the tension, and when Paige spun it a third time, it landed on Kara. Kara shrugged her shoulders in her easygoing way and said, "Okay, here goes." We lifted our towels like capes to shield the families nearby from our junior-high debauchery. We giggled and watched Phil and Kara lean in and French kiss each other. It felt funny watching two people kiss five inches from my face, like I was pressed up against a TV screen watching a soap opera.

The bottle spun onto Phil again. This time, Paige was the lucky contestant, spinning it right back at herself. Paige wasted no time. She came at him before he had a moment to think, and his eyes went wide with surprise. We all laughed, including Paige and Phil while they were kissing.

The third time it spun to me. I had kissed two guys before, one guy at sports day camp the summer before eighth grade, and Greg Wallace, my boyfriend for two months in eighth grade. Still, it was different with an audience. I remember hoping it would be Dylan because every girl wants to know what it's like to kiss the hot guy. But it landed between Paige and Carson. "Close enough," Paige said. "Carson, you're up."

No one knew that Carson and I had just had a sort-of argument. I'd never thought about kissing Carson before, but I figured it'd be like talking to him, easy and fun, with no thinking involved. But when I looked over at him and saw his shy eyes dart back and forth across the sand, something dropped in the bottom of my stomach. I wiped my sweaty palms on my towel. It felt too intense, especially with people staring. This guy knew too much about me, and kissing would take us somewhere I'd never been. It would force me to think about him in *that* way, the one way I'd avoided since I'd met him.

Carson scooted closer to me. "Whatever, right?"

"Yeah." I lifted and dropped my shoulders. "Whatever."

We both wanted to play it cool, so we kept our eyes open, like it was no big deal. But when our lips touched, we discovered what we both knew all along: We *clicked.* We clicked in the obvious ways, ways that everyone else could see—the way we talked and never wondered about what to say, the way we laughed and nudged and play kicked each other—but in this moment, I realized that we clicked in the ways that everyone *couldn't see*, too—the way that our kiss fit like two puzzle pieces, and how secretly on the towel, our pinkies reached for each other like they belonged to the same hand. I suddenly understood why I never had to explain myself, why he just *knew*. When I pulled away and looked at him, his eyes were bluer than I remembered, and his smile curled in a way that made me want to find it again with my lips.

"Whoa!" Paige yelled.

"Whatever," I said, embarrassed. My eyes were watering

because I hadn't blinked the whole time.

"It's okay, Paige. I'm just *cute Carson*. Right, Alexa?"

I couldn't decide if I was angry or relieved that he didn't know what I'd felt at that moment, but the lifeguard broke us up. "Hey, kids, some parents are complaining about what you're doing." I looked to the left, and two young boys, caked in dried sand, were pretending to kiss their hands, slobbering and giggling. Apparently, our towel walls had a few cracks. "Why don't you go for a swim?" the lifeguard suggested.

I jumped up and sprinted for the water. I hated that my feelings were bigger than me, that there I was, locking legs under the breakfast table with the hot guy, but having more feelings for his not-as-hot best friend, more feelings than I'd ever felt in my life. And no one knew.

Before we left that day, Paige invited the boys to her birthday party the following week. It'd been planned for months; in fact, she'd invited all seventy students in our eighth-grade class, and now that list included Dylan, Phil, and Carson. "I asked my dad to invite some of his casting-director friends," she said, winking at Carson. Her wink bothered me. "We'll have an open mic and do some improv. Sooo much fun. Oh, and bring your board shorts. Hot tub!"

On the car ride home, Paige whispered in my ear, "So what was it like?"

"What?"

"Kissing *Carson*? I see you watching Dylan like a hawk." She grinned. "You and Beth can have dibs on him. Carson is way adorable."

Shock paralyzed my thoughts. *No.*

"So what's it like? Kissing him?"

"I don't know, Paige." She stared at me, disbelieving. "He's just, I don't know, he's *cute* Carson. He's little."

"Like his tongue's little?" she whispered. I fidgeted with my seatbelt. I didn't want her to like him.

"Yeah, it was gross. He's like my best friend. It's like you kissing your brother."

She erupted in laughter. My mom looked at us through the rearview mirror. I ignored them both and stared out the window.

Chapter Nine

It's almost sunset when I arrive at Heidi's house. Heidi lives about a mile from school, so whenever I don't have a ride after cross-country practice, I just walk to her house, and she drives me home after we do homework.

Lindsey's car is parked in the driveway when I arrive. No surprise. I let myself in and make my way to the back end of their house. Heidi's room is a jungle. Her potted plants litter the floor, leaving only patches of visible carpet. Five different types of cacti line her windowsill, and miniature bonsai trees perch on her desk. More plants hang from the ceiling, and even ivy snakes up her walls.

Two steps in, I freeze.

"Please don't be mad," Lindsey starts.

There, draped across the ivy, are two large maps taped to the wall, one of the city of Los Angeles all the way out to the Pacific Ocean, and the other of Hollywood only. Across Heidi's bed are posters and cutouts of Carson from teen magazines, articles from TMZ.com, and printouts from IMDb.

A Carson Knight bedspread.

Lindsey holds up a photo. I stand there like an injury, limp and unable to move. Carson is no longer a boy. His blond hair is darker, still falling in that boyish way, but more like it does so on purpose now. His eyes, still piercing blue, shoot through the photo like they're looking at me, the way they always did. His face is carved now—no longer roundish—and a shadow of stubble covers his jaw. His frame is broad, and gone are the bony shoulders I rested my head on. Who knew that behind the little boy I climbed high places with was the most gorgeous man I'd ever seen.

"Well?" Lindsey asks.

I can barely muster words. "He's tall."

"Six foot two!" she squeals. "Oh my gosh. You've never seen him? How could you NOT? What about magazine covers at grocery-store checkout lines?"

My mouth is dry. "I, uh, never look."

"So what do you think?"

"Why?"

"Because it's *time*. I don't care what went wrong. Look, you have to watch his movie for Captain S, right? So! Being the greatest friend in the universe, in many universes, which we learned last night in the ACT reading passage is called the multiverse—"

"Get on with it," Heidi says. "Her future grandchildren are yawning."

"Okay, okay! I thought I'd get your feet wet, and don't worry, I didn't tell *anyone*. Just Heidi because, God knows, I have secrets on her."

Heidi lifts her eyebrows and nods, like, *You've got that right.* She grabs a watering can and begins feeding her ferns.

"I did some research because I knew you wouldn't. You

might want to sit down for this."

Lindsey pushes some magazines aside and makes room on the bed. I plop down, my strength sapped.

"Okay, Carson Knight, renamed Cayden McKnight. I put that together in class because a lot of celebrities change their names. But I couldn't figure out why. It's the only thing I couldn't find on him."

I pinch the bridge of my nose and close my eyes. "Renamed by his agent. Carson Knight sounded too much like *Carsonite*—a person from the city of Carson."

"That makes total sense!" Lindsey says, and I open my eyes. "You know Jennifer Aniston's dad changed their last name? It was Anastassakis! Sounds like 'Anna's ass I kiss!'"

Heidi laughs and spills water onto the carpet. "Love it."

"Plus," I continue, "there was that actor Carson Pike at the time—"

"Yes!" Lindsey jumps in. "He was the actor on that law drama *Raising the Bar*. What ever happened to him?"

"No idea. Probably nothing. But at the time, the names were too similar. Carson was just doing commercials that summer, so he was only 'Cayden' for auditions. He met some big talent agent at my friend's birthday party. That was the last time we talked, so I don't know what happened after that."

"You never looked him up?"

I shake my head. *Look him up?* He wanted nothing to do with me.

She adds, "But you knew he was a big deal . . ."

"I do hang around people like *you*. And when I see his name scrawled on the bathroom walls, I'm guessing he's not just doing infomercials. I just never opened a magazine or turned on the television. So, no, I don't know everything."

"Well!" Lindsey grabs me by the shoulders, like she's won front-row tickets to a concert. "I've been working on this all afternoon, so let me give you a crash course on Cayden McKnight, son of Hilda Krause and Charles Knight II."

"Heidi?" I plead, but Heidi's hunched over, examining a browning fern leaf.

"I told her to let you be," Heidi says. "It's called 'the past' for a reason. I've got more important things to deal with, like this little guy here." She holds up the fern with wilting leaves. "He's like, 'You ever heard of water, Heidi?' "

"Okay, then, it's settled!" Lindsey bounces over to the map on the wall. With her teeth, she yanks the cap off a red Sharpie and gets to work, marking stars at the places she names. "Cayden's currently filming a Super Bowl commercial in downtown LA, off First and Broadway, but it's primarily night shoots. When he's not filming, he's been spotted at the following clubs." She jumps over to the Hollywood map. "Voyeur, 3two3, and the Viper Room. Typical. Mostly house parties, though, because he *is* only seventeen. Like that really matters when you're Cayden McKnight, but still. There's a new club he's recently been frequenting, called L'événement, on the cliffs in Malibu. Which brings me to where he lives." She fills her lungs like she's getting ready for the punch line, but she exhales the words, "I have. No idea." She pulls the map off the wall. Taped underneath is a piece of paper with names of girls and restaurants. "But! I do know the girls he's dated and the places he likes to eat." She pauses. "We'll skip the girls. Sore subject. Food: Johnny Rockets, Go-Go Fish Bar, and this coffeehouse called Sunrise on Sunset. On Sunset Boulevard, of course. Oh, and at Johnny Rockets, he orders a cheeseburger, no mayo."

"He's allergic," I say. "Eggs."

"Ha!" Heidi, amused, laughs one syllable.

"See?" Lindsey slaps the wall. "It's love!"

"Because I know his favorite condiments? Lindsey, no!" I pull down the maps and the papers and fold them up. "I did something to him that friends should never do, much less a girlfriend, and he's moved on. I've moved on. And this is nice, really, *really* nice." I hold her hands in gratitude. "But I'm not going to become one of *those girls* who thinks she can chase down some movie star because she used to sit next to him in third grade."

"Told you," Heidi says to Lindsey. She picks up an orchid. "Now if you'll excuse me. This one lives off humidity, so he gets to shower with me twice a week." She pokes her nose into the single white flower. "That's right, lover," she says, kissing its petals. She walks down the hallway to her bathroom.

"OMG, Lex, you are so stubborn!" Lindsey only uses text-message language when she's riled up. "Seriously, what the hell!" She stacks all her hard work in piles, then slams the piles together one by one. "W," she says, slamming papers together. "T." *Slam!* "H." *Slam!* "Look, I was giving you this crash course today because—"

Heidi flies back into the room minus the plant. "Ryan and John are here," she says. "I heard my mom opening the door for them."

Lindsey stuffs the papers into the closest backpack: mine. I glare at her, but she throws her hands up like, *Where do you expect me to put them?*

"Hey, girls," John says, walking in.

Ryan kisses Heidi's cheek. He turns to me, grinning. "S'up, yucker?"

I feel the heat in my cheeks. Guess everyone heard I threw up. "Just ate something weird," I say. We sit, the five of us, and recap the day. The guys ran lines at football, and John made some "sweet blocks." Lindsey tells John to demonstrate one. When he says no, she charges at him anyway, and he laughs, flipping her over his shoulder before gently setting her down. "Watch the fern!" Heidi shouts, but she's laughing, too. Lindsey has this way of bringing out the fun in everyone. I mean, it's not like John's boring. He's on student council; people like him. But I never seem to bring that out. As if he can read my thoughts, he puts an arm around me. I lean my head on his shoulder.

After an hour or so, Heidi's mom brings us pizza. We study some, talk mostly, and then, around nine, John offers to drive me home.

As we leave the bedroom, Lindsey stops me. Everyone else is down the hallway. She says, "Cayden's here, you know."

Jokingly, I look toward the hallway, then the window.

"Not *here* here, like Heidi's house, idiot. I mean, here. Las Vegas. Cayden McKnight is in the same city as you tonight. That's what I was trying to tell you before the guys came. Your Cayden crash course?"

My breath hitches, but I control it and look at her evenly.

"I don't know Cayden. I know Carson. *Knew* Carson." I take her hand and squeeze it. "Please, Linds."

I catch up with John and climb into his car, but Lindsey appears at my window. "Phantom Bar. Top floor of the Palms." I roll up the window and blast the air conditioning. I hear her as we drive away, "It's his favorite spot!"

"What was that about?" John asks as we pull onto Sahara Boulevard toward the I-15.

"Nothing," I say. "You know Lindsey and her hunt for celebrities. She follows any story. Probably some alien mating with a soap star."

He laughs. "Yeah."

We drive for a bit, and the stars seem brighter than usual. Or maybe it's the Las Vegas lights making me feel more awake. "Let's go someplace high," I say.

"I'm sorry?" he says.

"Like, Red Rock Canyon. Let's go night hiking. I bet the stars are gorgeous tonight."

"Uh," he says. I wait, but he doesn't say more than that. He doesn't change the direction of his practical and gas-efficient Camry, either.

"Okay, maybe that's far. Let's drive to Caesars Palace. You can hop down onto their roof from the top floor of the parking garage."

"Why on earth would you do that?" he asks, not being mean. He genuinely doesn't understand. But I do. John and I are an algebra equation. Plug in the right formula, and you get a perfect answer. But no deviations.

"I'm sorry. I've been feeling light-headed all day."

"Yeah, I've noticed. You're really not sick?"

He leans away from me toward his window, but I shake my head. "Promise."

Since John's past his curfew, he drops me off without coming in, probably hoping I wake up tomorrow as the girl he's dating. I pretend I don't have a key, so I walk around back, and he drives away. When he's out of sight, I lean against the wall for support and let my backpack drop against the side door to the garage. I kneel down on the hard-packed ground and trace my finger along a crack in the dirt, eyeing my backpack like a bomb might explode if I touch it. Gingerly, I peel open the zipper and remove the crumpled magazine cutouts. A few flutter out of my hands as I fish for the one I saw before. There. I turn on my iPhone light to look again. Just like before, Carson's eyes look directly into mine. *"Sure, I guess you can call me your best friend,"* I hear him say. "I'm sorry," I whisper, the back of my throat cramping. Suddenly, I'm desperate to see him. I want to look in those eyes, the ones that saw the life, the adventure, the completeness in me I'd always had but never known until he woke it up. I stick my ATM card and driver's license in my running shorts. I'm still wearing my running shoes, and it's only four and a half miles to the Palms as the crow flies.

★★★★★

The hotel is west of the Strip, the main road full of high-rise casinos, which means it's north of my house. It's a pretty fast run, not a lot of stoplights, just industrial buildings, undeveloped land, and way too much time to think. What do I say when I get there? How do I explain? *Hi, Carson, remember me? The one who embarrassed you in front of hundreds of people? Turns out I was in love with you. Can I buy you a drink?* A drink. Who am I kidding? I'm not twenty-one.

There's an unspoken waiver for Hollywood A-listers when it comes to clubs and bars. There's no such thing as a drinking age if they help with the publicity of the establishment. But I'm just a valedictorian-hopeful distance runner—which is enough to get me a Shirley Temple and a pat on the back as they escort me out and tell me to come back in four years. Maybe I can have the bouncer hold my license at the door and give me five minutes, although even five minutes with Carson makes me nervous. I should be in bed reviewing my vocab word—*exacerbate: to make a bad situation worse*—practicing the word *on paper* instead of doing it to my life! I'm running four and a half miles to see a guy whose last words to me were, "Don't *ever* talk to me again."

I hadn't planned to.

Until today. Today when I looked at him, at that picture Lindsey showed me, that feeling deep down inside me did a back flip, reminded me what it felt like to be truly *alive*. Now I need to see him, to find out for sure if the 3D version of him is the same as the two-dimensional photo. If what I feel is still there, not just a memory resurfacing.

I try to remind myself it was *junior high*. The summer before ninth grade. I wasn't old enough to be in love. Maybe when I see him, I'll laugh and think I made a big deal out of nothing. Maybe he'll laugh, too, and say he overreacted, and we'll both wonder why we ever stopped being friends.

Even while holding a clunky iPhone and rolling my ankle on a couple of dark patches through the desert, I make it to the main entrance of the Palms in a little over thirty minutes. I look down at my phone and see a text from Lindsey.

where r u?

I type back: nowhere

as in the Palms? Dropped by your house. Hmm . . . backpack in backyard. Forget to bring it in?

She's good. Before I can answer, she types: Meet me in front of the theaters.

Chapter Ten

As I step through the double doors of the Palms, the rush of air conditioning slaps through my sweaty clothes. I shiver and think of one more thing I forgot besides the underage factor: my attire. I don't believe the dress code for a Las Vegas club includes Nike shorts with a wick tank top over a sports bra. I shove the cold aside and dodge between clinking slot machines and a group of drunk girls celebrating a bachelorette party.

I make my way through the narrow Palms Casino, past the card tables down the long hallway on the right until I arrive at Brenden Theatres and IMAX at the Palms. I overhear a kid at the counter window arguing that he's thirteen *and a half* so they better sell him the PG-13 ticket to *Open Boat.* I shiver again, not because I'm cold, but because Mr. Kucan's words reverberate, *"Is love a force of nature? Is it controllable by choice, or are you at its mercy?"* Eleven movies are playing at this theater. Why couldn't I have overheard a conversation about a senior-citizen discount for *Old and Hairy, Part 4*?

Across the movie lines, I see that familiar curly brown hair bouncing up and down as she waves at me. "You!" I say to Lindsey when she's in earshot.

"What do you mean *me?* You're the one about to train

wreck." She holds up a ratty backpack, and I notice it contrasts with her Vivienne Westwood blouse and True Religion jeans. She's almost as tall as me with her three-inch heels.

"When did you change?"

She doesn't answer, but I take the backpack, knowing that she's packed me a club-worthy outfit inside. We head to the bathroom where I take a quick Euro shower, sponge-bathing the necessary areas. A few ladies stroll in, ignoring me. Not surprising. No one notices half-naked escapades in Vegas. One lady staggers in with a plastic toy guitar strapped to her chest. She sips from a long straw, and I notice that the straw's attached to the plastic guitar, which isn't a toy, but a container for alcohol. "Thirty-six ounces!" she boasts, which sounds more like "Firty-fix ounchezzz!" She sees me sponging my body in my sports bra and tiny shorts and screams, "Wild night, I know! Hell, yeah!" Then she leans up against the hand dryer and falls asleep on her feet.

I slip on the Rock & Republic jeans and a top that hangs low in the back. Amazingly, these jeans reach the floor, which means they definitely don't belong to Lindsey's 5′3″ frame. As I slip on a Joie leather jacket and heels, I say, "Linds, have you forgotten that my twenty-first birthday is in February—in *four* Februaries?"

She reaches into her back pocket and flashes two IDs. "You can thank Delaney next time she's in town." Delaney is Lindsey's twenty-two-year-old sister, four years older and four inches taller, and a girl who attends clubs like Catholics attend holy days. She's always telling Lindsey she needs to get out more. She probably gave Lindsey her and her friends' old IDs for Christmas. It explains why I look like I stepped out of the first limo on *The Bachelor*. After a quick makeover, we pucker our lips, blow a kiss at the mirror, and exit the bathroom.

"Ready?" Lindsey says, squealing in excitement.

"No," I say.

"Perfect. You'll come across more sincere."

I wrap my arm around her and bury my face in her ear. "Thank you." I feel my throat tightening, so I pull away and laugh, shaking my head. "This is crazy!"

"No. *That* is crazy." She points to the line snaking around the wall and starting at the elevator. "That's the elevator to the fifty-fifth floor."

I text Mom that I'm spending the night at Lindsey's, and as we walk to the back of the line, I pull up a vocab app on my phone and quiz her with the first word. "Myriad."

Lindsey looks at the blackjack tables like she's thinking hard. "Myriad. Noun. Meaning: buzzkill."

"Nope." Then I realize what she's doing, but she steals my phone out of my hand.

"Stop."

"What? We've got time." She rolls her eyes. "Look. I just need something, anything, to calm my nerves."

"So let's make a list. You like lists. Reasons why Cayden liked Alexa Brooks—"

"Carson—"

"One, NOT because you were a walking dictionary."

I feel my hands shaking. "Is there a two? Because if there's only a one, it's not really a list—"

"Oh emm geeee, stop! This wasn't who you were when you knew him. You were fun."

"I *am* fun!" I argue.

"Look, you have friends, so no, you don't have the personality of a plant. Your friends like you because you're nice and helpful and not creepy, and you laugh at bad jokes and you're thoughtful and we love that, yay, you. But remember in ninth grade when you demolished all the upper classmen at beer pong?"

I smile. "I was competitive."

"No, you were *fun*! That's the night I met you. And remember in tenth grade when you convinced Kim and Heidi to streak topless across the front yard of the old people's home during outdoor bingo?"

"It was truth or dare."

"But it was a crazy-fun dare!"

I laugh at the memory. "Remember the guy with the cane? Waving it in the air like a fist pump and shouting, 'Woo!'"

"Oh, you know that was the best damn entertainment he had all year. And when you tell me these stories of you and Cayden, it's like it's you but not you. It's the you that kills it at beer pong and gets ninety-year-old men to shout 'Woo,' but not just once in a while. Like, twenty-four seven."

"Carson made me that way."

"No. You *were* that way. That was you. That's *why* he loved you. So how about instead of stupid 'myriad' and her buzzkill, you spend a few minutes remembering who you are, who you *still* are somewhere under all those vocab words, so that when you see him in a few minutes, he'll recognize you. You want him to recognize you, don't you?"

"I don't know." I'm not sure he'll want to recognize me, because what he loved, he ended up hating in the end. I must be lost in thought because I don't notice the elevator ride fifty-five stories up, and I don't hear the bouncer until the second time he says, "Ladies?"

We look up to a large man holding out his hand for our IDs. I freeze—just stare at him like I'm deaf and he's asked me the capital of Jupiter—but Lindsey hands him both IDs. He looks at one, then the other, and then back at us. "Which one of you's Delaney?" We both raise our hands. Then we both point at the other. It's like a scene from a bad comedy sketch.

"Sorry," Lindsey apologizes. "She's Delaney. My name's Laney. I must not have heard the 'duh.'" She giggles, trying to warm him up. He looks at her without smiling.

"Well, then, Laney," he says, "the elevator's behind you. Your friend, DUH-laney, can go in. In fact, she can go in *twice* if she wants." He hands the IDs back to me. I examine them closely.

"Linds, these are *both* Delaney!"

"They're just supposed to check the *birthdate*!" she whispers. "The picture's close enough."

"It's two pictures of the same person!" I yell, but I know it's the nerves. I lower my voice and grab her hands. "Lindsey, I can't do this alone."

"Nice jacket," a girl says to me as she walks by in the VIP line. She's in the same Joie jacket, but she takes hers off and drapes it across her arm. "Look," Lindsey pleads with the bouncer. He doesn't look. Instead, he moves on to the next girls in line. He glances at their IDs and waves them through.

"Look, sir—"

"Devon," he corrects without glancing her way.

"Devon," she presses, "my friend needs five minutes to find Cayden McKnight."

Devon turns to her and raises an eyebrow.

Lindsey's gotten his attention and doesn't want to lose it. "She's afraid to go by herself because, well, because she's in love with him."

"Lindsey!"

At this, he laughs. "Yeah, you and every girl in America. Listen, kid, don't bother him. He's not nice to the girls he *does* know. So save yourself the humiliation."

"She *does* know him!"

"*Did*," I correct. I've never had a drink in my life, but right now, a shot sounds lovely. Maybe ten. Anything to stop this sudden uncontrollable shaking that's overtaken me. Lindsey grabs me by both shoulders, steadies me.

"Hey," she says. "Focus. You're Alexa Brooks. Soon-to-be-valedictorian. Senior class council. Cross-country MVP. You kick butt in debate. I know many guys who'd love for you and John to break up."

"Really?"

"No, but maybe if I think about it."

"Wait," the bouncer interrupts. "You have a boyfriend?"

Lindsey throws her hands up. "You *both* are missing the point!" She cups my face with her hands. "Nothing intimidates you, Lex! I don't know what the heck went on between you two, but just go in there, find him, and apologize. Get rid of three years of guilt. Go." She's right. And she's being an amazing friend, because I know that everything inside her wants to see Cayden McKnight face-to-face.

I rest my hands on my knees, like I'm recovering from a race, then stand.

"Okay," I say. As I walk by, the bouncer pats me on the back, hard enough to knock me forward a little. I catch myself on wobbly heels.

"When he's not at the VIP tables," Devon says, "he hangs by the lookout."

★★★★★

Phantom Bar reminds me of the Haunted Mansion ride at Disneyland: curvy tables like the curvy cars you ride along the curvy track. Fluorescent lights offer a ghostly glow to the dark indoor area. I rub shoulders with *myriads* of young men who brush my waist or the small of my back, not in a creepy way, just the casual passing protocol in a bar, apparently.

"Miss?" A tuxedoed man with white gloves touches my arm. "Your jacket?" I hand it to him, and he places a ticket in my hand, then disappears to a private room to hang it up. Outside, past the dance floor and bouncing heads, I see a silhouette leaning against the rail, and although I haven't seen him in years, I know it's him by the way one shoulder still drops a little lower than the other. My legs feel like they do in the final four hundred yards of my races—Jell-O. Determined, I wobble across the dance floor toward the lookout until I stand on the edge of a glass floor, where you can look straight down fifty-five stories. Carson stands at the other edge, looking out across the skyline of Las Vegas. We're less than twenty feet from each other. Before I can approach him, he turns to a server. She writes down his drink order, and he hands her a folded bill with one hand, touching her cheek with the other.

Over her head, he glances my way. His eyes stop on me, curious for a moment, until it hits him. He knows it's me. He steps off balance, catches himself. We stare at each other, and my heart would knock me over if my feet weren't drilled to the floor. There's no way to describe what another human being can do to you when they're *that* person—the one you meet and immediately feel as if your life is *supposed* to include them, and any day from then on without them feels incomplete and foreign. It's crippling; it's fantastic. And nothing changes it, not the twenty feet between us. Not the three years we spent apart. Not a Hollywood lifestyle of agents, publicists, and movie-promotion tours.

His blond hair lifts with the warm desert breeze, like it doesn't want to disturb his perfect face. If we could just look at the view together, the view that always made everything okay between us, then—But the moment is interrupted by a girl, the same girl who passed me in the VIP line, who walks up to him and slides her hand around his hip. Our gaze is broken, and he writes something on a slip of paper—a receipt?—and then turns to her.

He leans in and kisses her neck, looking at me while he nuzzles her. He slips a hand into her jacket pocket to tug her closer, all the while never breaking eye contact with me.

I'm real, I want to scream. *You're not imagining me!* My eyes are wild with apology, but he doesn't acknowledge them, or wink, or even blink. He stays with her. Doesn't come over. Doesn't find out why I'm here, why I've run four and a half miles at night across the desert just for him. Instead, he removes her jacket. I'm guessing she put it on again so she could feel him take it off. He breaks his gaze and motions for the white-gloved man, who appears out of thin air and retrieves the coat, replacing the tip in Carson's hand with a white claim ticket. As Carson continues to caress this girl's arms, he again looks my way, his eyes revealing nothing. Not that he's forgiven me, or the opposite—that he's angry and trying to make me jealous. His gaze is flat, not even a hint of curiosity. But it's no mistake that he's looking at me.

And that's when I know.

He *wants* me to see that I no longer exist to him. I back out, foot behind foot. My high heel twists downward, causing me to stumble and reach for a passing guy who steadies me. "Sorry," I mumble, and I can't tell if it was to him, or to Carson for ever thinking this would be okay.

I hurry to the coat check, but no one is present to receive claim tickets. There are only a few jackets on this warm summer night, mostly worn by those who spent all day in the air-conditioned casino. I can see the gold threading hanging closest to the door, so I reach in and slip it off its hanger, worried that my embarrassment will flood the bar if I stay a moment longer.

As I approach the entrance, I see Lindsey standing on tiptoes with one hand on the bouncer's shoulder for balance. "Well?" she squeaks. "Did you tell him? What did he say?"

"Let's go."

Lindsey looks at me, and then, on her tiptoes, she looks over the many heads at the bar. "Is he there? Did he see you? Maybe he didn't recognize that—"

"Let's go," I say again.

She nods, once to me and once to Devon, exhales deeply, and ushers me away with a hand on my waist.

★★★★★

On the drive home, I busy myself with the blurring lights of the buildings and passing cars. I haven't spoken since Devon said to me, "Told you, kid. He's a Grade-A piece-a-work. Not worth your time." Lindsey has been overly kind, not asking one question about what Carson looked like or what he was wearing. We drive to her house, west on Tropicana until the street becomes fewer hotels and more houses. Finally, she can't stand it anymore. "I should've warned you," she says. "I knew you hadn't read up on him, but I just didn't think he'd be that way with you. He's such a different guy in your stories." She taps the steering wheel, maybe waiting for me to say something, maybe trying to figure out how to start. "He's known as Hollywood's hardest star. Doesn't talk to anyone. Meets girls at clubs, doesn't date anyone seriously. He's got a season pass courtside to the Lakers, and he doesn't cheer when they score or even get mad when they mess up. They call him 'the Nodder,' because when he likes a play, or a slam dunk, he'll nod."

"And people like that?"

"Are you kidding? They *love* him. Guys think he's hella cool. Girls find him mysterious. He's a code they all want to crack." I try to absorb this, but I'm still numb. Lindsey's next words are a whisper. "So what happened?"

"Nothing!" Lindsey flinches at my volume. "I'm sorry. I didn't even talk to him. I just—" I hold my breath for a moment, trapping it inside my aching lungs. My aching everything. "I just *looked* at him."

"Maybe he didn't notice. Maybe he didn't remember."

"No, he saw me. He looked at me, too. *Really* looked." I chew on my lower lip. "And then he didn't."

"What did you *do*?"

"Nothing," I mutter. "I just looked at him. It was enough."

"I didn't mean tonight." Lindsey shakes her head and makes a slow left turn. "I mean, what did you do *back then*? At that party?"

I turn to my window. We're not going fast enough for the scenery to blur, but it does anyway as the memory comes into focus. With quiet words and a cramped throat, I take Lindsey back to the night of Paige's party.

Chapter Eleven

Paige's dad was a big-time casting director, and his house made sure we knew it. Modern furniture. Abstract art with splattered paint. It was like a field trip to a museum rather than a birthday party. All seventy graduating eighth graders congregated throughout the first floor and outside patio.

Most of the parents hid inside with their phones trying to snap photos of their children without being seen. There was even a dance floor and stage in the house, and every hour, the deejay would stop the music for skits. Phoebe Fairgano sang the national anthem, which we'd heard her sing five thousand times for school events. Two boys stepped onto the stage and started laughing. "You start!" one said. The other hit him and said, "No, you start!" The first boy said, "I didn't fart!" Then they laughed and walked off the stage, shoving each other. Paige begged Carson and Dylan to do the skit they did at camp, the one I had told her made the whole camp laugh.

The boys agreed and pulled a few other of our guy friends backstage. Paige had a catch, though. She wanted Carson to perform it with her dad, Mr. Connelly. That way, all his friends—the agents and directors—would watch, too. I knew it was her way of "winning" Carson.

Mr. Connelly was a good sport. He and the boys rehearsed once through, but they decided it'd be more fun if they improvised the dialogue. As silly as the skit was, it was a great chance to show off Carson's acting skills; however, I could tell the party made him uncomfortable. I wondered if he'd change his mind.

"Wow, was this lawn cut with scissors?" Carson asked as we walked along the winding sidewalk path in Paige's backyard. The grass on either side of us was trimmed like a mini-golf course. Paper lanterns lined our walk, and rows of fat bulbs crisscrossed over the pool, a combination of China and Italy at night. "I feel so out of place here," he said, motioning to the pool bar where a group of adults in expensive suits mingled. Probably the casting directors and talent agents that Paige was telling us about. "My shirt doesn't even have a collar."

"Don't be dumb," I told him. I leaned down and dipped my finger in the glassy pool. "No one here knows anything. Who cares about that, anyway?"

"Everybody," he mumbled. I wish I knew a magic trick that could make him less embarrassed about money. There was so much more to him. I looked around at all the tuxedos and fancy dresses. Everyone was dressed up except Carson, who was wearing jeans and a button-down long-sleeve. I thought he looked fine. Amazing, in fact, but I hadn't figured out how to tell him yet. I wanted to tell him that I liked him, that he was more than *cute Carson* to me. Didn't he see that this was the last chance for me to be with all the classmates I'd grown up with, yet I was spending my night with him? Couldn't he tell that I was more miserable about leaving him than I was about leaving all my friends combined?

I wanted to tell him how I felt. Tonight. Even if Paige or Dylan got mad, I wouldn't have to face them for long. It was a week before I was leaving the state forever. Besides, this was Carson. Everyone knew how close we were.

But now that Paige was planning on showing him off to her dad's friends, I was worried. What if Paige got mad, and I ruined his big chance?

"Well, *I* don't care," I said, throwing my arm around him. He threw his arm around me, too, and I smiled at how we linked together. "And after these TV and film people see how good you are, they won't care, either. They'll be throwing money at you to be in their movies."

He smiled and stood taller. The deejay over the loudspeaker said, "Dylan and the Motorcycle Gang, to the greenroom."

"All right then," Carson said. "If you say so, it *must* be true." He started to walk toward the small room next to the stage, but I held on to him. He stopped and looked at me. And it happened again. That moment where I felt that we both understood each other without saying anything. I knew we were staring for way too long, but neither of us stopped.

"Carson Knight, to the greenroom," the deejay interrupted. "Carson Knight."

I pulled away and gave a sheepish smile. "Sorry."

He kissed me on the cheek. "I'm not." He smiled and jogged away. The lights dimmed in the family room where the small stage was housed. Hip-hop music blared through the speakers throughout the house and also poolside. The deejay's voice shouted through the microphone, "Please make your way over to the stage for the eight o'clock performance and give a warm welcome to Dylan and his Motorcycle Gang. Special guest appearance by Paige Connelly's father, Mr. Patrick Connelly." Kids and parents gathered around. The music faded out. I saw Paige in the back whispering to her dad's friends, who in turn whispered to each other. They looked up at the stage, and I could tell Paige was nervous for Carson. I wasn't. I knew he'd be amazing.

Mr. Connelly and Carson enter. A spotlight shines on them. Paige's dad pretends to carry a lot of stuff.

MR. CONNELLY:

Why do I have to carry all your camping equipment?

CARSON:

It's what little brothers do. Now set it up.

MR. CONNELLY:

You're only eight minutes older than me.

(He rolls his eyes and pantomimes setting up a tent.)

CARSON:

Okay, yeah, thanks. I'll see you in the morning.

MR. CONNELLY:

Wait. I don't get to sleep in the tent?

CARSON:

There's not enough room for two of us. You can sleep on that rock right there. Good night!

(He pantomimes closing the tent. They fall asleep. Out of the greenroom, Dylan, Phil, and three other boys ride in on their pantomimed motorcycles, making loud revving noises. They stop at the tent. Both Carson and Paige's dad continue to sleep.)

DYLAN:

Hey, what are these guys doing on our turf? Let's get 'em.

(They form a circle around Paige's dad and attack him with fake kicks and punches. You can't see what's happening, but Paige's dad's arm appears and disappears, and a shirt goes flying out of the circle. Meanwhile, Carson sleeps inside the tent. The gang exits back into the greenroom, and Paige's dad screams for Carson.)

CARSON:

(yawning)

What? What's going on?

MR. CONNELLY:

They mugged me!

CARSON:

Who?

MR. CONNELLY:

The motorcycle gang. They came and they—

CARSON:

Oh no. You're having nightmares again. And look, you wet the bed. Again!

MR. CONNELLY:

No, there was this gang, and look, they took the watch Mom gave me. They tore my T-shirt, and they—

CARSON:

Shhhh.

(He strokes Mr. Connelly's hair.)

La-la-laaaaaa—

(He sings him a lullaby.)

MR. CONNELLY:

Okay, I'll go back to sleep.

(He lies down and falls asleep. Carson crawls back into his tent and zips it up. No sooner does he lie back down than the motorcycle gang comes revving up.)

DYLAN:

Don't these guys get the message from the Rebellious Rebels? What should we do?

MOTORCYCLE GANG:

I dunno, I dunno.

DYLAN:

Let's get 'em again!

MOTORCYCLE GANG:

Yeah!

(They attack Mr. Connelly again. A shoe flies off the stage and into the crowd.)

DYLAN:

I think I hear someone coming! Let's get out of here!

(They ride away to Mr. Connelly screaming for help. Carson groggily gets up, unzips the tent, and peers out.)

CARSON:

What is it?

MR. CONNELLY:

It was them again. They came again! They beat me up. They stole my clothes. My duffel bag.

CARSON:

Oh, geez, you know what? This darkness is too much for you.

MR. CONNELLY:

No, it was them. They—

CARSON:

Why don't you sleep in the tent, and I'll sleep outside.

MR. CONNELLY:

No, I'm scared, I— Wait. Really?

CARSON:

Yes, go ahead.

MR. CONNELLY:

Okay. If you insist.

(He crawls into the tent. Carson climbs into the outside sleeping bag.)

CARSON:

I insist.

MR. CONNELLY:

Thank you.

CARSON:

You're welcome.

(Lights go down.)

CARSON:

And don't disturb me again!

(They fall asleep, and the motorcycle gang rides up.)

DYLAN:

What are they still doing here? What ARE THEY DOING HERE?!

MOTORCYCLE GANG:

I dunno. I dunno.

DYLAN:

Let's get him again!

(The group goes in to attack, but Dylan stops them.)

Wait, wait, wait. This guy's had too much. Let's get the guy in the tent!

MOTORCYCLE GANG:

Yeah!

(Lights go down on them attacking Mr. Connelly in the tent, while Carson sleeps peacefully outside.)

I was so proud of Carson in that moment. His humor. Timing. Improvisation. He sang to Paige's dad, stroked his hair, yelled sarcastically at him. He could deliver the lines with such dry sarcasm that the crowd roared with laughter every time he opened his mouth. It was such a dumb skit—nothing to show off Oscar-worthy acting, but still, Carson had "it"—that shine that fixes the audience's eyes on him no matter how many people are onstage. I searched the crowd for Mr. Connelly's industry friends. Would they see it, too?

As the audience dispersed to the dance floor and the backyard, Paige appeared like a tornado and jumped onto Carson, wrapping her legs around him and practically knocking him over. She was at least two inches taller than he was and no stranger to affection. I stood in the back of the room and watched. She grabbed his hands, scratched his back, flung an arm around him.

Maybe tonight wasn't the night to tell him. Maybe I needed to wait and let him have his moment. I wandered into the greenroom to give him some time; besides, I couldn't stand watching Paige fondle him any longer.

The greenroom looked like a large outhouse made of plywood. It was built just for the party, as Home Depot sheets of lumber didn't fit with the Eames décor. Most of the time, the deejay was on the stage, encouraging people to dance, but he popped in every few minutes to change the playlist. There were wires and buttons everywhere. His laptop was open to some playlist streaming into the speakers. I saw a microphone hooked up to a small box. I reached up to touch the box, and my Apple Watch glowed to life as I lifted my wrist, the same wrist wearing the bracelet Carson had made for me.

I unbuckled the watch and checked the battery life. Low, but not dead. My heart thumped wildly, a mixture of jealousy over Paige, excitement over seeing the beginning of Carson's career, and fear that I was about to enter the unknown with Carson and me. I'd record everything on my watch—voice memos—give it to him at the end of the night, and that way, I wouldn't ruin his moment or his chances. Then he could hear it privately and have it forever, even after I moved away. I never used my watch anyway. Just like I had a piece of him wrapped around my wrist, blue-and-black plastic that reminded me of high places, risks, and holding hands in the dark, now he could wear my honesty around his wrist, too—a reminder of how he wrapped around my life and fit perfectly.

I couldn't bear thinking of being three hundred miles away from him. Imagining Paige and him made me crazy. Without thinking, I opened voice memos and pushed the button. "Hello? Am I recording?" I put my mouth closer to the watch. "It's Good, or Alexa, or whatever. It's August 18, and I'm at Paige's party. Well, *we're* at Paige's party. I really don't know what to say because I feel dumb talking to this thing, but this is the most spontaneous thing I could think of doing, which reminds me of you because it's something you'd do, well, only better because you always do everything better—I mean—better than anybody, at least to me." Words usually came so easily, but now I was rambling. It was time to tell him. I took a deep breath. "Look, I know this may come as a surprise to you because it came as a surprise to me, too . . ."

★★★★★

Lindsey and I are parked in her driveway. I don't remember us getting here, or which part of the story I was at when she cut the engine and turned off the headlights. I've been at Paige's mansion in my head since we left the casino. By the look on Lindsey's face, I can tell my story has taken her there, too. She reaches over the parking brake and clasps both of my hands.

"Then what?" she says. "What did you say next?"

My eyebrows form a wrinkle between them. Everything is so vivid—every detail down to the texture of the fabric on Paige's furniture—but when it comes to what I recorded, it's blank.

"I don't remember."

Lindsey rearranges her body so that she faces me. She rests her ear on the headrest and frowns. "Please, Lex." She squeezes my hands. "I won't tell anyone, I promise. Like you said, it was three years ago."

"That's just it," I say. "I honestly don't remember what

I said. It's like this giant, blank spot in my memory. I only remember what happened after."

She waits a minute, but patience isn't her gift. She sits up from the driver's seat and peels her shirt from her body, which has stuck itself to her back from her perspiration with the warm night air. When I don't say anything, she leans back onto the seat and strokes my arm. "What happened after?"

I fight hard to remain stoic, but a single tear escapes. Quickly, I smear away the snitch. "Not tonight, Linds." She blows the air out of her puffed cheeks. Something in her knows that I'm not going to change my mind tonight, and it's part of what makes us such great friends. What most people would call stubborn, she calls decisive. She leans over and kisses my forehead, and without another word, reaches for her backpack and opens the car door.

Chapter Twelve

With only three hours' sleep, Friday is a bad day for Lindsey and me. I tap my foot to stay awake through AP Lit and take furious notes in AP Calc. Ms. Meckel is our savior, though, announcing that she'll guide us through a meditation exercise the whole period with the lights off. You can do anything in Ms. Meckel's room if you have a creative-enough excuse, so Lindsey and I raise our hands with a request "to get closer to the earth." Ms. Meckel places a hand over her heart, so proud of our boldness. She allows us to pull our limp bodies onto the carpeted floor. On her laptop, she starts a track of harp music against the backdrop of crashing waves, and I do my best to ignore John, who I know is eyeing me weirdly. As Ms. Meckel tells us to go to our "special place," I drop into sleep before she even cracks open the Emerson and Thoreau poetry book.

The bell rings, and the fluorescent lights blare on. I open my eyes to John staring down at me. He's wearing his #82 jersey like he does every Friday. Tonight is a home game, and it's the last place I want to be, especially with the ACT tomorrow, but it comes with the territory of "tight end's girlfriend." Supposedly, he's been getting as much action as the wide receivers, and he's pretty adamant that I witness it. Plus, as part of student council, I'm expected to sit in the front row with the other officers.

"Up late studying?" John says, pulling me up with a firm hand.

"Definitely up late."

He puts his arm around me, and I lean against his shoulder, more from fatigue than anything else. As we walk the halls, I ask him, "John, am I fun?"

"Sure."

"No, really. Do people say I'm fun?"

He pauses. "Since when do you care what people say?"

"You're right." John's been solid, my rock, for the past fifteen months. In a burst of gratitude, I jump on him piggyback, but instead of catching my legs, he stops walking, cranes his neck to look at me.

"What're you doing, Lex?"

I let go, sliding down his back until I'm standing again. "Sorry. I dunno. I just—"

"She was just tired," Lindsey interjects, who's overheard the interchange. Aw, Linds. She knows how withered I feel after last night. "I kept her up wayyyy too late."

"You two and your texting," John says. "You gonna be awake enough to cheer on your starting tight end?"

If he had meant it jokingly, it might've been charming, but I wrap my arm across his chest anyway. Captain S passes us in the hallway like an army sergeant. He nods once here and there, smirking at the students who are afraid to make eye contact. A memory pops into my head: How Carson and

I would try to figure out people by the cars they drove or the items in their shopping carts. "You ever wonder what Captain S buys at the grocery store?"

"Why would I wonder that?" John asks.

"No, you wouldn't. I wouldn't. I just meant, like if you could imagine—"

"Tampons," Lindsey jumps in, saving me. I giggle, imagining Mr. Kucan slapping the box down at the checkout counter. Even John smirks.

"And muscle milk," I add.

Lindsey belly laughs, and John shakes his head. The one-minute bell rings. He kisses me on the cheek before jogging off to his next class.

Lindsey leans into me, grinning. "There you are," she says, and then scampers away.

The football game is against Valley, a team with a history of only two losses against us in nine years. Just after dusk, their red uniforms jog onto the field behind our gold ones. Calista Roberts leads her squad in a dance to an edited-for-families Travis Scott song, which is pretty much his beats without any lyrics. Lindsey, head of the pep club, along with varsity swimmer Sean, starts the wave. Lindsey's flopping ponytail and squeaky voice get the whole front section riled before the coin toss is even finished.

I sit in the front row next to Joshua-not-Josh, senior class president, on my left and the four other representatives on my right. After the wave, Lindsey, who's also senior class secretary, climbs in behind me, and when I lean back against her knees, Joshua-not-Josh scowls at me. He always does.

It goes back to freshman year, only two weeks after Carson and I stopped talking. Joshua was curious about the quiet girl who'd just moved here. He asked me to the homecoming dance, and I said, "No, thank you."

It had nothing to do with him. I didn't want to talk to any guys at that point, even the popular ones. A month later, it all changed, thanks to Joshua, actually.

I'd spent the first three weeks at my new school sleeping through classes. Sleeping when I got home, too. One day in PE, we were getting ready to run a timed two-miler when Joshua and his bruised ego said, "Well, if it isn't Rip van Winkle." It wasn't all that mean, but I was never the person made fun of. As soon as the teacher said, "Go," I made sure I couldn't even hear Joshua's footsteps behind me. In fact, by the eighth time around the track, I came within twenty feet of lapping him twice. The teacher sprinted over to me. "How'd you like to join cross-country?" she said while dialing the varsity coach on her cell.

As I gulped air, hunched over with my hands on my knees, I realized something. For twelve minutes, I hadn't thought about Carson. Not once. I hadn't tortured myself with the what-ifs. For the first time since the night at Paige's, I felt like I might be okay again. I finally had an answer for my pain. "Yes," I said to the teacher. Yes, I said to everything.

That night, when Carson started to creep into my thoughts, I busied myself with cleaning my room. At first, it was to block him out, but as I organized everything, I loved that my Vegas room looked nothing like my old room in California. No hints of who I used to be.

The next day, I joined every club and after-school activity I could. I bought that huge calendar pad of paper where you can pencil in your own months and days. In one day, I planned out the next four years of my life on forty-eight pages of calendar paper and picked a college with an engineering program as far away from Carson as possible: Boston College. Every day, every hour, every minute was filled from that day forth, and it got easier and easier to forget I ever knew him.

★★★★★

We win the football game by one touchdown. Normally we'd go celebrate afterward, but most of us are taking the ACT tomorrow, so after a sweaty hug from John, Lindsey drives me home. I've had my license for almost a year, but my parents need both of their cars for work, so I only borrow a car on the weekends.

I'm in bed by nine, and I stare at the ceiling trying to will myself to sleep. I study the crown molding. I notice that my ceiling fan is dusty. I click on my phone to see the time, the screen's bright glow piercing the darkness. It goes dark after a few seconds. I wait for what feels like an eternity and then click it on again. Only six minutes have passed. I click and click and click. My screen glares like it's annoyed that I keep waking it up. At ten o'clock, I'm no closer to sleep, which makes no sense when I remember how much my body pined for it through every class today. I sit up, my mind restless. I want to see Carson again, look at him, say that I'm mad at him for pretending he didn't recognize me after he'd recognized me. *"That's a blatant lie!"* I'd yell. I bury my face against my knees. Who am I to talk about lies?

Dad left his car keys for me on the entryway table. They're loaning me the car to drive to my ACT as if it's a favor to me, but really, Mom gets to sleep in, and Dad gets his weekly Saturday-morning date with college football. I can see the light through the bottom of their bedroom door, but I don't poke my head into their nightly reading time. Instead, I stick a Post-it on my headboard, saying that I left early to get in some last-minute cramming. I don't specify that it's nine hours early. If they check on me tonight, they'll assume my note meant that I drove to Lindsey's, which according to the last three years of my life would've been accurate. Just not these past three weeks.

Instead of Lindsey's house, I make my way to the tall and narrow casino, leaving my car with the valet. Inside the Palms, I walk to the theater and look at the show times. I don't think. I don't feel. I just speak. "One for the ten forty of *Open Boat*." It's an assignment and nothing more. I don't know if Carson's taken his private jet back to his private life in his private Malibu mansion. I don't know if he's still at the Palms, but I know I won't find him watching his own movie in some casino movie theater. Still, I like the thought of being close to where he was just twenty-four hours ago.

I sit down in the back row as the beginning credits appear. For the next two hours, I watch Carson's face, his body, his tormented character as he chooses between saving his girlfriend or a group of thirty students trapped in the boat's cabin. I study every expression and muscle movement in his jaw. I look into his greater than life-size blue eyes as if they're looking back at me. At one point near the end, when he's on the raft with four others, he drops his head in agony at what he's discovered about his girlfriend.

Something in me breaks; I've seen that look before, directed at me. I never wanted to see it again; it's the reason I couldn't finish telling Lindsey the story. Now here it is, twenty times the normal size, staring into me. I rest my arms and forehead on the seat in front of me, and my throat closes up. I swallow and swallow again, but my body starts shaking from trying to hold it all in. The tears fight each other to be first out of my eyes, and once it starts, I weep until none are left. Luckily, I'm toward the back, and no one is sitting in my row to see my quiet collapse.

I never look up for the rest of the movie. I let my body empty itself until my face is dry and sticky, and the credits roll.

★★★★★

I don't drive to Lindsey's after the movie. I end up at Denny's, where my four friends plan on meeting at 6:00 a.m. for some breakfast and last-minute studying. It's close to 1:00 a.m., and the waitress who seats me isn't happy that I've made her look up from her phone. She drags the menu behind her like it weighs a thousand pounds. The place is empty, but she groans when I ask for a booth. "If it's just you, let me seat you at a table," she says.

"No, thanks, I have friends coming."

"When?"

I look at my phone. "In five hours."

"I usually have a minimum of one meal an hour at this table." I'm too drained to argue, so I tell her to bring me one breakfast every hour on the hour. She's never heard this request before, I can tell by her blank face and gaping mouth. She turns and walks away, leaving me with a coffee and my stack of notes.

I try to focus on practice problems, but my head starts doing the drop-forward-and-snap-up routine, so I lay my head on the table and begin doodling in my notebook. I write words like "open boat," "force of nature," "nature—natural—nat—root word—to be born." I think about how I'm filling pages with useless doodles, and then I start writing, "filling pages—pages—Paige," and my green notebook reminds me of the greenroom, and suddenly, as I scribble, I'm back in the greenroom with Paige.

★★★★★

My heart was hammering as I confessed everything to Carson onto my watch. "And although people might say we're crazy 'cause I'm fourteen, I just want you to know that—" The door to the greenroom opened, and I tapped the stop button on my watch. Nervously, I tapped it a few times just to make sure. The door opened farther, but the greenroom was so small that it knocked me off balance, and I stumbled toward the sound equipment, knocking over water bottles and pushing a bunch of buttons. Lights turned on, blinking, glaring at me for knocking all the flyers off the table. I scrambled to catch them, but the table tipped, and they fluttered everywhere, while the water bottles, the table, and I all crashed to the ground.

"There you are," Paige said, looking down at me. "Whoa . . . Oh wow, Lex, you okay?"

"Yeah, I was just untangling cords," I responded, my hands a web of cables and wires.

"Here." She unwrapped the cords tangled up in my arms and legs. "Careful, that's like ten grand in sound equipment. Here, let me help you up. Watch my nails. I just got them done for tonight. Do you think Carson noticed? God, he's soooo cute."

My whole body tensed. And where was my watch? I knelt back down, searching through the mess of flyers. "Yeah, about that. Paige, I don't think you should date him."

She stopped stacking the papers back on the table. "Why not?"

I didn't answer. I couldn't think of what to say.

She answered for me with a question. "Do you like him?"

There was a long pause. Uncomfortably long. It'd be easier to confess the truth. I knew that. But I was still worried that she might sabotage his career if I opened my mouth. I mean, Paige was nice, but what if I messed it all up, and she decided to tell her dad not to help out Carson after all?

"Because he likes you, doesn't he?" she guessed.

I paused, then caught myself. "Don't be ridiculous."

"I've watched him look at you." I liked hearing that, especially after tonight when I thought I saw him enjoying

Paige's hugs too much. She hesitated, before adding, "Do you like him, too?"

"No." If I was going to admit this, I wanted Carson to be the first to know.

"I don't believe you." She crossed her arms. "Why not?"

"Because she's more into his best friend," Dylan interjected, walking through the open door. This room was too small for three people. The proximity and the lies were making me claustrophobic. I needed to get out.

"Hey, Dylan," I said. I tried to ease around him, but his elbows blocked my exit. He was holding a handful of hors d'oeuvres in each hand. He popped one into his mouth and winked at me.

"You and Dylan?" Paige said. "You didn't tell us."

This wasn't going the way I wanted it to. "I didn't want Beth to know," I said. That much was true. "You know how she cries."

"Amazing!" Paige exclaimed, visibly relieved. She grabbed both of our hands. "So I can date Carson. Yes!"

"No!" The word shot out before I could suck it back down.

"Why not?" Paige asked.

"Yeah," Dylan added, "why not?"

"Because," I responded. And then again, "Because."

"Because?" Paige let go of my hand. Dylan cocked his head, waiting for more. There were so many answers I could've given right then. *Because I liked him first. Because I just poured my heart out on a voice memo. Because I'm in love with him, and you're not. Because we're about to start our lives together—tonight. Because because because.* Any of those would have sufficed. But instead, something different came out.

"Because he's poor."

I couldn't believe I said it, but I knew it would catch Paige's attention. She was rich, really rich. She loved all the perks of being the daughter of someone in "the biz," and I wasn't sure if it mattered, but I had to try something because I felt like I was losing him fast.

"He is?" she muttered. Yes! I had struck her Achilles' heel.

"Like dirt poor," I added. Anything to make him less appealing. "Like embarrassing-to-your-parents poor. He didn't even pay for camp."

"You're kidding." She slouched, looking deflated.

"She's not," Dylan confirmed. "But he hates it if people know. I only know because our moms are best friends." He shook his head. "I can't believe you know. As long as I've known him, he's never told anybody. Like NO ONE."

I felt nauseous, but I figured if I ended things with Dylan soon, I could tell Carson everything, and it would be okay. "Dylan, can we talk privately? I need to tell you something important."

"Yes," he said, taking my hand to lead me out. "As soon as I give you this." He popped an hors d'oeuvre into my mouth. Tuna. Before he could see my green face, I ran to the bathroom to spit it out. Carson would've known never to bring tuna near me, and I was more convinced than ever that I *had to* end things with Dylan.

Chapter Thirteen

I wake up in Denny's to my phone vibrating under my hand. A text from Lindsey: You already there? 2 min away. I lift my head and wipe the stream of drool connecting my mouth to the table. Gross. Four plates of pancakes and eggs surround my head in a semicircle. I hear my friends approach just as a server brings a fifth plate of food. She's a different lady than the disgruntled one hours ago.

"Nice," John says, admiring the food and sitting next to me.

"Hi, I'm Catherine," the server introduces herself. "I took over for Rhonda. Can I heat these up for you?"

I nod, and Catherine stacks three plates on one arm and one on the other, whisking them away before she can see John's face fall. I slide him the one leftover hot plate. "Here." I hand him a fork. "You can start without us." He digs in while Kim, Lindsey, and Heidi squeeze into the booth on both sides of us.

"How long have you been here?" Lindsey asks, watching the trail where the waitress left with the cold food.

I shrug. "Big test today, right?" Lindsey gnaws on her fingernail, but I ignore her. "The sum of the positive odd integers less than fifty is subtracted from the sum of the positive even integers less than or equal to fifty. What's the resulting difference?" Everyone starts scribbling, and Lindsey reluctantly opens her notebook. As usual, Heidi's the first to exclaim, "Twenty-five," and she's hardly written anything down. When the food comes, we hammer one another with questions between forkfuls of syrup-drenched sausages.

By the time we start the actual ACT two hours later, we're warmed up and amped on caffeine. The fluorescent lights in the classroom hum, and the test proctor's heels click as she paces the aisles. I tune out any lingering thoughts of Paige's party and open the test booklet, losing myself in the world of multiple choice and the squeaking of pencils. I breeze through it, even the science section with all the tables and graphs. I'm reminded of how well I can do when I stay focused. My future doesn't have time for memories of Carson.

Six hours after we finish, John and I go out on our usual date. This week it's at Timone's, the same restaurant as two weeks ago. We talk about the ACT, where we struggled and where we shined, and it feels normal and comfortable. This is my high-school life.

After dinner, we drive to Heidi's house. Her parents are away on some law conference, so a bunch of us stop by to keep her company. It's only 10:00 p.m., and already the house stinks of stale beer and weed. Lindsey and her curls bounce over to hand me a Sprite. No one ever bothers me about my non-alcohol habit, probably because I can kick anyone's butt at beer pong and never *have to* drink.

In ninth grade, after the "Joshua/homecoming incident"

and two-mile craziness in PE, more people waved at me in the halls, which was nice and distracting. It pushed the guilt of Carson further away. That's when I decided that as soon as I graduated, I'd get as far from him as possible. When I Googled "East Coast schools," Boston College popped up. After a little research, I learned that BC wouldn't offer admission just because people waved at me in the hall. I had to run for office, but first I needed to meet more people. I overheard that people were playing beer pong at some upperclassman's house party that weekend. I searched the game on YouTube, set up the cups on our Ping-Pong table in the garage, and practiced. Every night that week, whenever Carson's face would surface in my mind, I'd grab another Ping-Pong ball. I practiced for hours.

At the party that Saturday, I met a really fun freshman named Lindsey who became my cheer squad that night. I was crowned ultimate champion and had made twenty new twelfth-grade friends. Plus, because I went undefeated, I'd stayed sober and could actually remember their names. It's amazing how many underclassmen want to talk to you once you know upperclassmen. The next thing I knew, Lindsey and I were attached at the hip, and I was being voted in as student council representative. No, not class president, but for a shy new kid who'd been invisible, it was miraculous. Too bad I can't write a college-entrance essay about how to climb the social ladder through the mastery of drinking games.

Tonight, I wander through Heidi's house, talking to as many people as I can, which keeps my mind off anything that wants to slide back in. John and I stay sober, so at the end of the night, we split up to drive people home. It's sensible. Responsible. *Like us,* I think as I climb into bed and under my unwrinkled sheets. We work, John and I. Why would we break up? What reason would I ever have—

My hand grazes Carson's bracelet, still tucked under my pillow from the night Lindsey found it. I pull it out and look at it. My phone vibrates.

Night, John texts.

Knight.

I shiver at his timing. Still. Why would I break up with him just because I still have feelings for a guy I knew years ago? Especially a guy who definitely hates me now. I mean, if every girl in America who found Cayden McKnight attractive decided not to date anyone, we'd have a nation full of single teenage girls. I lean over the side and toss the bracelet underneath the bed, somewhere into the dark space where I won't see it.

You good? he texts again, and I almost drop the phone. Maybe John's right. I'm not every teenage girl in America. I'm *Good,* or at least I was. Could I ever be her again?

Home, I text back.

★★★★★

The following two weeks, I stick to my calendar. Mondays, ASB leadership council meetings. Tuesdays, cross-country meets. Every other Wednesday, volunteer work with Key Club. Thursdays, debate. Reviewing for upcoming tests. Fridays, after-school tutoring for freshmen, followed by the football game. Saturdays, cross-country invitationals. I work on my Boston College application for early decision, which is due November 1. My days fall back into the methodical pattern.

Except for one thing.

I start writing again. It's a hobby I loved back in junior high, but in ninth grade, I stopped because every poem or short story would bring me back to Carson. Instead, I threw my energy into math. Math had definite answers. Engineering would be a solid choice for a college major. But recently, weeks after my camp story for Ms. Meckel, I sat down and wrote more. It was short. A memory. But it felt good. Now, instead of the two hours of ACT studying before bed, I write. Try to remember instead of forget.

One night, I pull out my old box of letters and locate Carson's postcard—something I thought I'd never want to see again. It was the only letter he sent in the mail. July, the summer before I moved. I'd just sent him a care package full of Good & Plenty's two weeks after camp:

> Thanks for the huge box o' candy, Good.
> It was plenty.
> Xoxo, Carson Knight

I trace my finger along his signature. At least the "Knight" part of his name hasn't changed.

John and I continue to have our Saturday dinner dates, but lately, we limit our talking to school and sports. We never mention *us*. I'm sure John notices the lack of texts, the distance between us. Sometimes I think he's not that into our relationship anymore, either, but neither one of us wants to start the conversation.

★★★★★

On Friday, October 15, I miss the football game because I'm in a fifteen-passenger van with Lindsey and the rest of our varsity cross-country team, heading to Southern California for the Mt. SAC Invitational.

I've been to Southern California many times since I moved, but only for school conferences or competitions. Whenever I'm here, I always make a point to focus on the task and not the scenery. But on this trip, I find myself looking out the van window at the freeways, the distant mountains, the street signs, the people. What I once called home.

At around 9:00 p.m., we check into the Woodlock Inn, a four-story motel on a hill in Diamond Bar, a petite suburb of Los Angeles about fifteen minutes from the race. It isn't much, but at least it has a pool and a hot tub. After the seven girls distribute their luggage in the two rooms, we meet up in the guys' room for a quick pre-race meeting.

This is Lindsey's first trip with the team—her first trip to LA ever, actually—and she's convinced that movie stars hang out at every corner. She even looked for them at the gas station in Barstow on our way here. After Coach reviews tomorrow's race strategies, she charges back into our room and jumps from bed to bed. "We're in LA!"

"Diamond Bar," I correct, jumping up on the bed with her. "It's hardly LA."

"It's totally LA!" she squeals. "Come on, girls, let's put our star goggles on!"

The girls change into their bathing suits for the hot tub, so I do, too, but I sit down at the desk.

"You coming?" Lindsey asks.

"Of course! Just need to finish my *Gatsby* chapter, and I'll meet you."

"Hello?" Lindsey knocks on my forehead like I'm a door. "Knock-knock. Hey, Fun, are you in there?"

"Fiiiine," I say, and we walk hip to hip down to the pool. I'm watching my friends chicken fighting in the water, when I look up and see the flat roof. Carson would've loved it. I imagine him watching us from up there, which makes me smile. "Hey, I have an idea." I make the guys partner up and compete in synchronized swimming routines. I convince the girls to be the judges, but they have to imitate teachers from our school.

Lindsey leans over to me in a laughing fit. "See? Fun Alexa. I knew it. She's in there."

She is. I look back up to the roof. I miss that girl, too.

★★★★★

Saturday morning, the girls race first, one hundred runners from all over California, Nevada, and Utah. Mt. SAC is a notorious cross-country course through dirt trails that feel constantly uphill. Steep switchbacks as high as Mount Everest, and when you've barely survived those, there's still Poop-out Hill and Reservoir Hill before the finish line's even in sight. Lindsey and I finish sixth and tenth overall, setting a new record for our school. After my legs stop feeling like oatmeal, I wait at the finish line to cheer for the boys. They've just started their race, so it's going to be a bit before any runners are in view. That's when I hear it.

"I can't believe you like him," one girl says. "He's such a jerk."

"Are you kidding?" a second girl answers. "Who *doesn't* like Cayden McKnight?"

The sweat doesn't keep the hairs on the back of my neck from standing on end. I turn to see two girls looking through a *Celebrity Herald* magazine.

"Me," she says. "*I* don't like him. He's a creep." I swallow my annoyance with a gulp of Gatorade.

"Whatever. Look at him there. In Vegas. He even holds his drink hot. You can't deny he's hot."

"A hot *creep*. I hear all the directors in Hollywood hate him. And he goes through girls like they're a flavor of the week."

"That's not true," I say, keeping my eyes on the finish line. In my peripheral, I see the girls stop turning pages and look at each other. They must decide I wasn't talking to them because they continue.

"Oh, please, like you'd mind if you were one of his flavors."

"I would!"

This is too much. I lock eyes with them. "He's not like that," I say. A few onlookers eye us, their curiosity piqued.

"How would *you* know?" the girl holding the magazine says. Her eyes narrow to slits.

"Because I know him." *Knew,* my mind argues. I feel the

crowd turn as one to see this person who supposedly knows Cayden McKnight. No one's watching for runners anymore.

"Oh *really*?" the girl says, doubt in every syllable.

I step toward her. "Yes, really. He's not a jerk. And he's not a creep." I square my shoulders and cross my arms, daring her to challenge me. "He's the most amazing guy I've ever met in my life."

The girl rolls her eyes. "So what flavor were you?" Her friend cackles. Usually I would never stoop to this level, but without thinking—I charge. I ram her like one of John's tackling dummies, knocking her backward and toppling us to the ground.

"What the hell's wrong with you?" her friend screams. Strangers pull us apart and stand between us. I shake off the arms holding me and stride away, mumbling an apology.

Coach grounds me from shopping with the team after lunch. It's fine by me. I close the hotel-room curtains and sprawl out on the bed, prepared to finish my calc homework until I remember that I left my book in the van. Instead, I start my second draft to Mr. Kucan's essay. His comments on the first one were harsh, and if I don't make some serious revisions, I could be looking at my first B. I wrote that love isn't a force of nature, but a controllable choice. He said that my paper lacked sufficient evidence and that I didn't prove my thesis. In terms of my writing, all he wrote was, "Shallow."

★★★★★

That night, no one mentions anything, but I know everyone's dying to know. Alexa Brooks, sweet and kind study girl, *attacked someone*. They convince me to go to the pool, and I know they're expecting the story. But at the elevator, I say, "I'll meet you guys down there."

We've stayed here for the past three years, so I don't know why I've never noticed the sign at the end of the hall. Big black letters: "Access to roof." After everyone disappears, I head up the stone stairwell and push through the double doors. The night air floods my lungs, and I exhale the cold air in long, cloudy puffs. The roof is laden with white rocks, which crunch and grind as I step, reminding me of the rocky beach at camp.

I sit and dangle my legs over the roof's edge. Below me, our boys' team is cannonballing into the kidney-bean-shaped pool, splashing the girls who tiptoe into the hot tub. I watch the cars driving down the street, and I wonder if Carson still tries to guess what people are like by how they drive. The door behind me creaks open. I can tell it's Lindsey by the way her steps limp along the crunchy rocks. She gets blisters during every race, hobbles for two days afterward, and then repeats the process the following week.

"Hey." She eases down beside me, removes her Ugg boots, and dangles her feet over the edge, too. I don't say anything, so she hands me my small black leather coin purse. "You left this in the car."

"Yeah, that and my calc book."

"It's so not like you."

I move my legs side to side, swinging Lindsey's with mine.

"John texted," she says. "Asked if you lost your phone because you haven't texted back." I shrug. "They won the football game." I shrug again. "Maybe you should try out. Heard you had a pretty sweet tackle."

I shake my head in disbelief. "It was like"—I try to find the right words but there aren't any—"that girl's words did something to me."

She grins. "Ya think?" I don't say anything, so she ventures, "Do you want to tell me what happened?"

"No."

"That probably means you should."

"Maybe I was trying to prove to Carson I'd stand up for him, ya know?" I blow air into my hands to warm them. "A little late for that."

"I don't mean about today. I'm talking about Cayden, sorry, *Carson*. You haven't finished the story."

I crack my knuckles and look at her peeling, raw toes. It's true. I always stop short of the ending, like if I never get there, it never happened.

But it did.

I take Lindsey's hand, and together we go back in my memory to Paige's house.

Chapter Fourteen

Tuna. The stench of it from the trash can in the bathroom corner made me gag. I took it as a sign. For some reason, Dylan shoving my least-favorite food into my mouth was one more reason I needed to stop this whole "us" thing. Now.

I always loved Carson. Only Carson. Why had it taken me an entire summer to admit it? After I ran my mouth under the sink and convinced myself in the antique mirror that "you can do this," I charged out of the bathroom and found Dylan on his last jalapeño popper.

"I need to talk to you about Carson," I said in one big breath before I could second-guess myself.

"Yeah. I can't believe you knew he was poor. As long as I've known him, he's never told anybody. Like *no one*. Guess he doesn't care if people know anymore. Good for him."

"No. Not about that. Us. You and me. I can't do this anymore." He stopped chewing, and I grabbed his hand and squeezed it. "I don't like keeping this secret. It was fun at first, but now it feels, I don't know. Wrong. And I just, I'm done with it."

"Done with it being a secret?" He smiled.

Smiled? I balled my fists and released them, then balled them again. "No . . ."

Before I could finish, Carson charged in between Dylan and me. "I do *not* have a small tongue," he said, eye to eye with me and royally annoyed.

"What?" I tilted my head, confused, but Carson didn't budge.

"Paige just said you told her I had a small tongue." His words slapped me hard. *The car ride home from the beach.*

I looked at Dylan, chewing noisily and grinning. "Sorry, Dylan," I said. I'd have to break things off with him later. I pulled Carson outside next to the pool. The water reflected in his piercing look, making waves in the blues of his eyes. No one could hear us over the buzzing of the hot-tub jets, but I whispered anyway. "I never said that."

"Why would she lie?"

"Because she likes you." This made him blink. A small smirk started at the corners of his mouth, and it made me as queasy as the tuna. He *liked* the idea, which meant he might like her. He needed to know how I felt. Soon. "Carson, I haven't been totally honest."

His brow furrowed, like he didn't believe me. Like he thought I was being dishonest about being dishonest.

"But I'm leaving," I continued. "In less than two weeks. And it'll kill me if you don't know." I twirled his bracelet nervously, like when I was up at Hiker's Peak and didn't know what to say. I noticed the strange tan line on my wrist and suddenly remembered that my Apple Watch was still in the greenroom. I took his hand and interlocked my fingers with his. He looked down at our hands and then at me. "Come with me," I said, barely getting the words out.

My heart pulsed in my throat. I took him to the stage area. This was it. "Wait here." I poked my head into the greenroom, and the deejay was there stacking the last of the flyers. "Hey, did you find a watch?"

"Were you the one who cannonballed through here?" he said, handing me my watch.

"Yeah, sorry. I tripped." I opened the watch to voice memos. "Can you put this up to your microphone?"

"You got a request? I can pull up any song online."

"No, it's my voice memos." I handed him my watch. "It's like a prerecorded skit. For Carson Knight."

"Funny kid." He took it and scrolled with his finger. "Which one?"

"The last one?" There was only one voice memo, so I didn't know why he was squinting at the watch face like it was hard to read. "Thanks." I stood tall, steeled myself, and walked out.

"Attention everyone," the deejay announced from the greenroom. "Carson Knight is back to perform a little something they prepared." The casting directors walked in from the pool area. Carson smiled, eyeing me like it was a joke.

After a few seconds, I didn't hear the familiar beginning, "Hi, it's Good, or Alexa, or whatever . . ." Instead I heard a crash. A *recorded* crash.

Carson reacted to the sound effect like it was a comedy show. He gracefully tripped me but caught my fall on the way down so it looked like something huge was falling on us. I could hear the crowd laughing as my legs and stomach dropped to the ground. This wasn't the recording I made for him. Paige's recorded voice blared through the loudspeakers, "WHOA . . . OH WOW, LEX, YOU OKAY?" My watch. *Oh God,* my watch. I lay stiff on the ground, horrified. When Paige had interrupted me in the greenroom and I'd knocked the table and flyers to the ground, I'd pushed stop a moment before she entered. But to make sure, I'd pressed it a couple of times. Oh God. I'd started a new recording. That's why the deejay had asked which voice memo.

Meanwhile, Carson, standing onstage with me and thinking this was planned, immediately pretended to be Paige when he heard the words, "WHOA . . . OH WOW, LEX, YOU OKAY?" He pranced around me in a circle, then lifted my head in both hands to check on me. Laying me flat, he performed fake CPR, which I think I needed at that point. The crowd erupted in more hoots and applause. The recorded voices were so loud. I sat up as my recorded voice said, "YEAH, I WAS JUST UNTANGLING CORDS."

"HERE," Paige's voice said. Not knowing why she said that, Carson improvised and handed me his shoe. I wanted to run backstage, but I was paralyzed, gripping the shoe with both hands, wishing for a blackout—something, anything—to kill the electricity. But Paige's voice continued, and Carson acted out everything she said. "CAREFUL, THAT'S LIKE TEN GRAND IN SOUND EQUIPMENT." Carson snatched the shoe out of my hand and stroked it as if it were an expensive pet. "HERE, LET ME HELP YOU UP." He helped me stand on wobbly legs. My shakiness made it look like I was actually acting. "WATCH MY NAILS." Carson slapped my hands away, and the crowd giggled. "I JUST GOT THEM DONE FOR

TONIGHT." He held his hands up for everyone to admire. "DO YOU THINK CARSON NOTICED THEM? GOD, HE'S SOOOO CUTE." He clapped his hands and twirled in a circle like a little schoolgirl in love. Out in the crowd, a man's deep laughter bellowed from the back wall. They were loving him.

Panicked, I shouted at the deejay, "Cut it!"

The deejay, smiling, yelled, "No way, you're doing great!"

My voice came on again. It sounded weird and foreign. "YEAH, ABOUT THAT." I moved toward the greenroom, but Carson took my hand, so I gave the deejay the cutthroat sign, begging him to stop, but he thought it was me acting the line, as the voice said, "PAIGE, I DON'T THINK YOU SHOULD DATE HIM."

Carson stopped clapping and twirling. He dropped his hands to his sides. It fit perfectly with Paige's voice. "WHY NOT?"

I stared at him. Just like I had stared at Paige when she asked me the first time. Stupidly.

"DO YOU LIKE HIM?" her voice pressed. Carson put his hands on his hips. He arched one eyebrow my way, waiting for my response. We looked at each other, and although he was acting, I knew everything in him was waiting for my recorded response. "BECAUSE HE LIKES *YOU*, DOESN'T HE?" Carson nodded at me, acting like Paige, but I knew he was telling me onstage that it was true. He did like me.

"DON'T BE RIDICULOUS," my voice said. Carson flinched, like the words were a pinprick.

"I'VE WATCHED HIM LOOK AT YOU." He immediately jumped back into character. "DO YOU LIKE HIM, TOO?"

"NO."

Something shifted in his eyes, like the real him was accepting my answer. *I lied!* I wanted to scream. I shook my head to tell him it wasn't the truth, but it looked like I was shaking my head with my own recorded voice saying, "No."

"I DON'T BELIEVE YOU." He folded his arms like Paige had done in the greenroom. "WHY NOT?"

"BECAUSE SHE'S MORE INTO HIS BEST FRIEND," Dylan's voice interjected, and the real Dylan leaped onstage and joined us. He must've thought Carson was in on this. That he'd okayed this reenactment.

I couldn't get out any words. I couldn't move. All I could do was keep shaking my head. *No, this is all wrong.* "HEY, DYLAN," my voice said.

"YOU AND DYLAN?" Paige's voice said. If these words hurt Carson, he didn't let on. He slapped both hands to his cheeks and dropped open his mouth like this was the best gossip on the block. "YOU DIDN'T TELL US."

I could hear myself give a big, dramatic sigh through the loudspeakers. "I DIDN'T WANT BETH TO KNOW," the recorded me said. "YOU KNOW HOW SHE CRIES."

"AMAZING!" Paige exclaimed. Carson jumped up and down. "SO I CAN DATE CARSON. YES!" He did an awkward cheerleader kick, and the crowd clapped in delight. He danced a goofy jig with his butt sticking out.

"NO!" There was clear distortion because of the volume in my recorded voice.

"WHY NOT?" Paige asked. Carson stopped, his hands on his knees and his butt pointed up in the air.

"YEAH," Dylan's voice added, "WHY NOT?" Dylan threw his hands up in an overacting gesture.

"BECAUSE," my voice responded. I shook my head. I wanted this to stop so badly, but I couldn't breathe. My vision was blurry. "BECAUSE."

"BECAUSE?" Paige's voice said. Carson kept dancing in front of me, facing the audience, his back to me.

"BECAUSE HE'S POOR."

I watched, horrified, as Carson stopped dead. He turned around and stared at me. With his back to the crowd, his look of betrayal was evident only to me.

"HE IS?" Paige's soft voice murmured. I felt the color draining from my face. I watched as the color drained from his.

"LIKE DIRT POOR," my voice added, and the dagger I twisted into Paige was twisting into me now. "LIKE EMBARRASSING-TO-YOUR-PARENTS POOR. HE DIDN'T EVEN PAY FOR CAMP." I could see Paige in the audience nervously gnawing her thumb. She was self-consciously looking at people's response to her voice, but everyone was laughing. Carson fell to one knee and then the other, and it fit perfectly, as Paige's voice said, "YOU'RE KIDDING." Only I knew he wasn't acting. Not even Dylan, from his angle on the stage, could see Carson's expression as he knelt before me, staring into my eyes, confused, bewildered, trying to find a way in his head that what he was hearing didn't really happen. But it did.

"SHE'S NOT," Dylan's voice confirmed. "BUT HE HATES IT IF PEOPLE KNOW. I ONLY KNOW BECAUSE OUR MOMS ARE BEST FRIENDS." I don't remember what Dylan was doing onstage at this point because my eyes were locked on Carson, the painful words wrecking me even more.

"DYLAN, CAN WE TALK PRIVATELY?" my voice said, but I didn't acknowledge Dylan onstage. I couldn't take my eyes off Carson. "I NEED TO TELL YOU SOMETHING IMPORTANT."

"YES," Dylan's voice said, and the real Dylan approached me. "AS SOON AS I GIVE YOU THIS." Instead of popping a tuna hors d'oeuvre into my mouth, he planted a huge kiss on me, right in front of Carson, dipping me for the audience. They clapped and cheered. He definitely thought Carson was part of this. Still too frozen to do anything, I let it continue until the lights went out, and Dylan whispered in my ear, "Guess we're done with it being a secret." I peeled myself away from him, looked around. Carson had left the stage. I scrambled down into the applauding crowd, who patted me on the back as I weaved through them. I found him in the foyer heading toward the front door.

"Carson," I yelled. "Wait. Please. It's not what it looks like."

He whirled to face me, and I screeched to a stop. "That was your voice," he said. His breath was labored like he'd just finished a 5K.

"No," I begged.

"That was *you*!" He spat out the words, tears filling his eyes. He looked away from me, blinked them away before they could betray him.

I put my head down. "Yes," I whispered. "But I was lying."

"Like you lied about Dylan?"

I opened my mouth. Nothing came out.

"That's why you brought me onstage? Confessing your love for my best friend. And then." He paused, swallowed, tried to control his shaking. "In front of all those people, telling them I'm so poor, I'm an *embarrassment*? Why didn't you start a GoFundMe? I mean, fuck, Alexa, you could've just given me food stamps." I'd never seen him like this. He stayed standing, but his body collapsed on itself, and all the anger drained out of him. When he looked up at me, it was pure hurt. The next words were strangled. "You *planned* all that?"

"Yes!" Paige squealed, appearing out of nowhere and attacking him with a huge bear hug. "I didn't even know that was recorded!" She turned to me and said, "And I can't believe you thought of having Carson reenact it. Brilliant. You totally got a great reaction. Look at them." She motioned over to the men in suits. "See that guy, the tall one, heading this way? That's David Allen, the top theatrical agent at CYA. He only signs the best. Which means"—she kissed him on the cheek and then said in a sultry whisper—"you did it." Any concern she'd had about his poverty was erased by the limelight and the possibilities coming his way.

His face softened at the sight of Paige, probably remembering the words of the skit where she confessed her attraction. He smiled at her. "Thanks, Paige."

The man approached. "Hi, Carson, I hope I'm not interrupting."

"No," Carson said, looking at me. "We're done," and I knew he meant our friendship, not our conversation. He leaned into me, and I hugged him tight, begging forgiveness with all of my strength. He whispered in my ear, "Don't *ever* talk to me again." Then he pulled away, as if he'd just said a friendly goodbye, and turned back to David Allen. I backed away, watching more people approach: giggling girls, telling him how funny he was; proud parents, shaking his hand at his performance. Every person who approached felt like one more wall stacking up, building upon building between us. I waited for him to glance my way, to tell me we'd talk later, we'd work through this, but he never looked. Finally, I stumbled to the front yard and called my mom to pick me up.

For the next three days, I played the sick card, hardly leaving my bed. But then Mom found Carson's lanyard bracelet in my trash can and wasn't so sure about my flu. Without asking my permission, she signed me up for a math enrichment class to fill my final week in California while my parents finished packing. Mostly I kept my head on the desk and stared blankly at the computer screen during the practice tests. At the end, I could tell how well I did by Dad patting my shoulder and stating, "Told your mom we should've looked into sports camps."

Once we moved to Vegas, I tried calling Carson on his cell, but it always went to voicemail. He didn't return my emails or texts. Then he changed his number. I was desperate, but not desperate enough to call Paige. The one thing I didn't want to know was how *they* were doing. I did ask Dylan about Carson, but he was oblivious and said Carson was busy with a bunch of auditions. At first, Dylan tried asking if I wanted to hang out the next time I was in town, but I didn't have the energy. I stopped returning Dylan's calls, and after three weeks or so, he stopped calling altogether.

Chapter Fifteen

"Oh, Alexa." Lindsey strokes the Ugg boots in her hand. Everyone below us has moved from the pool to the hot tub, all twelve of them, and they laugh hysterically as the guys sit on one another's laps. Three girls are making those hairdos where they put their hair forward and then flip it back. They all look like George Washington, even from here. Lindsey sets her Uggs on the ledge. She starts to say something. Instead, she leans her head on my shoulder.

"All I had to do was run backstage and stop it. I just stayed there like an ass."

"Oh, Alexa," she says again. I know it's bad when Lindsey doesn't have anything to say. I guess I was hoping for one of those "It's not as bad as you think" pep talks.

I stand up. "I should get my calculus book."

"Alexa . . ."

"No, don't worry about it. I need to get the van keys from Coach before he falls asleep."

She slips her Uggs back on. I hear her hobbling along behind me as I walk back to the stairwell. "Wait, I'll go with you."

We have to knock three times on Coach's door before we hear movement. Two muffled swear words later, Coach cracks open the door, the room dark behind him. He frowns through squinty eyes when I ask for the keys. I hear him fumble around and knock something over. Finally, he grabs something that jangles.

"Thanks, Coach," I say when he drops the keys into my hand. "I'll get them back to you in five."

He shakes his head, unhappy at the prospect of staying awake that long. "Bring them to breakfast," he mumbles. I start to walk away. "And Brooks?" I turn around. "The keys stay with *you*."

"Got it, Coach."

"I'm holding you responsible, which after your display today—"

"Got it, Coach," I repeat. Convinced, he closes the door. Lindsey doesn't say anything the whole walk to the van. When I unlock the door, I reach up and turn on the back seat light. My book's under the seat in the third row, so I climb in. On the row in front of me, I notice a *Celebrity Herald* magazine. "That yours?"

She snatches it up. "Yes. Well, sort of. I bought it for you today, but now, well, I had no idea . . ."

I climb over the seat and sit down next to her. "Lindsey, I'm *fine*. I've been fine for over three years."

"It makes sense now," she says, flipping pages in the magazine.

"What does?"

"Why he's such a jerk."

"What?"

"Cayden—sorry, *Carson*—believes that he missed out on

you because he was 'the nice guy.' *Cute* Carson. He was good to you, and you walked all over him, I mean, not really, but he thinks you did, which wouldn't have been *that* big of a deal had he not been in love with you. And so Cayden was like, cay-rushed by you, no offense, but he was. Crushed, capital C. And he vowed never to let it happen again, and then he put up a wall and changed his personality. At the same time, he became famous, so all the girls liked him just because he was famous, but he thought it was because he was a jerk. He vowed never to be 'the nice guy' again, the same way you vowed never to think about him again, and he's been a jerk for so long, and you've been studying for so long, that now he's truly an a-hole, just like you're truly the boring girl with the highest GPA."

"You realize you're crazy, right?"

She tilts her head, and I burst out laughing. I grab the magazine and hit her shoulder with it.

"Come *on,* Lindsey! Put yourself on playback."

"Isn't the part about you correct?"

I don't answer.

"Okay, great, yes. So couldn't it be possible, stop rolling your eyes, Lex, and go with me on this, couldn't it be, maybe just maybe, that I'm right about Cayden, too?"

I marinate in the possibility of that ugly truth, then I snap my head up. "No, Linds. This isn't about me. I know you'd love to believe that all his roads lead back to Alexa Brooks, but no. Just no."

Like lightning striking, she snatches the keys, crawls into the front seat, and starts the car.

"Linds?"

She starts typing street names to her phone's GPS. My heartbeat knocks like a pinball against my rib cage. I climb into the passenger seat in a panic and look at her phone.

"Lindsey? What are you doing? Lindsey. Coach Jiménez said—"

"Coach is dreaming about the Ironman for the next eight hours." She giggles deviously and clicks her seatbelt on. "I have some cash. You have your ATM card."

"For emergencies!"

"Okay, this qualifies."

"No!" I jump out of the van, plant my feet on the parking-lot pavement. "First of all, celebrities don't hang around on corners waiting for people to find them."

"Oh, Lex, not after you told me that." She shakes her head like she's dodging an annoying housefly. "We're not chasing after Cayden tonight."

I peer at her with one eye, curious.

"Hulloooo! Two words. Holly. Wood."

"That's one word. And please no," I say, but it's weak. I hold on to the open passenger door for support.

"I've never been to Hollywood, and we're so close," she pleads, her eyes doe-like and sincere. I look at the cross streets on her GPS, then look back at the hotel. The base lighting shines like flashlights against the plants and pathway to the lobby. I turn away, and it reminds me of another time I clicked off a flashlight and kept walking, hand in hand up a mountain. Possibilities began that night.

I groan. "Back in three hours with a full tank of gas?"

Lindsey claps excitedly as I climb in and click my seat belt.

"And you're paying for it." I lean my head back against the headrest. "This is so unlike me."

"This is *exactly* like you!" she squeals as she puts the van in reverse and rolls over a speed bump toward the exit. "And that's not a bad thing. It's *Good*, if you know who I mean."

"Don't," I say, and look out the window. It's nine o'clock on a Saturday night. We're wearing sweats over our bikinis, and we're heading to Hollywood.

Chapter Sixteen

Hollywood is nothing like the movies. One street is glittery with flashy plastic signs, and the next is dark and ominous. Luckily, Lindsey knows exactly which streets to hit to make sure she's not disappointed.

Forty minutes after we leave Diamond Bar, we're cruising down Sunset Boulevard, slow enough for her to point out facts about the buildings we pass. Like Chateau Marmont, and how Cayden is often spotted there at night, having cigars with his buddy Scott Shamus, some other actor I've never heard of. How the Roxy is the place where some bands got their start and is totally approachable, unlike 3two3—"Really trendy, we'd never get in."

She turns right on La Cienega, then right on Hollywood Boulevard. We pass by the TCL Chinese Theatre. Lindsey says something about the handprints in the sidewalk, but I only half hear her. "—costs fifty thousand dollars to get your star on the Walk of Fame, fifty thuh-OW-sand," she rambles on. I think of Carson's handprints, his hands, and how they used to match mine as we linked fingers and swung them to and fro. I try to imagine his hands now. We pass by the mall on Hollywood and Highland with the curved blue glass surrounding the stores and restaurants and the Gap sign that might as well stretch to the moon. She exclaims, "No! Way!" and points to the opposite side of the road, where a guy in a collared black button-down and a red bowtie with red suspenders is looking at the flat tire on his pickup truck.

"Do you know him?"

She makes a U-turn and then pulls onto a nearby residential street. With a lot of grunting and twisting of the wheel, she parks the fifteen-passenger monstrosity under an oak tree.

"Let's go." She hops out of the van.

"Where?" I ask, jumping out after her.

"Dodge!"

"Lindsey, stop! Is that the guy's name? Is he some movie star? I don't think Dodge wants some randoms harassing him for an autograph."

"Come on!" she yells over her shoulder, her Uggs clomping ahead of me. "Ah, blisters!" she complains, but she doesn't slow down. We jaywalk, or more like jay*run*, across a side street with way too much traffic. A symphony of car horns follows us to the other side. We slow and sidle up next to the truck with the flat.

"Hey," Lindsey says to the guy in suspenders. He's leaning against his hood, texting on his phone. "You heading to work?"

He glances up at us, stressed. He has friendly eyes; he's maybe in his midtwenties. "Sort of. Private event. But yes, at my work."

"Can we help?"

"Not unless you have a spare tire."

"Maybe," she says.

I look at Lindsey, my eyes widening. I try to explain through my arching eyebrows that this is a bad, very bad, idea. "Look," I say, "you can't just throw any spare on any car."

Lindsey slaps the side of his truck. "Exactly. You'd have to have a Dodge. *We* have a Dodge."

"Uh, we have a soccer-mom van. This is a Ram." I know if we were sitting at a restaurant, Lindsey would be kicking me under the table. But there's no way I'm getting in any more trouble with Coach.

He shakes his head. "Look, thanks, really—coulda used the extra cash tonight—but I'm supposed to be there in twenty-five minutes, so I think I'm out of luck. Triple A says they'll be here in forty, so I'll wait it out." He tells us how he'd run there if he could—it's less than a mile—but he can't leave his car on Hollywood Boulevard without getting towed.

"You don't have any friends you could call?" I chime in. He says no, that he just moved here three months ago, and his girlfriend's visiting family, and his roommates are gone for the weekend.

"Since it doesn't matter anyway," Lindsey starts up again, "why don't we try our spare on your truck? If it works, we'll follow in our van, and Triple A can meet you there." She's operating on some plan, but I can't figure it out.

He pauses. Briefly. "Yeah, sure," he says. Lindsey charges back the block and a half to our van, and I nip at her heels. She locates the spare and as we unscrew it, I ask, "Are you gonna explain at some point?" She nods, and together we heave the thirty-five-pound tire onto the ground.

As we roll it down the street toward his truck, the competitive side in us kicks in, and we pick up our pace, like every second counts. When we cross the side street to where he's parked, he already has his truck prepped with his jack in place. Lindsey introduces us as "Laney" and "Delaney," and I barely have enough time to glare at her before he exclaims, "Well, hot damn."

The tire fits.

Lindsey's mouth drops open, and she looks from me to the truck to me again, as if I did something magical. "What?" I ask.

She shakes her head, then grabs my hand and says, "We'll get the van!" We sprint back and unlock the doors, whip the van into gear, and Lindsey drives onto Hollywood Boulevard and stops next to him. I roll the passenger window down.

His truck is purring, and he leans out his window. "I'm a bartender at 3two3. Know where that is?"

Lindsey smiles shyly. "I figured that by your uniform."

He looks down at his red suspenders and bow tie. "Yeah," he laughs. "It's a clear giveaway."

"We'll follow you," I tell him. I roll up my window just in time.

"3two3!" she shrieks for all of Hollywood to hear. "He works at THREE! TWO! THREE! Do you *realize* how much Cayden McKnight frequents 3two3?"

"No." I scrutinize her with squinty eyes. "Wait. What's the deal? What does Cayden have to do with anything?"

"Nothing," she says. "And that's why it's EVERYTHING. That's why it's *fate*!"

"What is?"

"Think about it! We're driving through Hollywood when we see someone in a 3two3 uniform. That's Cayden McKnight's favorite bar. And *then* . . . the guy's tire is flat, and we *happened* to have the same EXACT make—a Dodge. *Then* the tire actually fit! That's when I knew!"

I'm afraid to ask. "Knew what?"

"Don't worry, you'll see."

"Linds—"

"I don't want to jinx it," she whispers, as if the jinxing gods might hear her. I groan, but Lindsey doesn't give.

We pull up to 3two3 eight minutes after his shift starts. From the outside, it looks like a bungalow house. Nothing fancy, except for the girls lined up outside who look like they've spent five hours getting ready.

"Hey, Sasha," one of the valets says to him as the three of us get out of the vehicles. Sasha hands the valet his jack and some tools.

"Take care of these girls," Sasha says. "Get their tire back to them." He turns to us. "Thank you. I'd invite you in, but I'm not sure they'd be up on your attire."

"It's okay," I say. "Private party, right?" I know Lindsey's screaming inside because she didn't think to pack a clubbing outfit for her trip down to the hotel pool. Her bikini strings are dangling from her neck, and she stuffs them into her hooded sweatshirt.

"Do you see a lot of movie stars here?" she asks.

Sasha laughs. "Yeah. Yeah, I do. Scott Shamus, Randy Hall, Kirsten Davison . . ." He trails off, and Lindsey's eyes grow wider with each name. "Sometimes they come for birthday parties, or wrap parties, like when a film is over. That's tonight's gig here." He glances at his cell phone.

"You better go," I say.

He waves me off. "Not my usual shift. Just making tips helping out the boss tonight. Delaney, right?" I nod. "Why'd you girls charge across traffic? What is it—like a community-service thing?"

"Kind of," Lindsey takes over, and I'm so glad because I'm dying to know as much as Sasha is, and I'd been wondering if Lindsey was ever going to spill. But as soon as she begins, I freeze. "You've heard of Cayden McKnight, right?"

"Of course."

Lindsey knows my laser eyes are boring a hole into her, warning her not to mention my past. The valet attendants gather around, and she beckons them closer. "A few months back, Delaney here got a flat tire in Malibu at, like, two in the morning. She was coming home from a house party, and it was one of those mountain roads, not a car in sight, totally dark. Then someone drove by and pulled over." She pauses. "It was Cayden McKnight."

"You're kidding," Sasha responds, and all eyes look at me for confirmation. I press my lips together and force a slow nod. "Huh," he says. "I've seen him here before. Usually at a private table, but sometimes at the bar. He lives in Malibu."

"Delaney doesn't like to talk about this"—and Lindsey pauses, so I nod numbly—"but she was crying, and he was super nice to her, told her it was going to be okay, put on her spare, took his tools back to his car. She thought he was coming right back, but then he started his car and drove off. She never had the chance to say thanks. Then she saw you, and it reminded her of all that. And she was like, 'Stop the car!' and I was like, 'Hell yeah! Let's do this!' She figured it would be her secret way of thanking him."

"Like a pay-it-forward thing," he says, smiling at me. "That's great. Really. And amazing to hear. Everyone thinks Cayden McKnight is a"—he stops, catches himself—"Glad he did that for ya."

"Don't believe everything you read," I jump in, and then stop. I don't want to be obvious. "He was one of the nicest strangers I've ever met."

Sasha glances at his phone again. Pulls a business card out of his pocket. "Here. Shoot me a text the next time you're dressed to impress. I'll get you into the club, no cover. That'll be *my* way of saying thanks. First drink on the house. You old enough?"

"Of course we are!" Lindsey answers for me.

"You don't need to thank us," I say.

Lindsey almost falls over. "Actually, thanking us would be fine. Totally fine. We'll call you."

"No," I say, but Lindsey grabs my wrist in a death grip.

"Actually"—Lindsey releases her hold on me—"can you do us a favor? Would you pass that story on to anyone who asks about Cayden McKnight?"

"I will," he says. "In fact, when my boss hears that Cayden McKnight's the reason why this random girl helped me get here, I think he'll overlook that I'm a few minutes late."

With a quick goodbye and another sincere thank-you, he

disappears into the club. One of the valets gets to working on Sasha's car, removing the spare and replacing it in our van. He gives us permission to leave the van at the club while we "run a few errands," and Lindsey and I take off toward Hollywood Boulevard hand in hand, half jogging, half skipping.

When we're out of sight, I grab her by the shoulder and whirl her around.

"What was that? What're you doing?"

"It's what *you're* doing," she counters. "And that would be changing Cayden's reputation." A scheming grin creeps across her face. "One gossiper at a time."

Chapter Seventeen

It's simple to Lindsey. If I'm the reason Carson ruined his reputation, then I should be the one to fix it. Of course none of that's true, but I'm surprised at how right it felt to give Carson a good name, even if Lindsey invented the whole story. Maybe it's the closest thing I've felt to penance for what I did on that stage three years ago, since a do-over isn't an option. My grin matches hers. "This'll never work!"

"Then you have no idea how quickly celebrity gossip spreads, girl. But tonight you're getting your first lesson." She wraps her arms around me. "Think of all the things that just *happened* to happen to us. It's gotta be a sign." Her smile practically bridges her ears.

I have my wallet and an ATM card with $8,000 in college money available. What's a couple of twenty-dollar bills? I withdraw three hundred, and we spend the next two hours spending "Cayden's" money. In a burger restaurant, we see six high-school students celebrating their fall formal. I ask for their bill, informing the waitress that I'm the daughter of Cayden's publicist. I tell her that Cayden drove by and saw the group. How it reminded him of the high-school life he missed out on, so he called my mom. She was busy, so she had me cover their meal at his request. The waitress's eyes water. On our way out, I see other servers crowding around to hear the story. The girls hug their dates and bounce in their booth. They gawk in amazement, phones out, snapping updates.

For the next two hours, Lindsey and I hit up souvenir shops, buying everything from sodas to lollipops to keychains. Each time we hand out a trinket, we make up a new and fun story about Cayden McKnight. We pretend to be Cayden's cousins, his friends, strangers who've run into him, schoolmates from back in junior high, actors who worked with him on a movie set. Some of the stories are ridiculous, but they all paint him in a positive light: He bought a round of drinks at a bar one night, anonymously paid for a cancer patient's hospital bill, consoled us when Uncle Jimmy died. Lindsey tells one guy that Cayden got her off the streets and made her stop working at a strip bar because she was underage. Not once do we say that Cayden *told us* to give these gifts away. We say he was so kind, we feel *compelled* to do something kind, to pay his kindness forward, no matter how minor.

At midnight, we head back to our van. As we unlock the doors, I notice there's still ninety dollars in my pocket. "Hold on, Linds." According to Lindsey, the cover charge to get into 3two3 is thirty dollars. I walk to the front of the line, where an employee collects the money. She stands next to a large man with tattoos stretching across his hands like tight-fitting gloves. I can tell by the way his eyes scan my clothes that he's decided never to follow me on Instagram.

"Sorry to bother you," I say, as if I normally walk through

high-end Hollywood in a bathing suit and workout sweats. "Cayden McKnight's publicist is my mom."

Now I have their attention. "My mom—his publicist—just called me." I'm making it up as I go, praying that bouncers and valets don't swap stories. "She knew I was in the area. She's in New York. Business. I guess Cayden was here recently. He was impressed with the service, so he called her, asked her to do something for this club." I notice more people in line quieting down, trying to listen in. "Anyway, if you could let the next three people in for free, Cayden'll cover them." I hand over the cash. "It's a good way to promote your club, you know, tell everyone what Cayden did, maybe Trip Advisor or Yelp'll hear, give your club more notoriety." I smile at the girls who are about to go in for free. "Everybody wins!" People start whispering. Phones appear. I imagine the flurry of snaps, tweets, and IG stories. I turn my back so they can't get a photo of me, but a bright flash in my face startles me. A guy behind a wall holding a camera has taken my picture.

"Out!" the tattooed bouncer shouts. The photographer darts off, but I'm uneasy about the way he looked at me. On the drive back to Diamond Bar, Lindsey assures me it'll be okay.

"They'll never print your photo in a magazine. No offense, but you're Alexa Brooks. AKA *nobody*. The slimy paparazzi guy just doesn't know it yet." We laugh when we imagine him at TMZ, sharing his news, showing off my picture, only to discover I'm a fraud. "Plus, three people, Lex? Cayden would've paid for a hundred."

"Nah. *Carson* would've . . . if he had the money. But not

Cayden. Do you think it'll do anything?" I ask. "All that we did?"

"I guess we'll see, right? I mean, you didn't touch a textbook all night. So, heck, anything's possible."

★★★★★

The following Monday, at our weekly student-council meeting, we're planning the Christmas dance, which is our version of Winter Formal. It falls on the Saturday before Christmas break, which means a red-and-green theme with tacky tinsel everywhere. I'm searching TMZ.com on my phone for any news of Cayden and his one-hundred-eighty-degree flip toward decency. Nothing. I search keywords: *Cayden McKnight club free entry*. It brings up articles about Cayden clubbing, but nothing about what I did. *3two3 Cayden*, I search as I type. Still nothing. Articles about area codes pop up. "Hollywood clubs," I mutter as I add those words to my search.

"Yes!" Lindsey says and slaps my back. I look up at the group, startled to see everyone looking at me.

"What?" I ask.

"That's a perfect theme for our dance. How about *Christmas in Hollywood*?"

"I dunno . . ." Joshua frowns. "It sounds kind of girly, if you ask me."

"Whatever, Josh!" Lindsey says.

"Joshua," he corrects.

"What if," she says, thinking aloud, "we have a red-carpet

entrance? And decorate the walls with—ooh!—street signs of famous boulevards in Hollywood!"

The Christmas dance is Lindsey's baby. It's the senior class secretary's job to plan it. Lindsey's been anticipating this event since she was voted in last spring, and now it's going to be based on her all-time favorite subject: movie stars. She's in heaven, but Joshua-not-Josh is having none of it.

I'm about to defend her, but John beats me to it. "I like it. We could decorate the back wall to look like the Hollywood Hills," he offers. "Complete with the Hollywood sign."

Lindsey beams.

"And another wall with a bunch of paparazzi taking pictures," she adds, looking at me—I can feel it—but I'm watching John. Has he always been this creative?

"Nice!" John says. I think if I had suggested it, he would've looked at me like I was from Mars. "We could set up a Walk of Fame on one wall," he continues, "and instead of clay handprints, we could use tempura paint, and each couple at the dance could make a set of handprints for the wall. Like my right hand and Alexa's left hand." His voice is steady, but his eyes ask me, *Are we even going to the dance?* We're texting less, talking less. We both feel it, the weirdness, but neither of us wants to say anything.

"I'm not sure," Joshua objects.

"I absolutely love it," Lynecia, our treasurer, pipes in, and her rich voice quiets him. She's great at math, but she could easily have a career as someone who records audiobooks. Or sleep apps. Or the one who narrates nature documentaries and makes an antelope death sound romantic. I'll never suggest it, though. Won't make that mistake twice. I think back to the time I told someone to pursue an acting career.

"Hello?" John says to me.

"Hi." It's the first time we've spoken today.

"Lynecia just asked if you'd help her paint the Hollywood sign."

"Did she?" I turn to Lynecia's waiting eyes. "Yes, of course I'll help."

"Oh, and music?" Lindsey offers. "Can you take care of the deejay?"

"Done!" I say.

"Okay, let's talk decorations," Lindsey continues. She types on her laptop as we throw out suggestions.

By Thursday, I've given up Googling our weekend. Luckily, Coach never noticed the extra hundred miles on his odometer. John and I walk out of fourth period together each day, holding hands like usual, but barely talking. When we greet each other with a kiss, it feels more like a transaction. Like he's just doing his job, and the kiss is my receipt.

Tonight, I'm sitting in the stadium bleachers trying to block out my receipt kisses by cheering for him. We're playing our rivals, Durango, and I clap and stomp and do my best to play the "good girlfriend" role. Lindsey appears down by the cheerleaders, searching the crowd, and when she spots me, she holds a magazine over her head and shakes it triumphantly.

Four rows away from me, she climbs into the stands and waves the magazine. She mouths the words, *It's in here!*

"No way!" I belt out.

The refs have called a foul on Durango, and everyone turns my way.

"No way!" I repeat. "No way you're gonna beat us, Durango!' "

I duck my head, embarrassed, and Lindsey covers her mouth with her hand to hide her shaking laughter. She hurdles and stumbles over rows of students to meet me in the student-council section, then flips open the newest edition of *Celebrity Herald*. There, on page thirty-two, in the bottom left of the "Verbosity Page," I read the following paragraph:

> Rumor has it . . . RANDY HALL spotted leaving the Viper Room with KIRSTEN DAVISON at 2:00 a.m. in the same car. On again after the breakup? MICHELLE ARMINTA eating sushi with friends at Go-Go Fish Bar in Santa Monica. The server claims she ordered albacore and chicken teriyaki. Not as vegan as she claims? CAYDEN MCKNIGHT paying the bill for an entire group of six at Luxe Diner in West Hollywood. Turning over a new leaf of charity? Is Hollywood's bad boy going soft?

Lindsey and I jump up and down, holding each other's hands, and dance in a circle like maniacs. "I hope that's not a victory dance," Joshua says drily. He's sitting behind us. "Durango just scored."

"Oh," we say in unison. We pause. Look around. No one else is standing. For a moment, we feel bad, but then we can't help it. We jump up and down again, squealing and hugging and dancing.

★★★★★

When Lindsey drives me home, we stop for ice cream to celebrate. "We're published!" she says between licking her mint chip and driving her stick shift. "What're we gonna do next?"

"I don't know. I haven't thought that far ahead."

"You?" she says, like, *Yeah, right.*

"Not with this," I say. "It felt good, though, you know? Like saying sorry in a way. But I need to leave him alone, Linds."

"Maybe if his reputation changed, he wouldn't hate you so much."

"What if he likes his reputation?" I steal a glance to gauge Lindsey's reaction, then look back at the road. "What if . . ." I pause as Lindsey downshifts before a stop sign. "What if this is who he is?"

Admitting that out loud makes the butter pecan hard to swallow.

Lindsey's eyes are steel. "It's not."

We pull up to my house, and I reach into the back seat for my backpack.

"Linds." I set my ice-cream cone in the soda holder and touch her shoulder. I know I've deflated her. "Look, maybe I deserved it, but he was an a-hole to me at Phantom Bar. And we're talking big a-hole, not little a-hole."

"But the size of his a-hole-ness is in direct relation to the size of his love for you!"

"Are we really talking about Cayden McKnight's a-hole?" I joke.

She laughs but quickly sobers. "You're just trying to play this down."

"Okay, fine, what if your crazy theory is right? He vowed never to be the nice guy again. Carson's gone."

"Is he? You vowed never to think about him again. Pretty sure you broke that."

She lets that hang in the air as we listen to the car idling. Neither of us speak. Lindsey flips through the pages of the magazine. Carson's on the page where they show celebrities doing everyday things, like grocery shopping, hiking, getting coffee, walking dogs. There's always a cheesy caption like, "She likes lattes without foam!" or "He buys eggs and milk just like you!" In this photo, Carson's in a jogging suit adjusting his wireless earbud. Underneath it, a caption reads, "He listens to his music while working out!" I stare at Carson's face, angled to the left, maybe checking to see if he's being followed.

"You can't see his eyes," I murmur. "In this picture. You could tell a lot from the way he looked at you."

"You mean the way he looked at *you.*" The silence thickens.

"Linds, it was the summer before ninth grade. You don't fall in love. It doesn't happen at fourteen. It doesn't even happen at eighteen."

"Okay, that's between you and John, but as for fourteen, it so can totally happen at fourteen because Jack Black is married to his high-school sweetheart."

"Who's that?"

She rolls her eyes at me, makes a left into my driveway, and parks the car. "Okay, Tawny Sparks?"

"The singer girl," I say, thinking back to sixth grade. "Isn't she divorced now?"

"So? She was in *love* at the time! That's the point. Okay, what about Terrance Light and Kate Morgan Thomas? Fell in love at sixteen on Disney's *Kids Rock America*. Kristin Cashe and Tony Wallaker—they met on the set of *Beneath the Fog*. They were twelve." I shake my head. She could be reading names from her sister's yearbook for all I know. "Are you serious? You don't know who Kristin Cashe is? Where have you *been*? Okay, fine. Mary, the mother of Jesus? Ever heard of her?"

I roll up the magazine and smack Lindsey with it.

"Aha! You know her. She was, like, fourteen when she got pregnant."

"With the son of God, you idiot!"

"What-EV-er!" Lindsey grabs the magazine and smacks me back. "Joseph was *totally* hot for her. When he found out she was knocked up, he coulda had her *killed*. But he didn't. Why? 'Cause he was *in love*. Love, love, love."

I look back to the picture of Carson jogging, and I wonder if he was thinking about love as his head turned to the left. What girl filled his mind as he ran, well, got ready to run? He hadn't quite started, I could tell by the way he fiddled with his earbud, the way his clothes were fresh and loose, not damp and stuck to his body.

Lindsey takes the magazine and stuffs it into the side pocket of my backpack.

"I don't want that."

"Yes, you do," she says. "Be normal for once." She kisses my forehead, and I climb out of the car. "Don't forget about Christmas in Hollywood! Best dance ever!" she shouts as she drives away. I take the rolled-up magazine out of my backpack, intending to throw it in the outdoor trash can.

But I can't.

Frustrated, I stomp inside and throw it onto my bedroom floor. Pages splay in all directions. "What're you holding on for?" I growl at myself.

Chapter Eighteen

Saturday night, I'm picking at my grilled-chicken salad at Timone's. I move pieces of my salad from one side of the plate to the other. Opera voices sing through the speakers, and the lights are dim. John, eating his massive block of lasagna, sits across from me.

"That new?" He waves a fork at me. I'm wearing the jacket that Lindsey loaned me the night at Phantom Bar.

"No."

"Different." I'm about to ask if different means good when he says, between mouthfuls, "You usually get chicken."

"This is chicken." I stab a piece on my fork to show him.

"No, I mean, you always get the chicken marsala. As long as I've known you."

"I know," I agree. "So boring." John stops chewing his lasagna for a moment, the same lasagna he's ordered every time we've eaten here for the past year. It wasn't a dig at him, and I start to correct myself, but something crinkles in my pocket against my arm. I pull out a slip of paper and instantly recognize the handwriting. "No," I whisper.

"What?" John looks concerned, but more for my sanity than my well-being.

"Nothing," I say. "Girl problem. Would you excuse me, please?" He relaxes, knowing every girl is capable of having *girl problems*. I scamper away from the table and lurch through the bathroom doors before rereading the slip of paper:

We should do this again. Call my manager. Tell her you're Graceland.

There's a phone number scribbled below the message. Carson's writing hasn't changed, and although I hope beyond hope that he pulled a Houdini and magically slipped the paper in my pocket from across the room that night at Phantom Bar, I know it's not possible. The note wasn't for me. The other girl. The one with the matching jacket. I flash back to that night and see Carson writing on a receipt—leaning in close to her—and slipping his hand into her pocket.

Of course.

In my haste and confusion of kicking myself out, I grabbed the first jacket I saw in the coat check, assuming it was mine.

It was hers.

With shaky hands that can barely press the correct numbers on my phone, I start to dial.

What am I doing?

I stop, erase the numbers, and text Lindsey instead.

We need to talk. ASAP. Carson.

I pour cold water on my face and let my wrists dangle under the faucet, trying to cool my pulse before I return to John. When I do, I attempt to recover from where we left off. "You played hard yesterday," I say.

"Thanks."

I can hear him chewing. My fork scrapes across the plate.

"Sorry." We chew some more. Eventually we talk about our college apps, which are due in nine days. My ACT score was a 31; his a 29. He could play for UNLV easily, but he's looking at Washington. My 5K times are too slow for a full ride to Boston, but they'll probably offer something. The state-championship race in a few weeks might be a deciding factor.

As far as other colleges, deadlines aren't until January, but hopefully Boston will be a yes, and I won't have to submit to any of them. I wrote four different versions of college essays last spring, so I can just mix and match which essays fit which college.

"Efficient." John sips his water and nods. My planned life is like comfort food for him. An awkward silence sits between us. I think we both are wondering if the other is going to bring up the dreaded "Should we break up?" talk, but neither of us does.

When John drops me off after dinner, Lindsey's waiting in her car in front of my house. She waves at him, and he smiles more than I've seen him smile all night. When she exits her car, she fakes throwing a football to him, and he fakes catching it. She throws her hands up in the "touchdown" sign, and he honks his horn. She laughs. It bums me out that our friends can make him smile more than his girlfriend can, but I don't know how to fix that, or if I want to. I don't ask him to come in, and he doesn't offer to stay.

"Still haven't broken up yet?" she says after he drives away.

"No." I sigh. Even my friends can see it.

Once inside, Lindsey follows me into my bedroom. I hand Lindsey the piece of paper, and she scans it as if it's Greek.

"It was in my pocket." She shakes her head, still lost. "This isn't your sister's jacket," I explain. "It's the girl's—the one who was with Carson."

Lindsey slaps her hand to her mouth.

"Exactly." She eyes me, and I know what she's thinking. "Yes, it's his writing. I'd know it anywhere."

The weight of that pulls her backward, and she lands on my bed, bouncing on the springs. "Kucan's question. Remember? 'The Open Boat.' His question about love."

"What are you talking ab—"

"The girl Cayden was with," she interrupts. "And you. Having the same jacket? Think of the odds, Lex. It's like Kucan said about the universe. Love. What if it's *not* a choice?"

"It *is*. And Carson made his choice, remember? It was no. Don't you get it?"

She speaks all breathy, like Ms. Meckel reading poetry. "But the *universe* didn't say no. Love's a force of nature, Lex, and it's not just chasing you, it's *hunting* you. You have to call." She holds her phone out to me.

I shake my head, reach for the paper, but she blocks me with her elbow and dials the ten digits Carson scribbled for the other girl. Her hands are shaking, and she holds one of her shaky fingers to her lips to shush me, because the phone's on speaker.

A lady with a raspy voice answers.

"This is Kazinsky," she says.

The shaking from Lindsey's hands reaches her voice. "Hello." She clears her throat. "Excuse me, sorry. Hello." I feel light-headed, but Lindsey's composed herself and continues. "This is Graceland."

There's a pause, and I wonder if the word means anything to her. "Congratulations," Kazinsky says, like we've won some contest. She sounds accustomed to this plan, like this isn't the first *Graceland* note Carson's slipped in a girl's pocket. I wonder if the names he picks are all references to Elvis. I don't remember him being a fan. "His next scheduled outing is at the Viper Room," she continues, her voice a scratchy record. "Thursday night. And don't bring your friends. The guest list will have your name on it. No plus-ones. I'll let him know."

"Um," I interject, and Lindsey swats my arm. "You wouldn't have anything on the weekend, would you?"

Kazinsky laughs, and it sounds flooded with phlegm and cigarette smoke. "This isn't a Choose Your Own Adventure, lady." She doesn't seem to notice Lindsey's voice has changed to mine. "Graceland's on the guest list. Take it or leave it."

With that, she hangs up, and the loud silence echoes in my room.

"No," I say. Lindsey gawks at me like I've just dropped a winning lottery ticket in a toilet.

She stands and walks without a word to the front door. I follow, wary. "We'll go Thursday after cross-country practice." She speaks matter-of-factly, like she's reading the minutes at our student council meeting. "ETA ten p.m., stay until one a.m., and be back in time for first period, Friday morning."

"No."

"What were the chances of that ending up in your pocket?"

"Zero chances! Because it's not my pocket!"

"Or maybe the universe is intervening because—"

"It's not the universe!" I grip the front door to calm myself.

"It's this crazy, effed-up coincidence, and it's begging me to chase him like some lunatic fan. Don't make me be that girl."

"Hollywood's not safe for a girl alone at night."

I can't believe what I'm hearing. "You're blackmailing me with your safety?"

"Look, Cayden McKnight or not, this is a once-in-a-lifetime opportunity. A Hollywood club? I'm not missing it. If you're not gonna be Graceland, then I will."

"That's so unfair."

"Then be Graceland."

"I hate you. You know that?"

She does a little dance. "Yes! Thank you."

"But I'm only driving, not attending. No plus ones. *You're* Graceland. You're going. And you're not talking to him if you see him."

"I don't have to," she whispers. "If the universe wants its way, it'll have it."

"You're crazy, you know that?"

She giggles, kisses me on the cheek, and snaps the door closed behind her before I can change my mind.

Once back in my room, I look around my symmetrical bookcases. I love my order—I do. But lately, I've wanted something more, something wild and alive. Unexpected. Rearranging my books or moving my furniture doesn't feel like enough. I dial Heidi's number from my laptop. After two rings, her face appears on my monitor. She's pulling her hair into a messy bun.

"How'd he take it?" she greets me.

"What?"

"Thought you were calling because you broke up with John."

"No. Listen, if I gave you my debit card, could you"—I crack my thumb nervously—"*do* some things?"

Heidi frowns. "Wow. That's so specific."

"I mean for Cayden McKnight."

"Again, am I buying furniture or ordering a stripper?"

I laugh. I love that Heidi never presses me on particulars. "Sorry. Like what if we did a bunch of donations in his name?"

"It's all traceable."

My face falls.

"But there are ways around it," Heidi adds, and hope surges in me. "What exactly do you want?"

I lower my voice and lean close to my laptop. "When Lindsey and I went to Hollywood that night, it felt so good to do all those things for him anonymously. What if I did that, but bigger? You're a hacker, right?"

"There's no way I can break into his computer. He'll have firewalled the shit out of that."

"Oh no! I didn't mean that! I just mean you're computer savvy. You can figure out ways to do good works in his name, but on a bigger scale."

Heidi loves a challenge—I can see her mulling it over as she moves her jaw side to side. "How big?"

"I dunno. Whatever you can do. But anonymously. Make people think he's amazing."

"I can start some things," she acknowledges. "But I can't tell you where they'll end up. We're talking the internet. You light a match, and there's no saying if it'll spark a scented candle or a forest fire."

"Trust me. His reputation can only go in one direction." I point up. I notice the *Celebrity Herald* magazine that I threw on the floor the other day has been set nicely on my desk. Lindsey must've picked it up. "Also, I'll pay you."

"Don't be ridiculous. But I'll need your debit card for a few things. How much are you willing to go?"

My dad peers in through the doorway for the single-parent nightly check-in. "Hey, champ. Home early?" I nod.

"Hey, Heidi, I'll talk to you tomorrow at school." I close my laptop.

"Studying for the ACT?" Dad says, 'cheers-ing' me with the glass of water in his hand.

"That was last weekend, remember?"

"Right." He swirls the water around. "You taking them again next week?"

That's cute. Dad knows the ACT as well as Mom knows football. "Nope. I'm done."

He sips some water, swishes it around his mouth, and then swallows. "When do you hear if you passed?"

"You just get a score."

"When's the deadline for college?"

"For Boston? ED's November first." When he looks at me funny, I clarify, "Early decision."

He whistles low. "Better get started!"

I love his enthusiasm. There's no reason to tell him I've been working on applications since the beginning of my junior year, so instead, I agree.

"Heard you won the meet this week." He pumps a fist in the air. "Ready for Zone?"

"Yep." Zone is a race against all the high schools in southern Nevada, where the top twenty-five runners qualify for state. I've qualified every year, but this year, I know my dad's hoping for me to be the *first* qualifier.

"Mom and I will drive you there—Henderson, right?"

I nod and then remember I didn't see Mom's car in the driveway when I came home. Dad notices me looking over his shoulder toward their bedroom. "She left work early to visit Oma."

My dad's mom, my *oma*, lives in an assisted senior-living facility called Sunset Living. It's a community of seniors who live by themselves, but workers check on them throughout the day. Mom and Dad take turns visiting Oma throughout the week. I used to see her twice a week, but in the past couple of years, school has been overwhelming, so my visits have dwindled.

"Afterward, her boss called her back. Computer problems." Being the best programmer for the county has its downside. "That reminds me."

He retreats and returns with Mom's iPad. He licks his lips, shifts his weight from one leg to the other. "Listen, I found that magazine in your room." He points to the copy of *Celebrity Herald* on my desk. So it wasn't Lindsey. "Your mom saw me flipping through it, and she said that since you were reading it, you'd need this."

He hands me her iPad. Something feels funny about it all. "I have my own iPad, Dad, remember? Last Christmas?"

"Right. She said she downloaded some"—he pauses—"stuff."

"Stuff?"

"I told her you didn't watch movies, but she said you might change your mind. Is it a school project or something?"

Dad knows it's not a school project, but he's trying to make this easier on me. The iPad isn't heavy, but the weight of it pulls my arms down. I look at it with reluctant eyes. Of course, there's no passcode. I know there will be three movies downloaded, and I'm mad that Mom is so nosy and that she climbs uninvited into all the areas I'd rather keep private.

"Tell her thank you, but I don't need the *stuff* she downloaded." I hand the iPad back.

"You sure about that?" He opens the magazine to the page with Carson's photo. "Well," he says, yawning. "I'm turning in." He tosses the magazine onto my bed. As he leaves my room, he says, "Not a bad kid. He's paying for people's dinners. You see that?"

★★★★★

After brushing my teeth and changing my closet mirror to a new vocab word and a new to-do list, I crawl under my blankets still dressed. I text Lindsey: Mom downloaded Carson's movies to her iPad. :/

Lindsey texts back, I kno

seriously!

swear i didn't tell her anything. Has she been talking to the universe? ;)

I hang over the bed and fish underneath the bed frame until I find the lanyard bracelet. I snap it onto my wrist, and it fits perfectly. I place *Celebrity Herald* underneath my pillow, then rest my arm with the bracelet on the pillow next to me.

"Night, Good," I whisper. I picture him smiling at me the way he used to—the perfect smile that made me feel like the whole world was in love with me. I take my laptop off my nightstand, hug it close to my chest like a new stuffed animal, and imagine the way things could've been. Would we have gone to premieres together? Maybe he would've walked me across the red carpet and said things like, *"Don't be nervous. I'm right here with you."* And I wouldn't have been nervous. Not with him walking beside me. I would've felt the same sense of peace I had when he pulled the cactus spikes out of my hand.

My heart aches. All I'd wanted at Phantom Bar was a word, a nod, a sigh. Lindsey thinks he still loves me, but I saw the way he looked *through* me that night. There's no way I'd subject myself to that again at the Viper Room. I trace my finger across the smooth black screen of my laptop.

she also uploaded the files to your Google drive

Maybe I'll watch one movie. I know he's just reciting lines, but maybe I'll see the old Carson. Maybe his character will lift and drop a shoulder. Or look down to the left when he's thinking. Or link pinkies with the girl he likes. I don't allow myself time to think about how much I miss those things. Instead, I log into my Google account and open my drive.

Chapter Nineteen

"Wake up!" Lindsey shouts through the cell phone. It's 5:00 a.m. on Monday, and she's called me three times in a row. Finally, I pick up.

"This better be important," I grumble, buried beneath my pillow.

"Did you watch the first movie?"

"Lindsey, really? This couldn't wait until school?"

"Nope! Pick you up in twenty!"

★★★★★

Carson's first movie, *Against Life Expectancy*, is about five terminally ill orphans at a hospice. Doomed to die of cancer, they decide to seek death before it seeks them. They try to make a difference in the scariest, most dangerous places they can find, hoping to die of noble causes. There's other stuff, but that's the gist of my recap to Lindsey over Arizona Charlie's $5.99 ham-and-eggs breakfast. Lindsey nods as I talk; I'm sure she's seen the movie ten times. "So what's Cayden saying to you?" she asks.

"I don't know." I shake salt over my eggs. "Cancer sucks?"

"Come on! Play along." Lindsey's convinced that Carson's movies are his way of reaching out to me, of trying to talk to me after all these years. Honestly, the Carson back then probably *would've* made some crack about the suck factor of cancer, but I humor her.

"He's telling me to seize the day," I say. "Carpe diem."

"Yes!" She drops her fork and grabs my wrist. "And when he made that movie, things were bad between you guys, like cancer. You were his life, and that life was taken from him. Cancer said, 'You can't have life.' So he was like, 'Fine, I'll seek death.' But in the end, he still wanted life. You get it? He still wanted *you*, even back then!"

A piece of egg flies out of my mouth as I try to suppress my laughter. "Just stop, Lindsey!"

"I'm not kidding!"

"I know! Gosh, do I know."

She looks down at my wrist, which she's still holding, and notices the lanyard bracelet. She lifts an eyebrow, but I shake my head. Not up for discussion. "Okay, fine, what about the other movies?"

I focus on my slab of ham. I cut it into smaller and smaller pieces.

"You didn't watch them." One was plenty. My insides were twisted in knots watching Carson at that age. It was the age I remember him most. "Of *course* you didn't. I just think that if you learn more about his life, you'll crack the code of what he's saying to you in his movies."

"What?" I laugh through my bite of toast.

She ignores me. Pulls out colored index cards. "I've organized these trivia questions according to level. Let's study the green: easy." She holds one up. "What's Cayden's favorite color?"

"Blue," I say. "Navy, not sky blue."

"Food?"

"Pasta. Any kind." Lindsey's mouth falls open, impressed that I'm acing this test without studying.

"Fine. Let's go to the advanced stack. How old was Cayden when he learned to ride a bike?"

"Eight," I say.

"Geez," she says, flipping to the next card. "Not the most athletic kid. Eight?"

"Yep. His apartment was too small, and he was on the fourth floor, and they didn't have a garage, so when he was eight, Dylan's brother gave him his old bike, and Carson learned on his own at a park."

"Dang," Lindsey said. "*I* didn't even know that." She shuffles the stack and pulls out a red card. "Why was the movie *Against Life Expectancy* so life-changing for Cayden?"

"It got his mind off me?" I offer between bites.

"Close," she says, flicking me on the head with the card. "As in, not close at all. It was like the breakout movie of the new generation of teen actors. Three of the five have gone on to have successful film careers. The other two are still acting, one for television and the other for bit roles here and there. But it was a showcase of five talented young actors. Cayden was everyone's favorite, and he was nominated for a Golden Globe." She flips through the cards and stops at an orange one. "Ooh, wait! Here's a good one. And I'll tell you, since I know you don't know. Since his first movie, Cayden insists on having 'title' rights to his movies. Like, if he agrees to do the movie, he gets to choose the title."

"Weird," I say.

"Tell me about it. That's where his bad reputation began. Like, what actor demands to change the titles of the movies he's in? Who puts that in their contract? I'm thinking there has to be a reason."

"Your reason probably has to do with Carson sending secret messages to China's government."

Lindsey stares at me. "That's the dumbest theory I've ever heard. At least mine are believable. Anyway, after Cayden's first movie, he went on to do a critically acclaimed independent film with Timothy Hollingsworth called . . ."

She holds up a card to quiz me, but I shake my head.

"*Aruba*!" she says. "Seriously, Lex, everyone and their cousin's grandma's pet dog has seen *Aruba.* Anyway, he was nominated for that role, too, but didn't win." She fishes through my purse. "Do you have something to write on?" She finds a business card. "Hey, this is the card from the bartender at 3two3." Lindsey waggles her eyebrows and scribbles something on the back of the card. She stuffs it into the front pocket of my backpack. "I wrote down Carson's four movies in chronological order. Look them up on IMDb. Cross-reference them with any of the same cast or crew. Maybe there's a pattern."

On our way out, she prattles on about Cayden's vacation spots, his favorite places to shop, and how *Open Boat* didn't have a big-enough budget, so he took a pay cut because he wanted to act in it so badly. "People consider it his first poor choice as an actor, but the teen crowd loves it," she says as we pick up our car from Arizona Charlie's valet. We make it to school just before the one-minute warning bell, and I'm relieved that I don't have enough time to find John at his locker.

★★★★★

School feels different, and it's felt that way since my night in Hollywood with Lindsey. Now every lecture from my AP teachers becomes background noise for a montage of scenes from *Open Boat* and *Against Life Expectancy* juxtaposed with my own memories of Carson. I study his every expression in my mind, and it makes me feel closer to him again, like the way I can tell what my friends are feeling and thinking just by a smirk or a creasing forehead.

At Nutrition break, I wrap an arm around Heidi's neck and herd her into one of the library's study rooms. She leaves her cello outside the room. I drop the *Celebrity Herald*, folded open to Carson jogging, onto the table.

"How good are you at geography?"

She brings the picture of him close to her face, turns it sideways. "If, by geography, you mean Google Street View, that's not gonna be easy."

"So you can do it?"

"Let's pretend I can find his house. What then?"

"I dunno. I haven't thought that far."

"Okay, look at this." She pulls up a website, thankyoucayden .com. A banner of photos—all of Carson—frames each side.

In the middle of the screen are testimony after testimony about Cayden McKnight. The first one is titled: CAYDEN FILLED MY GAS TANK. I read the excerpt: "I ran into Cayden McKnight last week, and he filled up my gas tank. When I asked how I could thank him, he said I should donate blood. And I did! Thanks, Cayden. Who knows the lives you may have saved?" I don't read the rest of the stories, but I know what they're about based on their boldfaced title description: CAYDEN FED A HOMELESS MAN. CAYDEN PLANTED TREES AFTER DEFORESTATION. CAYDEN COVERED MY ELECTRIC BILL.

"What *is* this? Where'd you find it?"

Heidi rolls her eyes. "I built it, dummy. You asked me to start something. I created about twenty fake stories to start us off. And a fake email with a fake social media account, paid for some followers, and then posted a link everywhere I saw a fan base. I figured I'd add a few stories a day, but seventeen people already have sent emails sharing their own accounts."

"True stories?"

"Doubtful. Fans'll do anything to help the guy they love. But I ignore the trollers, proofread the good stuff, and publish them."

Lindsey flies through the door, making me jump. "Good thing I saw your cello! Took me forever to find you guys! Lex, did you see Heidi's site?" she squeals.

I glare at Heidi. "You told Lindsey?"

Heidi glares back. "I sure as hell didn't make up twenty stories on my own! You said you wanted help."

"And I also got her up to speed," Lindsey adds.

I wasn't trying to keep it a secret, but I feel bad that she didn't know, and Lindsey had to fill in all the gaps for her. Heidi harrumphs, waving it off. "Trust me, Lex. I didn't ask her to tell me."

"Oh! Guess what?" Lindsey interrupts, but doesn't wait for us to guess. "I contacted the director of activities at a children's hospital and said I was Cayden's personal assistant." Both Heidi and I turn to her, mouths agape. "Told her Cayden's manager is Kazinsky—which is true—and gave her Kazinsky's direct line."

"You didn't," I say.

"Sure did! Said that even though it had been three years"—at this Lindsey holds her phone to her ear and mimics her professional voice—"Cayden would like to show his appreciation to all the researchers and doctors at the children's hospital who supported *Against Life Expectancy* with their expertise."

I'm not sure what that means, but this isn't like dropping a few twenty-dollar bills to cover a prom dinner. I don't have two hundred grand just lying around to donate. I press the heels of my hands against my eye sockets.

"Relax. I said Cayden would love to attend a holiday party in the future and meet with the staff and children."

I peer up at Lindsey between my fingers. "What the heck? Children at a hospital? That's going too far."

"Not if it works. They'll call Kazinsky. They'll set something up. I told her not to tell the children until he confirms. Besides, he's not heartless. Just heart*broken.* Look, you sit in every class like a dazed puppy whose owner got deployed to some war zone. People are starting to notice. Did you see how happy that just made you?"

"No."

"Well, you're smiling."

"She's got a point," Heidi adds.

My smile immediately evaporates. "I need to talk to John," I mumble.

"Yes!" they say in unison.

"So," Lindsey says, "I might've told her that even if Cayden couldn't attend, we'd send a couple hundred for supplies, you know, cups and plates and stuff." I glare at Lindsey. "What! It makes us sound legitimate. And we can send a money order, and no one'll know it's us."

"I can't believe you," I say, but I'm laughing as I Venmo her.

I head home that day intending to give John a call after football practice. But instead, I block my caller ID and make calls, thanking companies on behalf of Cayden, claiming to be his personal assistant or Kazinsky herself. When I call Sony, I get transferred three times to managers of managers until some guy accepts my thanks for the quality of cameras used in Cayden's last movie. He's not the president of Sony, or even close, but at least word is spreading. So many people are tickled by these calls. Giddy. It feels so good that I forget none of it's really true. I doubt any of this will make the news, but the alternative is calling my boyfriend and telling him that even though nothing is wrong with him, I have to break up with him. Why is this so much harder than ending things with Dylan when I was fourteen?

I bury my thoughts by trying to get ahold of the CEO

of Southwest Airlines, which I learn is pretty much impossible, even when you're Cayden McKnight's assistant; however, I do find an email address. I create my own fake one—Kazinsky_2862—which isn't taken yet on Gmail, and I thank Southwest for the great customer service they've shown Cayden's family members when they fly to visit him on location.

After four hours of calls and emails, Cayden loves to recycle, encourage teen moms, and build houses in Mexico. I'm amazed at how little verification some companies need. The second I offer up the name "Cayden McKnight," I'm transferred to a manager who believes my words, no matter how far-fetched I think I sound. They lap up the praise and thank-yous like thirsty dogs. I guess deep down, no matter how much they deny it to their friends, everyone's dying to have a celebrity think of them. I know how they feel.

Chapter Twenty

On Tuesday after cross-country practice, I walk to Heidi's.

I drop onto her bed and stare up at the ivy across her ceiling. "Any luck?"

"Not yet," Heidi says, "but soon." She moves aside a lush fern and sits at her desk. Her laptop is open to Street View in some neighborhood. "According to the 2010 census, there are only six thousand one hundred twenty-six housing units in the area of Malibu he could live"—she shows me a thick stapled packet printed from the internet—"and I've pulled up the satellite pics on over three thousand of them to see if they match the photo you gave me. So far, I've ruled them all out, which means, hey, I'm halfway there."

"Unless you get lucky . . ."

"Unless I get lucky." She zooms in on a photo of a house, scans the front lawn, and hits the arrow keys to pan to the street. Next, she holds up the torn-out magazine picture of Carson getting ready to leave his house for a run. "Nope," she says after comparing the magazine pic to the photo on the computer screen, and she crosses out another address from the packet. She types in the next address on her list as she says to me, "Did you and John talk?"

I look away from her and gaze at her plants. "About what?"

She laughs to herself. "About what," she repeats.

I twirl one of her vines around my finger.

"Where were you last Friday?" she says, eyes on the screen. "John came to Calista's by himself." After cheering at the game Friday night, Calista had a house party. But it was the day Lindsey found the blurb about Cayden "turning over a new leaf." That night, I'd slipped out during the fourth quarter and stopped by a magazine stand. I bought all the latest celebrity magazines, hoping to find something else about our night rearranging Cayden's reputation. I'd planned on going to Calista's later, but I got sucked into the vortex of celebrity pictures and choosing who looks better in the same designer dress.

"I forgot."

"Mm-hmm," she says, squinting at a zoomed-in shot of someone's mailbox. She crosses out another address. Keeps typing as she says, "You flaked on Kim's birthday dinner last Tuesday, too, and you haven't even noticed that she's hurt and hasn't talked to you at school since Wednesday, and from what I've heard, you've missed two of your club meetings and didn't show up to tutoring on Friday. You and John walk through the halls like you're business associates, so I want to know when you're going to tell him."

I say nothing.

"Look, I couldn't care less that you're acting like a normal, irresponsible human being. But we all know that you've *never been* normal and you've *never been* irresponsible. So everyone in our friend group knows something's up, but you're not saying anything, and that doesn't work with people like you."

"People like *me*?"

"Come on, Alexa!" She stops typing. "News flash: You're a valedictorian dating a football player. You're like the geek who broke through the social ranks. People are going to start talking if you don't."

"I know. I just don't know how to bring it up."

"Well, don't put it all on you. John's got a God-given mouth, and he hasn't used it, either. Seems like both of you know something's off, but neither of you wants to be the first to say it."

I hug Heidi's pillow. John's the one solid pillar in my life of quicksand. He's part of what I know as "high school," and high school was the one thing that brought me comfort back when I lost Carson. "It's complicated."

"I figured," she says. "Which is why I'm helping you get to the bottom of whatever this is." She motions to the computer and her stack of paper. "As far as Cayden goes, it doesn't surprise me that he's messing with a girl who has a boyfriend. But you owe it to John. You owe him an explanation. I'm not quite sure what you owe Cayden."

"An apology," I say. "That's all. And Cayden's not messing with me. He wants nothing to do with me. I just want his address, his real one, not some P.O. box to his fan club. Maybe if I send him a letter explaining what I couldn't explain back then, maybe then I'll be able—"

"To have Cayden babies?"

"To move on." I look back at the ceiling and count the vines snaking in different directions. I notice they're held up with fishing wire. "Every bad part of Cayden—according to Lindsey—is because of me." I'm ashamed even saying it. "Nothing ever *happened* between us. Not then. Not now. And there's no possibility of anything ever happening. Ever."

"But if the possibility opened up tomorrow? Would you take it?"

My silence is all the answer she needs.

"You need to tell John."

★★★★★

I hang out on Heidi's bed and work on AP Physics while she switches between calculus homework and searching more Malibu addresses. Ryan comes over and they leave for the kitchen, returning with sandwiches for all of us.

I notice how everything's so natural between them. Heidi sits on Ryan's lap, and they play on the computer. He makes fun of her bony butt digging into him, and she jokes that all of her missing fat is hiding in his love handles. They don't talk about daily schedules or accomplishments—just trivial stuff, like the hiccups she gets after eating jalapeños, or how when he has a cold, his voice sounds like Mufasa in *The Lion King*. They look at each other when they talk.

Mom picks me up on her way home from working late again. As I leave, Heidi says to me, "What do you want, Lex? From all this?"

"I told you. To move on."

"Bullcrap. What you want is fine. Just tell John."

I look down at the doormat. "Home Is Where the Heart

Is," it reads, and I wonder how that works if your heart doesn't know where to be. I press my toes against the sides of my dusty running shoes. "I don't even know if it's worth it," I say. "Chasing after a *possibility*?"

Heidi shrugs her shoulders. She can't answer that for me.

★★★★★

Wednesday, I try to talk to John, but it's so hard. We're not fighting. Neither of us is being a jerk. I try to bring it up as we stand at our lockers.

"So I know it's been . . . you know," I say. I know he knows. His eyes search mine, wanting more.

"What is it?"

"I don't know anymore. I mean, do you?"

"About what?" He knows I'm talking about us—I bet he even agrees—but he won't be the first to admit it.

The one-minute bell rings. "We should head to class," I say. "Later?"

He shrugs, and we walk away.

★★★★★

It's three days before Zone, so cross-country practice is light and easy. We end early, and when I get home, I borrow Dad's car and drive over to Sunset Living. I knock on my oma's apartment door. After much shuffling, she answers it.

In the past few years, Oma moves and thinks slower, but she's still the same stubborn German woman. We take a walk around the grassy perimeter of the building, moving like molasses on Valium, but she refuses to lean on me for support, even when she loses her balance. She pats my arm a lot and never mentions how long it's been since I've visited.

"Oma," I say when we return to her apartment, "would you like to watch a movie with me?"

"Sure, sure," she responds. I remove my laptop from my backpack and make popcorn while she situates herself on the loveseat. I open Google Drive and place the laptop on the TV tray in front of her. The first scene is Carson walking along a beach, wind blowing through his blond hair, his bare chest toned and damp from the heat. I push pause.

"Oma, do you know who that is?" I point at Carson's face. His eyes even sparkle on freeze frame. She squints at the screen, her wrinkles burying her eyes. "It's Carson," I say. She looks at me blankly. "Do you remember the boy who spoke to you in German the night we went to eat at Hollywood Hal's? A long time ago." She thinks for a few seconds and then shows a faint sign of recognition.

"He was such a good boy," she says. "The German boy."

"He's American, but he spoke German to you, remember?"

"Of course, I remember. The boy from Germany."

"Yes," I agree. "The boy from Germany."

"Such a nice boy," she repeats. "He's the nicest of all your friends. Germans are good friends."

"Look at him," I say. "He's in this movie! He's an actor, Oma! A movie star!"

I could be saying that he mows lawns for all she cares. "Is that what he does now?" She looks away from the screen and reaches for the popcorn bowl. "Good for him."

"Isn't that amazing, Oma?"

She's not paying attention. Instead, she's tucking the blanket around her body. She reaches down and rubs her feet to get the circulation going. "Germans are hard workers. That's why he's such a good boy."

I tuck the blanket more firmly around her before grabbing my own bowl of popcorn and settling on the couch next to her. Oma lasts about ten minutes before she's snoring. I turn the volume up and submerge myself in Carson for the next two hours.

He plays Brad, a high-school jock whose girlfriend gets kidnapped while on vacation in Aruba. Everyone is supportive of his grief because the police reports show that they were attacked, and he was knocked unconscious. Only he knows the truth, and why he's so guilt-stricken: that even if he hadn't been knocked unconscious, he was too drunk to protect her.

Nine months later, he's dropped out of school and is living a hopeless life when he decides to head back to Aruba to find her. As he hunts down the kidnappers, he quickly becomes the hunted. After many dangerous close calls, he finds her and brings her home, but the kidnappers have kept her addicted to heroin for almost a year. Even after she's cleaned up, she's a shadow of what she used to be.

Two months later, she disappears again. She leaves a note for Brad, confessing that she's chosen to go back to her kidnappers. She longs for the heroin, and knows where it'll never be denied her. Now that she's eighteen, nobody has any power over her decision to leave, not Brad nor her parents or even the police. He's lost her forever.

I'm a weeping mess by the end.

I turn to Oma. Her blankets are tucked loosely around her, the edges dangling, her chest rising and falling to her rhythmic snoring.

"You're right," I whisper to her. "He *is* a good boy. I'll see you next week." I turn the lights off and kiss her on the forehead before locking up.

On my way out, I notice a dirt patch about the size of my bedroom. I stop by the manager's office and explain that Cayden McKnight's grandma and my grandma were childhood friends in Germany, and how Cayden would like to pay for a community garden for the senior citizens at Sunset Living. I offer to Zelle or Venmo him, but he doesn't know what I mean. He asks for a money order, so I set a reminder on my phone to get one. He doesn't know who Cayden McKnight is, either, but promises that the plot will have a placard that reads, "Donated by Cayden McKnight."

I know it's not from him. But it feels right, or at least the closest thing to it. Besides, it's a garden for old people. Carson would've loved it. Not sure if Cayden would.

Chapter Twenty-One

I knew pretending to be "Graceland" was a bad idea. Maybe our worst yet. But Lindsey's been so incredible to me through all this that when I see her excitement, I can't say no to her. She can't believe she has an invitation to a club where Cayden McKnight is going to be. "And it's the Viper Room!" she squeals to me at least once a day. She knows the rules—no approaching him, no eye contact, not even a mention of my name within fifty feet of him—but still, come Thursday, I feel like I'm going to vomit all day. I'm sure people notice my silence, but no one mentions it, at least to me. I remember what Heidi said about people talking, so I tell our friends at lunch how stressed I am about college apps due in a week.

Cross-country practice is a short three-mile jog. Since it's two days before Zone, Coach ends with an inspirational video on the Ironman. Competitors crawl across the finish line after surviving almost two and a half miles of swimming, one hundred and twelve miles of cycling, and over twenty-six miles of running. Fatigue has stripped them of their sense of balance, and many collapse, then stand and take a few steps, and then collapse again. Coach's message: Saturday's 5K is *nothing* compared to this, so if you're not falling over with dried spit caked on your face, you're not running hard enough. I think I'd rather do an Ironman than put Lindsey in the same room as Cayden McKnight, which according to my watch, is five hours away.

I busy myself by texting my parents and John that I'll be spending the night at Lindsey's. Lindsey tells her parents she'll be sleeping over at my house. We grab In-N-Out burgers before hopping onto the freeway, but I don't touch mine. I throw my bag of food in the back seat on top of Lindsey's suitcase. I was supposed to help her pack the "perfect outfit," but she said she'd take care of her own fashion since I couldn't even conjugate regular verbs in Spanish class. She gave me one job—bring a car charger since Lindsey's broke recently—and of course I forgot it.

I distract myself with music playlists for the first hour on the I-15, but when I think about where we're heading, I set my phone down and wipe my sweaty palms on my jeans.

"Lindsey, I don't know if we should do this."

"You're here to make sure I don't go alone. But you're just the driver, remember?" she says, even though she's currently behind the wheel. I don't think she trusted me to make it to California without a U-turn. "Remember what that lady Kazinsky said? No 'plus-ones.' It's just me going in. He won't know you're here."

"Right." I'm struggling to stay calm. "It's just all your 'universe' talk lately."

I reach in the back seat for my backpack and notice a rubber-banded rolled-up piece of butcher paper.

"What's that?"

A devious grin stretches across her face. "Something to keep you busy. Just a sign. Thought you could hang it somewhere in Hollywood."

I remove the rubber band and roll open the sign, the corners curling over themselves. Painted in green tempura is a trefoil with three faces.

"Girl Scouts? Linds, we're not Girl Scouts."

"Duh! But how good will Cayden McKnight look if the Girl Scouts of America are making signs for him?"

I snort with laughter. "You know some cop will tear that down the second I hang it."

"So? Someone'll see it. Just takes one snap. One photo. Besides, it'll last long enough to keep your mind off the fact that he's going to be in a two-mile radius of you."

I pinch the bridge of my nose and close my eyes. She's right. I say that I don't care. That I'm just here to be a good wingman keeping my best friend safe. But his proximity makes it difficult to focus. "This is crazy."

She reaches over and grabs my hand. "Right? Ohmigosh, Lex. I'm going to be in the Viper Room with Cayden McKnight! Same room!"

"Promise me you'll stay away from him."

She motions toward the sign in the back and holds up three fingers. "Scout's honor."

My stomach churns even as I laugh. "You're not a Girl Scout! Seriously, don't say anything. If you happen, you know—"

"Doubt I'll get that close. I'll totally text you through it all. You're going to get zero homework done, trust me."

I nod and squeeze her hand. A text lights up my phone. Heidi.

What did John say?

I text back: ?

U said you were going to talk to him

Told him I was staying w Linds 2nit

No. TALK TO HIM talk to him. About THIS. About Cayden. I TOLD you to tell him. 4th period yesterday.

Did u?

She doesn't text back, which means she did. I can't remember.

Sorry, H. This week has been all weird emotions for me.

"Who's that?" Lindsey asks.

"Heidi," I say, clicking send and pocketing my phone.

"Everything okay?"

"Yup. How about we talk about your Christmas dance for a while?"

"Yes!" It's a topic sure to get her amped and ready to take on the world. We talk about all the decorations, who is taking who, and what they're going to wear. Before I can say Hollywood, we're slowing to a stop on a side street off Sunset Boulevard. Lindsey motions behind us to where a line of clubbers snakes out of a door.

"It's right there." Lindsey lets go of the steering wheel and claps. I sink lower in my seat.

We drive down the residential street until it's dark enough for Lindsey to change her clothes in the car. She tosses me a designer dress and boots from the suitcase.

"In case you change your mind," she says. I climb into the driver's seat.

"You actually packed this? Not a chance. Besides, no plus-ones."

"The list just gets me in quicker," she says. "Stand in the regular line. It's not a private club."

"Wow, this is short!" I hold the dress across my body, and it barely reaches my thighs.

"Oh, please!" she says. "Our cross-country briefs are short." It's true. This year, Coach switched the girls' uniform to the brief-bottoms, which are really just glorified underwear. "Cayden's not the only one who's changed since junior high." She motions to my legs, but I ignore her.

"You ready?" I throw the car in reverse and park at the end of the two lines of people.

She opens the car door, then turns and grabs my hand. "Come with me," she pleads. "You can face him. You're Alexa Brooks."

I give her a rueful half smile. "He knows who I am. You'll have fun! Now go."

"Fine," she says, "but I'd rather have fun together."

"Text me," I say. "I'll be close."

I nudge her, and she jumps out of the car and prances to the line at the door.

Chapter Twenty-Two

Twenty minutes later, after driving aimlessly to calm my nerves, I'm hanging the paper sign on a chain-link fence in front of a car-rental place at a busy intersection. My phone vibrates.

Come! Bouncer says Cayden is a no-show.

I text back, Nice try!

I toss my phone into the car's center console, where I notice Lindsey's left me Delaney's extra ID. Go figure. For the next hour, I have a picnic with my calculus homework and *The Great Gatsby*, ignoring the urge to check my texts. Once my eyes start to blur at the pages, I finally reach for my phone.

There are twelve texts from Lindsey, mostly in caps. The most recent is in lowercase, like she's given up shouting and has resorted to on-her-knees groveling.

pinky swear. he's not here. when do you get the chance to go to a hollywood club on a school night? come onnnnnn, lex. plz

I look in the back seat. My makeup bag sits next to the boots, halfway open, with my mascara and eyeliner poking out. "Fine!" I yell at them and head back to find parking. I ignore Lindsey's stupid "What are the chances?" universe comments taunting me, pointing at the curbside space that miraculously opens up as I approach. "He's not here," I argue back. After wriggling into the sad excuse for a dress and zipping up the boots, I exit the car and head to the back of the line, which has since thinned. The bouncer takes my fake ID as someone lights a cigarette nearby. "Hey," he growls, "move it away from the building." He hands the ID back without even looking and waves me in. I hear Lindsey's voice again, *What are the chances?* I look up and glare as if I can see the universe smirking.

The club's on a hill, which means the entrance from the side street is on the lower level. The entrance leads me into a narrow, pitch-black stairwell going up, and I have to hold on to both handrails to find my way without tripping.

At the top, the room opens up to a dance floor the size of a large walk-in closet and a stage barely a step higher than the dance floor. Another entrance opening to Sunset Boulevard is on the far wall. Onstage, a band rocks out, flooding the room with a song reminiscent of those late-eighties ballads my parents always sing to. When the drummer pounds, I feel it on the inside of my ribcage, and the four male band members bounce in sync. The crowd's also bouncing, shouting the lyrics so proudly, you'd think they'd written all the words themselves.

I love that it's dark and crowded, that I don't have to worry about being seen. What if Lindsey's wrong? I walk the perimeter of the dance floor, searching. I've seen him only once since the summer before his freshman year, when he weighed in at a buck and was five-foot-nothing. At Phantom

Bar, we were out in the bright wide open. There's no way he'd be more than a silhouette in this lighting—would I even recognize him, with three years of height and weight added to him?

A pair of arms wrap around me. I gasp, even though I don't mean to, even though I know it wouldn't be Carson in a million years. Nerves.

Of course it's Lindsey. "Told you he's not here. Some other engagement, I guess. At least that's what the bouncer says." Her disappointment evaporates as she twirls in a circle. "But look around! Amazing, huh!"

Just to make sure, I lap the club in less than a minute. Lindsey's holding my hand the entire way, shouting facts about somebody named River Phoenix. I can barely hear over the music. Then, on the dance floor, I see a tall, thin shadow. His blond hair flops around as he bops to the catchy tune, a baseball cap in his hand. Tentatively, I walk closer, weaving through shoulders and hips until I'm behind him. His body's tall, like what I saw at Phantom Bar. *Please don't turn around!* In a panic, I back away, but Lindsey blocks my exit. "Where you going?"

She notices my wild eyes motioning to the guy. She laughs, reaches around me, and nudges him in the back. He turns around. His face looks nothing like Carson's, but the build, although skinnier, had me going. "Hey," the guy says to me, and keeps dancing.

"Hey," I blow out in relief. I turn to Lindsey. "He's not here."

"I told you that! Would you relax, Lex? Who cares? You're in the Viper Room! On the dance floor!"

"So?"

"So, dance!"

She has a point. How many seventeen-year-olds ditch Thursday debate club to go to an over-twenty-one club in Hollywood? I tap the guy on the shoulder. "Who's this band?" I shout.

"Who's this band!" he shouts back incredulously. "What planet are you from?"

"Las Vegas!" I yell, and he laughs and high-fives me.

"Well, 'Vegas,'" he renames me, "this band is called Departure Gates. My brother's the drummer."

"He's good!"

"Yahhhh!" He throws his arm around me, gives me a side hug, and releases me only after he has me hopping with him. Lindsey gives me the thumbs-up and starts jumping, too. We bump shoulders, backs, and fronts, and I see the way Lindsey throws her head back, so free and caught in the awesomeness of right now. I, too, want to lose myself in the music—kick out Carson and Boston College, regrets and worries—and I'm reaching for it, but then the song ends, and my new friend makes a beeline for the stage. I pull Lindsey close and shout, "Thank you!" She squeezes me, and I watch him say something to the lead singer, who laughs and nods. The singer leans into the mic and says, "Hey, Vegas, where are you?" He squints at the crowd, and my nameless friend lopes back, pointing at me the whole way.

"What are you do—" I start, but he's already clamped onto my wrist like a handcuff. Lindsey pushes me from behind, and he pulls me toward the stage as the singer continues to talk to the crowd.

"I've just been told that there's someone here who's never heard of Departure Gates." The crowd gives an exaggerated gasp. He extends a hand, and I hesitate before stepping onto the stage with shaky legs. The last time I was on a stage was—

"That true, Vegas? You a *DG* virgin?" I offer an apologetic grin. Lindsey's dying right now. I can hear her familiar scream above all the others. "Well, then." He produces a tambourine and hands it to me. "Looks like your world is about to change tonight, Vegas." I can feel his sweat and adrenaline. He's still on the mic so everyone hears when he whispers in my ear, "Don't worry, I'll be gentle." His fans laugh as he shouts to his drummer, "One, two, three!" The drummer pounds his intro, and the knots of people go wild. The singer faces me, and I still can't move, but the music is loud; it climbs inside and pounds on my chest cavity like it's trying to get out, a drug that makes me let go and forget. Because I don't know what else to do, I mirror his funny move, this wiggle that he does with his shoulders as he sings. The crowd cheers, and something within me finally cracks.

I hit the tambourine against my thigh to the beat of the drums. The singer and I dance around each other in circles, bopping and bouncing and hopping. It's the craziest adrenaline rush I've ever experienced, crazier than debate competitions, crazier than the state cross-country race before the gun. I hold the tambourine over my head, clapping it against my other hand to the beat. I turn and smack the bass guitarist's butt with it. As the song slows, the singer crouches down. I crouch down with him, eye to eye. The song pauses, and it's dead quiet. We don't blink. Then he jumps high, and I jump with him, the music starting in again, loud and wild. I jog across the front of the stage, slapping dancers' hands with the tambourine. When the song ends, I'm dripping with perspiration, and I can't stop smiling. The singer wraps his arms around me in a full sweaty hug. Holding the mic away, he says in my ear, "That was awesome."

"Thank you," I say. "I needed that." As he leads me with one hand off the stage, he grabs the mic. "Let's hear it for Vegas, fans!" They cheer and pat me on the back as I filter toward the back to get some air. A new song starts up, happy and hypnotic, with a volume that keeps earplugs in business. Lindsey's probably searching for me, but this place is small. She'll find me soon.

"What'll it be?" I turn to my right, where my elbow is leaning on the bar. The bartender's waiting on me.

"Uh, something simple," I say between labored breaths. He offers what sounds like "Roman Coke," so I shout over the noise, "Geez, they invented everything."

The bartender yells, "What?"

"You know," I say, "columns, concrete, and now, Coke!" He stares at me. "Never mind. Roman Coke. I'd love one." He grabs a glass and another person's beer right as the song ends. I hear a familiar snicker, and I turn, relieved. Lindsey.

Only it's not Lindsey. It takes a moment for my brain to catch up and realize the familiarity was not coming from her, but from a wisp of a memory. Carson.

It's Carson.

Chapter Twenty-Three

I flinch so severely that every part of me vibrates. Carson's standing shoulder to shoulder with me, leaning with both elbows on the counter. Something about what I said was funny to him, but the quiet laughter is short-lived. His face hardens.

The bartender returns with my drink. With fumbling fingers, I hand him my ATM card. "You wanna leave it open?" the bartender says. What does that mean? I can't think straight, so I shake my head, and he runs the card. I will myself to look ahead, elbows on the bar like Carson. Out of the corner of my eye, I see he's wearing a trucker hat low. I wipe my forehead with a napkin, and he sucks his drink through bared teeth.

As I'm signing the receipt, Carson says, "Nice show up there." He says it like he's Cayden McKnight, not Carson Knight, and for a moment I feel as if I'm talking to a stranger, an unapproachable celebrity.

"I had no idea that was going to happen," I stutter. *Stop*, I remind myself. This isn't some A-list movie star. This is Carson Knight, who pulled cactus spikes out of my fingers and swore we'd be best friends forever. After three years of not believing in second chances, we're having a conversation. This is all I've ever wanted. "I haven't been onstage since—" I falter, can't finish the memory.

"What are you doing here, Alexa?" His voice is icy. I'm glad I'm not looking into his eyes. We both stay facing forward, side by side.

From behind, Lindsey hugs me and squeals. "You. Are. My idol! Damn, Lex. How glad are you that you came now? Cayden's the one who missed out. If—"

"Lindsey," I warn, still looking straight ahead.

"No, really. Thank God for Graceland!"

"What?" Carson asks.

She whirls to Carson's face inches from hers. "Ohmigod." Her knees buckle, and she grabs me by the shoulder for support. "Ohmigod-ohmigod-ohmigod."

"Look, I didn't know," I say into my drink, and I know I sound lame. "I mean, the bouncer said you weren't here."

Lindsey starts panting like a pregnant woman in labor. "Ohhhmiiiigod," she sings high-pitched under her breath.

"When fans ask if I'm here, the answer's always no."

"I'm not some fan," I mutter.

"You never were."

His tone is mean. I stir my drink with the mini straw, but I can't get over how different he looks, even in my peripheral vision.

"You're tall," I murmur, eyes on my ice cubes. I haven't taken a sip yet. I probably won't. Even with all my years of beer pong, I don't think I've ever had more than half a glass.

"I'm not interested."

"No. I'm not— That's not why I'm here." I take a napkin and wipe the counter. "I'm not *stalking* you." He snorts derisively. "I have a boyfriend."

"Just one?"

I deserve that, and strangely, it feels good. The band transitions into a loud guitar solo. "I'm sorry," I shout, finally looking at him. "That's why I'm here."

His eyes flicker, just once, then settle back to their hard, unblinking gaze, still not at me. "Most girls *enjoy* screwing me."

Lindsey gasps. I forgot she was here.

"Stop it." I don't know why he's trying to be disgusting. "You're *not* that guy."

He laughs. "How would you know?"

"You're right," I concede. "I don't." I shouldn't be here. I hate this.

Lindsey says, "But maybe she wants to find out."

He finishes his drink. "No, she doesn't." He slams down the empty glass, and the ice cubes rattle. "Go home, Alexa." He walks away, toward a private, roped-off room, but before he enters, a security guard intercepts him, urgency in his step. I can't tell what he's saying, but I see Carson's body stiffen. Carson whips his head to the front entrance, the one opening to Sunset Boulevard.

"I'm so sorry," Lindsey starts. "He wasn't here. He wasn't. And then he was."

"Not your fault." I snake my way through the crowds and poke my head out the door. A team of paparazzi wait outside like a pack of wolves.

"Oh wow," Lindsey says when she catches up, seeing the swarm. I know without checking that the same number of photographers lies in wait outside the other entrance. Carson must be used to this, but his cramped posture and the way he tugs the brim of his hat suggest that tonight, for some reason, isn't a good night for this.

"The car's across the street by the food truck. Can you get it and meet me at the Sunset entrance in five?"

She smirks. "I love how you think. On it." She gallops out the door to the street. I speed over to Carson, and his bodyguard's hand almost clotheslines me.

"Not now, miss," he says.

I ignore him, fixing my eyes on Carson. "I can get you out of here without being seen."

Carson warily turns to me. I gaze at him like I used to, hoping he recognizes something familiar, something he used to love once. "Do you trust me?"

"No," he says without missing a beat. The bodyguard's stiff arm slackens, seeing that Carson and I know each other.

"Listen to me. There's so much more to that night—Paige's party—so much more I was supposed to say."

"Not the time." He looks away. And then, "I think you said enough that night."

"I know. And God, I'm sorry. I can't get rid of that, and believe me, I've tried. For three years, I've tried." His bodyguard drops his arm to his side, now engrossed in our story. Tears crowd my eyes, but I don't let them spill. "Please, Carson."

"Cayden," he corrects. "You gonna get me out of here or not?"

"Aw, c'mon, man," his bodyguard implores. "She's all tears."

"Don't be fooled," Carson says to him but locking eyes with me. "She's a better actor than I am."

I swallow hard, keep my chin high. "I'll get you out. Head to the bathroom."

"There's no window to the street," he replies, as if I'd ever have such a base thought. I ignore him.

"Can you do me a favor?" I ask the bodyguard. "For Cayden, actually. Clear out the bathroom?"

He turns, heads straight to the men's room. I dart through sweaty shoulders until I find my nameless friend who dragged me up onstage. "Hey!" I say. "What's your name?"

"Hey!" he says and hugs me hard. "Dan! You?"

"Alexa. Wanna make a quick hundred bucks?"

"Hell yeah!" He lifts his hand for another high five. This time it's me handcuffing him with my grip, and together we weave ourselves to the restroom, where the bodyguard stands watch. He lets us pass, and I go in with Dan, who has no time to prepare himself before he's face-to-face with Cayden McKnight. "Dude!" Dan exclaims. From the neck down, they're similar—tall and fit, but Dan's on the thin side. He lifts his hand to high-five Carson, but Carson doesn't budge.

"Switch clothes," I say. Dan giggles, but Carson glares at me. "I'll get you out of here, I swear." He still glares. "I get it, okay? This doesn't change anything between us. Just switch clothes, come on." I rush out of the restroom and tell the bodyguard to bring them to the front entrance when they're ready. "Oh, and get me Carson's jacket."

I charge outside the front door. It's as if the paparazzi

bred like rabbits while I was gone. Now some pedestrians are lurking with the photographers, whispering to each other. I open my Uber app—three on top of my GPS dot, so I confirm. Meanwhile, I see Lindsey driving up, so I hold up a finger to her—*Be there in one minute.* When I get back inside, Carson and Dan stand side by side in each other's clothes, with Carson's bodyguard blocking them from the back. They've even switched trucker hats. The bodyguard hands me Carson's jacket. I say to Dan and the bodyguard, "Tell Lindsey I'll text her where to meet up. See the purple Hyundai?" Dan nods. The bodyguard nods. "Head there."

And with that, I shove a hundred-dollar bill into Dan's back pocket, throw the jacket over Dan's head, and push Dan and the bodyguard out the door.

"No way!" I scream. "It's Cayden McKnight!" The jacket is draped over Dan's head, covering his face from view, but now he's wearing Carson's clothes from the neck down. Photographers swarm Dan, and the bodyguard fends them off.

I text Lindsey: Drive till ur far from here.

The two guys amble through the stampedes of footsteps and flashbulbs, until the bodyguard opens the back door to Lindsey's car and thrusts a hooded Dan into the back seat. The bodyguard climbs in after him and shuts the car door. The photographers crowd Lindsey's car and scream out in protest, demanding that Cayden answer some questions before he leaves. Lindsey lays on her horn.

She finally worms her car forward. A caravan of cars follows as she turns down the side street where the lower entrance is. Smart girl. No doubt she's rounding up the lower-entrance paparazzi on her drive. I look at the leftovers and shake my head. "I forgot about all the normal people." Even though the photographers are gone, there's still a group of bystanders. My cell rings—the Uber—and I spot the Prius twenty feet away. I take a deep breath, look into Carson's eyes. "You're tall," I say again. "That's gonna make it difficult."

"Make what difficult?"

I run out to the Prius, open the back door, and race back inside the club. "Can you carry me?" Facing Carson, I leap up on him, wrapping my legs around his waist. I'm eye level with him now. I pull his cap down as low as it will go without covering his eyes.

"What the hell."

"You're an actor," I say. "Just act. Head to the black Prius." And before I have time to think about it, I cup his face with my hands, covering him as much as I can, and then press my lips against his. "Go," I mumble against his lips. I wait for his rejection, but instead, he complies. He walks out the door, holding my legs around him, his face warm against mine, buried under my hands and lips.

The bystanders are still talking about seeing Cayden McKnight leave in a purple Hyundai. They don't notice us, but just to be safe, I keep Carson's face covered with my lips and hands. As he lowers me into the car, my head knocks the top of the door frame, his knee the bottom. We both wince, and he flops into the car on top of me. We are a mess of tangled arms and legs as the Uber driver confirms, "Hollywood and Highland?"

I can't suppress my giggle. "Or some place high," I say. I

see the faint trace of a smirk at the corners of Carson's mouth, but he quickly sobers when I smile at him.

He pulls away, shutting the car door and wedging his head between the door and the back of the front seat. He drapes his arm over his face so no one can see him from the sidewalk as we drive away.

We're quiet for a while.

"Why'd you have to sneak out tonight?" I ask. "Aren't you used to"—I wave an arm around—"photos?"

"Not your concern." He doesn't lift his head when he finally says, "If you're following me because you realized why I did the movies, you're wrong."

I cock my head. "Why you . . . did the movies?"

"Don't play dumb, Alexa. It was more of a superstitious thing. It wasn't you."

"I haven't seen all your movies," I confess. "Or your interviews or TV stuff. Before this week, I hadn't seen anything with you in it."

Carson peers out from his arm to measure my face, see if I'm telling the truth. He realizes I am. His eyes narrow. "Of course, you haven't." His words are dipped in acid.

"Carson, it's because—"

"What the—"

Something outside the window caught his eye, and I follow his gaze to the fence along the boulevard, where a huge poster reads, "Thanx, Cayden McKnight, for your financial contribution to Troop 425!" I hold back laughter, amazed at the odds. I couldn't have hung the sign at a better intersection.

"That's sweet," I say. "You support the Girl Scouts?"

"No!" Carson exclaims, peeved. "Something's going on. My publicist, my agent, even my friends keep hearing about—" He stops himself. "Never mind."

The driver pulls to the side of the road. "Hollywood and Highland," he announces.

"I'm not here because I'm hoping for a second chance," I say, tugging at my short dress, trying to cover my thighs, my nerves. "I saw you at Phantom Bar. I know you saw me, too."

"So?"

"So I saw the way you looked, I mean, *didn't* look at me. I'm not dumb. I can take a hint."

"And yet here you are," he says flatly.

"I didn't plan to be here. I mean, I did. But it— I'm here to apologize."

"With a tambourine?"

"No! That—look, it wasn't supposed to happen like this." I'm so frustrated I could scream. "I told Lindsey about you. About us. About how last I remember, you *weren't* the one everyone loved to hate. And now Lindsey's convinced it's my fault—your reputation in Hollywood—so she's been trying to—"

"You think *you're* the reason I'm this way?"

"No, not me. Lindsey. She—"

"Hah! Wow, Alexa. I thought you were arrogant before, but *now* . . ." He finishes his sentence with a condescending laugh.

"Wait." I'm annoyed and confused, and the driver sighs loudly, distracting me. "Look, I have two minutes with you, maybe. Can I tell you what happened that night at Paige's par—"

Carson's cell phone rings. He looks at the caller ID, then

answers, "There better be a damn good reason this couldn't wait." He listens for a moment. "What award? Huh? Oh, a *children's* ward." He looks away and lowers his voice. "No, I didn't schedule it! Did you? No. No. Well, forget it now—you can't cancel." He digs his chin into his chest, covers his mouth with his hand, but I still hear his muffled whisper, "Because they're *kids*. You can't spin that."

My cheeks warm, and I look away. I guess Lindsey's call to the children's hospital made it through to his publicist. He curses, hangs up, and then curses again.

"Hey, this your stop or what?" the driver says.

Carson says, "We're just dropping her off." He hands the driver a hundred-dollar bill. "I need you to take me somewhere else." I don't want to leave. I have so much more to say—but part of me feels like I'm talking to Cayden, not Carson.

I try again. "Why won't you just talk to me like Carson?"

"Carson's gone, Alexa." His jaw's clamped shut. Every time he calls me by my real name, the wind gets knocked out of me. It's a constant reminder that I screwed up too much to ever be called "Good" again.

"You're wrong," I mumble.

"Am I," he sneers.

I don't move, but instead look at Carson's blond hair, soft as a light breeze. His eyes—even narrowed and angry—remind me of diamonds reflecting the ocean.

"I loved Carson Knight," I say, and Carson blinks. No amount of acting could have prepared him for those words. I exit the car, and Carson slams my door shut and rolls down the window.

"Of course you did. He was your time filler while you messed around with his best friend."

"No," I say, but the driver starts pulling away. "That's not true!" I shout. The taillights glare at me, growing smaller until they disappear around the corner.

Lindsey texts me, I'll meet you there, but I haven't told her where *there* is, which worries me when it's Lindsey.

I text, U know where I am?

She doesn't respond, but I get a text from Heidi instead.

Just got off the phone w Lindsey. Crazy night about to get crazier. She tell you?

No what's up?

Found him.

Cayden?

Yes Captain Obvious.

Lol. Yeah I found him too. :(

No I mean his address.

If anyone could have sifted through six thousand photos and found the right one, it's Heidi. Such an amazing friend. I sigh when I think of all that work she did for nothing.

Thx, won't be needing it. Just got out of the car with him. It's over.

wtf!!! Lindsey's driving to his house. Thinks ur heading there.

No. This can't be happening.

Chapter Twenty-Four

I text Lindsey with frantic fingers: TURN AROUND!

She doesn't respond, and it doesn't show that the text delivered.

911! I try again. DIDN'T GO WELL!

Meanwhile, I text Heidi, Address?

And then a second later, I type, u still there?

And then a second later, HEIDI! ADDRESS!

Thirty seconds later, though it feels like thirty years, Heidi texts back, Wow. Calm down, crazy. 18216 Arminta Pasada. Did it really go that bad?

I request an Uber while I text back, The worst.

Sorry, Lex. Btw, Linds down to 5% batt.

She doesn't have a charger. I practically dive headfirst into the Uber as it rounds the corner. It's the same driver as before, and I think both of us can't believe it.

He pulls up the directions. "Malibu, huh?" He makes a U-turn and accelerates.

"Where'd you drop my friend off?" I try to sound casual, looking out the window as we drive past luxury theaters next to trashy lingerie shops.

"His car."

Could this night get any worse? I need to intercept Lindsey before Carson thinks I've gone mad with celebrity stalking. I can only hope he wasn't heading straight home.

It takes thirty minutes before we turn off Sunset onto Pacific Coast Highway. The streetlights send reflections across the ocean to my left, and I see the dark water crashing, churning into white wash, then slipping back out again.

Twenty minutes later, we've wound our way into the hills of Malibu, weaving through narrow streets and expensive cars, and he brakes in front of the street sign: Arminta Pasada. My head feels like a bowling ball. My vision blurs. I have the driver drop me off at an adjacent road. No need to call any more attention to myself than I need to. I clop uphill in my fancy boots along the curving road.

"There you are!" Lindsey squeals and appears out of the darkness, Carson's jacket in hand. When she throws her arms around me, I collapse against her.

"Where are you parked?"

Lindsey's looking past me. "Is he with you?"

"No. He's . . ." I shake my head.

She hands me my Asics, and I could cry. I wiggle out of my boots and slink into my running shoes. They cushion my feet like pillows.

Together we head toward her car, the road an orangey glow from streetlights, and she recaps her night. After she drove for three or four miles with Dan and the bodyguard, Dan took the jacket off his head and waved at his entourage. Once the disappointed caravan of paparazzi dispersed, Lindsey dropped the bodyguard at a nearby bar, where he called for a ride. A block from the Viper Room, she let Dan off, where he walked back to the club to meet up with his friends. He had one hundred dollars in his pocket, a great story to tell, and a pair of Cayden McKnight's pants.

"I totally thought you'd put Cayden into my car!" Lindsey laughs. "But it was Dan! That was such a cool move! Did Cayden thank you?"

"Not exactly."

I stop walking.

"Lindsey, where's the car?"

"Down the hill. There's no parking up here. Why?"

I remove the crumpled magazine photo from my purse, and in the dim streetlight, I hold up the blurry image to the clear real one in front of me.

I'm in front of Carson's house.

Panic ripples through me, but Lindsey says, "He's not home. Look." I step forward with lead feet, toward the ten-foot stone wall barricading his entire property. Beautifully groomed shrubbery hides the barbed wire perched atop the perimeter. The only place where the fence reprieves is at the two wrought-iron security gates.

I wrap my fingers around the gate and peer inside, wedging my face between two bars. The semicircular driveway has floor lights, illuminating a basketball hoop near the garage. There's a black SUV with tinted windows in the driveway.

"But—"

"I guarantee that's not his only car. See the other oil stain? Look at the house, Lex. It's like it's closed for the season, not really, but you get it. Nobody's home. That's why I thought he was with you. And don't worry. The Viper Room was probably just his appetizer. He's not coming back any time soon."

"Just like he was a no-show?"

"Oh, that's so unfair. The bouncer *said*—"

"I know, Linds. I'm not blaming you." I hug her. "It was fun, right?"

A corner of her mouth tips upward. "At least you get to keep his jacket."

The house seems lonely, too big for one person. Next to us is a security box. Three years ago, I might've cracked Carson's code by my third or fourth try. But I don't even know his shoe size now. I give it a shot anyway: 1105. November 5. Carson's birthday. It blares a rejection beep.

"What're you doing?"

"Reminding myself that I don't know him."

The house, though thirty yards back, is breathtaking, the size of a motel. I count the arched windows. Does he have an indoor pool? A small theater? The fourteen-year-old Carson wouldn't have a theater. He'd have a video arcade, possibly an indoor basketball court—at least a half court. But he's not a kid anymore. He's turning eighteen in a week. He's been clubbing and dating models for three years. We used to climb roofs; now, he's traveled the world. I knew him when he barely made the height requirement for Magic Mountain rides. Now we're almost old enough to vote.

"This is crazy." I laugh out loud. "I can't believe I actually hoped that—"

"So what happened?"

I blow out a mouthful of air, and my lips vibrate like a tired horse's. "You sure he's not coming home?"

"If he was at the Viper Room tonight? Not unless he was bringing *you* here—that's why I came. I really hoped—" She stops when she sees my face. "No, he has another crash pad in the Hollywood Hills. He's probably there tonight."

We sit down cross-legged against the stone wall next to the gate. I just want one last moment to feel close to him before I walk away from this. Small lights are built into the stone posts on either side of the gates, casting a soft light that warms the dark street.

I recount the night to her. She especially loves the part about the children's hospital. She says, "No way!" at least five times.

"And the movie part!" she yells, even though I'm right next to her. "Didn't I tell you? There's a *reason* he did those movies. He even admitted that you *figured out why he did the movies*! I bet I was right about how your relationship was cancer, and you were his life. But remember the ending? He dies. Maybe that was symbolic. He let go of you. And then the other movies represent different ways he's moved on. We just haven't figured those out yet." Her words shouldn't sting, but they do. Everything about tonight stings. I don't want to believe that he's moved on, but shouldn't he? I mean, haven't I? I'm the one with the long-term boyfriend.

"Oh, John," I groan, remembering.

"You still haven't told him." She sounds hurt.

"Tell him what? There's nothing to say about Carson. Can't you tell from tonight? I know it sucks, but Carson doesn't want to see me again. And according to you, he's done four movies saying that in four different ways. What am I going to do, bully him into liking me again?"

"Then you're staying with John?" She tosses a pebble and catches it with the same hand, but it feels staged, like she's trying to act like it doesn't matter.

"I didn't say that."

Lindsey's quiet.

"Wait, I thought you wanted me to chase after Carson."

"I did," Lindsey says. "And you did. And now it's over, but John, I don't know, maybe you should tell him. That we drove here. Maybe about Cayden, too. He's—been asking."

"When?"

"When you haven't been around, which is a lot lately. And"—Lindsey picks at a hangnail, avoiding my eyes—"maybe he's thinking what you're thinking. Maybe he's not, you know, so sure either."

"Why doesn't he just talk to me?"

"That's what he asks me about you! One of you has *got* to start the conversation. Heidi and I feel like jerks for covering for both of you."

Wait. *Both* of us? What's John been up to? I feel rotten that I didn't even know that they'd been talking about "us." John and I can't even hold a two-word conversation, and yet he's sharing enough with Lindsey and Heidi that they're "covering" for him? And Lindsey, who was Cayden McKnight's biggest advocate, is now advocating for John? What just happened?

"I thought you were excited to drive here."

"I was! I am! Oh my word, Lex, it's Hollywood!" She grabs my hand and squeezes it. "We went to the Viper Room! You danced onstage! We cruised Sunset and Melrose and Pacific Coast Highway! We're sitting in front of Cayden McKnight's mansion! But I realized tonight when I was driving Dan around—after I saw the way Cayden was to you—that if it didn't go well, then that should be it. You're gonna get hurt by Cayden, and you and John are gonna get hurt by each other. How can that be good?"

I feel like I'm missing a chunk of this story, but I can't figure out what. Why's she so worried about John? I'm about to ask when another car drones past. At least seven times since we've sat down, a different car has crept past Carson's property. Mostly older cars, definitely not from this neighborhood. Sometimes we saw a face; sometimes just a camera.

One guy slows enough to roll down his window. "Careful," he says. "Police cite for loitering around here."

"We should go soon," Lindsey says, but she drapes Carson's jacket over both of our knees. We sit in silence, and I trace patterns with my finger in the lining of Carson's jacket. I bury my face in it, drink in his scent. A dark Lincoln approaches, a sharp dent behind the right rear wheel. Through the rolled-up window, the driver looks at me, and my mouth falls open. "Who's that?" Lindsey whispers. Beneath Carson's jacket, I feel goose bumps lift the hair on my arms. It's the same man who took my picture at 3two3 the night I posed as Cayden's publicist's daughter. He's as surprised as I am, which means he remembers me, too. Without warning, he whips up a camera and takes a picture, then speeds off, which makes no sense. He must know by now that I'm a nobody. Nobody to him. Nobody to Carson.

"You're right," I say, my eyes heavy with sadness and fatigue. "It's getting late. We should hit the road if we're going to make it to school before first period."

But before we even get up, the gate suddenly creaks to life.

"No," I beg.

From inside the property, I hear Carson's front door.

"I thought you said he wasn't home!" I whisper.

"Maybe he was in the back of the house?"

"Lindsey!"

"What! I haven't studied his floor plan!" She takes my hand as reassurance, but her grip is fierce. She whispers, "He doesn't come home early! Swear. It's his MO to stay out till dawn."

I stay huddled with my back against the stone wall, my heart assaulting my rib cage. Carson emerges wearing AirPods and reflective running sweats, fiddling with his phone, probably finding a playlist. He stops directly outside his gates, less than ten feet from where we sit. His back is to us, and he reaches toward the ground, stretching. I don't move. I can't. He stands upright, rolls his neck and turns. And that's when his eyes lock with mine.

"Shit," he gasps, leaping back. I scramble to my feet, Lindsey right beside me. Once the fear dissipates, his eyes narrow to slits. "Seriously?"

"Okay, this part is my fault." My body betrays me, shaking so wildly I have to steady myself with a hand on the stone post. I let go and lift his jacket as a peace offering. He doesn't acknowledge it.

"Go away, Alexa." His voice isn't angry. It just sounds tired.

"I'm sorry I'm here," I say. "It was another mix-up. But—" I know how I sound. "But here's your jacket back."

He licks his lips, and with civil hands, he takes the jacket, sets it on the ground inside his gate, and presses a button to shut the gate. He stays outside, facing us.

"There's a recording," Lindsey blurts, like she's pitching a movie in Hollywood, and she's only got a few sentences before she gets the axe or the green light. "It was on her Apple Watch. That girl Paige might still have it." I want to crawl under a rock. Under one of Carson's fancy boulders brought in by some landscape architect.

"Seriously, Alexa," he says, "it doesn't matter anymore. Let it go."

"Just like you have?" Lindsey says.

Swear on my lanyard bracelet, he pauses. It's as if he's fighting to stay in control. But his expression hardens, as if I'm the one who said it.

"I'm not who I used to be."

I search his eyes for Carson, but I only see Cayden McKnight. Am I like Gatsby, falling in love with the Daisy of the past, blinded to the way he truly is now? I swallow the growing lump in my throat.

"She doesn't believe you!" Lindsey shouts.

"Lindsey!" I shout back.

He utters a one-syllable laugh without smiling or looking at me. And after adjusting one AirPod and then the other, he turns his back to us and gallops off on his run.

It's like I was never there.

Suddenly, Lindsey yelling things that I wanted to stay secret is just too much. It adds to my frustration with Carson from the night back at Phantom Bar, tonight at the Viper Room, and now him dismissing me in his front yard.

"Hey!" I yell, but he's either listening to his music, ignoring me, or both.

My insides are boiling, and I'm over him writing me off. I can barely hold myself back. I look to Lindsey, and she looks down at her feet strapped in high heels next to mine in laced-up Asics. "Go," she says, but there's reluctance in her voice. "I owe you. But remember . . . you owe John, too." I'm struck by that, but she pushes me. "Just go. I'll be in the car."

Chapter Twenty-Five

I catch up to Carson on the road, matching my pace with his. "Can we talk?"

"No." He spits to the left and accelerates. I let him pull ahead while I watch his pace and form. He runs like a basketball player, loping strides, in pretty good shape, but definitely no marathoner. His stride should be much longer than mine, but he runs more upward than forward, so our legs hit the pavement simultaneously on every step. I catch up again, and he shakes his head and speeds up.

I match it.

After five minutes of silent sprinting, I hear his breath, labored and angry. He doesn't know that I train like this every day. I don't want to build too much lactic acid for Saturday's race, but it feels good to push against the burn, to bite his heels with my sneakers. I follow him off the road and onto an unmarked hiking trail, steep and overgrown, him in his sweatpants and me in my miniskirt. We turn on our iPhone flashlights almost at the same time. The weeds brush against my thighs, slap and scrape my body.

At ten minutes, I can see his bare back through his drenched white T-shirt, shoulders and back muscles flexing at the pain of our pace. I'm off the skinny trail now, and the nettles and wild brush sting my legs, but I charge through them, my adrenaline surging. Side by side, we fly like the Malibu breeze whipping through the seaside cliffs. It's smooth sailing for another ten minutes, and we're almost to the peak when, like magic, a gopher hole swallows my heel. My ankle rolls under me, and pain screams through my body. Years of running have taught me to give in to the roll, but consequently, I tumble to the ground. I skid to a lumpy stop in the razor-edged weeds. Carson stops and turns. He looks at me, his eyes now adjusted to the dark, gauging whether this is a true injury or not. I wait for him to offer me a hand, run to my side, something. He doesn't. Instead, he rests his hands on his knees, wheezing and gulping air. "You're so stubborn," he gasps.

"Am not." I rub my ankle, still sitting neck-deep in weeds.

"Exactly."

I exaggerate my wincing, hoping for a response. I think back to when I fell into the cactus, how Carson reached for me, cared for me. Instinct doesn't change, right? But Carson stays where he is. I reach up a hand. "A little help?"

"You can manage."

He knows what I want. I almost yell that *he*'s the stubborn one, but instead, we look away from each other and out toward the horizon. His breathing is loud and labored as he tries to slow his heart rate.

The view is like a three-dimensional oil painting. A dotted landscape of brightly lit houses. A little farther, a sliver of a moon, glowing on the distant water, illuminates a shimmery blue-black ocean. I hope that in this moment, somewhere inside him, he longs for that summer, too—hiking to high places, back when everything was fun. Uncomplicated. Complete.

With shaky fingers, I pull out the folded magazine picture from my pocket. I wipe the sweat from my eyes and look closer. The light in the picture is low, not *dusk* low, but *dawn* low. "Since when do you run after midnight?"

"I don't." He licks his lips, still panting. "I needed to clear my head."

"So you do care."

"Carson cared," he wheezes.

"You *are* Carson!"

"Not to you!"

"Listen, please," I say, "before you can argue with me. My best friend brought me to Hollywood, and I wasn't supposed to go to the Viper Room—don't look at me that way, I *wasn't*!—and I wasn't even supposed to be at your house, but Lindsey's phone died, and I met her here, but then you started being all 'Cayden McKnight' on me, so I got mad and ran after you, because running is, like, the only thing I can do *right* right now. But that night at Paige's"—Carson starts to wave me off—"No, listen!"

"No, you listen!" he shouts, and his tone seals my lips. "You are *not* the reason Cayden McKnight is out there, so don't go patting yourself on the back." He pants, his lungs and anger burning together. "When I started acting, my agent back then hooked me up with a publicist who surveyed the teen actors my age. There were too many 'good guys.' If

I came into Hollywood the same way, I'd be another Disney wash-up. So he created Cayden McKnight, the edgy kid with the troubled past who wreaked havoc off-screen. Sure, he threw me into the independent roles, and that helped, but my greatest acting role is off-camera, every time I walk out my front door." He sucks in a breath of the crisp night air. "And he proved to me that the world loves a troubled kid with talent."

The breeze blows a wisp of hair into my mouth, and I peel it off. "So you *are* still Carson."

"To my *friends*."

I know what he means by that, and it breaks me into a million pieces. "Carson—"

"Cayden. I'm Cayden to you," and the way he says it numbs me all over. I want to stick my hand in a thousand cactus spikes to wake me up from the feeling that's closing in, a pain worse than the last tenth of a 5K. "My publicist is the one who killed off Carson, *not you*, as much as you tried to that night."

His phone rings, and he takes it as his cue to head home. As if our conversation's over. I follow, limping. My ankle stings, but it's nothing compared to Carson's words. We return along a path that cuts straight back down the mountain.

"Hey," he says to whomever answers. "You still up? Nah, Malibu. Just tonight. Call time isn't till five. We should talk. Yeah. Just, you know, shit." He laughs. "The *fifth*, bro. 'Course you're invited. It's my party." He glowers at me. "*Usual* place. Okay, later."

We descend quietly, our shoulders brushing each other

as we walk. I feel the heat from his body post-workout, and every inch of my skin pulses with awareness, a longing I can barely contain. How can he do that with nothing more than a brush of a shoulder? I pull myself together, force myself to talk. "Your birthday's coming up."

"Stop," he says. I stop walking. "No, I mean stop *this*. I don't know how the hell you're getting here, because I know you're three hundred miles away, but you need to stay there." He looks at the starless sky. "You need to forget you ever knew me."

I shake my head. My voice barely climbs out. "Why?"

"Because I don't care about you anymore, Alexa. Move on."

His words are cold. Honest. For the first time, I know that even if I told him about the recording, nothing would change. He's done. Maybe he's been done all along, but I let myself believe Lindsey because I so badly wanted to be wrong. We get back to his house, and he pushes the code, picks up his jacket, then walks through the gate. I follow, my mind spinning.

"Ma'am?" A security guard appears out of nowhere. He's a new one. I haven't seen him before. He must be a night guard for the grounds. He turns to Carson. "Cayden, this someone you know?"

Carson looks at me. "No."

"I'm sorry, Miss." The security guard apologizes, but his voice doesn't sound sorry. "You're going to have to exit the property." I stare at Carson, begging him to relent, to change his mind. As an answer, he removes his AirPods and busies himself by putting them back into the case from his pocket.

"Fine," I say. "Fine."

"And *Miss*?" Carson says, mocking the guard's name for me. "November fifth? It's a *private* event. Don't try to get on my guest list. 3two3's not as lax as the Viper Room. I *will* have you thrown out." He opens his front door, and a rottweiler shoots past him. The dog whirls back and stops at Carson's feet, wagging his tail. Then he sniffs at the guard, growls once, and turns, charging toward me. "Cooper!" Carson shouts.

"Hey, Coop!" I say and kneel down. The dog scurries to a stop and crouches below me, licking my chin like a lollipop. He pounces, knocks me over, and I can't help but erupt in laughter. "You still think you're a puppy, don't you!"

"He remembers you," Carson murmurs. I look up at his stunned face. Cooper's recognition makes Carson look at me like we're in some sci-fi movie and he's just discovered I'm an alien. He clears his throat like something's caught, preventing him from talking. "You need to go."

I don't know what else to do. I hold to the moment when we both stared at the view overlooking Malibu. When I apologized at the Viper Room bar, and his eyes flickered for a moment. When we shared our breath in the back of the Uber, and he smirked, just barely. I bury my face in Cooper's fur to hide the threatening tears.

"Coop!" he orders. The rott stops, then pounces again. "Cooper, now!" But he continues his lickfest, drenching my face, whining in delight. Carson stomps over to me, grabs the dog by the collar, and drags him toward the front door. He slams the door, and I lie there on the damp patch of grass with my wet face.

I wait, looking up at the starless sky, wondering if the last conversation I'm ever going to have with Carson Knight is one where the guard asked if Carson knew me, and Carson answered, "No."

The guard is close by, but the stiffness in his voice is gone after seeing Cooper's reaction. "Take your time. Let yourself out."

I nod.

"Kid's got a lot of walls," he adds. "Don't take it personally."

Easier said than done. I lie like a limp balloon until his footsteps fade. Guess I really am Gatsby.

"Lex," I hear Lindsey say, and it's so good to hear my best friend. She's at the open gate, leaning against one of the stone pillars, a sad smile and a crinkle between her eyebrows. Who knows how long she's been waiting while I lie there.

"I know. I'm coming."

I crawl to my knees and stand. As soon as I reach Lindsey, the gate roars to life and closes. How did he—and then I see the guard by the tree, clicker in hand. Of course. It's his job to keep people like me out. *People like me.* I'm no longer any different than the masses now that I'm back on the outside.

As we walk away, Lindsey says, "Oh my word, are you limping?"

★★★★★

Lindsey offers to drive the first shift. Gratefully, I crumple into the passenger seat. I owe her the story, but I can't right now, and she knows it. "Crappy runner," she starts, and it makes me smile. "And what's with November fifth?"

"His birthday," I say. "I mentioned it on our way down. He must've thought I knew about the party he's having. I seem to know everything else." I say the last part bitterly, and Lindsey bites her bottom lip.

"Speaking of parties—" she ventures.

"No, I didn't tell him about the recording." It comes out snappier than I expect, and Lindsey winces. "God, I'm sorry." I lean my head on her shoulder, and she softens. "I keep replaying the night, trying to think of what I could've done differently. But I tried."

I tell her the story of our run—the trail lit by our iPhones, the beautiful view, that darned gopher hole. And every cold word.

"Because I don't care about you anymore, Alexa. Move on."

When I finish, there's only the sound of the car humming. Even Lindsey knows this is where it ends.

At some point I must've fallen asleep, because I'm waking up as we pull into school. "Oh, shoot, Linds, sorry I didn't stay awake with you." She looks out the window like she's bothered, but maybe she's just tired. "I'll talk to John today, okay?" Her whole face lights up before it's overtaken by a gigantic yawn. It's five thirty. We're two hours early, so we change out of our club attire, I set my cell-phone alarm, and we pass out in the front seats of Lindsey's car until the bell rings to go to first period.

Chapter Twenty-Six

Saturday morning my parents do the *important race* routine. We've done it for three years, and it's no different this morning, as I prepare to race against all of southern Nevada:

6:00 a.m.—Alarm

6:05 a.m.—Wake up parents. Mom makes breakfast while Dad checks my sports bag for socks, running shoes, and watch.

6:10 a.m.—Put on cross-country uniform and flip-flops, brush teeth, throw hair into a ponytail, and amble half asleep to kitchen.

6:15 a.m.—Swallow half dry sesame bagel, half glass orange juice, and half banana. Anything more and I end up leaving it on the course, and that's never fun for the racer behind me.

6:20 a.m.—Drive to race, arrive by 6:45 a.m., fifteen minutes before check-in.

Everything goes as scheduled, except for one added feature on the drive.

6:22 a.m.—Open bank app to check balance after all the donations, Uber fares, gas money.

6:22:15 a.m.—Grip side-door handle of car. Panic.

6:22:45 a.m.—Breathe. Resist hyperventilation. Imagine rainbows and butterflies.

I usually sit in the back seat, eyes closed and earbuds in, Spotify set to my "Inspirational" playlist. My parents think I need this time to focus, which I do, but today I'm not "envisioning the victory." I'm praying they won't check my savings account. Mom's already suspicious.

This morning she saw my bare legs—the streaks of scratches from running in a miniskirt through dried twigs and bushes—and even though Dad said, "What the hell, Lexus? You fight a cat or something?" Mom frowned. It's the same look she's currently giving me through the rearview mirror when I peek, so I busy myself on my phone and text John.

Hey. We should talk.

John texts: Morning.

I'm thankful he doesn't mention how I ditched his football game last night. He also doesn't mention that he's on his way to watch my state-qualifying race.

I write, Where r u?

In bed.

I suppose that answers whether he's coming.

He adds, 2nite?

Of course. Our Saturday-night dinners.

Tomorrow's Halloween, and our entire group is dressing up as Christmas carolers. It was Lindsey's idea, which she came up with after losing one too many beer-pong games at Heidi's last party. I can't break up with him the day before Halloween. Not when our whole group is planning this fun thing. But if I go to dinner with him tonight, I'll have to bring us up.

Can't do date night, I reply.

?

School project w Linds.

It's sort of true. We do have Winter Formal to work on.

Ok.

★★★★★

Lindsey's the first one I see as we pull into the parking lot. Teams from all over southern Nevada are arriving in their rental vans. Lindsey jogs over to me. "You recovered?" and she doesn't mean my ankle. She means Carson. I lift a shoulder. She adds, "Okay then! Top two?" I lift both shoulders. Second-biggest race of our high-school careers, and I'm still trying to shake off Thursday night.

★★★★★

After we check in with Coach Jiménez, we run a warm-up mile with the team and then circle up and stretch. As we lunge into the dewy grass, Lindsey glances at me sidelong. "We missed you at the football game."

"Yeah." I wipe the loose pieces of grass off my knees. "I wanted to rest up before Zone."

"Ankle okay?"

"Fine. Just didn't want a late night."

She stops midlunge. "The games end by eight thirty."

"Oh." Shoulda stuck with the sore-ankle excuse. "Just . . . *stuff* to do." Like lying in bed and numbly watching *Against Life Expectancy* and *Aruba* again. I still haven't watched *Kicking*

Over Saturday's Rivers, but I will. No reason to avoid it anymore.

"Any of that stuff involve talking to John?"

I shake my head.

Lindsey looks up at the sky and then back at me. "I thought you said you'd talk to him Friday morning."

Guess I won't be telling her that I canceled tonight's usual Saturday-night dinner with him. "Soon. I will."

She nods. "Sorry about Cayden. He's a jerk, okay?" She grabs my hand and says, "You take all that, and throw it into this race, you hear me?"

★★★★★

The girls line up, the gun goes off, and I do what Lindsey says. All the anger, the swallowed passion, the frustration—right now into this moment. For the first mile, I focus on staying in the top ten. It's a fast start and a faster pace than usual, but it's a fast course. The second mile is through a dry creek bed, and Lindsey and I run stride for stride, passing one girl at a time. Every time we round a corner, we increase our pace and then settle back in on the straightaway. After almost four years of running together, we know when to accelerate and when one of us starts to struggle. For her, it happens during mile two. "Cramp," she mumbles.

"Thumb," I gasp, and she digs her thumb into her ribcage. She groans but keeps up. Even on my best race days, I start to lose my vision toward mile three. When I make it to the third mile marker, only a tenth of a mile left, my legs are Jell-O. I close my eyes, forget that I can't see, that ten thousand knives stab my lungs, and I fight toward the finish line like Carson is waiting for me there. I look up at my time as I run under the banner: 17:58. It's my first time breaking eighteen minutes. I fall over the ropes and cones, collapsing into my dad's arms. He's shouting and slapping my back like I've won an Olympic medal. I still can't breathe or see, but I know it'll come back soon. I've just won the cross-country championship for all of southern Nevada. Lindsey comes in third; a girl from Bonanza High passed her right at the end, but she PR'd and qualified for state, so she's ecstatic.

This is what I've worked four years of cross-country to see, and I only have one more race to finish strong: the state championship. My times only started being scholarship worthy last year during track season, and it took all summer to get the Boston College coach interested. He's flying into Vegas next week to watch state. But for today, I have so much to celebrate, and for a few hours, I forget about Carson entirely.

Then it's 2:00 p.m., and I'm back in my room, looking at my outfit from Thursday night strewn on the floor. I pick up the top, press it against my face, and inhale the faint scent of salty air and sweat. *What was I thinking?*

I can't chase after the old Carson. Turns out I'm not fast enough to beat the past. All these good things I've been doing to remake his image—they've been completely pointless. His reputation has nothing to do with me. Neither does his life, and he likes it that way. *Wants* it that way. Maybe some part of me was hoping that if I stopped trying to forget, I'd get a second chance.

"Because I don't care about you anymore, Alexa. Move on."

I look at my mirror, filled with my weekend to-dos. I take a sock and wipe the mirror clean. Every last corner. It's the first time there hasn't been anything written on it. I scan my reflection, all of myself, for the first time not blocked by dry-erase marker.

Well, Carson, it's a start.

"Cayden," I correct myself in the mirror.

★★★★★

The following morning, I pile on the couch with blankets next to Dad, watching Sunday football. I'm still there when Heidi shows up at 5:00 p.m.

"Hey. Happy Halloween. You trying to be a ghost?"

I guess everyone's been texting. I turned my phone off last night at nine. "Costume?" she says. I blink. "Okay, get in the car." We stop by Walmart, where they already have Christmas items on display. Heidi wins friend of the year and grabs two of everything so that I can come dressed the way my friends expect. She finds a turtleneck covered in rows of printed mini wreaths. "That's ugly," she says, snatching it up. Next to it is a red knit vest with sewn-on reindeer and bow-wrapped presents made out of sequins. Straight out of grandma's closet and hideous.

★★★★★

"Heidi!" Lindsey squeals as we meet up with the other four

at the high-school parking lot. Lindsey's donned a sugarplum outfit, with bright rosy cheeks and fistfuls of candy canes. Kim's dressed as a sexy Mrs. Claus, with a name tag that reads, "I'm a ho, ho, ho." John's a Christmas tree, branches and pine needles taped to his arms like splints. Ryan wears a box with holes cut out for his head, legs, and arms. On the box with a Sharpie, he's written: "Christmas Ornaments: Attic."

We drive to Summerlin, to the nicer homes, where parents dressed in witch hats and gory makeup open their doors. At first they stare open-eyed when we don't say the standard "Trick or treat," but they soon slap their knees and applaud our off-key renditions of "We Wish You a Merry Christmas" and "Silent Night." We even try out our Spanish with "¿Dónde Está Santa Claus?" It's a wonder that any of us have an A in Spanish 4. The parents fill our stockings with candy, and I do my best to match our group's energy, but I can only mouth the words to most of the songs. I overhear Lindsey and John saying silly puns to each other about their costumes. "Are you *plum* tired from the race yesterday?" he says, and she answers, "Yes! Don't you *pine fir* the good ol' days?" They're cracking each other up. John hasn't spoken to me all night, but on the way back to our cars, he approaches me. "I'll take you home," he says.

★★★★★

We drive for a long time. My house feels farther than usual. "What's up, John," I say.

"You tell me." He's taken off his hat with the star on top,

but he still has pine needles strapped to his body.

"I'm sorry. I know I haven't been—"

"I talked with Lindsey last night."

He lets the sentence hang.

"I wasn't with Lindsey last night," I confess.

"I know. Because you were with me. At least according to Lindsey."

Come to think of it, Lindsey didn't talk to me much tonight, either. Guess I wasn't the only one not feeling the Christmas spirit. "I'm sorry, John. I should've told you. I had something I needed to do."

"Like break up with me?"

I take one of his hands from the steering wheel. "Things have been weird for me these past two months."

"No kidding." He pulls his hand away and puts it back on the steering wheel. His grip tightens. "What's going on?"

I inhale through my nose, taking in the smell of cologne, car freshener, and pine needles. I try to remember the scent for later, when I begin to miss it, because I know where this is headed. "Lately . . . ," I start. I examine the upholstery. "It's been complicated."

"How?"

"I can't explain."

"Is it college? Key Club activities? It's okay if you're overwhelmed, but if you need help, you need to speak up. I can help you reorganize. Maybe you're doing too much."

I shake my head.

"It's none of that," he says, his voice flat. "It's us?"

"Maybe. Ah! I don't know, John!" I put my head in my

hands. "Do you ever wonder if this is all there is?"

"Like if there's life after death?"

"No!" I laugh. "I mean, like, good grades, and good colleges, and good jobs, you know, it's all good." I think of myself. "But maybe 'good' could be better."

"What are you talking about? You do great things. You racked up hundreds of volunteer hours in Key Club."

"That's just it! I mean, none of that's bad, right? But what if you're doing it just to do it? It's like us."

He pulls into my driveway and parks. "What's . . . like . . . us?"

"We get along. We're in the same crowd. We 'work,' ya know? It's 'fine.' But is it enough?"

He's silent, but I know he's been thinking about us, too.

How do you explain what's missing, describe that feeling you can't see? If you could see it, then it wouldn't be missing. "There's this. I just think that." I can't finish a sentence. Everything feels jumbled.

"I think I understand," John says, but I can hear the hurt creep into his voice. He nods as if I actually said something. When neither of us speaks for several minutes, John exits the car and walks around to my side. Opens the door. I take his hand, and he walks me to the front door. It's the slowest walk we've taken.

I hug him at my door. He reaches around me with one arm. "So is this it?" he says, and by *it,* he means the end of us.

"I think so," I whisper.

He pulls away, straightens. "Okay, then." He nods to no one. "See you Monday?" His words feel hollow. John used to be enough. I felt something for him; that part was true. I just didn't know that I could feel more. I didn't know that anyone could make me feel the way Carson does, where everything inside me feels wild and wrecked and put together at the same time. That's not John's fault, none of it is, and maybe that's why as he walks away, I watch him leave through blurry eyes, and I don't go inside until his taillights have disappeared into the night.

Chapter Twenty-Seven

By Monday morning, rumors have already spread. I notice the girls surrounding John at his locker, ready to be the one to "comfort" him. I leave him alone. During first period, the announcements mention Lindsey and me as the girls' cross-country state-championship qualifiers. The class applauds, and it reminds me that my running buddy hasn't spoken to me since the race. I find Lindsey before second period and apologize for lying about Saturday night. "Where were you?" she asks. I was actually doing homework, getting away from everyone and everything. Watching Carson's movies. Thinking about my life.

"Home. Figuring things out."

"I heard about you and John. I'm sorry," she says.

I shrug. "We're still friends."

"Of course you are." Her eyes don't match her words.

At lunch, Kim sits next to John. She thinks she's being secretive because she's usually big on eye contact, but today her eyes are glued to his like he holds the secrets to the universe, and I lose my appetite.

I skip practice and take the bus home. Today's the biggest day of my high-school life: early decision deadline for Boston College. I meant to send the application in Thursday, but I was too busy driving to California, running the hills of Malibu, killing my hope. The normal application deadline is January 1, but hopefully I won't need it. I don't plan on applying to any other schools. I reach into my backpack for my phone, but my fingers graze across a business card, and I pull it out. It's Sasha's card, the bartender at 3two3, who told us he'd get us into the club next time we were around. 3two3. The place of Carson's birthday party this Friday. Is that irony? Or cruelty? I look out the window like I'm expecting the universe to answer me.

I excavate my phone and check my voicemail. Zero. No texts, either. Absently, I play with the business card, holding it between two fingers, flicking it against my other hand. I recognize Lindsey's writing on the back of the card, where she's scribbled a list of Carson's four movies: *Against Life Expectancy*, *Aruba*, *Kicking Over Saturday's Rivers*, and his latest one, *Open Boat*. I think of the themes, the messages, the acting. I search for a connection to myself, but I think I'm wishing for something that's not there. He's moved on. It's time I did.

I stare at Lindsey's writing, how she makes each letter twirl and dip like roller-coaster loops. Suddenly, my heart drops as if I'm on one of the loops. I look closer. Then, to make sure I'm not imagining things, I tear out a piece of notebook paper and scribble, crossing out letters, rearranging. *Oh.*

My gosh.

I start to text Lindsey, then stop. Instead I text the number from the card:

Hey, Sasha. Remember me? I fixed ur tire.

Sasha quickly writes back, Delaney! You and your friend coming for ur drink?

I write, This Friday?

Sorry. :(Private party. What about Sat?

I take a deep breath and type, No-go for Sat. Only free on Fri.

Weird timing. Your tire-fixing actor rented out the place Fri.

Sorry. Any other night.

I dial Sasha's number. He answers on the first ring, his kind voice already apologetic. "Hi, Delaney, listen. There's a tight guest list. And there's two of you. There's just no way."

"Just me," I press. I know I must sound desperate. I relax my voice. "What if I'm working? Like, guest bartending? I wouldn't have to be on the guest list."

"I dunno—" He trails off. But all I hear is that he didn't say no.

"I know the drinks," I lie.

"Oh yeah?" He considers this. "I could use the extra help." My heartbeat shoots up to the back of my throat. He's thinking about it, but he reverses. "I know you'd want to thank him, but this just isn't the time."

"Cayden who?" I say, and he laughs. "Come on, Sasha. You said next time I was in the area. I'm only there Friday."

It's quiet for an interminable amount of time. I think I might've lost connection when he says, "Mayyyyybe."

My ribcage might explode. Before he can change his mind, I say, "Okay, great. Text me where to meet you." Then I click end.

If Carson won't let me inside, I'll have to *already be* inside. I have to. He needs to know that I know. I've figured it out.

I text Lindsey, so excited to tell her what she helped me discover.

You know how I was your wingman in Hwood?

Wanna be mine this Fri?

Cant. U neither. State!

She's right. Our state cross-country meet starts at 9:00 a.m. on Saturday morning. The Boston coach is flying in to see me. But state's important to Lindsey, too. Her times are just as scholarship worthy for some schools. I don't respond, so she texts again.

Whatever it is, no. You've worked four years for this Saturday.

My excitement deflates, and suddenly I don't want to tell her. I don't want to risk her telling me no, or to let it go, or that we've already followed this story down its dead-end street.

The truth is, I'm not asking permission. I've already decided I'm going. If it blows up in my face, no one has to know. But if it goes okay, then once I'm back and at the race Saturday, I'll tell Lindsey everything. She'll be the first to know.

Lindsey's car's no longer an option, but if I catch a 6:00 a.m. flight back to Vegas and head straight to the race, I should be fine. I'll have to pack my uniform.

After years of preparation, I imagined my final submission to Boston College would be at my desk with everything perfect and ceremonious, but I pull up the online application on my phone and squint as I proofread everything quickly. I check all the boxes and hit submit.

I've just applied to Boston College from a school bus.

I jump out at the next stop, a block from Barnes & Noble. There, I grab a set of bartending flash cards and head to the coffee shop to cram for the biggest exam yet: pulling off bartending when I've never had more than a beer or a Coke from Rome.

★★★★★

Since state is Saturday, cross-country practices are short, and I head straight home every day, burying myself in flash cards of how to make mai tais and Long Island iced teas. There's so much more: burnt squirrels, pink squirrels, banana banshees. What's with all the animals? I print out different alcohol labels, so I can recognize them on the bar shelves.

I skip debate and student council, but in the midst of sidecars and old-fashioneds and the ever-generic-but-classic gin and tonics, I revise my essay on "The Open Boat" for the millionth time. My thesis is that love is a choice; thus, it can always be contained and controlled. Kucan thinks so, too, according to his red marks across my paper. Maybe, like with a poorly mixed drink, I've got the right ingredients but the wrong proportions. Maybe love isn't a choice. Maybe it's like nature, uncontrollable, uncontainable, dominating anyone it wishes. And like nature—who could care less when she rips through a boat with her cold wind and dagger waves—love doesn't mind that it's opened my heart with a butterfly incision and made me feel things I've never felt before. I find another poem by Stephen Crane:

A man said to the universe:
"Sir, I exist!"
"However," replied the universe,
"The fact has not created in me
A sense of obligation."

Like nature, love doesn't care about me, whether I attain it or not. It taunts me with feelings that I try to deny, deny while secretly longing for them to be returned. And love has no obligation to be my friend. It rips through me and moves on, showing me what I can feel without satisfying that longing. In the garage surrounded by empty bottles and shot glasses, I tear apart my thesis the way love and regret have torn through me, and when I'm done scribbling everything out by hand, my new English paper is unrecognizable compared to the old. But it's backed with evidence from Fitzgerald, Shakespeare, Brontë, and of course, Stephen Crane. It's good, and I know even Mr. Kucan will agree.

Heidi sleeps over on Thursday, and in the garage late at night, I set up some of my parents' different glasses from the cupboards. I use water and food coloring to represent the different drinks. I mix and match as she goes through the list:

"A blue Hawaiian, biatch!"

"Blue Hawaiian," I say, grabbing the blue curaçao, which is really blue water. I pretend mixing a bunch of stuff.

"Call it out," she says.

"One and a quarter ounce light rum, two sweet and sour, two pineapple juice, half blue curaçao."

"Nice," she says, slapping the flash card down.

I pour two glasses of Red Bull and then fill two shot glasses with root beer to simulate Jägermeister. I drop the shot glasses into the Red Bull glasses, and together, Heidi and I down the drinks, slamming them on the counter. "Jäger bomb!" we shout, identifying the shot. It feels good to mix drinks and fall into where I feel most at home, in the world of test taking and memorization. Heidi knows I'm up to something, but she doesn't ask.

She traces the rim of a highball glass with her finger. "Lindsey says she talked you out of a bad decision." I open my mouth, but she cuts me off. "Don't say anything incriminating. I ain't lying for you, but I doubt she'll ask if our Thursday night involved mixologist training."

"I'll tell her. Soon." Heidi lifts a disbelieving eyebrow. "I will."

"You know if your arm was trapped under a rock, she'd gnaw her own off in solidarity." But before I can respond, she nods a, *This is your life, not mine,* and holds the glass up to me as a "cheers."

★★★★★

Friday, I skip tutoring for the third week in a row, head to my locker to exchange my school backpack with my faux-leather mini backpack of clothes, and take a Lyft from school to the airport. When my plane touches down at LAX, the clouds are sputtering rain on the runway. I nervously check my phone, but luckily, no one's texted or asked my whereabouts. I order an Uber from the airport, which is expensive, but I've already spent thousands on "Operation: Carson Knight," so what's another forty? I walk to the pickup spot, the rain dampening my clothes with every step. Thankfully, my driver's car is toasty, and I breathe in the warmth, trying to remain calm. For the next forty minutes, I focus on the rhythm of the windshield wipers and not on what I'm about to do.

He drops me off at a place called The Drunk Churro, where I'm meeting Sasha for dinner to go over the basics. It's the best Mexican food in Hollywood, he tells me, but I'm just thankful for the bathroom mirrors and outlets for my straightening iron. We're not supposed to meet for an hour, so I spend the time getting ready until he texts that he's here.

I exit the bathroom, and Sasha waves to me from a bright-orange booth. We're wearing matching black slacks with black button-down shirts. He hands me a pair of red suspenders. "It's our signature look," he tells me. His forehead creases as he sees me up close in good lighting. "You really twenty-one?"

"Barely." I fish out Delaney's ID. "Wanna check it, bouncer?"

He waves it off, laughing at how everyone in Hollywood looks fifteen.

Over dinner, we review the rules. "I'll show you the ropes once we're there, but you need to understand this is a high-end club, and even at private parties, *especially* at private parties, people expect their drinks quickly. But I'll help you, don't worry. I have to warn you, though." He pours some salsa on his burrito. "Cayden McKnight's going to be there. It's his birthday. I know he fixed your car, and you'd probably love to take a moment to thank him, but tonight, you're his bartender." He taps a tortilla chip on his plate, trying to remember all his points. "There'll be others, other actors and actresses, but Cayden McKnight makes girls crazy sometimes, so no requests for autographs or—"

"I'm not a fan," I say. He chuckles. "Really. I haven't even seen all his movies."

"First girl in America. Well, then, you'll make a great bartender for him. Make sure he gets everything he wants. He's a punk sometimes, but he tips well."

★★★★★

The party at 3two3 starts at 10:00 p.m., but since we finish dinner by eight, we head over early so Sasha can give me a tour. When I walk through the doors, I'm transported to Europe. We're still outdoors, stone floors below us, the cool air whipping through the banners of cloth that cascade from a high center pole to the outside walls. The walls are only about ten feet high, and in the summer when the cloth banners are removed, this dance floor is probably perfect for seeing the stars, and not just the ones from Hollywood. The workers are draping a canvas tent overhead to protect the dance floor. Already I can hear the rain pounding on the canvas, joining the music as the deejay performs sound checks on all his speakers. I poke my head inside and discover peach-tinted mirrors above curvy couches that remind me of Cleopatra. They encircle a second dance floor. I go behind the counter and make sure I can locate the alcohol in the dim candelabra lighting. The bar's in the shape of a large square, half outside, half inside, allowing the bartenders to serve the outdoor and indoor crowds simultaneously.

I must've lost track of time memorizing where the bottles are because suddenly people are flooding the patio floors. I'm sure celebrities are everywhere—I recognize some from all the research I've done—but I don't recognize them all. There are three other bartenders besides Sasha, all business. They walk back and forth, taking care of the stampede of drink orders from the outside and inside customers. Sasha sees me scanning the crowds as he's reaching across for a maraschino cherry. "Subtle, remember?"

"I don't know what you mean."

He grins. "Sure." He grabs a glass. "You want to shadow me?"

I shake my head. "I can do this." A woman waits behind two taller, more imposing guys. "What can I get you?"

"Fuzzy navel?" she says.

Sasha overhears. "Okay, for the glass, use a—"

"Highball glass," I answer. I reach below for the peach schnapps. "One and a half ounces. Where's the OJ?"

Sasha grins. "Nice." He hands me an orange-juice carton from the fridge. For the next two hours, I slam drinks onto the counter, run credit cards, open tabs. Convince groups to get a round of shots. Whenever they ask me to do a shot with them, I make sure to prepare it under the bar, out of sight, filling my shot with Sprite instead of tequila, Coke instead of rum. I need to stay sharp tonight.

Around midnight, a guy approaches me. He's dressed like my parents' accountant, his blue dress shirt tucked into his slacks. He wears a shiny, thin belt that matches his shiny shoes. "What can I get you?" I ask.

"A ride home." He's not totally wasted, but he'll be there soon.

"You want me to call an Uber or Lyft?"

"No way!" he says. "I've got a car. And I'd like to make you a business proposition."

Chapter Twenty-Eight

Business proposition? Suddenly, I'm imagining Rohypnol being slipped into my shot glass. A well-dressed man approaches a young girl and asks if she wants to make some money. Who does that? A drunk accountant, apparently.

"Oh yeah?" I say. Even Sasha's intrigued. He's stopped wiping the counter.

"I've gotta get home. I'm drunk. I'll pay you two hundred dollars to drive my truck home, and then I'll pay for your cab ride back."

"I'm sorry. I can't do that."

"Two hundred bucks!" he shouts. "I'll hook you *up*! Come on! I've gotta get home."

I look to Sasha for help.

"Sorry, man," Sasha interjects. "My girl's gotta work."

"No, no, after work," the guy tells Sasha. "Okay, okay." He leans his elbows on the bar, trying to look me in the eyes. His elbows wobble. "Here's the deal," he says with a slight slur. "I'm camping tomorrow, and my girlfriend said I wouldn't be ready if I went out partying. The camper's packed, I am READY TO GO. I just need. My truck. Home."

I shake my head.

"Okay, okay," he says and scoots closer. "What's your name?"

"Delaney," I say, while taking someone's drink order of cranberry and vodka.

"Jack," he introduces himself.

"Daniel's?" I joke, but he doesn't get it. I hand the drink to the girl who ordered, take her card.

"No," he says, like I've confused him with some guy named Jack Daniel's. "Here's the deal. My girlfriend will be pisssssssed if I'm not ready. You gotta help me. I'm hooking you up! Okay, three hundred!"

"Jack," I say, eye to eye with him. "I know there's some Jim Beam arguing with your logic, but I've got a question for you."

"Sure. Fire away."

"How wise do you think it is for a young girl to get in a car at two in the morning with a drunk man she's never met and drive to a location she's never been?"

He stares at me, and I can see Mr. Beam wrestling a good match. "Oh," he says. "Ohhhh. You may have a point."

I laugh. "Okay, then, so we're cool then with a no? I can call you a ride, or a friend . . . Now, if you'll excuse me." I wipe my hands with a rag. "I need to use the restroom." Sasha nods, okaying my exit.

★★★★★

I'm so caught up in what just happened that I don't notice Carson until he stops me midstride with his hand. I suck in a mouthful of air and recoil, shocked by being face-to-face and unprepared. I back against the wall of the narrow hallway, but we're still close. "What are you doing here?" he hisses. "I told you not to come. I told you I'd have you thrown out."

I think of removing his hand from my elbow, but he's not holding tightly, and a part of me wants it to stay, like it belongs there. "I work here." I prove it by flicking my red suspenders once with my thumbs. "So that means it's my job to throw *you* out."

He drops his hand. "What?"

"Bartending," I inform him.

"You're not twenty-one."

"Neither are you," I counter. I turn to walk away, but if he doesn't follow, or if he leaves the club, I have no shot. This is it. "I know why you did the movies," I breathe out. "All four of them." His eyebrows reach for each other, from worry or anger, I can't tell. "The themes are all about loss of some sort, just like you lost me and I lost you. I've gotta get back to work." I hightail it to the bathroom before he can respond or even offer a facial reaction. I lock myself in a stall, my heart drumming with the current band blaring through the speakers. Will he call my bluff?

When I return to the bar, Carson's surrounded by people. He doesn't look my way. It's his birthday, so his good friends are here, but I'm sure some guests are barely acquaintances, probably a second AD or lighting grip of his first movie, and pulling every string to be here, to be able to say that they attended Cayden McKnight's birthday at 3two3.

I lose myself in drink orders, trying not to think of my

heart sinking lower with every minute passing. Sasha fist pumps the air whenever I nail a virtually unknown cocktail. He doesn't know I've spent almost four years perfecting my memorization skills, and two hundred cocktails is nothing compared to Kucan's fifteen hundred vocab words in the first semester of AP Lit.

At around 1:00 a.m., the crowd begins to thin. The deejay lowers the volume, quieting the noise with a mellow set.

"You got any Cokes from Rome?"

At the corner of the bar, Carson waits, a crowd of people giving him his "star space." My eyes light up, but his remain glazed and unblinking. He watches me, his usually full lips a thin, tight line. I pour the Coke and the rum and try to be lighthearted. "You know the Romans are overrated. I mean, columns? Concrete? Really, I could've invented those."

A smile lifts one side, but he bites down on his lips. "Alexa," he starts.

I squeeze a lime into his drink. I can feel Sasha's breath as he stands behind me, wary of this interaction. I continue, "What did mathematics and democracy ever do for us?"

"Alexa," Carson says again. A few people are listening in, curious that Carson is talking to someone he didn't bring to the party, a girl who's not a model, not six feet tall nor wearing a loincloth.

"Now shampoo," I say, ignoring that Sasha's placed his hand on my shoulder, squeezing a gentle urge for me to stop talking. "There's something you don't hear the Romans praised for, but they started it, not even kidding." I hand Carson the drink. He holds my hand against the glass with his hand, curls his fingers around mine, and I lose all sense of where I am. I look down, choking on disbelief that his hand is touching mine after three years of believing it never would again.

"You're wrong," he says. "About the movies. That's not why I did them."

"I know," I say. He tilts his head, and I'm hoping he doesn't remove his fingers from mine. They stay there. Sasha watches us, confused, not sure what this all means, me talking nonsense about Rome to Cayden McKnight, Cayden McKnight telling me I'm wrong about his movies. "The titles," I say. "That's why you demanded title rights. The four movies. It's my name, Knight." His eyes flicker at his old nickname. "Alexa Brooks. Every letter of my name. They're the first letters of your movies."

He lets go of my hand, but I grab it and hold tightly. I'm whispering, and my breath comes out in short pants.

"You can't tell me you don't care."

"I don't."

"Bullshit," I hiss.

He looks to the left, then the right, seeing the five or so sets of eyes gauging his reaction. He looks over my shoulder, no doubt at Sasha, and peels my fingers off his. His eyes become narrow slits. "That's just a wild coincidence."

"Don't," I mouth so softly you can't hear me over the light rain overhead, over the instrumental reverberating through the concrete floors and the tented ceiling. "You do still care. You *do.*" I look down at the bar and then back at him. "You do, and I do."

He shakes his head, eyes innocent and apologetic, and if I didn't know he was such a brilliant actor, I'd believe him. He's so convincing. He looks at me like I'm some crazed fan, some nutty stranger who's convinced herself that a Hollywood star has a secret crush on her.

Suddenly Jack, the drunk accountant from earlier, sails toward me from the dance floor. "I've got it!" he shouts and slams his hand on the bar, rattling the ice cubes in all the nearby glasses. Drunker. No idea he's next to Cayden McKnight. "How about I get a cab, I'll sit in the cab, and you follow me with my truck to my house, and then you take the taxi back here."

"They still have taxis?" I feel the smile reaching across my face as I see Carson's alarmed expression. I look over my shoulder at Sasha. He shrugs and bobs his head from side to side, like he's my sports agent deciding whether the contract's worth my talent. That's when I know he believes me. He can tell that Carson and I know each other and that Carson is the one lying.

"You're free to go whenever," Sasha says, and then adds, "Alexa."

"No, you're not," Carson says.

"What do you care?" I snap.

Carson glares at Sasha. "Are you out of your mind? You're seriously going to let one of your girls do that?" He pulls out some cash and slaps it on the bar in front of Jack. "Here," he says. "Take a cab in the morning and pick up your car."

"No can do!" Jack says. "I've gotta be ready to camp, man! Hey, you look familiar."

"How'd you get in tonight?" Sasha asks Jack. "Private party."

Jack's hand dives into his pocket, surfaces with a crumpled invitation. "Troy Larkins. Location scout. Troy's a friend. He's out scouting, so I didn't want his invite to go to waste."

"Come on, Jack," I say. "Let's get you home."

"I'll send you a check in the mail," Sasha says, handing me my mini backpack from under the register. "Sorry I can't Venmo you, but it's from the restaurant."

A *check?* I had no idea I was making money for my work. "Can you send it to my old high school? Like, to their student-council fund? I'll text you the info."

"Sure thing."

I look at Jack holding the barstool for support. "What's your address?" He gives me his address, and I type it into Uber and text it to Sasha. "Let's do this," I tell my bartender/agent and give him a knuckle bump.

Sasha checks his text. "Be careful." Then he pulls me in and whispers in my ear, "If Cayden doesn't take the bait, you know I'm getting in my car to follow you and losing my job."

My eyes widen, but then he says loudly, "All right, get outta here."

"Hope you don't see me on the news tomorrow!" I wink at Carson, who's seething, his shoulders curling in anger. He knows all eyes are on him, and he doesn't want to break character. He would rather die than admit I'm not a stranger—that in fact, I'm the one he named his movies after.

★★★★★

I watch Jack crawl into the Uber. Behind them, I climb into Jack's truck, a light drizzle sprinkling down from the sky. I know I'm taking a huge risk, hoping beyond hope that Carson will get the address from Sasha's phone and follow us in his car. Jack pokes his head out of the window.

"Hey, don't steal my truck!" he shouts.

"I won't! I'm following right behind you."

"Are you serious?" he squeals. "You're so cool! Like a best friend. You're my best friend. What's your name?"

I turn the ignition, and the truck roars to life. I wave, and the Uber pulls out with me in tow. I look in my rearview mirror but see no sign of headlights following me. My heart sinks to my knees, but I hope I'm wrong. Maybe Carson is so good at covering his celebrity tracks that he's behind me somewhere, only I can't tell.

We stop at the bank so Jack can withdraw money. "Don't drive away with my truck!" Jack says again, then disappears for two minutes. Drops of water pelt the windshield, and I turn on my wipers. My phone vibrates with a text from Sasha: He took the bait. Headed your way.

I search the parking lot, but there are no signs of Carson, no signs of any car idling. When Jack returns, he hands the money through the driver's-side window and gives me an exuberant punch on the shoulder. "You didn't steal my truck! Hell yeah! I'm telling you, you are SO cool."

He splashes through puddles and climbs back into his Uber, yelling, "I can't believe you're driving my truck home. You rock!" At the next stoplight, he hangs half his body out the back seat window and shouts, "This girl rocks! Wooooo!"

We arrive at his house, in a quaint neighborhood tucked away in the hills behind a huge boulevard called Lankershim. I park the truck, and as Jack exits the Uber, he says, "This is SO cool! I want you to meet my girlfriend. She's wild." I tell the Uber driver that I think my ride is coming, but I ask him to wait five minutes. The street remains dark, the parked cars barely visible from the drooping weeping willow trees that block the streetlights. Maybe Carson changed his mind. I hand Jack his truck key and text Sasha, Safe. The rain is steady now, and I feel my shirt dampening. From the end of his walkway, the porch light flicks on, and the screen door whips open. Jack exclaims, "Karmen! I made it home."

Karmen, in a messy bun and sweats, ignores the rain and stomps toward him. "Enjoy the couch tonight, Jack."

He coos, "Baby! Don't be that way. I made it home. Look. This girl brought my truck home. Isn't she cool?"

Karmen is livid. She looks at me. "You, I like." She turns to Jack. "But you. The couch." Then she storms back inside.

"I'm so sorry," Jack slurs and then leans in conspiratorially. "She's on her period." He searches my face for understanding, like I would nod and say, "Oh, period."

Luckily, I see headlights appear from the end of the street just as a peal of thunder cracks and the sky downpours. A black sedan comes into view.

Carson. He came.

Chapter Twenty-Nine

The rain thickens, layers and sheets of it, the kind that bounces off the sidewalk, splashes up as much as it splashes down. Jack thanks me again, then wobble-runs inside, shutting the door on me and the rain.

I cover the top of my head with my hands but it offers little protection. I'm drenched within seconds. As the car approaches, I realize that it's a dark Lincoln. The dent near the back bumper. I freeze.

It's not Carson.

However, the Uber driver, assuming my ride has arrived, drives away.

Through the sound of the water slapping the pavement, I hear rustling on the side of the house, and a familiar voice hissing my name. Relief courses through me.

I steel myself and wave at the Lincoln, walk casually toward it, but then dart to the side of the house—toward the voice. I feel Carson's hand reach around me before I can see his face. "Let's go." He opens Jack's backyard gate just as the paparazzo exits the Lincoln from the street. I look back once, to the man's eyes boring into mine, with his hint of a smile, like he and I share a secret. Carson's pulling me along, but I grip his hand and run as the man shuts his car door and heads on foot after us. Jack's backyard is all mud, and Carson and I slide and sink. Mud oozes around my sneakers, sucks them down. I pry them free and reach the back fence. Carson gives me a leg up, and I leap over, landing in the grass of another backyard. I skid onto my knees, my mini backpack slipping off one shoulder, and Carson drops beside me. He takes me by the hand and pulls me toward another gate that he's found somehow, even though all I can see are the outlines of trees and the swampy grass. We head in and out of five backyards, and thank God there's not the cliché barking dog awaiting us anywhere. My faux-leather pack slaps my back as we dart across an alleyway and end up in an apartment complex. We zigzag through the labyrinth of buildings before he pulls me into a dark corner of the property. No one's awake, and the rain still falls, but quieter now.

I feel his breath on me, warm and rapid. "Is he gone?" I pant.

Carson holds a finger up to my lips, and I notice that it is the only separation between us. After a few moments, he nods, removing his finger from my lips.

"Carson," I whisper.

"What the *hell* were you thinking?"

"You came after me," I murmur.

"I want you out of my life," he snaps. "That doesn't mean I want you dead. I mean, seriously, Alexa. Jumping into a stranger's truck to fucking call my bluff?"

"Listen," I say, and he starts to interrupt, but I put my hand to his mouth. I feel his angry breath, hot against my cold, wet hands. He's staring at the bracelet on my wrist. His bracelet. I feel his breathing slow.

"Oh God, Carson," I start, but I'm choking on my words. Tears spring up. They join with the rain on my face, crawling down in different directions, dripping off my chin. "That night. That summer." I gulp down more tears. They've climbed into the back of my throat now, too, and it's hard to swallow. "Yes, I was keeping Dylan a secret, and I was *interested*, or whatever you are when you're barely out of eighth grade. I was figuring it out along the way, and then I started realizing . . . I started realizing that whatever I was trying to have with Dylan"—I look down, suddenly shy—"would never match what I had with you." When I look up, he grips my hand and gently pulls it from his mouth, telling me he's not going to interrupt. "And I didn't know what that meant. All I knew is that I needed to tell you, so I did. I recorded it. That night, I swear, I did. It was on my voice memos, on that watch I never used. Only Paige came in, and I lied to her because I didn't want her to like you. I said horrible things about you, but I swear I didn't know it was being recorded. I wanted to make you sound bad, so I could—"

"Humiliate me?" His tone is quiet, not angry.

"So I could have you all to myself." I wait for the strike of his voice, like fists against my heart. But it doesn't come. He watches me. I can't read his expression. "I left the watch at the party—I was so upset, I just wanted to be home—and I didn't even notice for a week. Anyway, Paige tried to contact me, but—well, I had moved, and it was a rough time—I figured it didn't matter. Nothing mattered for a while. I know she moved to New York, but maybe, maybe she still has my watch. I could try to find her on Insta."

"If not?" he says, his voice calm, practical. "How do I know you're not lying?"

"Because I'm not telling you this so I can date you now. Or because you're some Hollywood star. I'm telling you because"—I search for air, try to calm my ragged breathing through the tears—"I'm telling you because I can't live with you not knowing the truth. I couldn't back then. So for the past three years, I've pretended you didn't exist, which is no easy freaking feat when your name is plastered everywhere but on a milk carton. But." I stop. Swallow. "But lately, I can't get away from you, and not because Lindsey keeps taking me directly to you. I mean, you're everywhere, like your memory is chasing me, hunting me down, trying to kill me with guilt." I put my head down, like the weight is on top of me. "Oh God, the guilt destroyed me once. It swallowed me that year." He steps closer, and I'm surprised there's room for him to get closer. He holds my arm up, examines the braided plastic wrapped around my wrist. He traces his fingers across the bracelet, like he's reading our memories through braille. "And I could feel it coming back," I stammer. "Every time Lindsey chased you, but then I'd end up there, and, you'd look at me, and, and I'd see everything I did wrong like it was brand-new again. So I figured tonight if I chased you down first, said I was sorry, told you about the movies, then maybe, I don't know, I'd feel better, or my life would be okay, or I could move on, or"—I choke, lose my breath with my next words—"Only I didn't know—"

His hands reach through my wet hair and cradle my face. The heat from his body seeps through my clothes, and I swear I can feel his heartbeat thrumming near my ears as he looks down at me. "Only I didn't know," I stutter. "I mean, I've still never felt with anyone what I—"

His breath shifts, heavier now, like when he first stopped running. Only it's throatier. Controlled. My ability to speak is gone as he says, "Only you didn't know what?"

"Only I didn't know," I manage to get out, "that I'd feel *more.* That I'd—" His lips brush mine once, then twice. "Never felt with anyone what I—"

He stops my words with his mouth. We hold our lips together, standing perfectly still, not wanting to ruin it with any movement.

"Felt with you?" he finishes, whispering into my mouth. I nod once; it's all I have the strength to do. "Me neither," he says, and kisses me full, every part of him enveloping me. I want to drown in his embrace and the rain. "Good," he whispers, and all of me falls into him at the sound of my name.

"Knight," I whisper back.

"I know I've been unfair—" he starts.

"Stop." I rake my fingers through his wet hair, sob, and then laugh, and then kiss him again.

His hands caress my shoulders, my back, hands that are three years older and more experienced, more aware of what they're capable of doing with just the right movement. "Stay with me tonight," he murmurs, and I'm not sure how he means it, but I nod anyway. I want this moment to last forever. He pulls his cell from his pocket and texts someone to pick us up. Within ten minutes, a driver pulls up to the cross streets where we wait. Carson's hand is in mine. We're both sodden, our hair splayed in all directions, our clothes slathered against our bodies with dirty rainwater and mud. But we're grinning like back in junior high.

★★★★★

When we pile into the back seat, the driver looks over his shoulder at us. The bodyguard from the Viper Room. The one who told Carson to be nice to me. "Well, I'll be damned," he says. "Glad to see you again."

We start toward Carson's Malibu house, but I have a moment of clarity. "Tomorrow," I gasp. It's only the most important event of my high-school life. What's happening to me lately? "Cross-country state finals. Can you get me to the airport by five?"

"A.M.?" he asks. "What time's your race?"

"Nine."

He looks at the digital clock. It reads 3:04 a.m. "In *Vegas*?"

I nod, but I say defensively, "To my credit, I'm not usually this irresponsible."

"Rick," he says to his driver. "Take the two-ten to the fifteen. We've got a race in five hours." Carson and I look at each other, trapped in our smiles. "I just want to talk. I don't care where, but I'm not dropping you off in two hours, not if I can have you for five." I lean back against his chest. His arms circle across me. I tip my head up toward his.

"I recognized him," I whisper. "That guy we ran from. I saw him the night I was outside your house."

Carson nods. His chin rubs my cheek. "Longtime follower. Name's Antonio, I believe. Remember a couple of years ago when"—he stops when I shake my head—"Right, no TV. Well, anyway, he got a little aggressive, and one of my security punched him, and it was deemed self-defense. He's had a personal vendetta since then. I'm sure he's behind all the fake good press I'm getting lately." My chest cavity clamps down like a fist. I've stopped doing anything in his name, but I need to talk to Heidi and make sure the website's taken down.

"About that," I start.

"Yes, about that. I've told you you're *not* the reason I'm such a Hollywood jerk, right? So take that guilt off your shoulders. I've gotta keep it going, though. It's taken too long to build what I have, and I can't chance it by redesigning myself."

My chin falls to my chest. I know what this means. I can never be seen publicly with him. I'm too normal, too non-industry, too *good*. Carson doesn't exist in Hollywood. Just Cayden. Suddenly, I don't care about confessing the good things I've done in his name. It doesn't matter either way. Carson's not coming back.

"Hey," he lifts my chin up, kisses me softly. "We'll find a way around it. I'll find a way to see you."

"I can't tell *anyone* about you, can I?"

He shakes his head. "Not if you care about my reputation." Of course I do, but still, it stings. "It's not just for my sake. I wouldn't want Antonio harassing you, either. And there are one hundred 'Antonios' out there. Why do you think I got dropped off a block away and sneaked over?"

I think of Lindsey—all we share—and how badly I want to tell her about tonight. It's like Carson can read me, the way my eyes look down and my hands play with his fingernails. "Not even your friends," he adds. "Promise me."

My eyes, unblinking and rich with sincerity, lock with his. I can't bear the thought of losing him again. "I promise," I say, and by his kiss in return, I know he believes me.

He tells me of the great lengths he goes to keep his life private. Few people know where his mom lives, and that's why he was worried the night at the Viper Room. He was staying at her house, celebrating her birthday the following morning, and he needed to get there without being seen. But after everything, he thought it was safer to head to his Malibu house. So we weren't even supposed to cross paths again that night. And even if he stayed there, we shouldn't have seen him. He never runs, but he was shaken up after riding in an Uber with me. Old feelings crept up.

"Oh my gosh," I say, slapping my forehead. "Happy birthday!" I look over at the digital clock and groan. "Belated birthday." He kisses the top of my forehead, but I push off of him. "Wait, you're eighteen! Rick, see that gas station sign? Can you—" Rick flips his blinker on and exits the freeway. When he parks, I jump out. "Well, come on!" I say. Carson doesn't move.

"Lex, I can't."

At first, I don't understand, but then it dawns on me. He can't be seen on his way to Vegas, can't be seen so unkempt.

Can't be seen with *me*. I shrug it off and use Delaney's ID to go buy a lottery scratcher without him. Since we've stopped, I use the restroom to change into my racing bib and shorts. I bring him the lottery ticket, and he smiles. *I guess not everything is the same*, I think sadly as he scratches the card with a quarter.

As we drive through the high desert over the next few hours, we recount our lives to each other, filling in the gaps of the past three years. The sun glows red as it rises, outlining the distant mountains with a soft orange. I tell him of Boston College and cross-country and student council. How I plan my days with dry erase. He tells me of the countries he's visited. How he loves basketball. That he could never play a Spanish-speaking character because he can't roll his R's.

"There's so much I don't know," I say.

"Valedictorian?" he jokes. "I'm sure you know everything."

"I don't know your shoe size."

"Eleven and a half. Now you know everything."

I swat him playfully. "Why the movie titles? Why my name?"

"The first wasn't on purpose." He caresses the inside of my wrist with his thumb. "I didn't even notice until my agent texted me a reminder for a talk-show interview he scheduled for me to promote *Against Life Expectancy*. Only in the text, he abbreviated the movie 'A.L.Ex.' I canceled the interview. It wrecked me for days, reminded me of everything that had happened between us. How I wanted to hate you, but you were the whole reason I was anywhere in life. So I made a deal with myself. I'd at least give you credit by name, and then be done with you. It was my way to say goodbye. The next movie originally took place in Cancún, but I told them I'd only sign the contract if they changed it to Aruba." He talks to me as if we never stopped talking, as if just yesterday we were hanging out in the lifeguard tower watching the waves. His voice is both familiar and new at the same time, and I can't get enough of it.

"And the others?" I ask.

"In the next movie, *Kicking Over Saturday's Rivers,* the character's original name was Wednesday, so I made the studio change her name to Saturday. The final letters to your name were B and O, and I wasn't about to do a comedy with that title, so when the script for *Open Boat* was being passed around, I attached my name to it without even reading it."

"Risky," I say.

My head, resting against his shoulder, lifts and lowers with his shrug. "It's Stephen Crane. It's a classic. I can always fall back on that. So I finished spelling out your name, finally let you go, and right then, you started appearing in my life again."

"Ha. Universe," I mumble. My eyelids start to sag, but I force them open, afraid to miss a moment, afraid I'll wake up and none of this will be real. I trace my fingers across Carson's body, his chest broader, his arms thicker than I remember. I lace my fingers through his, and they link, still look like they fit better together than apart. Rick gets the address from me, types it into his GPS, and I nod off, my head buried in the cleft of Carson's neck, two perfect puzzle pieces.

Carson's sliding his fingers through my hair when he

wakes me up. "Good," he murmurs into my ear. "We're here." I sit up, rub my eyes, and look through the tinted window. The field where the race begins is a half mile away. Down the hill, I can see the specks of runners in their brightly colored uniforms dotting the landscape. Somewhere down there, Lindsey's warming up without me, my parents no doubt searching for me. I reach into my pack and fish around for my phone. Carson hands it to me. "No passcode? Also, you didn't have my number saved," he says, with a peck to my cheek. "Now you do. It's under 'Will.'"

"Clever," I laugh. *Goodwill.* I look at my phone: 8:15 a.m. There are four texts, all from Lindsey, all in the past hour.

"*Good* . . . luck," Carson says, cupping my face in his hands. My chest tightens. This is the end of the line for Carson. To everyone else in the world, I'm sitting with Cayden McKnight, and Cayden doesn't go support an old friend in the biggest race of her life. He kisses me in the protection of the car, and I know I should be thankful. He's forgiven me. He still loves me after all these years. But even with that, all we can ever have now must remain behind tinted windows.

I let my lips linger longer than they should, closing my eyes and inhaling so I can get drunk in the memory of it later. Then I jump out of the car and sprint down the hill toward the start line, the cold wind slapping me back to reality.

Chapter Thirty

I should be getting mentally ready for the next three miles, but I'm a cocktail of emotions—one shot elation, one shot deflation, and a floater of secrecy. I scan the crowds, blowing hot air into my fists, when I hear Dad behind me. "You ready for this, champ?"

I turn and hug him. The smiles on my parents' faces drop. "What happened to you?" Mom says. I bring my hand to my face, feel the rough texture. Dried mud.

"Oh," I say. "That." But I can't think of a good excuse.

"It's mud," Lindsey pipes in, appearing in the nick of time. "She's going for the intimidation factor." She reaches down to the wet grass, digs into the ground, and wipes the dirt underneath her eyes. "Scary, huh!"

"Oh, honey," Mom says. "It's all over your new shoes."

"I like it," Dad says, slapping me on the back. "Get in their heads!"

Mom eyes me warily. "Lindsey said you went out to get breakfast. That's new. You didn't eat too much, I hope."

"Nope, I'm ready to go."

"You feel all right?" Mom presses. "Your eyes are really red."

"No, I'm fine," I say, turning my tired eyes away. "I gotta

run, Mom. I'll see you at the finish." I speed off before she can interrogate me further.

As we jog, Lindsey grabs my hand. "Okay, story please! Where *were* you last night? Your parents thought you were with me."

I don't want to lie to her, but I don't know how to tell the truth without breaking Carson's promise. "I can't tell you."

Lindsey's hand drops, and she halts, running shoes planted. "What do you mean?" She cuts straight to it. "Were you with Cayden?"

The fifty-degree wind gusts between us. I stall by rubbing the goose bumps that have spread across my legs. "No," I say, and technically, it's not a lie. I was with *Carson*, not Cayden. She waits for more. I bend my knee and grab my foot behind me, losing myself in stretching.

"Fine," she says, the word drenched in hurt. "You don't have to tell me." And she jogs off toward the start line.

I don't know what to say to fix it, and I can't think of anything before the gun goes off. Already in the first mile, my joints ache from lack of sleep, but I push through it. For two miles, Lindsey and I run tandem, not a word of encouragement between us, not a word of who to pass and when. We're not working the way we usually do, and we both can sense it. She spits to the side forcefully. I see someone in a purple jersey ten feet ahead.

"Come on," I say, starting our usual sprint. Lindsey doesn't follow. "Come onnn!" I shout, but I look back, and Lindsey is still at the same pace. I pass the girl in the purple jersey and keep my eyes straight ahead, hoping with each step that I'll hear Lindsey's pounding feet catching up.

I never do. Finally, in the last half mile, I forget about her anger, forget about the guy who can't be with me and the other guy who I've recently broken up with, and drive into my physical pain. My legs are struggling, most likely from fatigue, and my mouth feels like cotton. In the midst of serving alcohol last night, I forgot to hydrate with my usual six cups of water. I pound my feet against the hard-packed dirt, every step sending shooting pain through my joints. Wavy lines swamp my vision, and I think only of the finish line.

When I glance at the official clock as I stagger across, I know it's in the seventeens, a record for me. I finish second, only behind Tara Lockner, the same girl from Reno who's beaten me four years in a row. Before I can turn and search for Lindsey, I hear, "Nice job." Coach Jiménez is standing with my parents, next to a man wearing a Boston College sweatshirt. The coach. His gloved hand reaches out for a handshake, the culmination of what I've been building toward for years. My spirit soars, then immediately sinks when I look back at the finish line. No sign of Lindsey, who's usually less than a minute behind.

"So your parents tell me you've had your eye on Boston since freshman year."

Mom and Dad are beaming. "I'd be honored to run for you," I gasp enthusiastically, my lungs still grabbing for air. Wouldn't I? Do I still want to be that far away? In my peripheral vision, I see at least ten girls cross the finish. *Come on, Linds.* Finally, as we talk sports, scholarships, and the state of Massachusetts, Lindsey jogs in at twenty minutes, her worst time of the year. Coach politely excuses himself once he spots her, but not before I ask what happened.

"She choked," he says matter-of-factly. "Just picked the wrong race to do it." I watch him approach, muss her hair, hand her a bottle of water. She bows her head, shrugs her shoulders. She doesn't look for me.

★★★★★

Sunday, Carson is in meetings and rehearsals, and he promises to call by Monday. He still manages to text me emojis and questions like, "Largest land mammal, Valedictorian. Thirty seconds. No Google searches allowed." or "Man in line just bought beer, chips, and Scooby-Doo Band-Aids. Predict his night." I still don't know what to tell Lindsey, and I feel awful for her bad race. I text her Sorry, but she doesn't respond.

On Monday, John and I still haven't spoken. It's been over a week, and school definitely feels different without him by my side during passing periods. He surprises me when he sits down beside me at our student-council meeting after school, asks me what my plan is for Winter Formal. All day he didn't even make eye contact, not through the three classes we share or during lunch. And now, while Joshua-not-Josh goes through all the boring business of upcoming events and club activities, John won't take his eyes off me.

We both know our relationship was pretty perfect as far as high-school relationships go. He's everything a high-school girl could want: football player, senior class representative, gelled hair, and enough ego to make you think you're lucky to have him. And I look good on his resume, too. Two months ago, it would have been enough for both of us. Now we know there's more than what looks good on paper. Maybe he's asking because it's not like it would kill us to go to Winter Formal, especially if we have no other options. This is my senior year, and if I don't go with John to Winter Formal, does that mean I'm not going at all? It's not like Carson's about to show up. "I don't know," I say. John turns away.

"No, you *wouldn't* know about that, Alexa," Joshua says, referencing something he just mentioned, "because you weren't there. In fact, you've missed the last two student-council meetings and three Friday tutoring sessions. There are plenty of capable students who could take over the position of representative if it's no longer on your list of priorities."

The other eight students on council hold their breath. A few shift in their seats. I look around, but no one makes eye contact. Lindsey, who's ignored me all day, busies herself on her iPhone. "I—" I start, but I don't have more than that. "I—" I say again, hoping for more than a vowel. My phone vibrates with a text.

Hey Delaney/Alexa, u survive? Text me your address. Got a $1,000 check for your alma mater's student council.

Sasha.

"I'm sorry," I say. "I know how much this Winter Formal means to Lindsey." Lindsey peers up from her phone. "So I raised some money. Secretly. It's one thousand dollars. I didn't want to tell you." The group erupts in questions. Where did I raise that kind of money? How long did it take?

"That's where you were on Friday," Lindsey says. "Secretly raising money?" I don't want to lie, not to Lindsey. I sit like a mute, but she wraps her arms around me, sending me inadvertently into John. John excuses himself from the meeting early. Lindsey watches him leave, then looks questioningly at me.

"I don't know," I say. "But let's focus on Winter Formal!" We spend the rest of the meeting mapping out the final details for the dance. While we plan, I text Carson, and Lindsey texts someone else, and both of us don't ask the other about who we're texting. While Lynecia and Joshua discuss how we're going to do the ballots for Winter Formal court, Lindsey leans her chin on my shoulder. She apologizes for Saturday morning, and it feels as if my insides crumble to a heap at my feet. She's the one who choked at state! Choked because I wouldn't tell her where I was, and it hurt her feelings and derailed her race. And now she's apologizing to *me*.

My head feels swimmy. Where does my loyalty lie? With my best friend of four years? Or the guy I loved way before that? I can't fathom hurting him again. On the other hand, I wouldn't have him without Lindsey pushing me back into his arms, so don't I owe it to her? Shouldn't I tell her? *"Not if you care about my reputation,"* I hear Carson saying.

"And to think," Lindsey says, showing me her phone, "I thought this might've been you."

The TMZ website is open. The article says, "Spotted: CAYDEN MCKNIGHT having a heated discussion with a mysterious girl at 3two3. Birthday blues?" There's a fuzzy photo taken from someone's phone, and thank God, Carson's body blocks me. We're in the hallway, and he's gripping my elbow. Aside from my elbow, the only part of me exposed is my shoes. I feel the blood drain from me, but I manage to say, "Huh."

"I thought they were yours, because who wears running shoes to a club? But they're totally too white to be yours."

"Yeah," I say. "Did you see the mud on mine? They're practically black."

"What was that about, anyway? All the mud?"

I could tell her a little. I could tell her I made money at a bar for Winter Formal. But what bar? And why the mud? There would only be more questions.

"Was out in the rain Friday night. Thinking about things. You know."

She nods understandingly, assuming I mean John and our recent breakup. "Hey, can we talk about that?" she says softly. "And about Winter Formal?"

So she's wondering, too. I shrug and shake my head. "I don't really wanna talk about it right now."

★★★★★

When my "brush your teeth" alarm chimes Wednesday morning, it reminds me of the ways I organized and filled my life to push out thoughts of Carson. Before I know it, I erase every alarm—the "plan your outfit for tomorrow" alarm, the "study for ACT," the "go to bed" alarm. I have a new schedule now, already memorized after three days. Carson and I talk twice a day, and my phone doesn't beep a reminder. I just know. I call him during lunch from a private study room in the school library, and he calls me when he gets home at night. Sometimes it's 2:00 a.m., and we still talk for three hours, but there's no greater reason to sleep through first-period AP Lit than being up all night talking to Cayden McKnight. It makes me smile, even when Mr. Kucan slams his fist on my desk to rattle me awake.

Thursday during sixth period, I receive a text from Lindsey with a link to TMZ Videos.

I know you used to be friends, but I think he's worse than Ms. Meckel's stringy hair.

I send a thumbs-up but don't click on the link. She texts again.

Saturday? We're all going out. Been forever. John isn't going, so you better for sure go!

I park myself at a nearby computer and search TMZ.com, scroll through the latest videos until I find Cayden McKnight. It's nighttime, and Carson's walking toward a parking garage, ducking low, an arm shielding his face from the constant flashing. Questions fly at him like gunfire, but only one gets a response.

"Cayden, are you dating anyone?"

Carson laughs. The reporters quiet, dying to capture even his laughter on their recording devices. One reporter presses, "You've been seen with the model Chloe Shauntel—"

"She's been seen with *me*," he says, still walking.

"Does Chloe know about the mysterious girl at 3two3? Who was she?"

He shrugs. "Nobody."

A finger shuts off my computer monitor, and I'm actually thankful. I didn't want to watch more. It's Mr. Weaver, my AP History teacher. "Miss Brooks, this is work time."

"Sorry," I say. "I got distracted."

"That seems to be a new habit of yours." He walks away, scissors in hand, back to help another group with their project.

I text Carson: So I'm a "nobody?"

My phone vibrates. Carson's breaking our two-call-a-day rule. "Put it away, Miss Brooks," Mr. Weaver says, even though his back is to me.

"Sorry, Mr. Weaver. I gotta get this."

"No cell phones."

"In the classroom!" I shout, running out of the room and into the hallway. I answer without a hello. "I'm a '*nobody*?' "

"Aw, Good," he drawls, and already my knees buckle.

"Knight," I complain, but it's soft like my knees. "Why'd you say that?"

"I didn't," he says. "Cayden did." He sighs into the phone. "I wish you could understand, but there's just no way."

"Try."

"Okay." He waits. Thinks. "Here it is: I can't let people know too much. People love the *mystery* of celebrities, and the ones they like the most are the ones they know the least about."

I'm glad it's a good explanation, because I think I would have forgiven him even if it were a bad one.

"You been home today?" he asks.

"No. Why?"

I can hear the smile in his voice. "No reason. Call me later."

Chapter Thirty-One

Mom picks me up after practice, which is strange, since Dad usually does the pickups. On the drive, she asks the obligatory "How was your day?" questions, and I answer the vague "Fine" and "Not much."

"Your recommendation letters?"

I shake my head. This week I was supposed to request letters from a few teachers to send to my backup colleges come January, but I haven't gotten to it. It's okay, though. I know I'm going to Boston College. "I'll get them in. Mom, look back at the road. It's fine."

She does, but her eyes linger on me for as long as possible. "I talked with Mr. Weaver today. Answering your phone in class? And your leadership adviser, Ms. Pohl. You've been missing meetings and tutoring. Something going on?"

"It's my senior year. I've been distracted, you know, with John." I feel bad that I'm playing the John card, but it's my only out. "We've been, I don't know, having problems."

"You've been awfully happy for a recent breakup," she notes.

Now I'm annoyed with Lindsey because how else would Mom know about the breakup? "It's been a couple of weeks." I see her looking at the top of the windshield, and I know she's doing math in her head, calculating the last two weeks with my recent attitude, which hasn't shown much sadness.

When we get home, I enter my room, and I'm greeted with a vase of flowers on my desk. The long-stem roses and stargazer lilies make me gasp.

"They were delivered today," she says, appearing in my doorway. I stare at them, forgetting Mom is staring at me.

I love Carson all over again.

I'm captivated by the pink and red lighting up my bland room, and I can feel his arms around me as we slow dance at camp. *"Okay, sure, I guess you can call me your best friend."*

"They're quite the bouquet."

Her tone makes me respond, "Just lilies and roses."

"Gathered with ruscus, salal, and bear grass." Mom worked at a flower shop while she was getting her degree back in California, and somehow, she means something by her list of ingredients. "And a crystal vase."

"Yep."

She gives up and says, "They're expensive." I bite my lip and don't look at her. She hands me the card affixed to the flowers: *Can't wait for our next muddy all-nighter.—Will*

"Who's Will?"

This might be difficult to explain. "Just a guy," I say. "He's playing around. Come on, Mom."

"Muddy all-nighter? And 'Will' *who*? Have I met him?"

I think of the most generic surname, where there's sure to be one at our school. "Smith, and please don't embarrass him, Mom. He was just joking. I tutored him. Told him to imagine girl mud wrestlers any time he started to fall asleep while reading." This is getting ridiculous, so I snatch my clothes for a shower, even though I took one before school.

At night, amid texting Carson a bazillion thank-yous, my phone buzzes with a text from Lindsey.

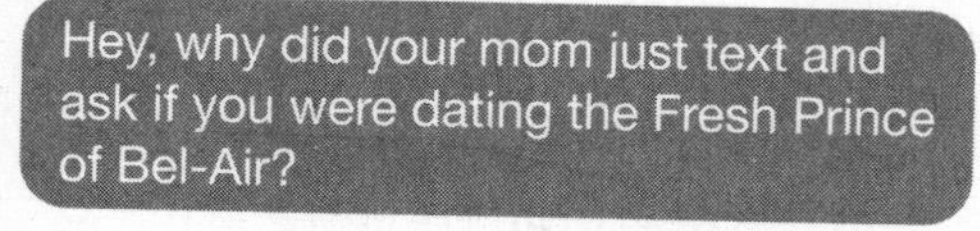

?

Will Smith? Really, Lex?

Lol, I write, and I'm actually laughing out loud. I hadn't put that together when I said it, and thank God, neither did Mom.

★★★★★

Saturday evening, Dad's watching a Lakers home game, and I'm lounging next to him on the couch. Tonight, they're playing the Houston Rockets. I'm supposed to be out with my friends, but I know that Carson will be on TV in the front row, and I'm dying to see him any way I can. The crowd stomps and waves their hands, an undulating sea of purple and gold, and Dad claps with them like he's there. I glimpse Carson every time the players cross from one side to the other, and all I want is for the teams to constantly change possession. He sits midcourt, close enough to the players to feel their sweat when they wick it off. He lifts his trucker hat and leans over to a tall, slender girl. She, too, is wearing a baseball cap, shielding her face from us common folks. Her legs look long enough to trip the players on the court. Carson tells me that these models are all show, that he escorts them to the games, they get free publicity, and he in turn keeps up his reputation. "Do you ever like them?" I asked him this week on the phone.

"I dated Karina Svoboda for a year," he said. My stomach churned, even though he used the past tense.

"And now?"

"Now she's dating the quarterback for the New York Jets."

"No, I mean, now who's the latest girl?"

"Now, I hang out with Chloe Shauntel, Kirsten Davison, Ali Lombar—Lex, why does it matter?"

"Do you like them?"

I thought for a second that we had lost connection. "You've only been in my life recently," he finally said. "The public is still going to see me with them. But trust me, when the cameras are off, a lot will be different than it was, okay?" Then he said it again, "Okay?" Like he believed it and was waiting for me to believe it, too.

I'm brought back to the present by the squeak of the sneakers and the feathery sound of baskets swooshing, but my eyes are glued to the girl with Carson, watching their interactions every time the ball is at midcourt.

After halftime, the game resumes but on a small screen in the lower corner. On the main screen, they show a recap of halftime. They replay highlights of the Laker Girls' dance routine, then a game in which a selected fan ran back and forth across the court dumping balled-up dollar bills into a water cooler using only a shovel. He got to keep everything in the water cooler, and the camera cut to the fans cheering. Carson, stone-faced, watched, and I have to remind myself I'm looking at Cayden. The Carson I know, the one who pied me in the face with a Frisbee full of oatmeal, would've been clapping and hooting for the guy. As the game was cleaned up, the announcer said, "And now, if you'll direct your attention to section three thirty." A spotlight fills the entire section with blinding light, and the Jumbotron displays a group of about fifty Boy Scouts donning their khaki uniforms. They each hold a bag of popcorn, and with fistfuls of it, they wave at the camera. "Congratulations to troops twenty-nine, forty-two, and forty-nine of the South Bay region for their generous contribution to the community. They've just rebuilt a nursing home that was destroyed three years ago during the Malibu fires." The Los Angeles and Houston fans stand and applaud. It cuts to Carson, who claps absently, leans over to Chloe/Karina/hot girl/whomever and whispers something. The announcer continues, "And a big thank-you to Cayden McKnight and his generous support of these Boy Scout troops." Carson is scratching his jawline and stops midscratch. Even his eyes freeze.

He's clueless, and his reaction scares me. Did Heidi—

"During the second quarter, Cayden bought popcorn for every troop member as a way of saying 'Thank-you for your care of the elderly!'"

If he's shocked, he doesn't show it. The camera closes in on him offering a casual wave. The crowd erupts in cheers. The clip disappears, replaced by the live game, and an announcer saying, "Well, there you have it, folks. I wouldn't have predicted that one."

The whistle blows, out of bounds midcourt. I see Carson

whip out his phone and type with fingers that are frantic or furious, or maybe both.

I pull out my iPhone and text him: Miss you. How r u

There's a short delay. Then I see him on my television pausing to read my text. He types something. Moments later, my phone vibrates.

Been better. Someone's out to kill my rep. Destroy my career. :/

I write back: Bad rumors???

He writes: Worse. Good.

Good like me?

One Mississippi, two Mississippi . . . and then on the fifty-two-inch flat-screen in front of me, I see him throw his head back and grin. Everything in me warms. The camera cuts away, but not before Dad says, "Hey, that's your Hollywood pansy. See? Good kid. Gettin' popcorn for Boy Scouts."

My phone vibrates, and I look down at it.

Lol. Why so damn cute? Ur ruining my bad mood.

I write, When can I see u?

Minutes pass before I feel my phone again: Don't know if that's a good idea.

Y NOT? I write it in all CAPS, but my body feels like it's dropped to lowercase. As if on cue, the TV shows him in the background staring at his phone, staring at my "Y NOT?" He shoves his phone back into his pocket, resumes watching the game. I text him, Hello? But he leans forward, elbows on knees, focusing on the court, the game. Not me. I leave my heart stuck somewhere between the couch cushions and borrow Dad's car in the middle of the third quarter to make it to my friends.

★★★★★

My friends love to meet up at the Gold Coast Casino for late-night bowling. It's a bit divey, but as long as we don't touch the slot machines, the employees never bother us about breaching curfew. "Hey, birthday girl!" I say to Kim when I sneak up behind her.

"Where've you been?" she says, hugging me and sort of slow dancing, and I'm thankful she's forgiven me for missing her birthday. "This is our last game. Here, play for me."

"Hey, stranger," Ryan says. Lindsey points out Ryan's comment with her eyes.

"Yeah, *stranger*," Lindsey says. "Where ya been all night?"

"Sorry, guys," I say. "I had some errands."

Heidi rises from Ryan's lap. "Errands, huh?" She picks up a bowling ball and dangles it from three fingers, waving it back and forth. "You find what you were looking for?"

"Yeah," I say. "But it's more complicated than I thought."

"It always is—" she throws the ball down the lane, and all ten pins topple, echoing like hollow thunder—"if it's worth something." She wraps her arms around Ryan to emphasize her point.

He plants a kiss on her. "Nice job, baby."

"That's hot," Kim says to them.

I ignore that Lindsey's looking from Heidi to me to Heidi again. I ask Kim about her birthday, and for the next hour, I'm distracted by my gutter-ball bowling skills.

Ryan feels for his phone, then asks the time, and when I look at my watch, Kim points at me. "You haven't beeped all night." Everyone's used to my alarms: study time, practices, club meetings.

"I know," I say. "I turned them all off." Lindsey pauses drinking her soda. Kim falls into a chair as if knocked off balance. Even Heidi and Ryan stop their groping and stare like I'm some lifelong addict suddenly sober. Wow. Was I always this bad?

I pull Heidi aside and tell her about the Boy Scout popcorn debacle. She swears she has nothing to do with it.

"Then how?" I ask.

"Told you," she says, shrugging it off. "The internet's a scented candle or forest fire. No telling which way the wind blows. You started something."

"We have to stop it."

She shows me her phone. Opens it to a website. "I shut down thank-you-Cayden-dot-com the second you told me it was over. Thank-you-*so-much*-Cayden-dot-com started a day later. Six more websites—there could be more, that's all I've found—have copied ours. And TikTok? Just look up the hashtag thankyoucayden, and you'll see. Even Instagram has accounts you can share to. Everyone's on board—joking or not—with making up stories about his kindness. Some of those accounts got over ten thousand followers in less than a month." She tucks her phone back in her pocket. "Forest fire. You gotta let this one burn."

★★★★★

I do my best. I get back to tutoring, club meetings, and

after-school runs, but I miss most lunches with my friends because I'm in a library study room, ear to ear with Carson. My friends have stopped asking, and I've stopped offering excuses.

One day, I make it to the lunchroom because student council is hosting Thanksgiving spirit week with games and contests during both lunches. "Who's Will?" Heidi asks as we're packing up after the bell rings. Everyone else has left already. My jaw juts open. She hands me my phone, which I must've left on the table. The text reads: Missed your call today.

"Just a guy," I say.

"Mm-hmm." She throws an arm around me. "Come on," she says, lugging her cello behind us. "You're gonna get yourself in a load of trouble, dumbass."

Chapter Thirty-Two

On Tuesday, November 23, Carson texts during a late dinner with my parents. Dad is normal as ever, shoving buttered rolls into his mouth and discussing why pre-season football is a waste of time. But Mom watches me read my text. It's from Will: Miss u like crazy. Have interviews tomorrow. Need to feel normal. Can you catch a flight? I'll pay for it.

It's a school night, and Thanksgiving's in two days. Something's going on.

I write: Can't you come here?

Can't risk it

There's a two-minute pause. Then he writes again.

PLZ

I don't know if it's the please that gets me or the capital letters or that he's so desperate that he abbreviates, but I write brb and then check flights on my Southwest app. They're all unavailable.

"Can I borrow the car tonight, Dad?"

"No," Mom answers for him.

I keep my voice even. "Why not?"

"It needs a tune-up."

"Nah," Dad pipes in. "Car's fine."

"No," Mom says again. "I want a tune-up. I'll drive you where you need to go."

"Fine," I concede. "Can I stay the night at Lindsey's? We gotta work on Winter Formal."

Dad says, "I can take you, Sport."

In the end, Mom takes me. I can tell she's suspicious, so on the drive, I ask her about Winter Formal—what colors go well together, what flowers we should use, what her high-school dances were like. I text Lindsey, When I ask, say that you have an extra. We arrive at Lindsey's, and she runs out to greet us. I look in my bag and roll my eyes. "Dangit, Mom, I forgot my toothbrush. Can you come back in a few hours and bring it?"

Lindsey jumps in, "It's okay, I have an extra."

Mom's shoulders relax. Now that I've asked her to come back, she trusts that I'm staying here. She won't come back to check on me, and I can safely borrow Lindsey's car and head to LA. "I'm sorry, sweetie," Mom coos when she hugs me goodbye. "You haven't been yourself lately. I had to check."

"It's fine," I say. "Really."

Inside the house, Lindsey says, "I thought you totally forgot about the dance by now. You haven't mentioned anything except at the student-council meeting."

"Yeah, right," I say, because how could I possibly forget the single-most-important event of my best friend's senior year? I'm too ashamed to borrow her car, even for the guy I love who needs me tonight.

She leads me by the hand to her room. "Then let's figure out what we're missing and make it better than any dance this school has ever seen. Better than the Oscars!"

"Oscars!" I say. "How about making two statues at the entrance?"

"That's brilliant!" She hugs me and starts drawing something in her sketchbook. My phone buzzes, and I look down.

On your way?

My heart belly flops in disappointment. I excuse myself to the bathroom. He answers on the first ring. "Hey," he says. There's something like gravel coating his voice.

"Hey."

"God, I miss you." His words stroke over me so softly that for a moment, I think I might start jogging the three hundred miles there.

"What's happening? You okay?"

I hear a sigh crawling out of him. "I got roped in to this hospital visit today. Someone signed me up for it a while ago, and it was for a bunch of children. I didn't expect it to affect me so hard, ya know?" I guiltily recall Lindsey's call a few months back to the activities director of the children's hospital. He sniffles, his voice wobbly. "And it was like, I dunno, that stuff isn't supposed to happen to little kids, you know?" I nod as if he can see me through the phone. "Anyway, the whole time, all I kept thinking was, 'Alexa would know what to do here. She'd make things make sense.' And then it hit me." He coughs to clear his choked-up throat. His voice is rough, weathered, broken. "You make *me* make sense."

My knees give, and I sit down on the edge of the bathtub. "I'm so sorry, Carson. The flights are booked. I can't get there."

He laughs. "It's probably better." His voice grows lower,

tangled up in desire. "I want all of you tonight."

I'm not quite sure what that means, but it sounds dangerous and exciting, and my body radiates like a furnace. I hug my knees to my chest.

A loud knock breaks up the moment. "Hey, Lex?" Lindsey's on the other side of the door. Carson hears it, too.

"Should you go?" he asks.

"Probably. Unless you want people to know who Carson is." I don't say it like it's a bad thing, but he laughs like it is.

"Got it. Yeah, I'll let you go. I'll be out there in December, okay?"

December feels like years, but I agree, and we whisper our goodbyes.

When I leave the bathroom, Lindsey says, "Who was that?"

"Nobody," I say, just like what Cayden said of me to the reporter. "It was nobody."

★★★★★

Lindsey and I spend the next two hours taking notes, transforming our high-school gymnasium into the lights, camera, and action of Hollywood. Lindsey writes a list of items to buy while my head swims with thoughts of Carson.

When we lie down to go to sleep, she turns to me and asks, "Are you gonna go with John to Winter Formal?"

I lift my shoulder, the one not on the pillow. "I don't know. We could go, you know, as friends. We don't hate each other."

"No. I guess not. But John's a rule follower. He won't ask anyone to the dance if he thinks it'll make you feel bad. I just think that if you're going with someone else, you should tell John so he doesn't end up holding out just to protect your feelings."

"Who are you going with?"

She shifts under the sheet. "I don't know."

I lace my fingers behind my neck and look up. Lindsey has glow-in-the-dark stars stuck to her ceiling. They're all in the precise locations for a summer sky.

"Will you please make up your mind soon? Chad asked me."

"Ew!" I giggle. "Chad, I-Only-Date-Freshman-Girls Chad?"

"He's cute. But if John's flying solo, I'd rather go with him because we've been friends way longer." She pauses. "But only if you're okay with that. And maybe you should tell him. Like, if you're okay with it."

I don't say anything. I'm actually fine with it. But if she goes with Chad, then maybe I could go with John just to have someone to go with. It's not like he has plans, either.

Lindsey adds, "Plus, I want to protect him from Kim, who totally likes him, if you haven't noticed."

"My head hasn't been *that much* in the clouds."

"Trust me, you could see that even through the clouds."

We laugh. Shortly after, we fall asleep, but at 2:00 a.m., I wake up for no reason. I stare at the glowing constellations overhead. They're faded now, not as bright as when we first turned off the lights. Restless, I text Carson: You up?

He doesn't write back. I think sleepily that maybe I should've texted Cayden.

★★★★★

Thanksgiving is traditional. Well, traditional in our sense of the word. We do the turkey trot like every year, but we always run it as a family, so it's more of a turkey walk. We're home by eleven, prep the sides, and then throw the turkey in the oven by noon. For the next three hours, we watch football while Mom cooks, which she loves, so it's not a big deal that Dad and I don't leave the couch except to refill the salsa bowl. After dinner, Dad and I clean the kitchen while Mom showers. She returns with a book, Dad turns on the recorded morning football he missed, and I head out for Heidi's annual after-Thanksgiving poker party.

Heidi's parents are there, which means it's a sober event, although the punch bowls are refilled without the parents' help. We play at four tables with blue, red, and white chips. "Just for fun," Heidi tells her parents, but we all know that the Venmo buy-in for tonight is forty dollars. Everyone gets the same amount of chips, and once you're out, you're out. The three remaining players split the Venmo pot. John's here, but thankfully he's at a different table.

By ten o'clock, we're down to two tables, and I'm still in the game. The ones who are out have made their own dance floor in the living room, and, by their moves, I can tell they're enjoying the party punch. I sip my water and look across at Calista, trying to read her, wishing I'd paid more attention to her face when she cheered at the football games. Lindsey was the second person out, and she shares my chair, watching my cards. "Raise," I say to Calista, putting two blue chips into the pot. She tugs at her frizzy ringlets, then throws out one red chip to match me, calling me.

I throw down my three kings. She grimaces, drops her three tens. I rake the pile of chips toward me, a strong win. My phone vibrates. I shield the screen from Lindsey.

At Phantom. Meet me? Code word to bouncer: Good.

I haven't seen Carson since his birthday, almost a month ago, and he wasn't supposed to be here until December. It takes all my strength not to throw over the poker table that stands between me and the door and bolt out of there. I lean into Lindsey's cheek. "Can I borrow your car?"

"Can I go with?" she whispers.

"No," I say apologetically.

Lindsey fiddles with the chips. Finally, she mutters, "I'll have John take me home." She takes her keys from her pocket, hands them to me under the table.

"Hey," I say. "Win for me, okay? You can keep all of it." I kiss the side of her head and stand. "Sorry, guys. I gotta head out."

I hear murmurs. Someone mutters, "Big surprise."

"Lindsey's taking over for me."

Joshua complains, "You can't hand off your chips. That's an automatic forfeit."

"Oh, Josh." Lindsey rolls her eyes. "Have some punch."

"Joshua," he growls.

As I head for the door, John locks eyes with me from the other table. We still haven't talked about the dance. I walk over to his table, kneel down next to him. "Hey," I say.

He focuses on a chip in his hand. "We're not doing this now."

"No, of course not. I just think we should talk."

He looks away. "Go do what you have to do. Find me when you have time." He adds, "Alone."

I slip out, but as I start the car and throw it into reverse, Heidi runs out to meet me. "So," she says, when I roll down the window. "Late night with Will?" She uses air quotes for "Will."

I don't answer.

"Right." She holds up a trashy celebrity magazine and waves it in the night air. "You know what you're getting yourself into?"

"I think so."

She slaps the hood of my car twice. "Be careful, dumbass."

★★★★★

At the Palms, I park in self-parking, area G2, and sprint to the front doors. I bypass the line that wraps around the bottom floor. "The guest list should say 'Good,'" I say to the guard at the elevator.

He allows me into the elevator with the next group. At the top, I tell the bouncer the same, and he escorts me into Phantom Bar and to a private table cordoned off with a velvet rope. I walk up to the table and look down as Carson, leaning back, looks up. Our eyes meet, and it all makes sense again, how I'd abandon poker parties, friends, the entire world, to have those eyes look at me the way they do right now. I smile, biting my bottom lip. He's sitting next to a girl, the same one from the Lakers game.

"Chloe, this is Alexa," Carson introduces, his voice dry, and

I can't tell if he's Cayden or Carson with her. "Alexa, Chloe." I reach out and shake her long, slender hand. Even her nails look like they diet. Her grip is firm, and she doesn't smile; she smirks. "Alexa, do you like views?" Carson says, and I look away from her smug eyes and smile at him.

"Yes, as a matter of fact, I do."

"Funny," he says, standing up. "Most people do."

I grin. "Why *is* that, do you think?"

"I don't know. Why don't we go find out?"

Chloe stands, puts a hand on his shoulder. "Don't," she says. It's a warning, but she's not angry. He considers, then turns to me and holds out his hand. I place my hand in his, for the first time ever, where others can see. We walk out to the view, where we can look at the skyline of Vegas, the thousands of hotel rooms winking back at us. We're back to the exact spot where I first saw him in September. I grip his arm tighter, shivering from the wind. He removes his leather jacket and drapes it over my shoulders. I can feel everyone's eyes on us instead of the view. I know there are camera phones everywhere.

I try to ignore them, focus on the view and why everyone loves it. "Maybe it's because you always feel so small," I continue, "and then when you see something this majestic, this overwhelming, you realize, it's okay that I'm so small. Everybody is. Even you, Hollywood."

Someone behind us shouts, "Cayden!"

"Tell that to *her*," he says, and I know what he means. I bet sometimes he'd love to be one of these twinkling hotel lights, a glimmer in the vast dark sky, and not the whole skyline.

Maybe not all the time. But right now, for sure. He searches the moon, across the horizon, and then looks down at the red spots of taillights below. He adds, "I think it's because we're fifty-five stories above where we have to live our lives." A girl approaches us.

"Excuse me," she says. "Can I take a picture with you?"

"Nah," Carson says in that lackadaisical Cayden voice. "If I agree to one, I've gotta agree to all." She scowls and takes a picture of his back. He says to me, "Not quite the same view as Hiker's Peak, is it?"

The people are behind us, but it still feels suffocating. "I have an idea," I say. "Come on."

Chapter Thirty-Three

We walk through the crowds. Some follow, pretending not to, and we reach the elevators. The bouncer lets us have the service elevator alone, and instead of the first floor, I push the button for the third. On the way down, I remove the leather jacket from my shoulders and say, "Bend your knees." He does and, once at my eye level, kisses me. I laugh, pull away, and throw the jacket over his head, just as the door opens to the High Sierra Ballroom. "Act drunk," I say, and he staggers obediently. I guide him through the private banquet and search for the emergency-exit stairs. Once inside the stone stairwell, I pull the jacket off.

"*This* is your idea?" he jokes, looking at the metal handrails and stone floors. "The décor is really not all that."

"Come on." We dart down the stairs to the first-floor exit outside. I throw the jacket over his head right before we push through the doors into the night air. He bends and staggers again, and I lead him to a cab. I guide his head into the back seat, and his body follows. "Hey," I say to the driver. "Can you take us to the top floor of the parking garage at Caesars Palace?"

The driver says, "Yeah, wherever, miss. Make sure he doesn't yak on my floor." I text Lindsey that I'll pick up her car later.

Nm, she writes. Never mind? I can't tell if she's mad or not. She asks where it is.

I text: G2. Palms.

I'm about to ask her if she's okay when Carson pulls me under the jacket.

"I should fire my bodyguard, agent, and publicist," he whispers. "Who needs them to get me around? You could sneak me into the White House."

"You wanna go? I'm on it."

★★★★★

The top floor of the parking garage is open to the night sky, and the driver parks in front of the double doors to the elevators down to the casino. I pay him and lead Carson out of the car. Just then a group of thirtysomethings exits the doors. Carson pulls me under the jacket with him, and we kiss and laugh while they pass by us. "Get a room," one says, but I can only see their shoes and Carson's lips. Once they're gone, we remove the jacket, and I pull him to the parking garage ledge next to the double doors. Over the ledge and below us is the top of the casino or the Forum Shops or something. Something with a completely flat roof. I know because my friends and I used to order pizzas and sneak down here on Friday nights to eat dinner overlooking the Strip. We've only been caught by a guard once, so I know security is pretty lax. It's an eight-foot drop to the roof. Carson looks down. "Really?"

"You afraid?" I say. I swing my leg over and drop.

"A-list movie star dies while running across roof of local casino," he says, dropping onto the roof with me. We jog to the edge and climb onto our stomachs, our heads hanging over the ledge looking down on the streets below. We listen to the symphony of Vegas: people shouting, laughing, singing; cars revving and honking over live music, and somewhere deep in the distance, the chimes of slot machines. Up here it feels silent and perfect. I rest my chin on his arm, and we enjoy quietly breathing. As if even *that* is an activity we do best together.

After thirty minutes, Carson's phone vibrates. He reaches for it, scans the text. "I'm going to have a lot of explaining to do," he says. "It's already reached my publicist that I'm with you." I hate that this is a bad thing. I hear Heidi's words reverberate: *You know what you're getting yourself into?*

"Knight," I say, and Carson turns his head so our noses almost touch and our heads rest on our arms. I search those eyes, deep as the ocean, the ones that can drown me with one look, and I have to ask. "Are you embarrassed by me?"

His expression doesn't change, and I wish it would. This is where he should look shocked—appalled, even—that I'd ever suggest such a dumb thing. But he doesn't. When he speaks, it's slow and calculated, and he watches the cars below.

"Did I ever tell you why I hated that I was poor? Why I never wanted anyone to know—why I hated you so much for telling people?" I shake my head. He stays stomach-down but hoists up on his elbows. "My mom was from Germany, you knew that. Dad was from here, New York. Old money. He fell in love with my mom when he was vacationing in Germany;

she was working at an art gallery, doing okay. Anyway, it was like you and me, you know? When you both just *know*." I lean over, brush my lips against his shoulder. "He postponed his trip for a month, convinced her to move to the States, marry him, start a better life for herself here. She did." He reaches over to tuck a strand of hair behind my ear. "They lived in California, waited for the marriage licenses to get approved. Then she got pregnant." My mouth gapes. He nods. "Yeah, they decided to hold off on the marriage until they got things settled with me. It was too much to think about, wedding, baby, I guess.

"Five months later, his family found him. He knew they'd never approve, so he hadn't contacted them. Since Germany, he'd been MIA. At first he ignored their calls, said he was going to do damn well what he wanted. Then his brother showed up at the door one night, took him out to dinner. They talked periodically over the next couple of years, sometimes in person, sometimes over late-night hushed phone conversations behind closed doors. Mom thought he was trying to work things out with the family's finances. But there was no more talk of marriage, and one night when I was two years old, he went out to dinner and never returned. Mom thought he was in an accident. Called every cop in town. Then she found his note tucked under his pillow. 'I'm sorry,' was all he wrote.

"She searched for two and a half years; when she finally located him, he was back in New York, married to a wealthy socialite, living the life that his family had planned for him before he was born. He never sent a check, never sent a letter, never gave my mom the life he'd promised her. I was an American citizen, so she toughed it out, gave me a shot at the American Dream."

"Has he tried to find you now?"

"Oh, yeah," he says, a disgusted laugh between his teeth. "Now that I have something to offer *him,* of course he'd seek me out."

"Maybe he wants to apologize?"

His eyes are steel, unblinking. "Not interested." He rakes his hair with his fingers. "Money broke up my family, broke my mother's heart. My dad chose his family's status over Mom. Growing up, I hated that. I felt like my dad rejected us because we didn't have enough. So I hated money, and I never wanted anyone to know that we didn't have any. I could keep my head up in this world as long as no one knew the truth, ya know?"

His eyes are soft, but his words carry a rigid determination. "So now, I've beaten money. I have more of it than I know what to do with. *I'm* giving my mom the life that my father should've given her, and it's all tied to Cayden McKnight, not Carson Knight. Knight is my father's last name, and he never gave me *anything*. McKnight is what *I* created, and I'll be damned if some lowlife reporter is going to destroy what I've built. Not my dad. Not some reporter. And not all this fake charity crap."

"Nothing's wrong with doing good things."

"It's not what Cayden McKnight would do, Lex. Whoever's doing it is trying to kill my career. If I ever find out who's behind it all . . ." He trails off, venom in his voice, and I'm glad he doesn't finish because already, I feel like I'm going to be sick. I have to tell him. He stands, gently pulls me up. He takes my face in both hands. His touch is delicate, like he's holding a wounded butterfly. "So, no, I'm not embarrassed by you," he says, "But you're too amazing, Alexa Brooks. You're no good for Cayden McKnight."

"The first night Lindsey and I went to Hollywood," I start.

"The Viper Room?"

"No, before that. You hated me, and so I thought if I did something good—"

"I never hated you," he confesses, not realizing that it's me who's trying to confess. We're interrupted by a car horn from the street below us. The man behind the wheel lays on his horn like he's fallen asleep against it.

"Damn," he says, watching an old man climb out of the car. He's hunched over, but he keeps screaming at the valet, waving his arms. "Who do you think *that* guy is?"

I chew on my lip. Accept that the moment is lost. "Ex-mafia," I say. "It's Vegas."

He adds, "Distant cousin to Bugsy."

"Twice removed." A young midtwenties girl climbs out of the passenger side, puts her arm around the hunched angry man. "And that girl's inheriting the biz. Daughter?"

"Hardly," he says. "Girlfriend who's offing him later tonight for five grand and two backstage passes to the newest boy band headlining at the Bellagio."

"Oh, Knight," I laugh, throwing my arms around him melodramatically. "How did I know anything about anything without you all these years?"

"You were existing, Saturday . . . not living."

"What?"

"Oh man, you haven't seen the movie, have you?" My blinking eyes answer his question. "It's a quote from *Kicking Over Saturday's Rivers.*"

"Let's go watch it," I say. "Come on, there's no photographers lurking outside my house."

Chapter Thirty-Four

We call an Uber to the rooftop parking, and on the way home, we're both underneath his jacket shielding our faces from the front seat. He looks at me with this intensity that makes me feel naked and wild, and I'm drunk on the adrenaline. "Take me to Winter Formal," I blurt out.

"What?"

I pull myself out of the jacket, roll down the window, and stick my head out. "Carson Knight, take me to Winter Formal!" I shout at the city. Carson tugs me back inside. He holds up his jacket between the front and back seats, blocking the driver's view of us. "Look," I say, grabbing hold of Carson's free hand, feeling his heat, making sure my voice isn't loud enough for our driver to overhear. "This all got messed up in junior high because I was too afraid to be honest. And now, you're too afraid because America loves the 'bad boy.'" He looks away. I grab hold of his waist, move my hands to his chest, then back to his sides. "But I love the other guy. The good one." He looks pained by my stubbornness. I know he just finished telling me about his awful dad and why Cayden McKnight needs to keep going, but I can't help myself. "I really think they'll like you no matter who you are."

"Cayden is still me. He's a little more guarded, sure." He sees my eyebrow lift. "Okay, a *lot* more guarded. I'll give you that. But my life isn't jail—it's different than how you do things, and maybe that's hard for you. But I chose this for me. And I wouldn't trade it in."

Our Uber pulls up to my house, slows. Carson must know his words sting, because as he retreats under his jacket, he adds, "But I also wouldn't trade in being here with you right now." I pay the driver, then lead Carson to my front door.

My parents' light is off, so we tiptoe into my bedroom. I take my laptop from my desk. Carson is twirling in a slow circle, taking in the personality of my room. His fingers trace the books on my bookshelf, all arranged by color. "You've become so . . . practical."

"It works." I look down at the pile of dirty clothes on the floor, the mess of papers on my desk. "Used to, anyway. You're hardly practical."

He sighs. "I know. Remember you had a fish named 'Fish'?"

"See?" I laugh. "*That* was practical."

He pivots to me, gently removes the laptop from my hands, places it on the dresser. His hands start at my shoulders and trace the outline of my body in front of him. They stop at my hands. He lifts them to his lips, kisses them each.

"We should watch the movie," I breathe out with about as much strength as my legs have.

"Mm-hmm," he says, and one of his hands reaches through my hair and cups the back of my neck. His other hand lowers me onto the bed. What I should or shouldn't do is swimming in my head. What I shouldn't do is drowning, and

I'm about to lose myself in the moment without caring about consequences or the fact that, to everyone else, I don't exist to Carson. Cayden. Carson.

"There's not a lock on my door," I say, struggling for air.

"So practical," he whispers with a smirk.

"Not about you." I hug him, our bodies not able to get close enough. "Does this mean we're going to Winter Formal?" I say in his ear.

I feel his muscles tighten. "Lex, I can't show up at some high-school dance."

The words cut deeply, but they shake me into sobriety. I push away, lean up onto my elbows. "No, of course not."

I want to tell him that it's important to *me*. That I'm not a Hollywood star, and that this *is* my red-carpet moment, and all I'm asking is that he show himself with me somewhere besides a drunken club.

I stand and grab the laptop from my dresser. Carson reaches for me with loose arms, but I back out of reach and head for the hallway. When he doesn't move from the bed, I whisper, "No way. We are *not* risking my parents walking in my room and finding a guy on my bed. My dad will NOT care what movie you've been nominated for when he grabs his shotgun."

We make our way to the living-room couch. I flip the laptop open and sign in to my Google Drive. I rest my head on his shoulder, place one of the AirPods in my ear and hand him the other, wondering if one day, Carson's going to think this is too much for Cayden's reputation as well. I'm frustrated and sad, but I cling to him anyway, my arm across his chest.

At first it's weird seeing Carson next to me and on the screen at the same time. I guess I forgot that these actors onscreen are real, three-dimensional people who have real lives, and it's strange that one of them is sharing his life with me at this very moment. In the movie, he plays Quinn, a depressed kid who's always in the shadow of his older sister, Saturday. Saturday is a champion swimmer, but she's in a car accident that leaves her blind. Quinn was driving the vehicle illegally when it wrecked, and now he's so ridden with guilt that he tries to kill himself. The parents feel no sympathy because they always favored Saturday, and they fault Quinn for her loss. Quinn falls into a deep depression until Saturday releases her bitterness and asks him to secretly train her in the pool at night.

Carson's phone vibrates constantly during the movie, and I fall asleep to its vibrating rhythm. I remember Carson waking me in the middle, joking, "Do I bore you that much?" I laugh halfheartedly and drop off again. I wake up when Quinn and Saturday are yelling at each other on the bank of the river, something about Saturday not listening to Quinn. They're both wearing life jackets, I'm not sure why, but suddenly, Quinn throws Saturday into the river, jumps in after her, and shouts that she better listen to him. She struggles, and swallows water, and then starts listening to Quinn's commands, right before she slams a shoulder into a rock. He keeps her afloat, gets her feet downstream, calms her, tells her which direction to swim to avoid rocks. She rides through the rapids on his voice commands. Then they're in calm water, and they swim to the edge and sit against the rocks. They hold on to each other with a deep family love.

"Aww," I murmur. "You're so sweet."

Carson looks at me and rolls his eyes. "You're lucky you're cute."

"You're dumb."

"*You're* dumb. Go back to sleep." I do. His warmth reminds me of home, of where I belong, and I bury myself in the peace my body feels next to his.

He nudges me awake a while later. "Here's the line," he says. "The one I quoted to you earlier." I blink my eyes awake, and the blurry screen comes into focus.

"What's the difference?" Saturday sputters between tears. "Why now?"

"We were *existing,* Saturday . . . not living." Carson says the line out loud to me along with the recorded version of him. "Mom and Dad. They're still existing."

"You think they'll ever live?" she asks him.

Quinn rakes his hand through his hair. "No," Quinn and Carson say together.

"Hey," I say, my voice hoarse with grogginess. "You pull your hand through your hair like that. Your character totally stole that from you. I hate him." I nuzzle into the cleft between Carson's chin and chest. "I hate him like I hate Cayden." I'm too sleepy to take it back, and I can't open my eyes to see Carson's response. But he doesn't say anything, which probably means he's thinking something. He plays with my hair until I fall asleep again. Sometime before dawn, he wakes me.

"Good?"

I open one eye.

He whispers, "I gotta run, sweetheart. I had a driver come

to the house, and they'll get me to the airport, okay?"

I rub my eyes awake. "Wait, what's going on?"

"One, it's probably better your dad doesn't find me here, shotgun or not. Two, I'm in a load of trouble. My publicist has organized a meeting with my agent and me to deal with my upcoming events. I'm scheduled to talk on *Wake Up, LA*, *Guy O'Rourke*, and *Jimmy Fallon*. I guess my good deeds are quite the scandal in Hollywood." He gives me a rueful grin and then leans down to kiss my forehead. "And Winter Formal," he says. "I'll be out here. We'll work around it. And I'll definitely see you somehow that night, okay?"

I nod, accepting the best he can give me. "Good luck this week."

★★★★★

Carson ends up having the opposite of good luck in every magazine interview, live talk show, or online blurb about him in the following weeks. He gets body slammed from every direction for every good deed. His picture splashes the front page of *Celebrity Herald*, and the article is daunting:

> Cayden and "wild" have always been synonymous. It's what we've loved most about him: the fits on the set, the high demands on movie studios, his audacity to change movie titles and film locations. Without that, what's left? We already have Rick Cayell and Timmy Tibbles cornering the market in the "nice actor" category. But the question Hollywood wants to know is this: What has led him to

> this change of behavior? Sources say that he is lonely and isolated. "He's desperate for companionship," one source close to the actor reveals. "He's reaching out."
>
> Many aren't surprised by this behavior. "He always brought a girl home," one model says. "But the one time I came home with him, he left me alone while he was called away to 'unforeseen business.' It was obvious that he had intimacy issues. I think he's finally hit rock bottom."
>
> Others believe his good deeds are still a by-product of the bad boy, claiming they will no longer endorse any Cayden McKnight films, and over fifty organizations have signed the petition. Apparently they have received laughable five-dollar donations from Cayden McKnight, and they believe he is mocking them by offering pitiful amounts. One organization states, "He is clearly telling us that we aren't worthy of a large donation." Needless to say, his STARmeter has dropped 22 percent in the past month, a drastic decline in popularity that America hasn't witnessed since rapper Jaysen Lazy's 2017 scandal.

I stop reading here. I have no idea who's behind the new five-dollar donation trend, but why does he have to give a ton of money just because he has it? If every person in America gave five dollars to their organization, they could change the world. Why's he getting slammed for it?

The live interviews are rough; I can tell by his eyes. He keeps his stone-faced "I don't care what people think" expression, but he shifts in his seat way more than usual. When he's asked if he is behind all these good acts, he doesn't reply or deny it. He asks in that Cayden drawl, "And what if I am?" like he's really not, but he wants to challenge them on it.

On *Wake Up, LA*, the host says, "America wants to know what's behind all these acts. What's your motive? Too many sources are saying the same thing. Websites, personal testimonies, hospitals, all claiming Cayden McKnight is not the bad boy everyone loves. Some people believe you're doing this because you're lonely, others believe you're sick of people, some say you're kind, and others say selfish. We're all left wondering one question: Who is Cayden McKnight?"

"Who do you want me to be, Alice?" he says seductively to the host, and she laughs nervously. Even this middle-aged woman is flustered by his charm.

They mention Instagram accounts and some websites I've never heard of. It's now become a "thing" to do things in Cayden's name. Heidi started something (well, technically, it was me), and it's remarkable how many have jumped on this bandwagon. Clearly, truth has no boundaries on the internet.

He handles himself well when Jimmy Fallon asks about the girl in his leather jacket at Phantom Bar in Vegas.

"She was cold." He shrugs.

"That seems awfully *sweet*."

"Sweet-*talkin*," Cayden counters.

"A little short for your taste?"

"Why, you want her number?" The audience claps, and even Jimmy Fallon laughs.

I call Carson afterward. "You did great," I say.

He breathes audibly. "Lex, I don't know about this." His voice is strained.

"Yeah?" I say, but I don't know what he means.

"It's so hard. I want people to know about you. I want to say, 'Screw it. This is Alexa Brooks, everyone, and I love her.'"

Everything in me absorbs his words, and I have to sit down from the weight of it. "Really?"

"Yeah," he says, his voice deep and gravelly.

Nothing can erase the smile on my face. "That's good enough for me right now." I don't care if the world doesn't know how he feels. I do.

"I gotta go."

"Hold on." I need to tell him I love him. I need to. It aches inside me, and I want so badly for him to know it.

"Hold on to what?" he says.

"Oh my gosh, you're so dumb."

"*You're* dumb," he says. "Damn, I really gotta go, call you later, bye."

He clicks off the phone. I wanted to say, "I love you," and I ended up saying, "You're dumb." Nice job, Alexa Brooks.

Then I don't hear from him for three days, which makes it worse. I leave voicemails and texts. Nothing. Finally, in frustration, I write, Btw, TMZ hasn't reported your death. He immediately writes back, lol sorry crazy week.

I wonder if this is the norm for dating celebrities—radio silence followed by apologies—but then he writes, Been thinking a lot. Dyin w/o you in CA. Talk Fri.

Winter Formal is only a few days away, and I've decided to go alone. When I tell Lindsey she should bring John as a friend, she says, "Did you talk to John?"

"No, but—"

She interrupts me with a clipped voice. "Didn't think so. Well, he said he'll be busy with the lighting all night." Besides, she tells me, she already agreed to go with Chad, which makes me cringe, but I don't say anything because she seems annoyed with me. It sounds like John's made up his mind—busying himself with lighting—so it shouldn't matter. He hasn't approached me, texted, or called, so I stay away. I figure I can always help with setup and cleanup and dance with my girlfriends. A few months ago, this would've felt like a letdown, but right now, it's not a big deal.

On Friday—finally!—Carson texts: Talked with my mom.

I text back Yeah? pretending this week hasn't been pure torture.

There's a two-minute pause.

You get a date for Winter Formal?

What does this have to do with talking to his mom?

No. Going solo. You still want to meet up afterward?

Then he texts back, and I have to read it four times before I believe it.

Can't have a pretty girl going solo. Some guy at the dance might mistake you for single. Pick me up from the Palms at 7 tomorrow?

I can't stop smiling as I type: Welcome to Hollywood, Carson Knight.

Chapter Thirty-Five

On Saturday, I can wring my clothes out from all the sweat. I'm literally shopping for a dress on the day of Winter Formal. Mom takes me to one store, and I pick a BCBGMAXAZRIA silk strapless gown. The price tag makes her almost fall over, but I convince her it's my one big senior purchase from my college fund.

Afterward, she drops me off at the nail salon, where Lindsey and Heidi meet up for manicures and pedicures, followed by hair appointments. As we sit with our toes propped up, Lindsey says, "So, you've decided to go stag?"

"Actually, someone's taking me."

I expect Lindsey to be excited, but she scowls. "Why didn't you tell John?"

"I just got asked yesterday," I say defensively. "And besides, John's not talking to me, if you haven't noticed, and you told me he was doing the lighting."

"So who's taking you?" she says with way less enthusiasm than I expected.

I bite my lower lip and grin shyly.

It's Heidi who says first, "No way." When I don't deny it, she makes a weird squealy noise in her throat—nothing

I've ever heard out of Heidi—and whips her legs around toward me. The lady painting Heidi's nails paints a huge red streak across Heidi's leg and yells at her in another language.

"Sorry," Heidi says and moves her legs back in place. "Shut *up*!" she whispers to me. "Your friend Will—*Will Smith*—the guy we're talking about—said he's taking you?"

I nod.

"When did you fix everything?" Lindsey says, her tone crisp. "When you abandoned my car in a parking garage?"

"Linds, I'm sorry. It was a while ago, and I wasn't allowed to tell you. He was too afraid of it leaking and becoming something bad. He made me promise. And I was so afraid of losing him again. You know what happened the first time."

Lindsey swallows. "I get it, I guess. It's just"—she plays with a nearby nail-polish bottle—"why didn't you say something to John about Winter Formal?"

"Carson decided yesterday. Oh, and it's a surprise, so don't say anything, okay?" I squeeze her hand. "But I wanted you at least to know."

Lindsey squeezes back, but it's faint. I really owe her more than that.

"Remember when you wrote his movies on the back of the business card?" I say. She tilts her head, curious. "The first letters were the first letters of my name."

There is a lengthy silent pause as she processes this. Then she claps a hand over her mouth.

"I know!" I say. "It was his way of trying to let me go."

"He did care," she says breathily.

I nod but wave it off. "Forget him for a sec. This is about

you. If you hadn't hammered me over the head with the idea or written those titles down, I wouldn't have noticed or ever taken an airplane to chase him down and tell him."

"You took an airplane?" she yells delightedly.

"Again, not the point. The reason we fixed things? It's because of you." The corners of her mouth lift. And she can't take her coldness anymore. She leans over to my chair and flings her arms around me, jostling the lady working on her pedicure, who throws her hands up in annoyance.

"Cayden McKnight is showing up to a dance that I planned?" she says into my ear. I nod into her shoulder and she pulls away, displaying such a wide smile that I swear I can see all her teeth. "Seriously, the best Winter Formal *ever*."

"You know it," Heidi adds.

On our way out, Heidi whispers to me, "You sure he's going to come through for you?"

"You don't know him like I do," I say.

"I hope so."

★★★★★

Lindsey has her short, curly brown hair straightened strand by strand with a flattening iron, and Heidi wears hers half up and half down, loose curls at her shoulders. I opt for the basic French twist with little wispy pieces framing my face. Elegant and classy. Like a movie star.

Mom, of course, takes way too many pictures of me and laments how tragic it is that I'm going solo to my senior dance. I think of telling her about Carson. She'd be elated for me, but there are too many questions that I couldn't answer without getting in trouble. I'll surprise her and bring Carson home to meet her after the dance.

After she practically fills up her phone storage from photos, I borrow the car to meet up with Lindsey, Chad, Heidi, and Ryan for dinner. The boys look sharp in their black and white, and the girls sparkle. We joke the same as usual through dinner, but the guys act more gentlemanly, opening doors and pulling out chairs, and the girls even eat more delicately, smaller bites on their forks, napkins on their laps. About halfway through dinner, I excuse myself. With huge grins and golf-ball eyes, Lindsey and Heidi wave goodbye.

Twenty minutes later, I arrive at the Palms Casino. Carson has left me a key to his suite at the front desk, and I feel the air-conditioning on my back as I head to the elevators. Every sense is heightened. This is the moment when the world will know. The moment when I'll be free to love who I've been dying to love since I was fourteen.

Instead of using the key card, I knock. When he answers, the door yawns open like a movie in slow motion. We look at each other. He's wearing an Armani tux, and it cuts against his shoulders as if the seamstress sewed it around his body while he stood there.

"Wow," he says, his eyes following the top of my dress to the floor and then back up to my eyes.

I recall the first time I saw him up close at the Viper Room. "You're tall," I murmur.

He pulls me in close. "You're hot," he says. We kiss, but he pulls away. "C'mere. Look at this." He guides me by the hand into his suite. It's two stories, and I pass by a pool table and a full bar. He leads me toward the ceiling-high windows, but I'm staring at the basketball hoop and electronic scoreboard past the dining area.

"You have a basketball court?"

"Half court," he says. "Never mind that. Look." He turns my face, and in front of me stands the entire valley of Las Vegas. The night is crisp and clear, one of those winter days where you can see from the base of the hotels to the tip of the skyline to the top of the horizon where the full moon outlines the surrounding mountains.

"Oh," I gasp.

"I know, right?" he says. We stand hand in hand. After a minute, he says, "You know why *I* like views so much?" He keeps his eyes on the horizon. "It's where the idea of *us* first made sense to me. The night we were up at Hiker's Peak. That's when I knew. I mean, really knew. More than I'd ever known anything before."

My phone rings, and it's not an alarm. I push ignore and switch it to silent. We keep looking at the view, but my phone vibrates again.

"You're a wanted girl," he says. He holds an arm out as an escort. "Let's get you to your high-school dance."

★★★★★

Incredibly, it's just us in the elevator on the way down. Right before we reach the bottom floor, I say, "You ready for this?"

He smiles. "Are you?"

The door opens, and we walk arm in arm through the main casino area. I can feel eyes looking at us, hear the murmurs and the pointing, and I even overhear a lady say to her husband, "Hey, isn't that . . ." The rest of it is drowned out by the loud electronic dinging of a slot-machine jackpot. I don't think I breathe until we walk through the doors to the parking garage. We walk down a covered ramp toward my car.

"Wasn't too bad, was it?" he says.

My phone vibrates again. Carson takes it from my hand. "Shall I be your personal assistant?" he jokes. "Ooh, someone added a passcode."

"Eleven zero five," I tell him, and he unlocks it, smiling. His birthday. He scans it, and his smile fades.

"John says, 'If you wanted to go with someone else, why couldn't you just tell me?' "

"Long story," I say. "Please don't worry. That's not exactly how it sounds."

"Cayden McKnight!" a voice echoes from across the garage. We look over and see a photographer charging toward us.

"Get in!" Carson orders, and we sprint the short distance to my car and climb in, slamming the doors shut and locking them. It's like the photographer is the pied piper of paparazzi. Behind him, at least ten men and a couple of women with cameras appear, walking with slow, intentional steps like they have us cornered, and they do. I throw the car in reverse, and we lurch backward, the tires squealing in the enclosed building. "Okay," Carson instructs. "You're going to have to drive slowly. No running them over, as badly as you want to."

"What if they stand in my way?" My panicked voice doesn't match my car's crawl forward.

"They will," he assures. "Just don't stop, whatever you do. Slow, but don't stop."

"Great," I grumble. We approach the vultures, their eyes gleaming at their prey.

"Cayden," one shouts, knocking on the car window. "Who's the girl?" A ton of pictures snap, blinding me with flashes in the dimly lit garage. I shield my face from them, but it doesn't help.

"Come on, Cayden," another says. "Five minutes. Give us a five-minute interview. We'll leave you alone."

"Where you going?" another says.

"Are you trying to run us over?"

Carson reaches over and honks my horn.

"Come on, Cayden. That's not polite. Tell us who the girl is."

"You wanna fight us, Cayden?"

Someone slams the side of my door with an open hand. It reverberates in the car.

"Hey!" Carson shouts back. "Seriously!"

"Are you angry, Cayden?" he taunts. "Come out and fight me. Come on, you know you want to." He smacks my car with his hand. I haven't stopped driving forward, but it feels like we've only gone inches.

"Keep going," Carson encourages. "You're doing fine. It's okay." His voice calms my heartbeat, and I set my focus the way I do on that last mile in my cross-country races.

"Well, well," a familiar voice says. A flash blinds me. I blink, and when my eyes focus again, I'm inches from a man on the other side of my window. The man who drove up to Jack's house. The same one from outside Carson's house. And 3two3 the first night. Antonio. "Well, well!" he says. More flashes. "Who do we have here?"

"Don't listen to him," Carson says. "Keep driving." I continue my one-mile-an-hour mad dash out of there.

My stomach roils, and I want Antonio to disappear under my tires. He smirks. "You might want to ask your lady date a few questions." I drown out his voice with a slam of the horn, blaring through the garage with a deafening honk. He walks around to Cayden's side, and no amount of honking can smother Antonio's shouting. "Ask her why she's posing as your publicist's daughter."

"What's he talking about?" Carson mutters.

"I don't know."

"Oh, you do," Antonio yells through the glass. "Tell him how you paid for the girls at the club. Bought dinners. How you organized hospital visits. All from Cayden McKnight's publicist, who suddenly has a daughter. But funny, she doesn't recall giving birth."

Carson turns, looks at me. Doubt is creeping in, I can tell, but he fights it off. He wants to believe me, even though I've lost all color in my face.

"Oh, and the five-dollar donations," Antonio continues. He shouts so close to Carson's ear that he spits on the window.

"That wasn't me!" I scream. I slam the horn again.

Antonio continues, "Very clever. One hundred pathetic donations to the most needy charities. And all those websites. I should've hired you years ago."

"Tell me the truth," Carson says evenly. I could lie. I could say the man is crazy, keep driving, and leave it in the wake of the flashing bulbs behind us.

But I put the car in park with shaky hands and take my foot off the pedal. I feel my phone vibrating again. I ignore it. "You remember how Lindsey thought it was my fault that you were a jerk in Hollywood?" I start, hoping the people outside our windows can't hear us. "Well, she tried to fix it, and I helped. We did some good things in your name. Little things. When you finally told me the reason behind 'Cayden,' I had stopped by then, but somehow, it took off beyond my control. I swear, Carson, I didn't know it would hurt you. In the beginning, I thought I was helping." He listens. Doesn't respond. "Please, Carson, I swear on everything, that's the truth."

"But you never told me." It's not a question.

I shake my head miserably. "I started to . . . but then I never finished."

"And more kept happening. But you still didn't tell me."

I don't say anything.

He adds, "Even after I told you it was hurting me."

"How would that have helped?"

"Because it would've been the truth," Carson says.

"You lied, too! You lie every day about who you *are*!"

"Not to the people I love."

My eyes fill, and I wipe them away so I can see his face. I'm so afraid. "But I'm telling you the truth now. And maybe it was hurting Cayden, but Cayden's the guy who calls me a nobody to reporters and denies that he knows me at 3two3, and stays in a car while the girl he supposedly loves competes in the biggest race of her high-school career."

"I wanted to believe that I could trust you." He's hurt, not angry, and his voice is eerily quiet. "Were you lying about the night at Paige's, too? Was there really a voice memo? Did you really record what you said you did?"

"God, Carson, yes!" I plead. I feel him slipping. "You've got to believe me."

"Who's John? Why did he send that text?"

I don't want to lie at all. I want to roll out my heart before him and tell him everything. "Because we broke up. But we were thinking of still going to the dance together."

He nods slowly, trying to process.

"It's hard to explain. High school was all I had before you. John was part of that. We were like an algebra equation that worked. We're broken up, though. We are."

"Does he know that?"

"Yeah," I say.

"When you were at the Viper Room. When you ran with me. Were you broken up then?"

"No."

"So you were chasing after me, while you still had John. Just like eighth grade, how you had me but chased after Dylan." He's mad now.

I shake my head. "It's not like that," I try, but my throat is tight. "It's nothing like that."

"Did you ever tell him about me?"

"You told me I couldn't tell anybody."

"Bullshit. You didn't have to say my name. You could've offered him the decency—"

"What was there to tell?" I shout. "Cayden hated me. And I hated him back. He kept me from you!" The reporters must hear because tons of blinding lights respond, flashes from every direction.

"You started it all. The Cayden campaign. Everything I've been going through. You *started* it?"

"I never meant . . ."

"And you thought what? That by bringing 'Carson' tonight, you'd make Cayden McKnight magically disappear into the sunset of a high-school prom?"

"No!"

"Well, good, because look around you." He taps the car window with an angry finger. "Cayden's not going anywhere." More bulbs flash around us. The photographers shout and jostle for position.

"I hate him," I whisper. "I just want Carson."

"There's no such thing anymore," he says. "And neither of them trusts you." Carson opens the car door.

"No," I say. "Please." I grab for his sleeve, but he rips it away and climbs out of the car. The crowd parts like the Red Sea for him. He walks briskly back toward the double doors to the casino. The photographers snap hundreds of pictures, and I watch out of my rearview mirror. I see when Antonio says something to him with a smug smile, and Carson winds back and punches Antonio in the chin. Antonio falls to the floor, and I can only see the blinding flashes surrounding the scene. Carson shakes out his hand and darts through the double doors while everyone is distracted. My phone vibrates again. I answer it. "What!" I yell into the receiver.

"When were you planning on having the deejay arrive?" Lindsey's angry voice yells back. I pause, shocked and confused, and then it hits me: in the midst of everything in my life and all of my back-and-forth, getting rid of all my watch alarms, reminders, to-do lists, I must've erased the note. I forgot to do the most important thing—the *only* thing—I was in charge of: booking the deejay.

"Oh my gosh, Lindsey, I forgot—"

"I trusted you!" she screams. The phone goes dead before I can respond. I try calling her back, but it goes straight to voicemail. I speed out of the parking garage with no trouble at all, the paparazzi now vanished as quickly as they appeared.

Chapter Thirty-Six

On my way to school, I search my iPhone for entertainment groups, deejays, and party planning. I call as many as I can. It's Saturday night, and, of course, all of them are closed or working a gig already. I try them anyway.

When I show up, cars are emptying out of the lot. From my parking spot, I see students filing out of the school gym. I unstrap my high heels and race barefoot to the entrance. Along the way, I hear a couple say, "Nice job, Alexa."

"Yeah, way to plan. Amazing dance." Their sarcasm stabs my ears, but I keep running. Once inside the gymnasium, I look around. The decorations are exquisite. It looks like I've walked into a Hollywood props warehouse. Couples stand in various corners, and they turn and glare as one when I appear in the doorway. An iPhone plays through a mini speaker system. The sound is at its loudest, distorted and scratchy in the cavernous gymnasium. I spot Lindsey in the far corner at the end of the red carpet. Her arms are crossed. She leans up against the bleachers, next to the backdrop of the Hollywood sign across the mountains. Chad stands next to her.

"Lindsey," I say, out of breath. "Why don't we call Mr. Avery? Have him open his room?"

Mr. Avery, our audiovisual teacher, has speakers in his storage area. I'm sure that he can drive the keys over to us.

"Out of town," she says flatly.

"Well, I'm sure we can find someone with speakers."

"It's too late!" she screams. "Everybody's gone, and those staying around are doing it out of pity. You had *one* job! One! But no, you were too caught up in chasing after your Hollywood jerkface to think of your best friend for one minute."

"Lindsey, that's not true—"

"It's totally true!" The gym is silent, all eyes on us. "And where is he now? Your best friend's here, she's always been here, but where's *Cayden*?"

I look down at the streamer draped across my bare foot.

"Yeah, that's what I thought," she says, bitter and quiet. I stand there stupidly for a minute, until she turns her back to me and faces the Hollywood sign. I walk the red carpet back toward the entrance, feeling the stares slapping me with their disgust. I step outside into the cold night air. The biting wind whips at me, but I don't feel like going to the car to get my jacket. I'm numb, frozen in place with my bare feet stuck to the grass.

"Hey," someone says.

John is sitting next to a bush in the dark, his hands resting on his knees. I shift unsteadily, not sure if he's about to yell at me, too.

"You wanna sit?" he offers.

I trudge over, sit next to him. No one can see us here in the shadows. More couples file out of the gym. Nobody looks happy.

"You really blew it tonight," he says.

We're silent for a few minutes, watching the fog emerge from our mouths as we breathe.

"Why didn't you just tell me you were bringing someone?"

I look at him. "You and I broke up. Why did it matter if I—"

"Why couldn't you just say it?"

I put my head down. "I don't know," I say into my knees. "I didn't think it mattered."

"You know Lindsey wanted to go to Winter Formal with me?"

"I know," I say. "She felt bad for you."

"No, I mean she wanted to go. We talked about it. She's not as obvious as Kim when she likes someone. I told her I wouldn't. You're my ex-girlfriend. She's your best friend. I needed you to tell me it was okay. Just based on principle."

I feel like an even worse friend. All along, she'd liked John, and I hadn't noticed. "And you?" I say. "Do you like her?"

He looks at me with no emotion, but no anger, and that feels comforting. "I'm starting to." It should be weird, talking to my ex-boyfriend of a few weeks about the possibility of him dating my best friend, but it doesn't feel strange for either of us. "She talked me through a lot of stuff these past three months." Of course I hadn't noticed, and maybe I should be angry that my best friend was secretly talking to him, but I don't think she ever kept it a secret. She told me they had been talking. I saw the way they interacted. The way he lit up around her. Their silly jokes. She always brought something out in him that I never could.

"I can't believe I didn't notice," I say.

"I can," he says. "You should've seen yourself these past few months. Your life's kind of a mess." He pauses for a moment, then asks, "Was it worth it?"

His kindness makes a few tears leak out. John is John, practical and reliable. He's not mean. I wipe my face with my hands and then wipe my hands on the grass. Pieces of grass cling to my wet fingers.

"I dunno. I thought so, but now . . . things kinda blew up before I got here."

"Rough night for you." I don't know why, but the understatement makes me laugh into my knees. He adds, "So where is he now?"

Carson's face comes to my mind—the confusion and the hurt—and I need to find him, talk with him. Terror grips me when I think of losing him again. I crawl to my knees, find the strength to stand. "I should go."

He stands and faces me. "So are we good?"

I cringe that he uses that word to describe us, but I try not to show it. "I dunno, are we?"

He sighs, pity deep in his eyes. I don't think I've seen pity in John's eyes before, and it makes him look sweet, like the eyes of a protective parent. "You have enough people hating you right now."

The truth of that pulls my head down, and I nod. I walk out of the shadows and into the parking lot toward my car.

★★★★★

Back at the Palms Casino, I fish the hotel key out of my purse to gain access to the elevator. It rejects my card, so I take it to the front desk, to the same guy who gave me the key. "Hi," I say. "I was here earlier. It was for the Oakwood Suite."

"Yes," he says. "I'm sorry, miss. The gentleman registered to that room has checked out."

Panic seizes my lungs.

"Miss," he says. "Miss, are you okay?"

I call Carson the entire way to my house. Every time, it goes straight to voicemail. My parents are awake when I get home, and I tell them we'll talk tomorrow. They see my tear-streaked face and let me retreat to my bedroom. I continue to call Carson until exhaustion pulls me into a restless sleep.

I don't get out of bed all Sunday. In the morning, I text Lindsey apology after apology, but she doesn't respond. Mom tries to wake me around noon. "Sweetie," she says and strokes my mascara-stained cheeks. "Is this about that 'Will' character?"

"Yeah," I say.

"Or should I say Carson?"

I don't even care how she found out or whether she knew all along with her sixth-sense mom thing. It's such a relief to know that she knows, and tears awaken all the dried mascara, smearing it farther down my chin and neck. "I messed up back then, and I just messed up again, and now, and now, and . . ." I can't finish, the tears gripping the back of my throat and making me gulp between each word.

"Shh," she says. I sob into my pillow, and she soothes me by playing with my hair the way she did when I was a child, back when I would wake up with nightmares. Only now I can't wake up from this nightmare, and I sob until I have nothing left.

It's dark when I wake up. Mom's brought me chicken soup. She's perfect in that moment, not asking questions. When I finish, she takes my bowl and says, "Tomorrow's Monday. Last week before Christmas break." In other words, tomorrow's a school day, and she's not writing me a sick note. Before bed, I try calling Lindsey instead of texting, but of course, she doesn't answer.

Monday morning, I ignore my alarm until Dad marches in. "Hey, champ," he says, lifting my blinds. I squint up at him. "Breakfast is getting cold. Let's go."

"I don't feel well."

"That never works for a race, does it?"

"No."

"So get up. Come on, let's go." He throws off the covers, and cold air rushes around my body, shocking me awake.

A few minutes later, I'm staring at my closet. I have no idea what to wear. Nothing makes sense. Heidi storms in just like my dad did. "Morning," she says, as if she comes every day into my room before school. She fishes around my closet, pulls out a tank top, a V-neck boyfriend sweater, and a pair of jeans. "Get dressed. I'm gonna go put your breakfast in a Ziploc bag. Don't *make* me have to come back in here."

When Heidi returns, I'm dressed but sitting at the edge of my bed, staring at the baseboards in my room. Instead of grabbing my hand and yanking me out of there, which I'm expecting, she sets my backpack down and eases next to me.

"If I'd just made that stupid phone call for the deejay," I say to the floor. "You know? If I would've just told John, 'Hey, go to the dance with Lindsey.' Or if I'd said, 'Hey, let's break up,' way back when I first thought of it. If I'd let Cayden's reputation be. If I'd told Carson that . . ." My throat closes on his name. "Oh, Carson . . ."

"Quit it, already," Heidi says. "If frogs had wings, they wouldn't bump their asses every time they jumped. You can't beat yourself up over the 'what-ifs.' You messed up with Lindsey. She'll come around. She's Lindsey. You gave it a shot with Cayden. You lost. Alexa Brooks has eight million other things going for her that people would die to have." She slaps her hand on my thigh and stands up. "Half the school isn't your biggest fan right now, but by the time we come back from Christmas break, there'll be some other drama to take the spotlight. Everyone'll get over it."

"And Carson?"

She scratches behind her neck and pulls her hair out of her face. She looks at her watch. "Come on, Lex, go wash your face. I'm not getting a third tardy in Mrs. Dubois's."

★★★★★

I temporarily forget that I'm entering a war zone. It's not until I stop looking at my feet that I notice it's "Narrow Your Eyes at Alexa Brooks" Day. I head to the library at lunch and sit in the study room, staring at the phone that carried Carson's voice to my ear for so many weeks. Today I push the side button over and over, revealing the screen that displays

12:02, December 13. I push it again. 12:04, December 13. 12:05, December 13. I never need to unlock my phone to read a text. It isn't until sixth period that my phone finally vibrates. We need to talk, Mom writes. I'm assuming she's ready to do her "Mom job" and hear the details of my heartbreak so she can console me in great Mom fashion. Not sure if I'm ready.

At the ASB meeting after school, Joshua runs through the upcoming schedule of events for January. The tension is thick. Everyone avoids eye contact, even with each other, so I know something's up. Our adviser, Ms. Pohl, addresses what everyone but me knows is coming. "Alexa," she starts. "I'm terribly disappointed in the lack of responsibility you displayed at our Winter Formal this weekend. But there's a bigger issue at hand. The check that leadership received was from a nightclub in Hollywood." I look at Lindsey, but she keeps her eyes fixed downward. "I called to verify your fundraising efforts, and they informed me that you guest bartended for a night." She pauses, and then just in case I don't know what bartending entails, she adds, "You served alcohol?"

"I did," I admit.

"You realize we can't endorse illegal behavior without throwing the school district into the possibility of a major lawsuit." I'm not sure where she's going with this, but her voice is all business, which is worrisome. "We've voided the check and phoned your mother. She assured me that you'd reimburse the school from your own funds." And suddenly, I understand the text from my mother: We need to talk. It's not going to be about my heartbreak, but hers.

"Oh no." It escapes my lips before I notice.

"Yes, and unfortunately, we've discussed this with Joshua and the other advisers, and we believe that you need to step down from your office as representative." My head snaps up. No, no, no. "We've asked Lindsey, class secretary, to assume your duties along with hers until we find a suitable replacement from the senior class." I turn to Lindsey, but her eyes don't leave the table. "You should feel fortunate that we're not pursuing this further, but the principal felt your record had been spotless before this."

I want to argue, but I don't have the strength. I shake my head, like I still can't believe it, but finally, I mumble, "Okay." My face is hot, and I'd probably cry if I had any tears left. "Thank you." I stand and lift my schoolbag to my shoulder. I step outside through the double doors. There are snow flurries in the air, and I blow past them, past the late buses, and walk the eight miles through the streets and desert to my house.

★★★★★

It's dark when I arrive, my hands numb all the way up to my elbows. The lights are on, and the garage door is open. Both cars are parked in the driveway, though usually one is still at work at this point.

Mom and Dad are sitting on the couch in front of the television, except the television is off. I walk into the room, pull up the piano bench, and sit down. I flex my hands, trying to get my circulation going. Mom starts with the facts, and Dad gets right to the questions.

"I withdrew from your account today to cover for your bartending trip."

"What the *hell* were you thinking?" Dad hollers.

"Then I checked your balance . . ."

"What were you thinking?" he yells again, now the censored version.

"Alexa, there's one thousand dollars missing from your account, now two thousand with your slip-up."

Dad's not a man of variety when he gets flustered. "What the hell, Alexa! What. The. Hell."

"Honey, where did that money go?"

I don't know what to tell her. Gas money. Dance dinners. Souvenirs. Girl Scout signs. Website domains. Plane tickets. Cover charges at clubs. Hospitals. Gardens for the elderly. I mean, really, when I think about it, I did a lot for two grand.

I shrug my shoulders. "Wasn't it my money?"

"Yes, but it was supposed to go toward your future."

For the record, I did try to invest it in my future. I invested most of it in the lives of others. The rest was on my future with Carson, only it turned out to be a bad investment. "I'm sorry," I say. "You can ground me if you want. I don't feel like leaving the house much anyway."

They stare, mouths agape, not expecting me to treat their punishment as a reward. "What *happened*?" my mother asks, and I don't know if she means what happened to the money or what happened to their daughter. I know they're good parents and they deserve to know, but it feels like too much effort to start from the beginning.

"Dad, you know when it's the fourth quarter and you're

down by six?" He looks like an angry football player, but I have his attention. "And you've got sixty yards to go, but only seven seconds on the clock." Dad shifts forward, like he's waiting to hear my play, only he and I both know there's only one option. "So you throw a Hail Mary. It's all I had. Only my receiver didn't catch it."

"So you left it all on the field," Dad says, his voice much calmer.

I nod, squeeze my cold hands into fists, and then release them. I fiddle with my wrist for a moment, stand, and approach Dad on the couch. I drop Carson's bracelet into his hand. "And I lost."

Dad and I get each other at that moment. He looks at the bracelet in his hand, really looks.

"You would've done the same for Mom," I add.

His voice is tender when he speaks. "Go to your room, champ. Go study or something." I start to walk away. "Although I don't think you can get any smarter." I turn and smile at him, and for a moment, I feel better.

Chapter Thirty-Seven

On Tuesday in first period, Mr. Kucan hands back our essays. It's the third and final revision, our biggest grade, well, outside of our midterm and final exam. I'm confused when I see a big red F on the top of the page. Even Lindsey, who still hasn't talked to me, glances at my paper wide-eyed from her nearby desk. Surely there's a mistake, and he meant to write a letter A but forgot the final vertical line, so it just looks like an F. He hasn't drowned the paper with correction marks the way he usually does. It's definitely an A, I'm sure of it. After class, I approach his desk.

"Hi, Mr. Kucan."

"Miss Brooks," he says.

"I think you misgraded this," I say.

"I don't 'misgrade' things, Miss Brooks."

"It's an F, sir."

"That it is."

My heartbeat begins thrumming faster at his lack of surprise. "But it's a good paper."

"That it is."

I'm so confused. "But an F, then?"

He sets down his red pen, sighs like I'm missing the

obvious. "You changed your thesis. Consequently, you wrote a new paper."

"So?"

"This is a *revision*, Miss Brooks. Not a new paper. That makes it a late assignment, because the first paper was due months ago."

"But I no longer agreed with my thesis!" I argue. "How could I support it? I originally wrote that love wasn't a force of nature, but a choice, one that could easily be controlled. But it can't be. There's nothing in life that supports that!"

"A winning self-discovery."

I try to breathe normally, but I'm seeing spots. "Mr. Kucan, if this F stands, that means the best grade I can get in here is a B. I know how to calculate your point scale."

"Then you'll get an A in math."

"Mr. Kucan, please. I'm *valedictorian*."

He reaches for my paper, looks down at it, and for a minute I think he's going to change the grade. But he only looks for a quote from my own paper. "In the words of Stephen Crane quoting 'the universe,' 'The fact has not created in me a sense of obligation.'" I swear I could detect the hint of a smirk on his weathered face. He finds himself very witty.

The bell rings, and Mr. Kucan stands to begin third period. He doesn't write me a hall pass, of course.

★★★★★

On the bus ride home, I search Cayden McKnight on Twitter. I don't feel like reading full articles, so I've been getting all my updates in two hundred eighty characters or less. No one has seen him. Everyone has heard about his punch to Antonio, and most say "typical," but some are calling it self-defense or harassment. Word is he'll get community-service hours when he returns from filming his next movie, slated "soon." I no longer know anything more about Cayden McKnight than the average fourteen-year-old Tweeter.

When I reach my house from the bus stop, I'm frostbitten on the inside, not knowing how to feel. Maybe that's why I start laughing when I hear a ping on my phone and read the first line of an email: "We are sorry to inform you . . ."

Boston College.

I don't even click to read more. Only three possible responses to ED: acceptance, denial, or deferral to the regular-admission pile. "Sorry" wouldn't start off a deferral. For some reason, it makes me giggle.

Cross-country races, intervals, weight training at dawn. Now for a team I won't be running for. All I can do is laugh deliriously.

My best friend won't talk to me, and the love of my life hates me. I laugh some more.

Three and a half years. Studying and losing sleep and stressing and revising and perfecting. Volunteering, tutoring, and campaigning. My stomach aches from laughing.

I'm not going to Boston College next year. Denied.

I laugh and laugh and laugh.

Then I hurl my phone as hard as I can over the fence beyond our backyard into the desert wilderness. And I fall to the curb and cry.

I don't know how long I sit there, but the winter wind turns crisp, and my body starts to shiver. The light turns dark, and I hear cars crawl past. One parks nearby, probably a neighbor. But then I hear the crunch of gravel as a familiar pair of sneakers appears. I look up, confused. Lindsey stands over me, hands in pockets, looking like she's not sure why she's here, either.

"Hey," I say.

She takes her hands out of her pockets, blows on them to warm herself, then crouches down and sits next to me on the curb, facing out at the dark street. I think of how wonderful Lindsey's been, and how much I screwed up. The guilt clamps down my throat, makes it hard to talk. Instead, she does.

"Saw your grade in Kucan's," she says.

"Linds—"

"I know."

She knows I feel awful. Knows it even without my texts saying it. She knows because she's Lindsey, and she knows me without needing words. And for some reason, it makes me feel worse, not better. She shouldn't let me off this easy. But she holds out a pinky—and I guess I know her, too, without words—know she's referencing what Carson and I did under the table three summers ago. One more tear spills out, and I link my pinky with hers. It doesn't mean she's not mad at me anymore. Just that we're gonna be okay.

★★★★★

Everybody loves an underdog. By Friday, word has spread

that the Boston College girl is no longer going, and that Captain Sadistic successfully sank another valedictorian. Sympathy has replaced all students' previous animosity. They smile at me in a way that makes me feel like my cat's been run over.

Even my group has asked me to sit with them at lunch. I avoided them yesterday, but today, Heidi finds me in the library researching the University of Reno. The regular deadline for colleges is January 1. I'll go somewhere next year. Just not where I planned. "Come on," she says, dragging me like her cello to the cafeteria.

My friends don't talk to me, but they don't ignore me, either. Everyone smiles politely. I notice Lindsey and John sitting together sharing a sandwich, which doesn't make me jealous. But it does remind me of Carson, and my heart aches in every part of my body. Even my fingers ache. I know I'll be fine, but right now, I miss him so much. My shoulders sag, and I wipe a space clean on the table and rest my head on it. My friends don't mention it. They talk of the upcoming Christmas break in hushed voices.

I hear static on the speakers of the PA system. Muffled movement. Then someone speaks into the microphone. "This is Principal Vaughn. Could I please have the attention of the faculty and students?" Strange. Announcements are always after third period. Outside of that, they only use the PA for fire drills. Everyone quiets, curious about what this could be. There's more scratchy movement, and then a distant voice.

"Hello? Is this on?" she says.

I lift my head from the table.

Lindsey looks over at me. "Is that—" she starts, but the recording interrupts her.

"It's Good, or Alexa, or whatever. It's August 18, and I'm at Paige's party. Well, *we're* at Paige's party. I really don't know what to say because I feel dumb talking to this thing, but this is the most spontaneous thing I could think of doing, which reminds me of you because it's something you'd do, well, only better because you always do everything better—I mean—better than anybody, at least to me."

My friends are looking at me, so I know they hear it, too, but it feels like it can't possibly be real. I left my Apple Watch at Paige's party. Maybe the deejay found it, but Paige never sent it. Then again, I never asked for it.

My heart's in my throat. Everyone in the cafeteria is staring at me, wondering why this old recording is playing on our school's speakers. I hear the younger me take a deep breath before she continues. "Look, I know this may come as a surprise to you because it came as a surprise to me, too . . ." There's some background noise. "Oh, Carson. In the beginning of the summer, I thought I liked Dylan. I mean, I did. But then I didn't. And, um, well, I never told you 'cause I didn't know what you would say, and I didn't know what I would say, and I felt guilty, but I didn't know why. And then I realized people feel guilty when they're doing something wrong, and that's when I got it: Dylan was all wrong, and you, well, you were everything right. You kept reminding me of someone I knew, and as the summer went on, I realized that you weren't someone who I met long ago, but someone who I made up in my mind."

Some voices say, "Awww," but I can't see any faces because the tears are thick in my eyes. I want to climb back into that moment and redo it, tell him out loud without a recording. "Only it was too late to tell you, but now I'm so afraid, and I don't know how to tell you because I don't know how this works, I only know I can't, I can't, um, I can't imagine life without you. I think that sounds crazy, and you'd probably call me dumb, and then I'd say, no, you're dumb, but all I know is that things make more sense when you're around, and that's supposed to mean something, right? And although people might say we're crazy 'cause I'm fourteen, I just want you to know that—" Suddenly there's the sound on the speakers of a door opening, and I know Paige and Dylan are currently barging into the greenroom. My fourteen-year-old hand slams the stop button on the watch. Suddenly, the PA system goes quiet, but the cafeteria doesn't stay silent. There's a collective gasp, all three hundred students looking in one direction as Cayden McKnight walks through the double doors from the office and makes a beeline straight for me. I wipe my eyes to make sure I'm not seeing the wrong image. He stands over me.

"You never finished," he says. "You just want me to know what? Although people might say we're crazy 'cause you're fourteen, you just wanted me to know—*what*?"

I stand up on shaky legs, find the strength to say what I didn't say back then. I swallow. "That I'm in love with you, Carson Knight."

We don't move, don't blink, don't breathe. Even the air feels like it stops circulating, not wanting to disturb this moment. He breaks the silence and reaches into his pocket. He produces a blue-and-black plastic lanyard bracelet and takes my wrist in his hand. "Well, then," he says to me as he snaps it on. "Hello, Goodnight."

My voice is choked with sobs, but I croak out, "Hello."

I look at the bracelet, and he knows what I'm wondering. "Your dad. I stopped by your house. I figured your parents needed an explanation. And a two-thousand-dollar check, they informed me." At this, he smiles.

"But the recording." I motion toward the PA system. "The watch?"

"I took some time off this week, flew to New York to get away, think things over. Turns out Paige isn't so hard to find, thanks to her dad. Anyway, be glad she's such a pack rat. She still had streamers from that party." I chuckle, and it feels so good to smile again. "She said she meant to send it back, but you never wanted to talk to her after the party. Look, Lex, I've been given so much, more than I can spend, more than I know what to do with, but . . . but I always said I'd never be my father. He was afraid. He chose status over love." He steps closer to me, rests a hand on the small of my back. "He met love and walked away. I can't walk. I tried, but the truth is, I'd rather have you than anything the world promises Cayden McKnight." He leans down and smirks. "That kinda sounds like a movie line, doesn't it?"

I laugh through my tears. "A really cheesy one."

"Pretty bad, huh?"

"Like, the cheesiest."

He nods. "But true." And his lips reach for mine. I fall deep into his kiss until the entire cafeteria erupts in hoots and wild applause.

When he pulls away, he says, "I'm leaving to shoot a movie on Monday." My chin drops. Leaving *again*? "I'm playing Alan Webb."

"The track star?" I ask. Every runner's heard of Alan Webb, the first high-schooler to break the four-minute-mile.

"Yeah, that's why I've been training with the running. It's set in Reston, Virginia, but they're shooting it in Massachusetts."

"Massachusetts?" The word is painful to say. It's synonymous with Boston College.

"Your parents told me what happened. But you applied for engineering . . ." He pauses. "I talked with the track coach, who talked with the dean of admissions, and he said there are still openings in creative writing. English department. He wants you to submit a sample."

"What?" I ask, but I heard him perfectly.

He plays with my hair like there aren't hundreds of staring eyes. "What if you wrote our story? Might as well get it out there, let people know the origin of Cayden McKnight, and the girl who made him into Carson again."

"Wait." Is this real? Boston College might be a yes? "Wait, what?"

"Why don't you come over Christmas break and write for two weeks while I'm on set? We can visit the campus."

Hold on. I shake myself loose from his embrace. My parents agreed to this? As if he can read my mind, he adds, "Your dad said he could take some time off work. I'll set you both up in a hotel. So?"

Again. Did he just say that I might be going to Boston College next year? I look at Lindsey, and she's bouncing with excitement. "Say yes, you idiot!" she screams.

"Um." My voice is echoey in the silent cafeteria. "I picked Boston College in the beginning just to be away from my mistakes. But now." I look at Lindsey. "Some people are amazing enough to make you chase after your mistakes." Then I glance at John. "Or talk about them." And I grin at Heidi. "Or stick with you even while you're making them."

"Now who's being cheesy?" He smiles, but there's disappointment in his voice. "So you don't want to go?"

"No. I do." I squeeze his hands as reassurance. "I love Boston College. But—" Gosh, I can't believe I'm saying this. "For all of high school, I knew exactly what I wanted. I knew who I was. I planned out every single detail." I scrunch my eyes shut tight when I think of the embarrassment of saying this in front of the student body. "But it was just to avoid you. All of it. And now nothing's perfectly planned, and it's scary and unpredictable, and it might be bad. But it's mine. My life has to be about more than you. That okay?"

He laughs. "God, yes. That's better than okay. That's—"

"Good?"

He cups my face with his hands. "Good. Definitely good."

"Then yes," I say. "Yes, yes, yes, yes." And I keep saying yes until he shuts me up with another kiss.

★★★★★

Dear Boston College English Department:

I have enclosed the requested manuscript titled *Chasing After Knight*. Thank you for giving me the opportunity to apply to your program post deadline. You carry in your hands the story of my life with Cayden McKnight as best as I remember it. Some people believe that the brain changes your memories over time, makes you recall what you want to, and therefore, memories can't be trusted. If so, then I believe love is the only pure memory, because when you recall love, you can feel it as powerfully as if it were happening all over again for the first time. That is why I changed most of this to the present tense, so that you could experience it for the first time with me. And if all the memories in this manuscript were false or greatly exaggerated, then throw them all aside, and love still stands.

Throughout this semester, *The Great Gatsby* and "The Open Boat" have taught me that we are all open boats, unprotected vessels tossed around by love's uncertainties. Some drown, some survive, but love takes us all at some point. Gatsby's green light stands at the end of the dock, beckoning, calling, and reminding us that as we get tossed by love (the force of nature that doesn't care whether it fills us or shatters us), hope still shines in the darkness at the edge of the water.

The story is taken from diary entries, notes, old writings, and my memory. Everything is accurate, with one small addendum. In the beginning, I wrote that "we *never* actually dated." Carson didn't agree, but I shared with him what John taught me—that words are powerful, and until you say it, nothing is official. So since I've finished this, Carson has officially asked me (with words, not texts) to be his girlfriend, and I have officially accepted his offer. As for the future? The rest is a movie not yet made.

But I know of a great actor I could recommend.

Sincerely,

Alexa Brooks

Alexa Brooks

Acknowledgments

I've retold this moment so many times, it's probably nothing like the original. *Revisionist history,* I like to call it. But a decade ago, I met up with my agent, Michael Bourret, at a local NYC restaurant for a quick catch-up sesh, and I told a funny celebrity story that I only share over a cocktail. He surprised me with, "That's your next story." I blew off the idea. It really wasn't a story. "But you're a writer," he reminded me. "Make it one."

So I did.

It came in pieces—like stories often do for me—fragments of characters, shards of scenes. A best friend limping barefoot across a motel roof. A hand in cactus spikes and a plastic bracelet. Two pinkies linking under a table. A late-night run through the hills of Malibu. It all morphed into something, which stayed happily on my shelf, until a decade later, when Michael told me to revisit it.

So, first, Michael Bourret, thank you.

Chasing After Knight was your favorite from the beginning, and you always believed it would sell. I'm still pinching myself that it's actually a book.

Nathaniel Tabachnik, I don't know the odds of being assigned an editor who truly *gets* me, but it's gotta be up there with an elk sighting in Hermosa Beach. Receiving your edits each time was the opposite of stressful. People would ask, "Isn't it hard tearing up your work?" and I was like, "No, it's awesome!" I felt like I had this block of stone, and you were like, "Chisel *here*," and a gem would appear! I'm so proud of what this novel has become, and honestly, you're the backbone.

Thank you to everyone at Penguin Workshop: Francesco Sedita, Felicity Vallence, and everyone else working your tails off behind the scenes. Lynn Portnoff, again you secretly climbed into my brain and designed the perfect cover. It's creepy how you can do that so well!

Jamie Berggren, Vanessa Hernandez, and Megan Crabtree, when you were my roommates, you curled up on the couch and read my manuscript like it was a good *Gossip Girl* rerun (the original!). Thank you for letting your entire day stop just to find out the latest with Alexa and Carson. Scott Sussman and Lesley Downie, if cutting words were a career, you'd both be CEOs.

Kenneth Kucan, thank you for letting me use your name as a tribute to you. You were a wonderful teacher, and I'm glad my adult self finally read all the books you assigned back in eleventh grade. Lol.

Ms. Carrol Statom, you had nothing and everything to do with this book. There's not a scrap of you on these pages, but there's all of you in my work ethic and creative drive. Thank you for being the biggest bully of a high-school teacher I ever had. I love you to Vegas and back.

Carl and Clara (parents), Kevin and Tiff (bro and sis-in-law), thank you for reading my rough drafts as if they were gold (they weren't!).

Phil Blyth, there aren't enough words, gifs, poutine, or Spacedust to thank you. Love you to Bozeman and back.

Finally . . . Marci Hawkins, Guinevere Ervin, Leo, and Alex, thank you for giving me a canvas to paint. You get it.

I've been asked if this is a true story. Ha. No. But authors can throw in Easter eggs, and this book has a field full of them. Some of them are for my Las Vegas peeps—gems only for you. Sometimes it's just a line. When you recognize it, I dare you not to chuckle. And Danya, Elizabeth, Jen/Guin, Marci—remember what a big deal it was to go to an island summer camp—with boys?!

This book is entirely fiction, a world I built with this crazy imagination God gave me, chock-full of characters who made me laugh out loud as I brought them to life on paper. I've never met Lindsey, but I would follow her anywhere if I did. Alexa, like all my main characters, is far cooler than I will ever be in this lifetime, but as her author, I got to live my life vicariously through her in a love story I could only dream about. John is that guy so many of us have dated—where we hold on past the expiration date because he's one of the good ones, yet he's never quite a perfect fit because he was never meant for us. And Carson—well, who knows if the bedrock of friendship will last with the new romance it carries, but I like to end stories where we imagine that things can only get better. What is life if not for hope?